E.
Heatherington

Playing the Field

POOLBEG

Published 2009
by Poolbeg Press Ltd
123 Grange Hill, Baldoyle
Dublin 13, Ireland
E-mail: poolbeg@poolbeg.com

© Emma Heatherington 2009

The moral right of the author has been asserted.

Typesetting, layout, design © Poolbeg Press Ltd.

1 3 5 7 9 10 8 6 4 2

A catalogue record for this book is available from the British Library.

ISBN 978-1-84223-372-6

Typeset by Patricia Hope in Bembo 11/14.5
Printed by
Litografia Rosés, S.A., Spain

www.poolbeg.com

Note on the author

Emma Heatherington is a freelance PR consultant from Donaghmore, Co Tyrone. She is married to Dalglish and they have three children – Jordyn, Jade and Adam.

Read more about Emma at
www.emmaheatherington.com

Acknowledgements

Thanks to all at "Team Poolbeg", especially Paula, Niamh, David, Sarah and Conor for being possibly the best team in the (publishing) world.

Thanks to the wonderful Gaye Shortland for keeping me on the right track and for spotting little star players in the story and bringing them to the forefront.

To my agent, Ger Nichol, who believed in this story right from the very beginning and cheered it on from the sidelines with lots of support and early ideas. For helping me to get started, thanks to Shona, Emma and Maryanne for belly laughs over lunch when the book was born well over a year ago.

Thanks to everyone I asked about the offside rule, soccer agents, the transfer window and the whole mechanics of soccer. I am perhaps the un-sportiest person in the world, but the hunky footballers in the book – well, I was happy enough to research them myself!

And to the wonderful ladies in the "van" – here you go . . . your very own scene (it's near the end so no cheating!). Here's to keeping in touch, eating tinfoil (!)

and to always being able to reminisce about wonderful days gone by at St Joseph's Grammar.

Finally, as always, thanks to my family – all zillion of them, immediate and extended, and all the lovely people of Donaghmore in Co Tyrone (who are mostly related to me) who make the most fantastic supporters.

For my three wonderful children

PROLOGUE

Cara's rusting Fiat Uno grumbled along the country road, its wipers scraping the windscreen as the English summer rain finally subsided.

"Crap!" she said aloud. Was it right then left, or left then right? She couldn't remember.

She pulled the car in alongside a neatly trimmed hedgerow, turned off the engine and scrabbled in the depths of her handbag for the typed list of directions to Wimbledon that the recruitment agency had given her a few days before. Whoever her new boss was, she would not be impressed if her new "domestic assistant" was late.

List in hand, Cara turned the key in the ignition and the car spat back. Not a kick.

"Oh no, please don't do this to me now," she said,

patting the dashboard and looking around her for help. She wanted this job. She needed this job if her career break was to work out as she had planned. Her glasses had steamed up and she took them off, gave them a quick wipe with her sleeve and said a silent prayer that she wouldn't be late.

She turned the key again and, as if the car had just been giving her a warning not to doubt its capabilities, it shot forward. Cara clung to the steering wheel, her eyes pinned to the road ahead. Then the car slowed down to its usual struggling pace.

Indicating right she took off again, chugging along the road and surveying her surroundings for another few miles, until she saw a huge set of gates that matched the recruitment agent's written description. Then she saw chimney-pots towering over trees far in the distance and she knew this had to be her new workplace. Yes, there was the name: Summer Manor. She slowed down further, glanced in her rear-view mirror and took a right turn through the gates.

"Oh holy shit!" she said as she made her way through sprawling lawns up a winding drive which led her to the front of the house, a modern home based on an old design. Its sandstone walls were a background for tall Georgian windows and a huge red door which was framed with ivy. Who lives in a house like this, she wondered, and she fought an involuntary urge to let her mouth drop open.

She wound down the window when she saw an older man who was watching her approach with a friendly smile.

"Ah, hello there," he said, leaning on a spade next to a mass of greenery. A black Labrador circled his feet. "You must be the new start."

The man's skin was a weather-beaten brown and his face was framed at either side with soft white curls that looked like candyfloss. If everyone at this "Summer Manor" was as friendly, Cara reckoned she would feel right at home. He looked so cute in an old-man sort of way that she could have put him in her pocket.

"I'm Cara," she said, extending her arm out through the car window. "Cara McCarthy."

"Cara McCarthy. Well, that's a pretty Irish name," said the man. "I'm Sam Potts, and this old scamp is Buster. He belongs to the man of the house but sometimes he thinks that's me."

"Lovely to meet you, Sam," said Cara. "And you too, Buster." The dog wagged his tail and panted up at her and Cara reached out to pat his shiny black head.

"He likes you," said Sam. "That's you off to a great start. Now, why don't you park up and I'll show you around?"

Cara surveyed the magnificent landscape once more and realised that whoever lived in this glorious home would hardly appreciate her hunk of junk standing out like a sore thumb.

3

"No doubt my trusty little motor will blot the landscape around here but it's the best I can do at the moment. I'll just park between these two beauties, then?"

"No, no, better not park there!" called Sam but Cara was already nosing her way between a nifty MG and a BMW jeep.

She locked the Uno into reverse and tried to straighten up the tiny lump of green metal, feeling dwarfed among such grandeur and wealth.

"Is that okay?" she panted, wishing for power steering, which evidently hadn't been invented in the land of Uno pre-1997.

"Sort of," said Sam, his blue eyes wrinkling into a smile. "Your new boss likes to have plenty of room to manoeuvre in and out of here when it suits her. Best to stay well out of her way in future and park down the side of the house. But I don't think she'll dock your wages for parking in the wrong place on your first day."

Cara stepped out of the car and squinted in the morning sunshine. "Honestly, I'm normally an excellent driver but I guess I'm just a bit, well . . ."

"Nervous?" asked Sam.

"Yeah. Nervous." Cara shoved her hands in her pockets and then took them straight back out again, hearing her mother's "tomboy" remarks echo in her head.

"Don't be nervous," said Sam and he signalled at her to follow him towards the sprawling home. "There are a lot more rules to remember than parking your car in the correct position around here, but you'll soon get the hang of them, don't worry."

Cara closed the car door gently and followed Sam and Buster.

"I'm afraid I'm not very good at playing by the rules, Sam," she said as they made their way to the entrance of the magnificent home.

"Well, then that makes two of us," said Sam, opening the huge ornate red door. "Now, let's go inside and I'll introduce you to Sophia and Dylan."

"Sophia and Dylan?" said Cara. The names sounded somewhat familiar.

"They live here. Well, this is Dylan's home but his girlfriend Sophia moved in only a few weeks ago and already she's making her mark by making lots of changes around here. You, my dear, are one of them."

Cara followed Sam in through the front doors and into a wide, marble hallway which was the size of a small ballroom. Sophia and Dylan. Sophia and Dylan. She rhymed off the couple's names in her head. The house had a faint smell of summer fruits to it. Sophia and Dylan. Their names went together like tea and toast. They sounded all too familiar and then, like a slap on the face, the penny finally dropped.

She stopped in her tracks and stared at the gigantic

5

framed photo at the top of the stairwell and gulped in realisation. A striking black-haired girl lay with her head on the lap of her Adonis boyfriend and her eyes glared confidently in Cara's direction. Her brand-new boss was none other than Sophia Brannigan, the all-new high-maintenance, highly strung girlfriend of Premiership footballer and babelicious hunk in a pair of trunks, Dylan Summers.

"Yes, that's our Sophia," said Sam and he threw his eyes up towards the portrait, laughing at Cara's reaction. "She wasn't here five minutes till she had that portrait commissioned."

Cara let out a nervous giggle and pushed her glasses back on her face. Dylan Summers and Sophia Brannigan. She was going to work for Dylan Summers and Sophia Brannigan!

Oh holy, holy, holy shit.

1

Don't You Step in my Red Suede Shoes

"*Cara! Cara!*" The sound of Sophia's screeching tone pierced Cara's ears from the intercom that linked one room to the other at Summer Manor.

"Yes, Sophia?" Cara wriggled her way out from a pile of laundry in the utility room, wondering what the hell the demanding cow wanted now.

"Just an observation," called Sophia who was pinning her long, raven hair into a trendy twist in her dressing room, "that you have been here for weeks now and I am absolutely no further on in my career as a celebrity." She finished the look off with a pale pink neck-scarf and admired her own beauty, almost kissing the mirror. "To say I'm disappointed is an understatement." When Sophia was in a mood like this, her Liverpool accent became a little more posh.

Cara wondered how Sophia's celebrity career, or lack of it, could possibly be her fault, but then remembered that when Sophia went into a "poor me" rant, the world and his wife were to blame. Or the nearest person to hand: usually Cara. Fly in her chardonnay? Blame Cara. Lost lipstick? Cara again. War in Iraq? Cara, how could you be so cruel?

"I have to say I don't really understand what that has to do with me," said Cara as she folded the laundry, rolling her eyes as the intercom light flashed before her. "As you keep reminding me, I'm just your cleaner."

She could sense Sophia's frustration a mile off. It was one of those days when her boss would argue a black crow was white and no one would convince her otherwise.

"Well, you wouldn't understand," said Sophia. "You see, I am using your arrival as a yardstick of my success and if I do not make some progress soon, it can only mean one thing."

"Which would be?"

"That you are simply not a good omen."

Cara nodded to herself. She was not a good omen. She could live with that. She'd been referred to as frumpy, clueless, hopeless, useless and any other word with "less" at the end of it as a daily punishment-beating for just, well, breathing since she took on her job at Summer Manor. Being a bad omen was merely a minor flaw.

"I had hoped that by hiring you to keep this house

on its feet I would have more time for social networking and extending my contacts, but to date there has been no progress on my commercial success at all. Nowt. Nada. Nothing."

The intercom flashed off and within minutes Cara heard Sophia's stilettos march towards her. Then she appeared at the door, all dressed up to go out.

"I have some shopping to do for tonight," Sophia ranted. "So, don't expect me back too soon and if I were you I would start praying that some sort of miracle occurs in the near future that gains me the profile and publicity I deserve. Oh, and by the way, if my package from Belle's Boutique arrives, leave it upstairs outside my dressing-room. Goodbye."

Cara felt like the weight of a rhino had been lifted from her back when she heard Sophia's car vroom away from the house. "Don't expect me back." Those were her favourite words of all time from Sophia and they were normally only said once a week, whereas "do not go into my dressing room" had been drummed into her repeatedly since day one.

She looked at the clock. It was eleven o'clock. Sophia's shopping trips were usually all-day events so she would give herself an hour before she made her way up the stairs to see if she could get a peep at what all the fuss was about in the dressing room. Sophia always locked it when she went out, of course, but by now Cara knew where she kept the key.

Yes, curiosity about what lay at the other side of that door had haunted her during her brief employment as general dogsbody to Sophia Brannigan and now she was about to give in to temptation. Like a forbidden fruit hidden on the second floor of the luxurious residence, the room was calling to her, daring her to open its heavy, gilded doors, assuring her that no one was around to find out she had broken the rules in her brand-new job.

Come lunchtime, Cara tightened her pony-tail and glanced outside to make doubly sure the coast was clear, then took a deep breath and climbed the winding staircase. She retrieved the key from a drawer in the master bedroom and made her way to the dressing room. Her heart pounded and adrenaline pumped through her body as she turned the huge knob and pushed the doors open.

"Wow!"

She gave a ballerina twirl across the fluffy, cream-coloured shag-pile carpet, into the centre of a room which was even more lavish than she could have imagined.

It was huge. At least five times the size of the family sitting room she had been reared in back in Donegal and it was shelved from ceiling to floor with not an empty space in sight. The entire room smelt like new leather, with railings of clothes on hangers labelled by designer and boxes and boxes and boxes of shoes. The ceiling had so many lights that the room was almost floodlit, and a deep cream podium made a magnificent centrepiece in front of a floor-to-ceiling mirror.

Cara looked out through the window onto the extensive lawns of the house. She took a deep breath, longing to pinch herself back to reality but allowing herself just one more moment of fantasy where all of this was hers . . . A haven of luxury that was so out of her reach it was almost impossible to believe she was standing inside it right now. And she was getting paid for it. Not paid to stand around of course, but when the cat was away and all that . . .

She imagined the man of her dreams waving to her as he finished a game on the tennis court at the far end of the manicured walkway. She imagined her top-of-the-range sports car – no, actually, a Space Wagon – sitting on the golden stones of the gravel driveway, with baby seats for her adorable twin baby boys who were the spitting image of their father. Yes, in this dream she drove a top-of-the-range Space Wagon with tinted windows and a key code that would open the huge electronic gates of the big house especially for her.

She pictured herself chilling out in the heated, kidney-shaped swimming pool, after a hard day's shopping, or lounging in the extensive drawing room that was never used. She dreamed of choosing outfits for charity dinners and awards ceremonies, where she

11

stood right now in the long rectangular dressing room.

For a few precious hours every day, Cara McCarthy truly loved her job. As she scrubbed and cleaned her way around its nooks and crannies with no one to disturb her, she would allow her imagination to run wild and pretend that she was the true lady of Summer Manor. Tucked away in the country-style suburb of Wimbledon Village, where rolling hills and country hideouts hid the fact that the bright lights of London were only a stone's throw away, its private grounds were a nest of tranquillity and the perfect space for a dreamer like Cara who could easily lose herself in a world of peace and luxury.

She allowed herself to run her hands along the Prada section, she tried on a Galliano scarf and put it back exactly where she found it. Then she felt brave enough to go a little bit further by trying on a pair of Sophia's high-heeled shoes which luckily were just her size.

"Where did you get those shoes?" she asked her reflection, then stumbled and fell into a clumsy bundle before pulling herself together again.

She stared in awe at how dainty her feet looked in the full-length mirror and how lean her calves when she didn't try to walk, or move or breathe. The shoes were blood-red pure silk, with a fine, real-platinum slinky heel and a pretty red bow which sat on the edge of dainty peep toes.

"I think I've discovered fashion," she laughed, realising she was actually enjoying herself more than she had in a long time. "Have I really been missing out on so, so much?"

Cara didn't normally talk to herself, but then again, she didn't normally try on shoes either unless she really had to. Unlike most women, Cara McCarthy had always viewed clothes as one of life's necessities rather than an adrenaline-inducing passion. In fact, if push came to the shove and her life was in danger, she would actually confess to preferring hiking boots to high heels.

But these shoes were different. These shoes had beckoned to her from beneath their bed of soft, cream tissue paper. She'd even taken a quick peek at the label which was still stuck on the box and had almost choked at the price tag. To own only one of them she'd have to live on Super Noodles for at least a month and hobble to work because she wouldn't be able to afford petrol for her clapped-out motor car, let alone afford the match of the shoe.

"Perfect, just perfect," she whispered, wishing she could keep the glorious beings in her possession forever and take them home to the poky apartment she shared with her friend Natalie. She would never, ever wear them outside of course, but would just stare at their beauty on a daily basis as they lay in their shiny box, and when she'd feel like it, maybe once a month or so, she would put them on and dance around in the safety of her own apartment.

Hell, she wouldn't even show them to Natalie and she always made sure she showed every item of clothing to Natalie. As her best friend and fellow "let's spread our wings and see the big smoke" buddy, Natalie was the one who had eventually told Cara that navy and black didn't go and that horizontal stripes made you look like a fat zebra, unless you had a frame like Kate Moss.

Feeling foolish, but brave, Cara maintained her balance and opened the heavy doors that led back onto the landing of Summer Manor. She made her way towards the stairs where the sassy drumbeat of a Girls Aloud song called to her from the kitchen.

Pretending she was as tanned and gorgeous as Cheryl Cole, Cara shimmied down each step of the spiral staircase in Sophia's stilettos to the beat of the music and made her way in the direction of the succulent aroma of her roasting chicken which filled her senses and added to her good mood.

She made her way carefully across the reflective white tiles of the hallway, through the double doors that led to the dining room and through a huge open-plan area that brought her into the kitchen, allowing her mind to drift into a world of glamour, perks and parties where everybody knew your name and everybody wanted to be your best friend.

Into a world where the biggest daily dilemma was which shop to visit on which day of the week, where your diary was bursting at the seams with parties and where the man of your dreams played a poncy ball game for a living in return for a salary that would feed a small nation for the rest of their days. Into a world where jotting down a few remarks on other celebrities' fashion sense made you a "columnist" in a weekly magazine. She could be a "columnist." Not even a fecking problem.

But this wasn't Cara's world at all. This was Sophia's world. This was a WAG's world. But, right now, for a few stolen moments on a Thursday afternoon in August, Cara "Cleaner to the Stars" McCarthy was living it – and she was loving every flippin' minute of it.

Even her rubber gloves and checked apron didn't feel out of place when she slipped them on and continued with her chores in the kitchen. She turned the volume up to the max and allowed herself to feel the music as it took over her body. The shoes had become so comfy she would have forgotten she had them on only for her tendency to look down and admire how delightful they made her feet look, approximately once every ten seconds.

With a dramatic *whoosh* she wiped down the draining board, and then let out an "Ooh!" as she dusted the dresser. She felt her heart surge with excitement as the gentle clip-clop of the heels kept to a rhythm on the ceramic floor beneath her.

She lifted a photo from the solid oak dresser in an over-exaggerated sweep of her arm.

"I'll just give you a quick facial," she joked to it as she ran the duster over Sophia's glowing face. Sophia grinned back at her (it was an old photo – Sophia didn't smile any more in real life – she pouted) and she found herself giving the glass on the frame a little more elbow grease than she normally would with just a tiny pang of jealousy added in for good measure.

For Cara knew that the shoes she wore, the shoes that fitted her so well and introduced her to the dizzy heights of haute couture didn't belong to her and they never would.

They belonged to the real lady of the manor – the one person who could make Cara McCarthy feel like scum on her gorgeous shoes with just one sly comment or degrading cackle; the person who paid her a measly cleaning salary that was less than her own humungous weekly clothing allowance; the girl whose claws were so deep into her footballer boyfriend's existence that Cara could almost smell the gloss of the magazines she planned to sell her wedding to, if he ever proposed.

"Shallow cow," she said, vowing she would stop muttering as soon as she took off the shoes, which she would do in a few minutes of course, and she gave Sophia's rare grin another extra-hard polish. "Lucky, lucky, shallow cow."

The sudden crunch of tyres on the gravel from outside the house made Cara's heart skip a beat as she gave an extra fast dance spin on the kitchen floor. Who the hell was that at this time of day? Sophia didn't normally attract visitors. She didn't appear to have many friends.

"Jesus – shit," she stammered, glancing around and trying to decide on which direction to run. Sophia couldn't be back ... could she? Cara clip-clopped over to the window and peeped out to see her worst fears come true. Sophia was back early.

Her pinched face framed by a long ebony mane and clad in oversized sunglasses was all Cara could see as she drove down the side of the house, yapping nineteen to a dozen into a tiny phone. Her personal number plate was emblazoned across the front of the car, just in case anyone would happen to forget just who she was.

She was early and Sophia was never early. Not from a shopping trip.

And she was coming in through the back door. And the back door led through a cloakroom that led into a hallway that led to the kitchen, where Cara stood in Sophia's red shoes that still had the price tag on them. A price tag that was the length of Cara's mobile phone number. Shit, shit shit!

Cara glanced down at her feet and dropped the duster into her apron pocket, then made a mad dash for the main hallway and towards the stairs, praying that Sophia's telephone conversation might hold her back and give her a few minutes' grace.

"Shit – bitch," she said, not knowing which word to use first. "Shit, shit, shit, shit, shit," as she took the stairs, two at a time. Sophia would sack her on the spot if she found out that she had as much as sniffed her brand-new shoes. Hell, she only let Cara use the cooker because she couldn't be arsed to use it herself and had a terrible fear of everything domesticated and electrical unless it could straighten her hair.

Cara opened a window at the top of the stairs and listened briefly to Sophia's conversation from below as she to-ed and fro-ed from the house to the car in a bad temper.

"But, honey, you promised!" she heard Sophia shriek into her cellphone as her heels clicked across the patio. Sophia didn't call her phone a "mobile". No way. That was too UK. "I have everything organised and we simply *have* to work on your profile, whether you like it or not."

Cara heard the car door open and then slam. That would be to fetch her shopping. A mountain of shopping. Cara hoped it would take her ages to unload it without her help, which Sophia was sure to scream for any second now.

"With the Beckhams gone Stateside everyone wants to park their pert little bottoms on their vacant thrones," said Sophia, "and this party is the ultimate

opportunity to show the country that we have arrived."
A pause, then an ear-splitting yell: "*Cara! Cara!* Come
immediately and help me with all this!"

The intercom let out a shriek on the landing and
Cara raced towards Sophia's lavish dressing room, silently
complimenting herself on how she had learned to run
so easily in such glorious footwear. To hell with cat-
walks and premières, these shoes should be promoted
as road-runners.

"Shit," she said again as she opened the dressing
room doors. Then she reached down to take off the
shoes. Her right foot felt naked without its new
companion but she had no time to sympathise. She
had to be cruel to be kind.

But, as she reached to slip off the left shoe, she lost
her balance and bounced off the doorframe, then
wobbled back into an upright position. She pushed the
doors of the dressing room open further and hobbled
quickly towards a chair. Faster than lightning she
swooped down to remove the other shoe but suddenly
her heart stopped.

It didn't skip a beat this time. It stopped.

For Jimmy Left Choo was now injured. Fatally
injured. And Cara thought she was going to die too as
the heel broke from its base and fell into her hand.

2

Flaming Star

Dylan Summers glanced at the caller display on his phone and sighed. Having had Sophia rant down the phone about some stupid party of wannabes was bad enough, but now his brother was phoning him with more bad news.

It was always bad news these days. Living so far from home, when relations with his father were so strained, was tough at the best of times and now he had a feeling he was going to feel the pinch again.

"Things aren't so good, bro," said Mark Summers. "It's Dad."

It was always Dad and things with his dad were never good.

"What's up now, Mark? Tell me it isn't as bad as the last time."

Mark fell silent and Dylan got nervous. His brother was never lost for words.

"He's – well – he's gone again, Dylan."

Dylan stood up against a stone pillar on the perimeter of the football grounds as his heart sank.

"Again?" This was the second time in a week his father had gone missing after hitting the bottle and as always he felt so useless, so far away in his life of luxury and wealth. Signing a cheque or two wouldn't solve his father's alcohol addiction, no matter what direction they were fired in.

"Mum called and she's in a terrible state. He left last night and hasn't been seen since. Should I call the police? I know the moment I do he'll come sauntering in and I'll have to phone back and apologise for wasting their time. And I don't want to bring attention your way again."

"Don't worry about me, Mark. Don't worry about that end of it at all. Now, let's think. Where have you checked? The Strip? Have you done all the pubs along that way?"

Mark had.

"There has to be an explanation for all of this," said Dylan, his nerves shattered at the thought of his old man lying in a ditch somewhere. It was inevitable the way he was behaving lately and no matter how strained their relationship was, he couldn't bear to think of him that way.

"Look, Dylan," said Mark, "there is one other place I could check before I call in the coppers, but I can't tell Mum. I'm not even sure I want to tell you."

Dylan listened with dread. His older brother was always so protective of Dylan's feelings, not to mention his position as a high-profile footballer, but Dylan wanted to know exactly what was going on.

"Where? You have to tell me. Come on, Mark, I'm not a kid any more."

Mark's breathing was heavy over the phone and Dylan knew he had thought this all through before bringing it up.

"He's been, well, he's been hanging out with this woman at the pub and the last time I found him at her place in the early hours of the morning. I have a feeling he might be there again but I need your support on this if he is. We have to get his life back on track. This spells rock bottom to me."

Dylan kicked a few stones under his feet and nodded to some of his team-mates who were making their way from the changing rooms following the club's daily training session. He had so much on his mind lately and, with his father's condition worsening, things didn't look any brighter.

"I could ask for a few days off?" he said. "I could come up at the weekend? It's about time we faced the music and cleared the air."

Mark jumped in, knowing that the Prodigal Son's

return might not help matters, as much as his brother meant well.

"Look, don't panic just yet," he said. "I'll go and have a last look around for him and get him home and sobered up. Maybe it's best if you stay put for a while. You have enough on your plate with the summer transfer window coming up and all that."

"If you're sure . . ."

"I'm sure," said Mark. "How are things in that camp? Any news?"

Dylan sensed his brother was keen to change the subject. "I have a few more months left in my contract with Fulton but I'm more than happy where I am," he said. "I'll consider the options and follow my agent's advice."

"Too right. But, if Joe Buchanan or any of his sub-agents came to you with an offer from a northern club, don't say you wouldn't jump at the chance? You're no more a Londoner than I am, my boy."

Dylan laughed. Mark's heart was set in the north and where he was settled with his wife just up the road from his mum and dad.

"No, but can you imagine Sophia's face if I told her we were moving to Newcastle or Leeds? She'd go mental!"

"She'd blow a bloomin' gasket!" said Mark and bit his tongue when he realised he could say a lot more about Dylan's high-maintenance girlfriend. "Look, take care of yourself and I'll phone you later with an update on the old guy, okay?"

"All right, but I'm still open to making the trip if you think it would do any good. I feel a bit useless piling all this grief on you."

Mark lowered his voice. "Dylan, don't be. You've carried enough of all of this on your shoulders through the years while I was away seeing the world and I know you're still sore over that horrible press scandal last year. I'll keep in touch. In fact, I have some business in London some time soon. Maybe we could meet up?"

"Yeah, sounds good, Mark. Sounds good."

Dylan hung up the phone with a heavy heart and climbed the steps to the private car park reserved for players at the football club that had been home to him for three years now. With a transfer opportunity on the cards and his dad making all of their lives a misery, he wondered where exactly he belonged at the moment. He bleeped the alarm on his top-of-the-range car and sat still in the driver's seat for a while to gather his thoughts. He couldn't wait to get home to a long bath and some trashy television to numb his brain, but his daydreams were disturbed by his Fulton FC team-mate Paul Henderson, who rapped the car window and jumped into the passenger seat. Paul had been his closest football mate since they both signed up three years ago and Dylan was godfather to Paul's baby son.

"Hey, kid, what's up? You look like shit if you don't mind me saying so and your sprints sucked today."

Dylan laughed at Paul's honesty. He rubbed his jaw to find a two-day-old stubble and took a glance in the rear-view mirror.

"You are one hundred per cent right, Paul. I do look like shit but I've had a shit day. What's your excuse? You were a bit slow on the uptake yourself."

"Ooh, that's a bit low. Seriously, though. Is there anything you want to get off your chest? Anything Doctor Paul can advise you on? You do know you can talk to me about anything."

Dylan looked at Paul in surprise. "Since when did you become so caring and sensitive? Bring back the old 'I don't give a toss' Hendie that I know. Please! You're scaring me!"

Paul fiddled with the car's Sat Nav on the dash and ran his hand over the new motor's leather interior.

"Must be fatherhood, mate. It's got me all gushy and sensitive. I highly recommend it and pretty soon I'll be a married man."

"And they say it's all downhill from then on," laughed Dylan. "With a wedding band on your finger, you'll be well and truly under the thumb."

A group of young fans gathered at the gates of the football grounds, clad in Fulton FC's famous blue and black colours. They called to the two players to come and sign their kit and Paul pointed them out to Dylan.

"Hey. Do you remember hanging around your home club after pre-season training? It was the best time to meet the players before the pressure of the games had them rushing around at the end of summer. I remember every time I saw Kenny Dalglish outside Anfield I would nearly wet myself with excitement. This is Premiership football, Dylan, and we are living the dream. Can you believe it?"

Dylan fondly recalled his early memories as a fan at his own native Leeds United. His dad would take him to see every home game, rain, hail or shine and now here he was, playing for the newly promoted Fulton FC, and transfer whispers to no doubt an even bigger outfit and his old man was too busy drinking his life away to savour all he had dreamed for his boy to be.

"It's amazing, I know," said Dylan. "Here we are at twenty-eight years old and in just a few years we'll be retiring."

"Speak for yourself."

"I am! Have you ever thought what else you would have done if this hadn't worked out, Paul?"

Paul stared out of the car window onto the stadium below them, its overpowering stands towering over the pitch and the club's name emblazoned in huge lettering on its roof.

"No, never. I always knew I'd be a superstar."

Dylan opened the car door and playfully pushed his team-mate out.

"Come on, bighead. Let's go and sign some jerseys and then I'm off home to chill out for the rest of the day. Big time."

3

Hard Headed Woman

"Sam! Samuel! Hurry!" hissed Sophia as she dragged shopping bags out of her tiny sports car. "Why do I have to *ask* for a little help around here? Can't you see I'm struggling?" she said, referring to her mountain of shopping in the passenger seat of the MG convertible. "And where the hell is Cara?"

Beside the convertible's shiny silver exterior stood Cara's battered old green Fiat Uno and Sophia felt her insides burn with disgust. It looked like bloody Shrek! Why some girls settled for the bottom of life's barrel would never cease to amaze her. She strutted towards the house, not knowing which angered her more – Sam's pitiful stare as he struggled with her afternoon's shopping, her boyfriend's reluctance to join the real world of British Celebrity, or her housekeeper's insistence on taking that piece of scrap and parking it in full view right beside her home. The very sight of it, not to mention its ancient registration and disgusting colour turned her stomach.

"Really, baby, this is so important," she continued down the phone to Dylan who had eventually answered her second phone call in the space of ten minutes. She wagged an impatient finger in the direction of the sitting room for Sam to offload her countless bags and made her way to the kitchen where she flicked on the kettle with a sigh. "I cannot afford for Amanda Stewart to gossip if we don't show up tonight. Gossip is my job in my new column when I get it and I won't get it if I don't go to this flaming party! And what the hell is that noise?"

She marched towards the CD player with a face like a bitter lemon and ripped the blaring Girls Aloud CD from the system, then flung it in the bin. Letting out another sigh, that came from her toes this time, she then covered the end of her phone with her hand.

"Yes?" she said to Sam whose loitering at the kitchen door was grating on her already tortured mind. She'd only told him to leave her shopping in the sitting room, not lurch around her like a stalker!

"Am I done?" he asked softly, and then he winked as he saw Cara enter the kitchen carrying a laundry basket.

"Yes. Thank you kindly, dear," said Sophia through

gritted teeth, realising that Dylan could hear every word on the other end of the line. If her boyfriend thought she was being rude or ungrateful to old Sam Potts she would never hear the end of it. Never mind that the man was doting and way beyond retiring age. Couldn't Dylan just forget family ties – Sam was an old friend of his father's – and employ someone who actually made a difference to the lawns and was a bit easier on the eye? Plus his loitering around was getting on her wick. He had a home on their grounds so why didn't he just stay in it?

Her cold stare diverted to her housekeeper who was making her way across the kitchen floor, almost invisible behind the overflowing laundry basket. The very look of Cara and her clumsiness angered her even more.

"Hi, Sophia," said Cara, her frizzy hair hanging in her eyes. Yesterday it was fine and limp and today it was frizzy. Tomorrow it would probably be fuzzy or shaggy. Yuk!

"Afternoon," said Sophia and she looked Cara up and down, finding it impossible to hide her repugnance. Cara's skin was pale and her hair was as always tied back in a schoolgirl pony-tail. Her clothes were straight from the high-street bargain bucket and her shoes were, well – they were flat! What was the girl thinking?

"Look, darling, we'll chat about this when you get home," Sophia continued to her boyfriend down the phone. "There is still time to change your mind and to be honest there are ears everywhere in this house. It is good press we want. Not idle gossip from the hired help. Bye."

"You look good, Miss Brannigan," said Cara.

It irritated Sophia to always find her so chirpy. What did she have to be so happy about? She was a cleaner for Christ's sake!

"Mm," she answered with a fake grin. She knew she looked good and was hoping to make a living out of it if she got her way.

"Hi there, Sam. You working hard?" asked Cara.

"As always, my love. And has anyone told you how pretty you look today? That shade of blue really suits you."

"Oh, okay, save the small talk for Friday nights at the local, folks," snapped Sophia and she examined her freshly French-polished nails. "That will be all, Sam. Good day. Any messages, Cara?"

Cara shrugged in apology to Sam who sheepishly made his way outside again into the gardens where, as far as Sophia was concerned, was where he belonged.

"Er . . ."

"Yes or no? *Messages*? How many times have I told you to write my messages down? Your hesitation is highly annoying. And where were you just now? I was calling for you?"

"Em, upstairs, and yes, Assets PR phoned to discuss

your new strategy," said Cara, clinging to the laundry basket for dear life and reading from a notebook that sat on top of the pile of laundry. "I told them to try your mobile but they couldn't get through."

Sophia let out a cackle. "It's called screening your calls, darling, otherwise known as playing hard to get. Not that you would know anything about that. They waste my time, I waste theirs in return. Any deliveries?"

"Deliveries? What kind of deliveries?" said Cara, shuffling on into the laundry room.

"You know, shoes, clothes, shoes, more shoes – from Belle's Boutique?" called Sophia after her.

Cara knelt on the floor and peeped to the bottom of the basket where poor Jimmy Left lay.

"No, no deliveries arrived today," she shouted back, her hands shaking with fear as she searched for the mutated piece of evidence, the heel.

"Ah well," said Sophia.

Cara jumped. Sophia was right behind her.

"At least I have another few pairs I haven't worn yet. I won't be stuck. And what the hell is wrong with you today? You seem jittery."

"Jittery?" said Cara, her voice in a quiver. She would make a shit mass murderer.

"Yes, jittery. Nervy. Pull yourself together!" said Sophia, marching back towards the kitchen with Cara on her tail. "Oh, and how many times do I have to tell you, please do not park that ghastly vehicle in full view beside our house. It doesn't look right. Drive it around the back in future."

"Right."

"And do not let me hear that bubble-gum pop music blasting throughout the house ever again. I mean, if someone important came around!"

"Important like who?" asked Cara.

"Like Andrew or Paul or any of the other footballers," answered Sophia, her voice rising ever so slightly. "Or worse, their *wives*. They might think it was me listening to that trash."

Cara looked puzzled. No one ever called around to see Sophia.

"Trash? But it's Girls Aloud. I thought you said you were hoping to befriend Cheryl Cole?"

Sophia poured a cup of herbal tea, then changed her mind, threw it down the sink, opened the fridge and took out an ice-cold Evian. She marched her way through a set of French doors that led to her favourite sitting room where she plumped down on a luxurious sofa, crossing her long, spray-tanned legs.

Cara had dutifully followed her.

"Hoping to befriend Cheryl Cole simply means accidentally standing near her when the paps are around," said Sophia and she necked a mouthful of water. "I am hoping to become acquainted with the girl, not be her friend, Cara. There is a difference. There are very few friends in my world."

"Isn't that a bit sad?" Cara mumbled, knowing she would want to eat her words instantly. "I mean, to just have acquaintances rather than real friends. I'd imagine it's lonely. Very sad."

"Not particularly."

"My name means 'friend' in Irish."

Sophia wasn't interested. "I'd say going to the same local pub, week in, week out, wearing the same old fast-food-style clothes that would cost less than a good bottle of wine, in fact not knowing your Moët from your Manolos – I'd say that's sad, no?"

Her turned-up nose reached as high as it could and Cara was sure it looked more pinched than it did in her older photographs. Which screamed one word: surgery.

"No," said Cara. "I really don't think it is sad at all."

A blast of music and the sound of a vehicle on the drive interrupted her from further theorising and announced the arrival of Dylan Summers which saved Cara from being devoured by Sophia's sharp opinions, or Cara answering back once too often and getting the sack. The girls glanced at each other and Cara was sure she could see Sophia's face twitch as she transformed from the bitch from hell into the girlfriend from heaven.

Fresh from his training session, Dylan would breeze in with a friendly smile and a kiss for his girlfriend and Sophia would give an Oscar-winning performance as she did every time he was around and she wanted something.

"I'm in the sitting room, honey," she cooed and Cara's stomach turned sour at her sickly sweet act. Cue fluttering eyelashes, butterfly kisses and vomit-inducing stroking through his still damp hair. Cue a baby voice and a promise of lots of you-know-what and a glare for Cara to get out of the way. It worked every time.

"Something smells good," said Dylan as he breezed inside, a navy leather sports bag thrown over his broad shoulder and a white T-shirt that demanded that onlookers wear shades as it met his lean, tanned arms.

Sophia stood up to greet him.

"*You* do, baby," said Sophia with a flash of pearly whites that rivalled her boyfriend's T-shirt and she took the bag from Dylan's hand then flung it on the floor towards Cara, who could feel the bile rise in her throat.

"Sophia, really, I think I can manage to put my own stuff in the laundry room," he said and Cara's heart soared. She didn't know Dylan very well yet and her few direct encounters him had been brief, but at least he had some respect and didn't treat her like she was dirt. "I'm sure Lara has other things to do."

Lara? *Lara?* Cara's face fell. Did he just get her name wrong? She could feel her cheeks go hot and she stared at the discarded football bag.

"It's *Cara*, silly!" giggled Sophia, delighted at the chance to emphasise the fact Dylan had mucked up again. "Gosh, you can't even get our housekeeper's name right, darling, which just proves my point this afternoon. We need to socialise more. We need to get you out more."

Sophia's emphasis worked as Cara gulped back her disappointment. Dylan didn't even care to remember her name. After weeks of cleaning up after him and his snotty girlfriend. He was just the same as Sophia was, trapped in a self-centred, one-way vision bubble. A match made in heaven.

"It means 'friend', in Irish," she said and she instantly regretted speaking at all. "My, er, name, that is."

Now Dylan was looking at her like she had sprouted a ginger beard and a pot of gold and she could feel her face flush even brighter. She felt like a right leprechaun.

"Oh," he said and Sophia arched one perfectly shaped eyebrow in her direction, making Cara feel so pathetic.

She was acutely humiliated. This was Dylan Summers for crying out loud and she had just let herself down by trying to explain the meaning of her name to him. As if he even cared. He probably thought she was a right pancake. It was Dylan Summers! The few people she told about her new life in London tortured her for inside information on what the world of Dylan Summers and Co. was really like. Was it true he shaved his chest? (No. He waxed it. For charity. Only once!) Was it true he never wore the same socks twice? (Definitely no. She had washed at least twenty pairs at least twenty times.) Was it true he was even better looking in the flesh than he was in pictures? (Hell, yes!)

Now, as thanks for all her defence of him against such ridiculous rumours and the way she honoured his private life *and* Sophia's, not to mention the number of hours she had wasted dreaming that she could get to know him and be his best friend, he had just proved to her that she was simply the hired help who made him his favourite roast-chicken dinners, did his laundry and jumped to his girlfriend's every whim and he didn't even care to get her name right.

"Cara? Of course. That's a really cool name," he said eventually and he flashed a smile in Cara's direction. "I won't get it wrong again and I'm sure you have much more pleasant things to do than lift my sports bag around. I can do that myself. Now is that roast chicken I smell? Great, Cara. That's my favourite and I'm starving."

Oh my God, you are so forgiven, thought Cara. Back to the top of the class, Gorgeous. She noticed the snarl on Sophia's face so she scuttled away into the laundry room, realising of course that she had better things to worry about than Dylan Summers' inability to recall the name of his housekeeper. Like a broken shoe that cost a fortune, for example.

"So, ta-da! What do you think?" asked Sophia and Cara's ears pricked up as she passed the sitting-room door on her way to the kitchen. She was trying to keep busy and after her "it's Irish for friend" announcement, she planned to stay out of Sophia and Dylan's way until home-time. But of course she couldn't resist having just a little listen to their conversation on her way past. It was instinctive. It was only human to do so.

"Isn't it divine?" said Sophia. "I mean, come on, babe, how could you possibly say no to me when I've spent so much time in planning for this party? I've even sorted you out from head to toe. This shirt is perfect —"

"It's red. I am not wearing red, Sophia," said Dylan. "And I'm not going to Amanda's party."

Cara couldn't help but smirk. Dylan really was beginning to stand up to Sophia's demands. Like last week when he got to pick the movie they went to see at the cinema. He let her choose the restaurant beforehand, but still. He was taking baby steps to calming her spoilt-brat routine and it was a far cry from a few weeks ago when he gave in to her every whimper. It was amazing what you could pick up about relationships while doing someone's dirty washing and Cara had a ringside seat.

"But I am wearing red too. And you don't understand – we *have* to go," said Sophia, her tone heading closer to Destination Desperate.

You don't understand, we have *to go*, mocked Cara from the other side of the door.

"Look, babe. I am absolutely shattered. I've had a long day and I was looking forward to a chilled evening in front of the telly. You know, just you and me, being ourselves and not pretending to be something we're not just to keep up with the Joneses."

"The Stewarts, actually."

"Whatever. I just can't be bothered with all that. It's just not me. You know that. You know why."

Dylan made his way to the kitchen and Sophia followed him, pleading. Cara tip-toed to the kitchen door to have a better listen.

"But Dylan, I mean it. You don't know Amanda Stewart like I do. If we don't show up tonight, she'll spread the word that we're jealous of Andy's transfer to Arsenal, quicker than Emily Evans would take off her clothes at the flash of a camera."

"But we're not jealous. I'm delighted for Andy."

Cara couldn't resist peeping out through the slit in the door to where Sophia was giving her best shot to get her boyfriend to do what he was told.

"And so am I," said Sophia through gritted teeth.

She was delighted for Andy's promotion and Amanda's growing celebrity as much as she was delighted the day she found a grey hair in her glorious black mane. "But they have bagged a *Fab!* magazine photo shoot in their garden and we don't want to miss out on that."

"You mean *you* don't want to miss out on that," said Dylan, tearing off a piece of Cara's chicken to fight off his growing hunger, not to mention his frustration at Sophia's persistence. "You know I don't like to be splashed over glossy magazines. Been there, done that and have the scars to prove it."

"But Dylan!"

"Listen, Soph. If you really want to go, why don't you give Avril or Kirsty or someone else a call and take them along for the evening. I really don't mind."

Sophia drew a breath. "Avril is in St Tropez and Kirsty is otherwise occupied. With David."

"Who the hell is David?"

"Some property developer guy who just made his first million."

"Should have guessed," said Dylan. "This chicken is really good. It's delicious actually."

That was it. Sophia had to up her game. Her boyfriend was distracted by a chicken.

"If you don't want to come with me, Dylan, then I'll have to go alone, and you know what everyone will think then. That is how rumours in the tabloids start. Women on their own always attract male attention and –"

Cara gave a chuckle. Oh, Sophia was really grasping at straws now. She was trying to scare him into going. She was trying to make him jealous.

"– I am really dying to wear my new red Jimmy Choos!" finished Sophia.

Her new red Jimmy Choos?

Now Cara didn't chuckle. She thought she was going to choke. Did Sophia just say she was going to wear her new red shoes? Her new broken red shoe that still lay tangled in sheets at the bottom of the laundry basket? Cara had to interrupt them immediately and then get out of there fast and never come back. She ran to the laundry room, stuffed the broken shoe into her large handbag and popped her head around the kitchen door, wondering what time the next cheapie flight left for Belfast.

"Excuse me?" she muttered.

"Oh, are *you* still here?" said Sophia, more viciously than even she intended.

"I'm just about to go."

"Sophia," said Dylan, "there must be someone you can take to the party. Come on, you can think of someone!"

Sophia turned to him again. "I told you, I can't!"

"I'll be off then," said Cara but they didn't hear her. Good.

She turned to tip-toe out through the back door

and disappear back to her sad, but very welcome, life of takeaway clothes and disposable shoes which had just inherited one very pricey friend minus its very pricey heel.

"Take *her*," she heard Dylan whisper.

"Take who?"

"Take Cara," he said.

Cara froze. Had she heard him wrong? Was the guilt of her crime making her deranged?

"Cara! Just a moment!" he called.

Cara made her way into the kitchen where she found herself in the full glare of Sophia Brannigan and Dylan Summers. Two people, who despite their differences of opinion and current debate, still looked like they had stepped off the front cover of *Vogue* with their sickening beauty.

"Are you being facetious, darling?" asked Sophia. "Sorry, big word. Are you for real?"

"Oh, come on, Sophia!" he said. "I don't see why not."

"I can think of at least twenty reasons why not," said Sophia, giving Cara the once-over and Cara was sure her boss's fake tan was evaporating – she had turned the colour of a corpse.

An orange and white plane flashed into Cara's head beckoning to her to climb aboard. She had to get away. Fast. In the words of ET and Michael Bublé all rolled into one – she wanted to go home. Now.

"I mean, what would she wear?" hissed Sophia. "I'm not sure Top Shop fits with Amanda Stewart's dress code – and look at her nails!"

"Sophia is absolutely right, Mr Summers. Look at my nails."

"It's Dylan."

"Dylan," Cara continued. "I have plans for tonight, Dylan. Big plans."

"You heard her, she has plans," said Sophia and she turned to face her boyfriend. "Baby, *you* are coming to the party with me. Not our housekeeper."

"I'm sure you could wear something belonging to Sophia, Cara. She's about your size."

Cara sensed he was serious, while Sophia was on the verge of a stroke. It was true, though. They were roughly the same size – but Sophia would never admit that!

"I beg your pardon. I'm a six," spat Sophia. "Most of the time. Depends on the label."

Liar, thought Cara. I do your laundry. The only six Sophia had was the one on her forehead next to the other two. Then she noticed Dylan giving her a friendly smile.

"Look on it as doing me a favour," he said and made a pleading face behind Sophia's back. "I'm really wiped this evening. Hell, no, look on it as overtime, part of the job. Double time?"

"Triple," said Cara with a cheeky smile, remembering

she was quite skint at the minute and that he was loaded beyond belief.

"Sold."

Cara's insides glowed as Dylan made eye contact with her. He was so, so . . .

"Is anyone here on this planet?" yelled Sophia, snapping Cara back to the real world. "You heard her. She cannot go, she has other plans, she has nothing to wear. Is anyone listening to me?"

"I'm sure I could cancel my plans if this is work-related," said Cara and Dylan gave her a winning smile. "I can always make the pub quiz on another night and, to be honest, my team has won every week for the past few months. There are only so many bottles of cheap white wine a girl can drink and I quite fancy some champagne for a change."

Sophia was horrified but sensed she had been backed into a corner. She could go to the party with Cara or go alone. Or not go at all. Actually, that wasn't even an option. She had a columnist job to bag for *Fab!* magazine based on this party and her future career as a "celebrity" depended on that.

Sophia stared at the face before her and noticed for the first time that somewhere beneath the frizz and paleness, Cara had features that just might be able to pass. Somewhere beneath the frumpy clothes and flat shoes there was a figure that just might be able to carry off an outfit that wasn't from a charity stall.

As long as she didn't speak out of turn, this might just work. It was only for two hours anyway. It was a chance she had to take. It was business.

"Right, right, right then. You are hired for the evening," she said. "But these are the rules. Your name is Sara, not Cara. You are an old school friend of mine. You do not have time to talk, no matter who approaches you with questions or remarks about me or anyone else in the room."

"I can do that," said Cara and she realised that Dylan was finding this just as amusing as she was.

"I'll leave you ladies to it, then," he said and he headed towards the stairs, leaving a scent of pure masculinity behind him. "Thanks. I owe you one, Cara."

Cara blushed when he said her name like that.

Sophia circled around her like a silent hawk.

"Spray tan, manicure, hair styled and be back here for six," she said at last. "Then I'll try to find you something to wear. But remember, this is business, not pleasure. I have big plans depending on this party and you are merely my acquaintance."

"I'm pretending to be your friend. Sara. I've got it."

"That's right, Cara. *Pretending*," said Sophia. "Now go and get ready. If you mess up, you're out of a job and it's back to the bingo hall for you, babe – or wherever it is you came from."

4

One Broken Shoe for Saving

The battered green Uno started on its second go as usual when Cara left Summer Manor minutes later, armed with a list of beauty treatments she had promised to succumb to if she were to attend the Stewarts' ball as Sophia's old school friend "Sara" that evening.

She reeled off in her head all of the orders her boss had given her. Don't speak unless you are spoken to. Don't make eye contact with anyone. Don't tell anyone who or what you really are and, most of all, stay away from photographers. Oh, and journalists from *Fab!* too. This was Sophia's big night and no one nor nothing was going to ruin it.

For a moment Cara feared she had bitten off more than she could chew with her big challenge. After all, she hadn't been to a formal party since she was at high school and she avoided weddings like the plague for fear of getting it all wrong. What if she made an utter fool of herself? What if she tripped and fell in front of all of those famous people? What if she was photographed and slated in one of those trashy weekly magazines that preyed on Z-list celebrities who mess up?

There was only one person she could trust to help her get ready for such a big occasion and to coach her and reassure her that she could get through this all with her pride and dignity still intact. Natalie.

She dialled Natalie's number and hoped her friend would be able to take her call from her fruit-bowl-shaped juicing stall in an East End shopping mall. As well as being an excellent smoothie-maker, Natalie's previous life in Ireland before the Big Move from Belfast was that of a beautician. *Trés* handy really, in times like this.

"Natalie, listen to me carefully," said Cara as she chugged out through the gates of Summer Manor and through the luscious countryside that led toward the city. It took her forty minutes on a good day to get home from work and she prayed she wouldn't run into any school-time traffic.

"I'm sorry, you'll have to speak up," shouted Natalie. "I'm juicing here and the place is packed. I can't hear my ears. What's wrong? Have you done something illegal?"

Cara took a right turn onto the motorway. "No,

apart from talking to you on my mobile while I'm driving, which I suppose is pretty illegal, but no matter. I need your help. Big time, like now."

"Quick, quick, quick, tell me before I splash someone with citrus fruit. What is it? If it has to do with that brother of yours, forget it. He swore last night he saw Bono in the corner cake shop. His hallucinations are getting worse."

"It's nothing to do with Liam this time, I promise. Just meet me at the apartment in half an hour and get out all your beauty stuff – you know, make-up, tan, and all of that other stuff you use on yourself and try to force on me now and then. I need it all. Now."

Natalie left her juicer on auto. This sounded important. To even cut Cara's hair was like performing abdominal surgery on her friend. It pained her to sit still for so long.

"Okay, but tell me please. I'll burst with curiosity if you don't. Do you have a date? Did Dylan finally leave Sophia and seduce you over a sink full of saucepans?"

Cara smiled. She could sense Natalie was bouncing with nosiness at what was going on. The suspense would kill her.

"Of course not. Look, you're a sweetie and I love you. I'll tell you all when you finish work, but I don't have long and I need you to perform a miracle. And I am not joking."

"Okay, I'll be right there," said Natalie. "I'm nearly

done here and I'll be home as soon as I can. Is there anything else I can get for you? A man? Botox? Chicken fillets?"

"Ha ha, very funny, but now that you mention it, there is something else I do need very badly."

"What's that?" asked Natalie and Cara's stomach churned at the thought of the other task she had ahead of her.

"Em, I need some Super Glue. Extra strong. And please hurry."

Cara tried to remember the last time she'd succumbed to beautifying herself to the extent of transformation. On her Graduation Day she'd been forced into a dress that she swore made her look like Carol Vorderman – the frumpy version, that is, before the Countdown Countess became a cult and turned all sexy and vampy. The dress belonged to her sister Olivia and was two sizes too big but her mother had made her promise not to wear jeans or scary Goth gear on a day when other parents were present in Queen's University and her Uncle Jim in New Zealand would have to be sent photographs. He was already convinced Cara should have been born a boy.

As a teenager, when anyone would mention her love of rock music or Gaelic football jerseys worn as daywear, her mother would briskly change the subject and talk about Olivia's law degree or Liam's science experiments instead.

In fact, Margaret McCarthy often recalled, behind closed doors of course, how her only memory of her younger daughter's First Holy Communion Day was the huge chocolate stain she had to hold her prayer book over as she went up to receive the Body of Christ in front of the whole of Kilshannon. And worse, how the McCarthys were the talk of the village when Cara was spotted doing wheelies on her BMX in the park in the same white (and brown) dress on the very same day. The shame.

So here she was, a whole nineteen years later with a fashion conundrum that made her Communion Day and graduation fiascos look like they were as successful as a fashion show in Milan and Cara hadn't a clue where to start. She pulled into the car park of the poky apartment block and said a mini-rosary that Natalie had got there before her. If she was late for Sophia, she would be lynched. Well, she'd get the sack and she had rent to pay so that wouldn't do.

Besides, this whole scenario was an unexpected challenge and there was nothing that Cara McCarthy loved more than a challenge. She would show that stuck-up clotheshorse Sophia Brannigan that she could neigh as well as the rest of them.

"She's in the shower," shouted Liam McCarthy as he heard the door slam, marking Natalie's entrance. He was engrossed in *The Weakest Link* and was surrounded by empty crisp bags and cans of Coke, his bare knees peeping from torn, faded jeans and his white-blond hair spiked so high up it could poke your eye out.

"What on this holy earth is going on?" asked Natalie, unravelling her hairnet and picking out apple pips. "There's something just not right around here."

"Nothing ever is right around here according to you. So, what's up now?" asked Liam through a mouthful of Maltesers.

"Firstly, Cara needs to be beautified for an occasion I've yet to be told of and then you forget to insult me when I come in from work, plus you have no fake celebrity-spottings to share like you normally do every other day. And what is that mountain of junk all about? I thought you were on a strict healthy eating diet? Your mother would go mental if she could see you now."

"Two words, Nat. Chill and pill," said Liam. "I'll clear up once this TV show is over. Now, if I were you, I'd go and see to Cinderella. She's in some sort of serious tizzy and keeps talking to herself. I'm beginning to think it's a family trait 'cos I've been doing it a lot myself lately."

"Well, maybe if you'd get off your butt and get yourself back home to Kilshannon you wouldn't have to talk to yourself so often, would you?" said Natalie in a voice that would waken the dead and she made her way towards the bedroom. "Your flippin' weekend break has lasted almost three weeks now!"

51

"Oh yeah, well then I won't tell you who I saw at the market stall today buying a pair of flip-flops."

"Don't bother."

"Jack Nicholson."

"Bullshit!"

A loud crash sounded from down the hallway.

"Natalie! Is that you? Come here quickly," shouted Cara. "Bring the tan and the Super Glue. Please tell me you got me some Super Glue!"

Natalie and Liam glanced at each other.

"Tan *and* Super Glue? Strange ingredients for a makeover – I'm outta here," said Liam as he gathered up his mess. "I really don't want to hear any more. Good luck."

"I think I'm going to need it," said Natalie and she made her way to the bedroom where Cara stood in her underwear with a mask on her face that resembled guacamole, but smelt more like something which had been lying in the fridge way past its sell-by date. She was holding the heel of a shoe in one hand and its rightful partner in her other.

"Quick it. I mean, glue it. Quickly, fix it, Natalie. I can't look at it any more. Then you can fix me which may be even more difficult."

Natalie took the parts of the shoe in her hand and gasped. They could only belong to one person and one person only. Sophia feckin' Brannigan!

"How the hell do you get yourself into such

messes, Cara?" asked Natalie. "Sometimes I think you were destined for a life of mucking out fishing boats and playing football. Most girls would treasure a pair of Jimmy Choos. You, on the other hand, choose to break them."

"I only tried them on once and if she finds out I am so dead. And that's only the start of it."

"Why did I sense you were going to say that?" said Natalie as she examined the damage. With a sweep of glue she might just be able to make it look reasonably normal again. These shoes were *gorgeous*.

"She's planning on wearing the shoes tonight to Amanda Stewart's party and I have to get this one back in its box before she notices it's missing. Oh Natalie, please say you can fix it!"

Natalie took a step back. Did Cara just say Amanda Stewart? Queen of the WAGs, wife of the gorgeous Andy, mother of two beautiful princesses and icon of every female in England? Amanda Stewart! Natalie's favourite of all favourite celebrities of modern times? She plonked down on the bed and stared at Cara who was picking at the green face-mask in front of a full-length mirror.

"Wow," said Natalie. "Amanda fucking Stewart! Does Sophia actually know her? She wouldn't be fit to lace her – well, lace her bra."

"She knows her in an acquaintance sort of way."

Natalie was genuinely stunned. "Jeez! Swap jobs?"

she said. "I swear, you can juice on my stall in your flat shoes till your wee heart is content and I will happily clean up after Sophia Brannigan just to hear of all the parties and celebrity bashes she gets to attend. You are so wasted in that home, let me tell you. If that was me I'd be . . . I'd be –"

"Going with her?"

"Like, hello!" said Natalie. "Too flippin' right I'd be going with her! I'd be her best friend, bitch or no bitch. I'd be schmoozing and boozing and floozing and . . . oh my God tell me you are not going with her . . ."

"I am. Going with her. That's my problem."

Natalie gulped. "Yeah, right! No way."

"Yeah right, yes way," Cara nodded, not knowing whether to laugh or cry at the look on her friend's face. She knew exactly what Natalie was thinking. Natalie was thinking this was major. A major mistake on Sophia Brannigan's part.

"No, no, no, no!"

As much as she loved her dear friend, Natalie knew that Cara McCarthy was simply not the type of girl you would take to a celebrity party. Cara was adorable. Fresh-faced in a no-make-up kind of way. She was slim, with twinkling eyes and a wicked sense of humour and Natalie loved her to bits. But glamorous she was not.

As far as Natalie was concerned, Cara was destined to settle down back home in Kilshannon in County Donegal, surrounded by loads of children and football matches every Sunday and with the smell of fish from the nearby harbour seeping through her pores. In fact Cara was destined to do anything in life but live it up with celebrities.

"But how the hell did you get an invitation to Amanda Stewart's party? I just can't believe all of this."

Cara sat down on the edge of the bed beside her friend. "Because Sophia's desperate to go and Dylan won't and she has no one else so he suggested –"

"What? Hold on!" squealed Natalie. "*Dylan* suggested? Dylan suggested you go? This is just so surreal. *You* hanging out with *her*. And having little conversations with Dylan. And going to Amanda Stewart's party! It could only happen to you, Cara McCarthy!"

"I know," mumbled Cara. "I know."

"Right, let's think," said Natalie. "I really can't take this all in but we have to get started if you have to be back at Summer Manor on time."

"Six o'clock on time. I have to be back for six as Sophia is letting me borrow one of her outfits."

Natalie jumped up from the bed and burst into a mumbling rant. "She's letting you borrow an outfit. She's letting you borrow an outfit. Shit, I think I'm dreaming. Someone pinch me and tell me I'm dreaming." She began to wipe the green paste from her friend's face. "We don't have time to think. Just, well, oh, I suppose we should start with your eyebrows."

Cara closed her eyes and felt a sweat attack coming

on. "Oh no, Nat, please don't say the 'W' word. You know I come out in a rash at the very thought." She had the fear of God on her face.

Natalie left Cara to prepare her mind and then returned moments later with her waxing wand in her hand.

"Look, it's like this," she said. "At the moment you have caterpillars running along the top of your face and if you don't let me do this you soon won't be able to see out over them. Plus, they are going to crash into each other any one of these days, which is not a good look, believe me."

"Yes, I know, I know. They should be treated as siblings and not conjoined twins."

"Exactly. Now step into my boudoir and we'll make a start."

Natalie led Cara into her own much more untidy bedroom and somewhere amongst scattered CDs and bras and magazines, she flicked a switch on her waxing pot and Cara winced.

"And then what?" asked Cara.

"Then it's spray time," said Natalie and she laid out a huge grey sheet on the floor. The apartment wasn't very fancy but Natalie didn't think the splashed-tan look would match the décor.

"A spray tan? On *me*? Oh, Natalie, am I off my head? I should never have agreed to do this," said Cara. "And what am I going to do with the darn shoe that cost as much as our total monthly rent on this place?"

"Let's take this one step at a time," said Natalie, tilting Cara's head back and preparing to de-fuzz above her eyes. She had been longing to perform this particular operation for ages.

"What if we can't fix it? What if I mess up at the party? *Ow!*" The wax felt like scalding lava and brought tears to Cara's eyes.

"Cara Jane McCarthy, you are an intelligent –"

"*Ow!*"

"Educated –"

"*Ow!* Shit, that is sore!"

"– young lady and you will probably wow everyone you meet at this party. Of course you won't mess up," lied Natalie.

Then she lifted her tweezers and shaped Cara's eyebrows until her eyes watered, her nose was running and her face was almost unrecognisable in the nicest possible way.

"But I'm not allowed to speak to anyone," said Cara. "That's part of the deal. Telling me not to speak is like telling you not to buy handbags. It is impossible. You see, I'm only going because Sophia doesn't want to go alone and she can't miss it as she has some sort of business to attend to. *Ow! Christ!*"

"Wait a minute. She said you aren't allowed to speak? What sort of a muppet is that Sophia doll anyway? She actually expects you to go and stand like a dummy in the corner? How she snagged that gorgeous being she is living with I will never, ever know."

"Mm," said Cara in agreement, relieved that the plucking had come to an end. She felt like her eye-sockets were on fire. This beautifying was surely more bother than it was worth.

Natalie poked in a huge beauty bag and then stopped in mid-action. She stared at Cara as if she had been struck with divine inspiration.

"What?" asked Cara. "You've suddenly realised I'm the spitting image of Kylie Minogue after all?"

Natalie let out a deep sigh and sat down on the bed again. "Er, not exactly. Just . . . well, just remember, Cara. We are supposed to be keeping a very low profile over here for a year, not hob-nobbing with WAGs? I mean, aren't you aware that you actually lied on your job application?"

"Everyone lies on job applications, don't they?" said Cara. She couldn't back out of this now.

"A bit perhaps, but you just happened to wipe out about six years on yours."

"Eight."

"Eight. Right. Now, what if you happen to be photographed with Sophia tonight and it's published in a glossy magazine and someone from home spots it? It wouldn't take long for it to get out who you are or what you really do for a living. You'd get the sack from Sophia immediately and our Big-Move-from-Belfast plans would be scuppered."

Cara thought about it. Natalie was right of course. There were going to be a lot of celebrities and journalists at this party and it would only take for her to appear accidentally in one photo and for one of her former colleagues to spot her and her true background would be revealed. Then she would have to explain herself all over again.

"You're right," she said and she stood up. "That's it, I'm not going. You're right, as always."

"You think?"

"Yip. Put that bag of tricks away and we'll get on our jammies, order a Chinese and I'll get a job in a pub or something. After years of working in Graceland it would have been the sensible thing to do when we arrived here instead of trekking across town to clean up after that cow and then have to act as her friend because she doesn't have any of her own. This is Mental Mickey stuff and I'm not doing it."

Natalie nodded and another orange pip fell onto the floor from her hair. She blew a stray strand off her face and began to laugh.

"At the same time . . ." she said.

"What?"

"You just might meet the man of *my* dreams at this party tonight."

Cara was puzzled.

"I've just decided. You're going," said Natalie and she pulled Cara back down to her beauty throne. "I'm sorry for doubting your ability to mix with the A List in the first place."

"*You* just decided?"

"Yip. It's way too good an opportunity to turn down and I would never stand in the way of you finding my future husband for me. You can give him my number and I'll thank you for all your hard work by letting you join us for dinner at The Ivy. Now, let's get you ready and for goodness' sake just do what you're told. It will be safer that way."

Cara's face had a look of terror but, somewhere beneath it all, Natalie could sense her friend's trademark steely determination. She might not be the most glamorous chick on the block, but Cara had a brain and a heart that would blow anyone away. She just needed a little fine-tuning, that's all.

"Okay. I'll go," said Cara to reassure herself as Natalie continued her beauty regime. "Let's face it – Sophia isn't exactly Victoria Beckham and I am hardly the type of girl photographers will be falling over themselves to get a snap of. I will just be a wallflower and blend into the background as always."

Natalie shrugged. "Hey, don't sell yourself short, sweetie. They just might be falling all over you when I'm finished with you. Men with money and legs like rocks are few and far between where we come from and you might just blow the ones at the party away. Now, let me get my hair-straighteners and you'll be gorgeous in no time."

5

Lame and Fortune

Cara noticed how Natalie's mouth dropped in awe when she approached the famous Summer Manor as the clock struck six. She had heard all about it from Cara, read all about it in magazines way before Dylan Summers even met Sophia Brannigan but, despite what she'd heard or read, the real thing was even more magnificent than she could ever have dreamed of. Its sprawling gates opened automatically onto a gravel driveway and she almost apologised to the pillars for driving the pathetic heap of scrap she and Cara called a car up towards the sandstone home.

Miniature themed gardens were scattered across extensive lawns and Natalie recognised gingko in the Japanese section, round stone and barrel ponds in the water garden and miles and miles of greenery with not a daisy in sight. Natalie felt like she was in heaven, whereas in the passenger seat Cara was going through a living hell.

"Oh Natalie, I'm getting cold feet," she said. "Like, really cold feet. Freezing."

Natalie clung to the steering wheel in deep concentration, petrified she might run over some countryside animal or flowerbed. Cara had been moaning about this, that and the other since they left Ealing and no matter how Natalie had tried to conceal them, Cara's eyebrows still bore a pinkish glare from their overdue waxing. No amount of aloe vera had soothed them and no amount of high coverage foundation had disguised them as yet.

"Well, you will just have to suffer on because it's the middle of summer and there is no way I was going to let you wear tights. Do you want Sophia to have a fit? Plus, you can't expect to have a heater in a car that cost less than a Superser."

"I mean I've got cold feet as in I'm nervous, you clown. Not cold feet as in cold feet."

"Oh. Oh, well, of course you are nervous. You are just about to go to a celebrity party when the most you know about fashion and fame is what you learn from me."

Natalie started to laugh, but in reality she was a bag of nerves too.

"I am so out my depth here it isn't even funny," said

Cara in a whimper. "And I'm not used to being preened and primed like this, plus I still have to get this darn shoe into its box before Super Glam notices it is gone. Are you sure it won't break again?"

"Certain. Just as long as she doesn't decide to dance in them or anything, and for some reason, I don't think Sophia Brannigan is the dancing type. Now, fill me in here with all the palace gossip. Who's the old guy?"

Sam was pruning some roses at the back door but scuttled into the house before he noticed their approach.

"Oh, that's Sam," said Cara, checking the mended shoe at the bottom of her handbag. "He's a surrogate uncle to Dylan apparently, an old friend of his father's, and he likes to help around the house. He lives in the gate lodge and he's the only person who keeps me sane around here. Now, it's two minutes after six. I'd better get in there and face the music. How do I look?"

Natalie giggled. "You look gorgeous, babe, I swear you do. Just take that frown off your face and remember to stand up straight. Your hair is shiny, your make-up is perfect and minus the tracksuit bottoms and T-shirt, you have a figure to die for. Now, go for it. Go mingle with the stars. Go do yourself proud."

"Thank you so much, Natalie," said Cara, taking one

last look in the overhead mirror. "I'm almost un-recognisable." She felt tears sting her eyes and prayed they didn't spill onto her face and ruin her friend's good work. "Do you really think I can do this?"

Natalie let out a sigh, knowing she simply had to be honest.

"Look, I won't deny it," she said as she pulled up the handbrake, fearing as she did every time that it might uproot into her hand, "I did have my reservations at first, but now that I've thought it through, I know you'll knock 'em dead. You are just as pretty and intelligent as anyone who will be at that party and, as Sophia said, it's only for a couple of hours that you have to pretend you're her best friend. But if you do get any doubts as the evening goes on, just think of two magic words."

"And what might they be?"

"Triple time."

"Too flippin' right," said Cara and her face broke into a smile. "I'll fill you in with all the details when I get home. Wait up for me."

"I will," said Natalie and she said a silent prayer her friend wouldn't fall flat on her face, like she normally did. "And I'll happily settle for a man from the first division if you can't bag me one from the Premiership, so keep your eyes peeled. Or if the lovely Dylan needs company while you and Sophia are away, just give me a call. You hear?"

"I hear," said Cara and she took a deep breath and walked towards Summer Manor.

Judging by the sounds of hairdryers and commotion from upstairs, Cara guessed that Sophia was having her hair styled in her dressing room. She stood at the foot of the marble staircase and wondered should she announce her arrival to her boss or quietly hang around until the styling was over.

"Excuse me?" said an inquisitive voice from behind which made her jump. She turned around to see Sam standing defensively, clearly mistaking Cara for an intruder. "Ach, hen, is that you? Aren't you looking all glamorous and girly? Would you be offended if I said I didn't recognise you?"

When Cara caught a proper view of herself in the huge mirror that dominated the hallway, she could see why Sam was confused. Her dark hair was shiny, silky and straight and Natalie had tied it back into a sophisticated chignon. Her eyebrows were perfectly arched and shaped, framing her bronzed face which glowed with shimmer and her eyes which were dark and moody. Her teeth sparkled beneath a sweep of red lipstick. She looked good. Really good.

And it was terrifying.

"I hardly recognise myself, Sam. I'm accompanying Sophia to a party tonight and my stomach is in knots. Any tips?"

Sam smiled and put a friendly hand on Cara's shoulder. "Just be yourself. In that way, you'll be fine. That little smile of yours would melt anyone's heart and you look like a movie star."

"Oh, you are so nice. '*Say it again, Sam*'," she joked.

"In fact," he continued. "I'd say that pretty wee face of yours will upstage her majesty tonight and it won't do her any harm. Now, I take it you're not wearing that tracksuit to the party?"

Cara looked down at her grey marl bottoms and white T-shirt with a shrug. "No, I don't think I could get away with it, unfortunately. I'm going to be wearing one of Sophia's dresses."

"Gosh, aren't you the privileged one?"

"She's desperate."

"I see."

Cara smiled. Sam was such a gentle sort and it was a real shame how Sophia bullied him.

"I'll just wait here until her ladyship is ready to see me. She told me to be here for six. It's just after six now."

Sam shuffled away towards the kitchen and Cara sat down on the velvet throne-like chair in the foyer and took a deep breath. Even her nails were perfect and she reminded herself not to pick at anything in case she broke one off. She wondered how brides felt on their wedding day, all done up to the nines and almost afraid to breathe until the photographs were taken.

67

What if Sophia changed her mind? What if she took one look at Cara and realised it was all too far-fetched that she could be good enough to go to a celebrity party? What if Dylan had decided to go after all and they'd forgotten to tell her and she'd end up looking like a right Cinderella?

She stared up at the wall on the first landing where the huge portrait of Sophia, lying with her head on Dylan's lap and trying to look seductively into the lens, filled the wall. Everything about the woman was perfect, if not naturally so. Her porcelain face, her raven, bouncy hair, her impressive (if enhanced) cleavage, her trim frame. Everything physical was faultless, and to give Sophia her due, she worked bloody hard at looking that way. Cara doubted that she could ever sacrifice food in the way Sophia did. There had to be more to life than aiming to be a size zero.

"Oh, so there you are!" yelled Sophia from over the balcony. "Come this way and I'll see what I can find to, er, fit you. Do hurry, Cara. I cannot afford to be anything more than fashionably late."

Cara shuffled across the hallway in her trainers, all the time clutching her bag across her body.

"So, em, do I look okay?" she asked as she climbed the stairs and regretted it instantly.

Sophia looked down at her. "I suppose. You'll do," she said and marched onwards towards the dressing room, her skinny hips wiggling from beneath a cappuccino satin dressing robe. "You couldn't look any worse than before."

Cara was too worried to reply. She knew she had only one chance of returning the broken shoe. She'd have to try to distract Sophia in some sort of way so she could get the stiletto back into its place. Perhaps she could pretend she had a serious physical defect she didn't want her boss to see or that she suffered from a severe inferiority complex and couldn't undress in front of other people.

But Sophia had other ideas.

"You can wait in here and I will bring you some of my larger sizes to try on," she said, pointing towards one of the million spare bedrooms. "Don't be too fussy though. I can't stand fuss and after all this really isn't about you."

"Can't I have a look at what you have in mind?" asked Cara, a tone of desperation threatening to seep through.

"Do you mean, in my dressing room?"

"Uh huh," whispered Cara.

"Absolutely no way," said Sophia and she guided Cara into the adjoining bedroom and closed the door. "You know the rules."

Cara stood in the golden-clad bedroom and then plonked herself onto the king-size four-poster bed.

"What the hell am I supposed to do now?"

She could feel the fear rise from her toes as

she sensed her doomsday approaching. What if Sophia had already searched for her shoes and knew one was missing at this stage? What if she couldn't get to return it to its box? What if she could and the glue so carefully supplied and applied by her dear friend Natalie wasn't nearly strong enough? What if –?

She got to her feet and walked to the door. She *had* to brazen her way into that dressing room.

"Sophia?"

Cara's heart raced as she heard Dylan at the door. "What? Yes, I mean no!" she called.

The bedroom door opened and he burst in, then stopped in his tracks.

"Oh, I am so sorry," he said. "I heard footsteps and I thought Sophia was in here." He turned and headed for the door again.

"It's okay. Em, Dylan?" said Cara, not really sure of what she was hoping for. She hardly even knew the man but it was a risk she had to take.

"Yes?"

"Can I ask you something?" said Cara, her eyes shut tight.

"Of course."

She opened her eyes. He wore a light smile and Cara wondered how on earth God could make a man in such a model of physical perfection.

"You know the way you said you owed me one when I agreed to go to the party with Sophia?"

"I did," he said. He looked at her from beneath long dark eyelashes and Cara tried to ignore the fact that she was in a bedroom alone with a man every woman in Britain wanted to jump and she couldn't even make use of the fine facilities around her.

"Well, sorry to be so pushy, but I need a favour," she said at high speed, and she held Sophia's shoe out towards him in sheer desperation. "Can you sneak this into Sophia's dressing room? You see, I sort of . . . Well, I had a bit of an accident. When I was cleaning. Earlier. Today."

Dylan took the shoe and looked at her in bewilderment. She closed her eyes briefly again in anticipation of his response.

"I see," he said, examining the shoe. "Looks like a good DIY effort has been made on it anyway. Do you have the other one?"

"It's in the box. In the shoe closet. In her dressing room." Cara's heart was racing. What if he told Sophia? She would murder Cara for involving him in any of this, but then she figured that breaking the shoe was a crime anyway. What did she have to lose?

"Your secret's safe with me," he whispered.

Cara caught her breath. God, he was a babe. "Thank you so, so much. I'm not asking you to tell lies of course. If Sophia finds out, I'll come clean but . . ."

"It's fine. I won't say a word," he said, and put a finger to his lips. "I suppose this makes us even." He winked at her and then added as he walked out of the room, "Oh, and by the way you look really nice. Have a good time at the party."

And he was gone.

When the door closed behind him, Cara went and lay back on the super-king-size four-poster bed and thanked the Lord for sending her a bit of humanity in the shape of such a heavenly body. Dylan Summers had saved her bacon.

So some men *were* born perfect after all.

"Okay," said Sophia when she breezed into the bedroom almost fifteen minutes later. "I've brought you a size 14 which of course never fitted me, and a small size 12 which I am ashamed to say once did. They are so last year but that's about all I'm afraid. Take your pick."

She laid the dresses down on the bed and Cara scratched her head.

"I'll try on the, er, size 12 if that's okay?"

"It won't fit. Go for the 14," said Sophia, examining her nails.

Cara went into the en suite, undressed and slipped into the dress easily. It felt cold on her skin, its pale gold silk slithering down her body, and already she felt like a princess. If her mother could see her now! She wondered should she take a sneaky pic of herself on her mobile later when Sophia wasn't looking and send it to some friends at home. They'd never believe she had actually dressed up for once!

The back of the dress had a vertical row of tiny diamond-shaped buttons and Cara stretched her arms behind her back to fix them up but it was a stretch. Already she could feel herself break out in a sweat and she prayed that the extra spray of deodorant would see her through the evening. Imagine if she stained Sophia's dress with BO! She would chuck a mental even if the dress was a size 14 and was therefore utterly useless as far as Sophia was concerned.

Cara breathed out, then looked at her reflection in the mirror. Oh no. Oh no, this wouldn't do at all! The dress was like a tent and her head looked like a bobble on top. Sophia would not be accompanied by someone who resembled a tepee. She had to change it!

"Er, Sophia," she said when she emerged from the en suite, the dress still on, "I don't think it fits me."

Sophia was flicking furiously through a copy of *Fab!* Magazine. She didn't lift her head.

"Didn't think it would. I knew this was going to be a problem and my limo will be here in twenty minutes."

Cara shuffled from one foot to the other and then let out a cough. "Sophia?"

"What!" said Sophia and she flung the magazine onto a nearby table. "Oh crap, it drowns you. That can't be right."

She spun Cara around on her heels and yanked the label from the back of the dress.

"Huh! It says a size 14 but it couldn't possibly be. It must be faulty. It must be at least a hideous size 16. Try the 12. It's by a better designer."

"But, Sophia, I always wear 10. And sometimes 8."

Sophia laughed and Cara noticed a deep red flush starting to creep over her neck. "Nah, nah, nah," said Sophia. "Twelve. And hurry!"

Cara shrugged and lifted the ocean-blue size 12 and made her way back into the en suite. She pulled it over her head, zipped it up at the side, looked in the mirror and nodded. As predicted, it hung around her like a sack. She marched defiantly back into the bedroom where Sophia stood, hand on hip.

"Too big," said Cara.

"Faulty," said Sophia and she blew out a breath. "Right, I'll be back. If I'd have known it was going to be so much trouble . . ."

She slammed the door and returned moments later with the most exquisite specimen that Cara had ever seen. A long, slender, shimmering purple gown with diamanté at the bust and a long slit that went right up to the thigh. She could hardly breathe at the sight of it.

"It's a 10," said Sophia, almost choking out the dress size. "It will never fit you but desperate times. Give it a go. And when I say it's a 10, I mean –"

"It's a roomy size 10. I get it."

"Good. Now skedaddle!"

Cara stood up against the bathroom door and wanted to squeal with excitement. The dress had never been worn, like most things in Sophia's wardrobe, and it was Versace. It glimmered under the bathroom lights. She pulled off the blue dress, carefully placed it on its hanger and braced herself for her ultimate transformation. She raised her hands into the dress and let it drop to the floor. There were no buttons, no zips and no need for them either. This dress fitted Cara like a glove. And when she caught sight of her reflection, she couldn't help but gasp. It looked wonderful on her. The rich, princely purple made her blue eyes sparkle and her dark hair look even more glossy after Natalie's deep conditioning treatment. She squeezed her hands and did a mini Irish dance on the bathroom tiles with excitement.

She opened the door and saw Sophia was bent over, rummaging through shoe boxes.

"Don't tell me," she said. "It's way too —"

"Perfect," said Cara. "Just perfect."

Sophia pursed her lips and another flush crept up her neck. She squinted, tilted her head to the side and then to the other and finally spoke.

"Here," she said. "Put on these earrings, this necklace and these shoes and let's get out of here. I always knew that dress was a mistake. You look like a grape but you'll do."

Cara walked towards an ornate dressing table that sat under the window of the bedroom, clipped on the earrings, fastened the necklace around her long, bronzed neck and slipped her feet into the matching purple shoes. She took a final glance in the mirror and tilted her chin up with a smile. She didn't look like a grape, no matter what Sophia said.

She looked like a princess. In fact, she looked like a superstar.

Cara stretched her legs in the back of the limo and glanced across at Sophia who seemed to be inwardly chanting to herself in preparation for the evening ahead. If Cara didn't know her better, she would have guessed it was another nervous reaction, just like the way her neck broke out in pink blotches when she was jealous or angry or didn't get her own way.

"Wow! This place is amazing," said Cara, gasping at how Amanda Stewart's house made Summer Manor look like a Legoland bungalow.

Sophia shot her a dagger look. "It's nothing special. I've seen much more exciting properties in my circle," she snarled, but Cara doubted it very much.

Amanda's home was a magnificent blend of Tudor and modern, with acres of land that illustrated how, in comparison, Sophia and Dylan were like minnows in the big pond of celebrity.

Swarms of beautiful people mingled in the front

foyer that reminded Cara of a five-star hotel with its huge crystal chandeliers crowning its guests, and Emily Evans, the country's most photographed glamour model, was being snapped from all angles with her new footballer boyfriend. Instead of Sophia's tasteless thrones and huge self-portraits, the Stewart household had a glow of family about it, with photographs scattered around each room of various milestones featuring the couple's two gorgeous daughters.

Cara had to remind herself to stop muttering as she followed Sophia into the drawing room where the crème de la crème were gathered. She recognised a few soccer stars and for the first time in her life she longed for her brother to be in the vicinity to keep her right and to tell her who played for what team.

She was wearing Versace. She didn't even know exactly how to spell Versace, let alone how much the deep purple gown she donned might have cost. Her neck glistened with diamonds the likes of which she only ever saw in shop windows and she was afraid to move in case she broke one of them too. Costume jewellery this was not.

Sophia looked like a dream. Clad in blood red from top to toe, her wavy hair-extensions glistened under the lights and her velvet skin gave a shimmer that spelled luxury. She was amazing to the eye and she knew it. And the shoes . . . well, so far, so good.

"Don't move and don't speak to anyone,"

whispered Sophia and, before Cara could catch her breath, she was left alone in a corner with a glass of champagne in her hand like the wallflower she had promised to be.

Despite how many faces she recognised around her, she knew that to them she was an alien in their world. A pretender. A wannabe.

"Hi there! Welcome, welcome," said a husky voice and Cara turned to see, straight in front of her, the queen of the WAG world herself, Mrs Amanda Stewart. She suddenly felt faint as she stood before a face that she had only seen before in magazines and advertising campaigns for everything from smoothie drinks to sportswear endorsements. A goddess of the twenty-first Century she was, and Cara didn't have a clue how to respond.

"Hi," stuttered Cara. "It's an honour, I mean, a pleasure."

Oh holy shit. She was speaking to the woman like she was royalty. Pull yourself together, she thought. The next thing she would be doing was curtseying or drooling.

"Thank you. I take it by that beautiful accent you are not Sophia's sister as I first thought?" said Amanda, with an immaculate smile which would wipe the floor to perfection. Her legs were up to her armpits and her complexion was divine and, somewhere beneath the beauty, Cara sensed genuine warmth that almost put her at ease.

"Her sister? Er, no, I'm actually –"

"This is Sara, an old friend of mine. She works in PR," interrupted Sophia who had emerged once again from the drowning sea of celebrities. "She is just here for the weekend from, er . . ."

"Ireland," said Cara and Sophia glared at her in warning not to speak out of turn again.

"Thought so," said Amanda in sincere delight, "I have lots of friends in Ireland. What part are you from? Your accent is so –"

"Darling. I know, her accent really is darling," said Sophia. "But never mind that. Your dress is ever so much more so, babe. Do tell. No, let me guess. Is it John? No, Jean Paul?"

"It's actually High Street," said Amanda and Sophia winced and took a gulp of champagne. "I think it's just remarkable. You see, I'm endorsing a new clothing line for a supermarket chain and they insisted I wear this for the *Fab!* photo shoot. Can you believe it?"

Cara could see Sophia's amazement turn to seething rage at Amanda's latest product sponsorship and she found herself on her own again as Sophia led Amanda away into the crowd. She felt naked and no matter how many times she assured herself she was as good as anyone in the drawing room, she knew she was totally out of her depth.

"You look like you're enjoying yourself as much as I am," said a voice from behind her left shoulder.

She turned to see a handsome man with a camera that weighed almost as much as she did in his hand. He wore a dark grey pinstripe suit with a white shirt and no tie.

"Em, yes, of course," she muttered, remembering she was on business and she had rules to stick to. Photographers were a no-no.

"Can I take your picture?" he asked. "I'm with *Fab!*"

"No!" said Cara a little too sharply. "I'm afraid that's not such a good idea. And anyway, I'm sure you have many more important people to photograph than me."

She could feel her face burn under the intensity of the man's gaze.

"But I didn't say this was for the magazine," he said with a lopsided grin and Cara sensed he was as ordinary as she was. "I'm Bryan."

"Hi, Bryan," she said and gave a nervous giggle. Dare she be herself only for Sophia to re-emerge and cut off her identity in front of this stranger? She hadn't been chatted up by a man around her own age in years. Natalie had truly performed a miracle and it felt great. "I don't really think it would be a good idea for you to take my picture. I'm just here as a guest of someone. I'm not very important."

Bryan leaned over towards her and she could smell his cologne. It was musky, masculine and Cara swallowed hard and glanced around her like a nervous butterfly. She was sure her hands were shaking.

"Whoever told you that?" asked Bryan in a whisper. "I'd say you are one of the prettiest women at this party. So who is the lucky guy?"

"Guy?"

"Yes. You said you were someone's guest. I don't want some big football star to punch me up for chatting with his missus."

"Er, no, it's not like that. I'm actually with a girl."

Bryan took a step back, not knowing whether to appear shocked or impressed.

"Way hey, fair enough," he muttered. "That rules me out even more so, then, doesn't it? Or does it?"

"No, no it's not like that. I mean I'm with —"

"Ahem, Sara!"

Cara turned to see Sophia stood behind her, one hand on her hip and an icy glare in her eye.

"Oh my God, I'm in heaven," said Bryan and Sophia smiled at him seductively as he took her photo, then introduced herself as Dylan's other half, apologised for her pesky friend's behaviour and led Cara away to the far corner of the room.

"Just what the hell do you think you are playing at?" she hissed. "I leave you for one bloody second and you're schmoozing with photographers behind my back. Play by the rules, Cara. Remember, you are still my employee and if you mess up this evening, you are out of a job."

"It wasn't like that. I didn't – he came over – what was I supposed to do? I didn't want to be rude . . ."

Sophia wore a glazed grin on her face so that no one else would see her anger but she spoke to Cara through gritted teeth.

"If anyone in this place speaks to you again, just excuse yourself and walk away in the opposite direction. Do not, and I mean do *not,* converse with any of these people again. They are not your friends, they are not my friends and everyone here is at this party for the same reason that I am."

"Which is?"

"To impress the people at *Fab!* magazine so that they might consider one of us as the new columnist since Carole 'Simple' Semple mucked up and got the heave ho. Now, stand there and look pretty, or at least try to, because I have mingling to do and a sample column to write based on tonight's events. And I can't afford to miss a thing! If you want to be useful, take mental notes!"

Sophia stormed off in a haze of Chanel towards where the elite of the crowd gathered in the dead centre of the room. The group dynamics were crystal clear – Premiership players and wives in the middle of the room, the women chatting with confidence and false admiration of each other's nails, hair and lipstick, while the lesser known couples filtered around the sidelines, watching the key players in centre field and learning from their style.

So this column idea was the bait for tonight, thought Cara. All this arse-licking and air-kissing for a half-page blurb of drivel on page five of Britain's top glossy magazine. Profile and competition was the name of the game and Sophia was determined to play it, determined to outdo Queen Amanda herself who so far was always at least five steps ahead.

"Sara, you do look a little lonely stood there in the corner," said a friendly voice and Cara looked up to see Amanda approach her with two glasses of champagne in her hands. She gave one to Cara, who wasn't sure if a second glass when she was working was such a good idea, but she could hardly refuse the icon of every young girl in the UK and besides, it tasted a lot better than the cheap dirt she and Natalie drank most weekends.

"Really, I'm fine," said Cara, realising she sounded extremely staccato. She would have to excuse herself before Sophia noticed she was talking to her arch enemy. This was a job, she reminded herself, and she would not allow herself to take Sophia's comments personally.

"So, you are in PR, right?"

"Uh huh," said Cara, praying for some divine intervention to allow her to make an escape.

"Then I'm sure you are used to parties like this, where everyone pretends to be your friend and then two steps away they rip you to shreds in every detail from your hair to your husband. It's a false, wicked world we live in sometimes."

Cara looked into Amanda's eyes and sensed a tinge of sadness. Amanda blinked, and then spoke again.

"I don't know why I'm even saying this to you when it's probably your job to brief your clients on who is worth talking to and who is not." She let out a nervous giggle as if she knew she had said too much, or perhaps drunk too much. "Never mind me. Do you enjoy your job?"

"Um, well, I don't really do that sort of PR. I'm more into, er, well, I suppose it's more aimed at, um ... an ..."

The music had grown louder as the live jazz quartet had swapped places with a well-known DJ who Cara was sure was more famous since his girl-band girlfriend had a baby a few months ago.

"I'm sorry, I didn't hear you, Sara. I must get Andrew to arrange for the volume to be lowered before everyone starts to complain," said Amanda above the din. "Did you say you did PR for animals?"

Cara wasn't sure why, but she agreed. "Yes, er, animals. For an animal charity. Um, it's sort of like the RSPCA, only a smaller version."

"Ah, so you deal with real-life animals where here

we just have the odd snake or rat to contend with. I see."

"Or bitch," said Cara and found herself automatically looking in Sophia's direction. "Oh, I wasn't talking about anyone in particular! Me and my big gob!"

Cara exhaled in relief as Amanda laughed and spoke in a humorous tone in agreement, almost apologising for the behaviour of her circle.

"It's all a bit false sometimes," she giggled. "I mean, some of the other wives and girlfriends really don't realise how desperate for fame they seem to the outside world. It's laughable."

Cara checked around again for Sophia who was now standing centre stage, nodding and smiling inanely at a handsome grey-haired man. Sophia twirled a finger through her hair and laughed at the man's every joke, swaying ever so slightly to the music and fluttering her eyelashes into his face. Sophia was playing a blinder and had the poor man eating out of her hand.

"She really, really wants it, doesn't she?" said Amanda, shaking her head in bewilderment.

"What's that?" asked Cara.

"The *Fab!* column that's rumoured to be up for grabs. Sophia is desperate for it, I know it."

"And aren't you?"

"No, no, no," said Amanda with a smile. "She's welcome to it. I have enough on my plate at the moment with the clothing range and I'm in talks to launch a perfume, but I'm not sure if I'll go ahead with it. With two little ones and a busy soccer schedule, that's more than I need, believe me. Like I say, sometimes it all becomes a little pointless, for want of a better word."

Cara couldn't believe her ears. She couldn't wait to tell Natalie how refreshing and honest Amanda Stewart was in comparison to the bitchy and catty, overly ambitious Sophia Brannigan. This was a girl who was truly appreciative of all she had been blessed with and wasn't greedy for more. Cara was impressed. Her old inquisitive instincts kicked in and she longed to know more, now that she was reassured by the fact that Sophia was otherwise occupied with her audience of one.

"I'm really surprised you're so cynical about it all," said Cara. "Surprised in a good way, mind, and I'm beginning to see exactly what you mean."

Amanda gave Cara another of her stares. "You're not really an old friend of Sophia's, are you, Sara?"

"However do you mean?" Cara felt her heart race. She hated having to tell lies but she didn't know enough about Amanda Stewart just yet. It was too early in the day to be thinking she was best buds with one half of Britain's most popular couple.

"I grew up on a housing estate in Liverpool," said Amanda quietly. "So did Andrew. We have been together since we were sixteen and when Andrew signed for Fulton and then Arsenal this year, my life has never been my own. Yes, it has its high points and I don't knock it for a second, but sometimes I wonder why girls like Sophia want to give up their whole identity when they really don't know what they are letting themselves in for. I just don't sense that you are the type who would call Sophia a friend."

Cara gulped. If she was evil and twisted she knew she could make Sophia's life a misery by telling Amanda the truth, or she could go and sell her story of how Amanda Stewart's realistic take on the WAGs' world was so different to what the public believed it to be. Amanda was a smart lady, an astute businesswoman and a loving mother, but behind all of her glamour and riches, she seemed to be a vulnerable, lonely, twenty-nine-year-old girl who wanted her life for herself and couldn't be bothered with false, self-glorifying cling-ons like Sophia.

"I mean, look at the way she is blatantly flirting with Jake Johnston," said Amanda. "If she wins him over, she knows that *Fab!* column is in the bag. Look, she's taking him up to dance. I don't believe it. Go, go, Sophia!"

Cara's eyes widened in a blind panic. "What? They're going up to dance? Oh no, I can't let her!" Cara shoved her drink into Amanda's hand, knowing that she just had to halt Sophia's *Saturday Night Fever* impressions, no matter how angry she would be. "I've got to stop her."

"Why?"

"I just do," said Cara and she ran as fast as she could in Sophia's borrowed shoes, but she was too late.

Jut as Sophia went to twirl underneath Jake's arm for the second time, the mended red shoe snapped and she landed in a bundle at his feet.

The whole room turned towards her.

A camera flashed and so did Sophia's knickers, then Bryan the *Fab!* photographer left the party, knowing that he had just landed himself a small tabloid fortune which was a fair enough swap for the phone number he'd hoped to bag from the snobby bitch's friend.

"Ahh!! You clumsy, clumsy man!"

Sophia squealed as everyone glared, the men with their mouths open and the women covering their sniggers. She looked mortified. She staggered upwards with the reluctant help of Jake Johnston, then sheepishly fixed her dress and her hair, looking around for a sympathetic face but there were no takers to come to her rescue.

"That's one way of grabbing attention, Miss Brannigan," said Jake and he walked off in the opposite direction. "Enjoy the rest of your evening."

Sophia stamped her heelless foot off the dance floor in bad temper.

"Someone, somewhere is going to pay for this! I need a cab!" said Sophia and she hobbled off the dance floor in search of Cara.

6

Cryin' in the Kitchen

The tension in the sun room of Summer Manor the following morning was suffocating. Cara felt like an Oompa Loompa now, all spray-tanned in her working clothes of a tracksuit and trainers, while Sophia lay sobbing on a lounger, a duvet wrapped around her like a baby's comforter, clutching the red shoe, with various red-top tabloids laid out all over the marble floor.

"I am so, so humiliated. I mean, how can I come back after this?" she cried. "*Fab!* won't want to know me now, let alone take me on as their celebrity columnist. So much for sophistication and glamour and I was doing so, so well."

"Can I get you anything more?" asked Cara, leaving a tray of chocolates, grapes and a pot of tea – real tea – on the coffee table just as Sophia had ordered her to.

"A career? I mean, last week I was pictured leaving a nightclub behind Emily Evans as she staggered out high as a kite on vodka and Red Bull. I looked so good, so graceful in comparison, and now this!"

"Isn't there a saying that all publicity is good publicity?" Cara had definitely heard that so many times in her own previous career.

"Balls!" snapped Sophia. "I have a reputation I have been working on for three years now and it's all up in the air, literally, all because of those bloody shoes. I paid a fortune for those. Have the designers called you back since you made the complaint?"

"Er, no," mumbled Cara, failing to report the fact that she hadn't and wouldn't be making a complaint about a shoe that was already broken before it hit the dance floor. "But Assets PR called. They said this might be the big, er, break you were waiting for. Pardon the pun."

Sophia looked up, her face tear-stained with mascara stripes that ran into each other like a spaghetti junction. Her eyes were bloodshot from crying and she had a wild look that was far removed from her normally perfect self; and she had a chocolate mark at the side of her mouth, but Cara didn't find it in her to tell her.

"What? What? Are they having me on?" She sat up on her makeshift bed and gobbled another handful of chocolates. "There may be certain clients of Assets who thrive on getting their crotches out for the paps but, I, Sophia Brannigan, am not one of them. Do you hear me? I have more dignity than that! Didn't you tell them I have more dignity than that?"

Cara cowered as Sophia's voice hit a crescendo.

"I have morals, believe it or not, and I will work damned hard at turning this whole thing around!" She took a deep breath and pushed her hair out of her eyes. "Did they say anything else?"

"No, but Jake Johnston phoned straight after them."

"What? When?"

"Two minutes ago. When you were on the phone to Dylan . . . I didn't like to interrupt . . ."

"If I am on the phone to *Barack Obama* and Jake Johnston phones, for God's sake *interrupt* me! Now, what did he say? Is he going to sue for me for damage to his reputation? I called him clumsy! Oh, this is the worst day of my life!"

Cara was enjoying being in the driving seat for a change. She had vital information and she could withhold it for as long as she wanted.

"Er, he said . . . actually the line was quite bad. I hope I got this right . . . what *did* he say exactly?" She paused and leaned on the back of a chair, secretly enjoying how she could sometimes make Sophia sweat, now that she knew her agenda.

"Cara! *Where* is your notebook?"

Cara pursed her lips in thought, then slowly took her notebook from her apron pocket.

"Yes, I've got it now. Here it is. He said . . . he said that you gained the equivalent of half a million quids' worth of exposure for his magazine's sponsorship of Amanda's party in the tabloids today and if you can send him in a 600-word piece on last night's events by 3 o'clock this afternoon, you have the columnist job. If he likes your work, that is. Which I'm sure he will."

Sophia's face twisted a bit and then her tears and snot seemed to evaporate as her face broke into a huge grin. Cara noticed how her eyes didn't really change expression but then neither would yours if they were frozen solid from Botox. This lasted for what seemed like two days before Sophia finally spoke.

"You should have interrupted me! I mean, Dylan, Jake, Dylan, Jake." She illustrated her point by waving her hands from side to side. "There's simply no competition when it comes to my career. *Mwah, mwah!*"

Cara couldn't help but laugh as Sophia kissed the shoe which she had been cradling like a sick baby all morning.

"Good news?"

"Excellent news," she said and kissed the shoe again, then spoke to it directly. "I knew the moment I laid eyes on you that you were special. You little beauty! You may have just got me up another rung on the ladder of fame! Cara, forget complaining to anyone for the rest of the day. I have a column to write and I'm going to do it now. Do not disturb!"

Cara felt a huge relief now that the shoe drama had turned out for the best and she went out into the garden to make a sneaky phone call to Natalie who would be wetting herself at this stage for the latest information.

"Are you sacked?" Natalie squealed the moment she answered. "Juicy John's needs someone to work evenings. I've already put a word in for you."

"No, I'm not sacked at all," said Cara. "In fact I think I might have earned Sophia more column inches in the tabloids than she could have ever wished for."

"What? How?"

"Well, she is just realising how she can maximise all of this exposure to her own benefit. In an 'all publicity is good publicity' kind of way. I'm in the clear. Crystal clear."

Natalie excused herself to serve a customer and then came back on the line.

"You know what, Cara Jane McCarthy?" she said. "Sometimes I truly believe that if you fell into a pile of shit you would come up smelling of Chanel."

Cara giggled. "What's Chanel?"

"McCarthy, I am going to pretend you didn't say that."

"I'm joking! Look, I'll see you this evening. Takeaway for dinner to celebrate?"

"Deal," said Natalie.

Cara hung up, then took a good look around her. The grounds of Summer Manor were a paradise in their own right and the soft hum of the lawnmower in the distance mixed with the smell of fresh cut grass filled her senses. There was no doubt about it, if Sophia was out of the equation, this place would be heaven on earth.

She walked back inside the kitchen and continued with her chores, all the while wondering how Sophia was getting on upstairs with her column. Cara had always wanted to be a columnist. She loved reading the views of all sorts of opinion-makers in newspapers and magazines in Ireland and often scribbled down her own ideas. What angle would Sophia take in her efforts to impress Jake Johnston? Witty? Sarcastic? Droll? Bitchy? All of the above? She took her pen and notebook from her apron pocket and sat down at the breakfast bar. Where would *she* start, if it were her job to impress Jake Johnston and his team at *Fab!*? She imagined she would be quite tongue in cheek. She would give her readers little titbits of information that would let them see into this world of glamour with just a hint of a glimmer that it wasn't always as pleasant as it seemed, just as Amanda had more or less told her.

WAG Tales she began with a smile and the ideas began to flow. *By Sophia Brannigan. The benefits of wearing knickers,* she wrote, *even on a hot summer night was*

emphasised last night at the annual charity ball at the home
of Andy and Amanda Stewart. I'd always wanted to do the
foxtrot in a ball gown but instead I ended up in a pose more
suited to the Scissor Sisters than Strictly Come Dancing when
my brand-new <u>(insert designer name here as I have forgotten</u>
<u>already. Nat would be disgusted)</u> – stilettos snapped under
my enthusiastic disco moves. No doubt most of you will be
now familiar with my matching red thong but doesn't it pay
to do what your mummy used to tell you – as long as you
are fit to get up and enjoy yourself, do so with pride but
remember, your knickers must be a) on, and b) matching!

Now for the juicy detail on the shoes, news and views of
all those lucky enough to secure tickets to the hottest charity
event in town!!!

Cara took a sharp intake of breath when she heard
footsteps come into the kitchen as she dotted her third
exclamation mark. Could Sophia be finished already?
She couldn't have written a full review of the entire
evening in twenty minutes. The kitchen door swung
open and Cara stuffed the notebook into the nearest
drawer and pretended she was looking for a Brillo pad
as Sophia headed for the fridge.

"It's just not happening," she said, taking a long
drink of mineral water straight from the bottle. "I just
can't seem to get going at all. I hate doing things under
pressure. This sucks."

"Maybe you have writer's block?" suggested Cara,
scrubbing an imaginary stain on the draining board.

"Maybe you have writer's block!" mocked Sophia in a high-pitched tone. "Look missy, just because you accompanied me last night to a one-off event doesn't make you an expert in my life. I will get this column written. I just need to get a bloody starting point!"

Cara on the other hand was bursting with ideas. "Well, how about if you began with something self-deprecating, like . . ." She looked up from her scrubbing to see that Sophia's brow was furrowed, as much as it possibly could be under its surgical strain, and that no matter how stuck she was, she was not ready to accept her housekeeper's advice.

"Listen, sunshine," she said. "All that I can recall about last night's party is how you never obeyed one rule I set for you and how you chatted up photographers behind my back, not to mention chin-wagging with Amanda when I told you not to *and* when I fell over you conveniently were at the ladies' and didn't return until our cab arrived ten minutes later. Some chaperone you turned out to be!"

"Sorry, I couldn't help it. The champagne was running through me. I think it was off."

Sophia stared in disgust and then marched out of the kitchen mumbling and chanting positive thoughts to let her creativity flow.

When the coast was clear, Cara took out her pen and notebook again and continued to write until, half an hour later, her version of her column was finished.

She read it aloud to herself, giggling at some of her observations, like when the poor girlfriend of a junior player turned up in the same dress as the hostess herself, only to be asked to politely leave the party. As nice as Amanda Stewart seemed to be, she was not one to be upstaged at her own party in her own home.

She popped the notebook back into the drawer and sighed as she dragged her mind back to reality. This really was a dream world where there was plenty of activity and characters but no one seemed real, apart from Sam. And maybe Dylan. She thought of how it seemed like she was a million miles away from home in Donegal, where people were hearty and wholesome and real and in times of trouble they helped each other out. In Sophia's world, seeing someone in trouble was the best chance you could get to leapfrog them and take what was theirs with you on the way.

Maybe she *was* wasting her time here after all. Despite her physical polishing up, she wasn't really cut out for a life of cleaning up after someone and it was proving to be a little more stressful than she intended. She could have taken her "adult gap year" back at home and worked at the family pub. Graceland was becoming rapidly dilapidated and with her sister Olivia still behaving like a teenager, and brother Liam acting like someone out of *Crimewatch*, she knew if she didn't take it under her wing, no one would.

At the same time, a Master's degree and years of experience in a high-flying job in Belfast was a bit high to fall from to run a family business just because no one else wanted it. She needed time to think, to reassess her life and she had promised herself to let go of everything for just one year. She quickly weighed up her options – had she taken over Graceland she would have been jumping out of the frying pan and into the fire with refurbishments and accounts and staffing issues and she knew she would have to run the place well if she was going to do it at all. Here, the most trying task that came her way was which cleaning product to use on which surface, and whether or not she preferred the view over the swimming pool to the view over the tennis court at Summer Manor.

Yes, Sophia was a trying old bitch but she was a pussycat in comparison to Michael Bradley back in Belfast who had made Cara's life a misery, or listening to moaning locals who insisted that they preferred the rundown look of Graceland to Cara's more ambitious plans.

"So, how did my little Cinderella get on at the ball?"

Sam Potts took off his working boots at the back door and made his way across the kitchen, bringing Cara out of her career conundrum and back into the present. She lifted her head from the dishwasher and noticed how the old man's eyes looked tired and his skin off colour. Yet he still managed to give her his usual warm smile.

"Oh, I suppose it was okay," said Cara, closing the dishwasher door and waving away a puff of steam. "Not as fun as I thought it would be and I'm sure you've heard or at least read in the papers about Sophia breaking her shoe and falling on the dance floor."

Sam looked around before he allowed himself a chuckle. "I've been warned it's not a good subject to bring up at the moment. Poor Dylan left this morning for his training session with a right earache. How he puts up with all that newspaper nonsense is beyond me, but you know how it is. It's the back pages he needs to be concentrating on and not the front and he knows it, but if The Witch had her way she would have him in a double-page spread, selling his soul for celebrity."

"The Witch?"

"It's my new name for her. I think she has potions and lotions and a broomstick in that dressing room of hers upstairs. That's why she is so bloody particular about who goes in and out of it."

"Or a voodoo doll where she curses anyone more successful or glamorous than she is! I suppose that does make sense!"

Cara put the kettle on, knowing that at around this time every morning it was safe for her and Sam to share a pot of tea and discuss how they might change the world with their ambitious views and opinions on totally random subjects that came to mind. Tea breaks in Summer Manor were taken strictly on schedule when "The Witch" was around and they both knew, since she was in the house, this one would be kept short and sweet.

"It really was very funny last night, though. I can laugh now but I have to admit at the time I was terrified of how she would react." Cara's voice fell to a whisper and she felt a fit of the giggles coming on. "If you had only seen the position she ended up in! I'm telling you, all that yoga and Pilates sure comes in handy when you kick your heels too high."

Cara took the teapot and sat it on a table-mat in front of Sam who excused himself to wash his hands before they ate and drank their fill.

"She is a determined young lass, that's for sure," said Sam. "I'm just about getting used to her routines and moods at this stage and she's been living here for along time now."

He sat back down and licked his lips as Cara laid out a platter of cheddar cheese and biscuits she had hidden at the bottom of the fridge behind Sophia's cottage cheese and cracker bread.

"Did Dylan have any other girlfriends then? I mean before he fell head over heels with Sophia? Or was it she fell head over heels for him since she seems so good at it?"

Sam laughed and took a sup of his tea. He wiped the sweat from his brow with a handkerchief and looked at Cara. "Put it like this, he has never been short of female admirers, our Dylan. But he was badly scarred last year when his ex, Davina, sold nasty stories about him to the papers. Then he met Sophia and jumped right in. With anyone else, he is a big strong personality with lots of views and opinions but when she is around he is like a love-struck puppy. His father would never believe it, if he was here. Though I'm sure he is watching all of this and giving his own opinions to someone or other."

Cara noticed Sam's face drop sadly at the thought of his old friend.

"I'm sorry, I don't know much about Dylan's past. When did his dad die?"

Sam waved his hand as he put down his cup and swallowed a mouthful of tea.

"No, no, no. He is still very much alive, is our old Dave. He lives up North but I'm afraid he and Dylan haven't spoken in almost four years. As you can imagine, it hasn't been easy. I'm sure he keeps up with Dylan's life through the sports pages. And now Sophia's through the front pages."

Cara felt as if she'd put both her feet right in it. Dylan Summers was her employer and she had no right to probe into his personal life. She regretted everything she had just said.

"You'd be better staying well away out of it, hen," said Sam. "Indeed, sometimes I wish I had. It's a messy, messy situation."

"You're right, Sam," said Cara, cradling her hot cup of tea. "It's absolutely none of my business what Dylan does in his personal life. None. I won't ever pry again."

7

The Wonder of You

"She's got a dog!" said Sophia and she threw a copy of the *Daily* something or other on the kitchen worktop under Cara's nose. "I finally get myself some coverage and she goes and steals my thunder with her cutsie-wootsie photos of her two baby girls and a poppet of a puppy playing in the park. It's on every blooming front page of the evening news. Like, aren't there wars going on in the world? Shouldn't Amanda be even slightly hung over after the party last night?"

Cara studied the full-colour photos that graced the newspapers. They *were* sickeningly sweet as Amanda's perfectly made-up face gazed in adoration at her toddler twin girls who held between them a tiny white Chihuahua that looked like it would fit in your pocket. The babies were dressed impeccably in pale lemon and white sun-dresses while Amanda wore figure-hugging white shorts, a lemon vest top and a pair of must-have wedges. Her head was cocked to one side as she took in the playful pose her twins had adopted on a trip to the park. *"The Adorables"* read one headline, *"Picture Perfect"* said another. The article claimed that now that the twins, Abigail and Meg, were almost two years old, it was just a matter of time before modelling agencies would scramble over each other to sign them up for world-leading product endorsements. Opinion-column celebrity "experts" dismissed this claim, stating that Amanda and Andrew Stewart were way too shrewd to let their daughters be plunged so blatantly into the spotlight through advertisements and PR pitches. Amanda had class. Unlike other women in her field who would sell their placenta on eBay if it would increase their profile.

Sophia lifted the newspapers when Cara was in the middle of reading a sentence and flung them into the recycling bin under the sink. She had been like a demon since she hadn't heard back from Jake Johnston about her column. She strutted about like a peacock with a period, desperately trying to conjure up ideas for photographs and how to tip off the paps to catch her in an interesting pose that didn't show her knickers.

"Oh, I've had enough of this nonsense," she said. "I'm off for some therapy and then I'm having my nails redone. I can't be bothered with the stress of it all. Jake can stuff his column and Amanda Stewart can shove her perfection where the sun doesn't shine."

Cara thought Sophia was going to cry. She really did fear she was losing the plot and Cara felt just a tiny bit sorry for her.

"Give me your notebook, Cara," she demanded. "I want to leave you a to-do list and it all centres around making me feel better."

"It's in the drawer," said Cara and then she gasped. Shit! The column!

Sophia rummaged in the drawers around the kitchen, slamming each one.

"I'll get it," said Cara, but she was too late.

Sophia lifted out the notebook, flicked through the pages and then stopped.

"What's this?" she snapped, holding open the notebook where Cara's sample column was scrawled. She let out a guffaw. "Are you obsessed with me, Cara? Do you want to be me?"

Cara stuttered and felt her face burn with embarrassment. She hadn't meant for anyone, especially not Sophia, to find her ramblings.

"I . . . I can explain."

"Hush!" said Sophia and she scanned the page, her face twitching at every paragraph. She even let out a muffled giggle at one point. Cara was terrified and her heart jumped when Sophia viciously tore out the page. She folded it, stuffed it in her over-sized handbag then marched out into the hallway.

"I really didn't want anyone to . . . Please! You seem very upset!" shouted Cara, running after her. "I was just —"

"I am *not* upset," said Sophia as her heels clicked back towards where Cara now stood, mortified. "Look, little Miss I-can-do-everything-that-you-do Prim. From now on, just clean and do as I say, do you hear?"

"I hear."

"Now, I have business to attend to in my office, and then I'm going out for a few hours to let off some steam. Dylan is on the golf course so don't expect him back. Goodbye."

And at that The Witch was gone in a puff of perfume upstairs to her office.

"Shit!" said Cara. Now Sophia thought she was some sort of stalker!

Twenty minutes later she heard the front door slam and then the vroom of Sophia's car heading down the drive.

Cara looked around the house, which was eerily silent now. She wondered should she do the dregs of the laundry but she had most of it under control. Just a few bed sheets that had never been slept on needed ironing and she wondered how she was going to fill the last few hours of her Friday afternoon. The piano room was gleaming, the bedrooms were as neat as ninepence and you could eat your breakfast, dinner and supper off the bathroom floors. She let out a sigh, knowing the urge to snoop in the dressing room was beginning to niggle at her again. She lifted her notebook and pen and cringed at the thought of what Sophia had just read. She didn't want to be Sophia. She couldn't stand Sophia. But just a glimmer of the lifestyle would be oh so nice . . .

With Sophia now gone and her chores up to date, there was nothing else for it and before she knew it, she was back at the doors of the dressing room, key in hand, the same flow of adrenaline pumping through her body as before. And as much as the red-shoe alerts that flashed across her brain warned her not to, she went back inside.

She pulled up a stool at the ornate make-up table and looked at herself in the mirror. Anti-wrinkle creams were lined up in order of body parts, shades of foundations were sorted like soldiers in alphabetical order and there were eye-shadows in every colour of the rainbow.

Out of the corner of her eye she spotted, draped over a small chair, the Versace gown she had worn the evening before. It wouldn't do any harm to try it on again, would it? She walked over and let her fingers feel once more the soft satin finish of the deep purple dress. Then she lifted it against her body. Her hair was still straight from Natalie's fine efforts and her neck and arms glowed from the spray tan which was certain to last for a few more days at least. Cara laid the dress back down and slowly peeled off her T-shirt and then her elastic-waisted track bottoms, kicking her trainers across the carpet. She pulled the dress over her head. Then she walked across to the rows of shoeboxes and found a pair of silver sandals she had never laid eyes on before. They had been worn perhaps once she guessed, and she slipped her feet into them, adding a magnificent four inches to her five-foot-two-inch frame.

Then, she clipped on a pair of diamond earrings and pulled her hair behind her ears so she could admire her new image in all its glory. She looked good, so good. She had found the fashion bug after years of skulking about like something that was dragged out of a ditch and she could never go back to being Cara "Plain Jane" McCarthy again.

"Now," she said in a posh English accent, "I think I'll go and fix some afternoon tea."

She carefully strode across the landing towards the stairs and took each step as if she was treading on glass. There was no way she could go any faster in these shoes even if she tried. As she approached the bottom of the staircase, the shrill ring of the doorbell made her wobble and she turned to run back up the stairs.

Easier said than done on these heels. She turned and looked towards the door once more, urging whoever the doorbell ringer was to get tired of buzzing and buzz off.

After a short spell of silence she took a few steps closer to the door, hoping that the coast was clear, but a face was staring at her from the other side of the glass panels and she knew she had to answer the caller who had already seen her in all her finery.

Cara had to act fast. If she answered the door she could be Sara again, she supposed. She would take a message for Dylan or Sophia and the stranger at the door would never know any different. She cocked her head up and walked with false confidence towards the oversized front door and then opened it with a smile that almost broke her face. It was quite difficult to be so false.

"Hi there, can I help you?" she said, her insides churning with fear in case the mystery visitor should know she was a fake.

"Good afternoon, Miss – Miss Brannigan. I'm from Hastings Deliveries. I have a, er, I have a – well, a delivery for you, obviously. Can you sign here, please?"

Cara caught her breath, realising that the man in front of her had mistaken her for Sophia. So her hair was the same colour and she was tanned and wearing her clothes and shoes and earrings but surely that is where the similarity ended? Well, she hoped.

"Hello and thank you so much," she muttered to the young man who she guessed was no more than her own age. He seemed nervous in a gentle way and his eyes gave away the fact that he was in awe that his delivery schedule had brought him to the doors of Summer Manor.

Cara took the pen from his clipboard and scrawled Sophia's name so that it was illegible. She took the package from his hands and nodded with a smile.

"So how do you enjoy working for Hastings Deliveries? I hope they treat you well?" she asked.

The man stepped backwards, clearly in shock that the woman he had been warned might bite his family allowance off was being so normal. And nice.

"Er, it's really, well, interesting. Let's just say I get to see a lot of the countryside. And the city of course. I like it. So far."

"Good," said Cara. "It's important to be happy in your work. I truly believe so," she said and the delivery boy scurried off towards his red van. He stopped and looked back at Cara with wide eyes, as if he was dying to say something but didn't know whether or not he should. Then he pushed his shoulders back and took a few steps closer to the front door again.

"I know I really shouldn't say this, but I'm going to anyway," he said. "Those pictures of you in the paper today when you were at the Amanda Stewart party? They don't do you any justice at all. You are much, much more beautiful in real life."

He turned again and ran to his van, jumped in and

zoomed towards the gate where Sam let him back out.

"Christ!"

Cara stood against the back door and breathed in, then out again. What the hell was she playing at? She had just pretended to be Sophia! She had to stop this. It was going too far. She would pull herself together over the weekend and decide once and for all if this job was going to be more trouble than it was worth.

Project Graceland with its leaky roof and smelly toilets was becoming more and more appealing.

Sophia Brannigan held her mobile phone in her hand and sobbed like a baby. No news was good news, she tried to tell herself, but she knew her hopes of winning the columnist job were disappearing fast. She had parked her car in a country lane a few miles from Summer Manor to gather her thoughts.

Why did she have to work so damn hard for everything? She was so close yet so far away from everything she had ever wanted. All her life she had dreamed of a life of glamour and luxury and a career where she wouldn't have to do much but be admired for her beauty by everyone who met her. She deserved it, she told herself, and she would keep knocking on doors until she got it. Look how far she had come in just a few years. Back then, she had been working in a nightclub and modelling part time when she met Dylan Summers on a sportswear photo shoot. He was shy and nervous, where she exuded confidence and experience and within months she was mixing in circles she only ever dreamed of.

Where Dylan preferred to stay in the background, Sophia would push to the front, being the proverbial social butterfly mixing and mingling with wannabes and watching the experts work the media and make a career out of nothing. She watched wives and girlfriends of soccer stars rise to the top of the media ladder, publishing autobiographies before their twenty-first birthdays, endorsing clothing lines on the High Street, launching perfume ranges and building a brand around their celebrity, ensuring they had security should their footballer other half run away with the nanny. Even politicians' wives were making a name for themselves on the back of their other half's profile and, everywhere you looked, the wife of a celebrity chef was producing her own cookery books as quickly as she produced additions to her growing brood. It seemed so goddam easy.

But Sophia was struggling. So far, she had lost an underwear campaign to glamour girl Emily Evans, she had been pipped at the post for a TV advertising campaign by a soap star and now it looked like she couldn't even blag herself into *Fab!* magazine which was a haven and a cert for C-Listers.

She lifted her red shoe from its resting place on the passenger seat of the car and felt like flinging it out into a nearby field for some stupid farm animal to feast on, but something caught her eye. A fine sliver of what looked like glue ran around the heel exactly where it had snapped and her heart pounded in her chest. Had she been sold a dud? Her temper rose once more. That snobby shopping assistant would find herself at the end of the dole queue when she reported this little faux pas. No one messed with Sophia Brannigan's credibility and got away with it. She lifted her phone and dialled home to speak to Cara.

"Get me Belle's Boutique's number right now, Cara. Someone is just about to lose their job over there."

"Er, I'm sorry Sophia, what do you mean?"

"I mean I was set up. I always knew that blonde bitch with the cow's lick in her hair had it in for me. She sold me a shoe that was already broken! Can you believe it? I will ruin her and that jumped-up doll that owns the place. She is history. Get me the number. Now!"

Sophia could hear Cara rummaging at the other end of the line and it was getting up her nose.

"What is the name of the shop again?" Cara asked.

"Oh for Christ's sake, Cara, wakey, wakey! Actually now that I think of it, *you* can call her. That's what I pay you for, isn't it? I mean, why should I get my hands dirty by telling some pathetic little princess she has made the mistake of her career? You tell her. Tell Belle to sack her assistant or I'll go to the press on this. And I mean it!"

Sophia fell silent and Cara was having palpitations at her hesitation.

"Sophia?"

"Her name is Charlotte. I've just remembered. She must have been trying on the shoes behind Belle's back. Tell Belle to sack Charlotte! Simple as that!"

"Sophia, it was me."

"I beg your pardon," Sophia stuttered. "Why does everything have to be about you? It was my shoe!"

"I, er . . . I broke your shoe," said Cara and the earth fell silent as both women swallowed what had just been confessed. Cara took a huge breath. "I'm so, so sorry, I tried to fix it, well my friend did. But look on the bright side – you've got all this publicity and –"

"*You . . . you* broke my shoe?"

"Yes. But –"

"You let me wear that shoe knowing that I could have broken my back by wearing it! You let me dance with Jake Johnston knowing fine well that I was taking my life, and more importantly, my career into my own hands? You cheeky, no, you evil little bitch. You're fired, McCarthy!"

"But, I tried –"

"Fired! Sacked! You know, given the boot, the elbow, whatever way you want to put it. No one snoops around my property and gets away with it. Now get your things and leave my house immediately!"

Sophia hung up and with all her might she flung the broken shoe out through the far window into a ditch, not caring that she had stunned a cow in the process. She vroomed down the laneway, swerving at the last minute to avoid an old farmer on a bicycle and stood on the horn in frustration.

Her mobile rang with no caller display and she stared at it, contemplating whether or not to take the call. Eventually she pressed the answer button, realising that her day couldn't possibly get any worse.

"What?" she sniffled. "This had better be bloody well good news because so far I am having a shit day and I don't think you want to add to it if you value your life!"

"Darling, it's Jake Johnston, *Fab!* magazine. Can you talk? You seem a tad flustered?"

Sophia straightened herself and dabbed her eyes. She had to pull herself together, win, lose or draw. She still had her dignity, somewhere. She stopped the car again in the middle of the country lane.

"Yes, yes, of course, Mr Johnston. How are you?"

"I'm good, Sophia. Really good. Now, about the column. I read your piece."

Sophia gulped. "You didn't like it, did you? Look, never mind, I sort of gathered that by now, but –"

"You're right, I didn't like it." Jake Johnston let out a chuckle. "Sophia, Sophia, I absolutely loved it!"

"I beg your pardon?"

"I *loved* it! It's so refreshing to see one of you lot

115

with a sense of humour. How you could recount your fall in the middle of a dance floor with such honesty and fun! It's just what my magazine needs. My favourite line is – wait – oh, here it is . . . '*At least I was wearing knickers. Can you imagine the jealousy of all my fellow wannabes if I'd exposed more flesh than they had?*' Classic! And the name of the column is spot on. We'll run with it this week and we'll need some new photos to go with it. Can you wear red for the photo shoot?"

Sophia's eyes widened as she realised what she was getting herself into. He loved it! And then what he had said sank in. When she had found Cara's column, she had emailed it to Jake as a second option and now he had chosen it over her original. He liked her cleaner's column, not hers. Should she come clean? Hell no.

"Yes," said Sophia, almost biting her nails and then stopping herself just in time. False nails were so last year. "I can do that. I can wear red. I'll wear polka dots and stripes if you want me to. Actually, that's a lie. I wouldn't."

"Excellent," he said. "Wear red shoes like those you refer to in your story and a red thong just in case we need you to 'flash some flesh'. Oh, 'WAG Tales' is going to be fabulous. *You* are going to be fabulous. Welcome to the team, Sophia."

8

Bossy Nova Baby

Cara's second most favourite thing in life, next to her new-found passion for fashion, was her Friday night takeaway. But instead of marking the end of a working week, tonight's feast was set to mark the beginning of Cara's first stint of unemployment since she left college.

"Chin up, babe," said Natalie. "That silly cow doesn't know how sorry she'll be for letting you go. You are way better than her. Now, put your feet up and let's start our Friday night wind-down as we had intended to. It's takeaway time."

For as long as Cara could remember, Friday evening in Kilshannon was when Cara's mum took a night off from the kitchen and her dad would arrive home with a huge brown bag of fish and chips from the local fryer. It was something she and Natalie had carried on into their adult life as flat mates and it had always given Cara a sense of home when she left to live in Belfast, and now, as a big girl in London. As children, she and Liam and their older sister Olivia would salivate as the traditional fish supper was laid out on the kitchen table, with a glass of cold milk each and some bread and butter for chip butties and lots of salt and vinegar. It was her favourite meal of the week.

Now, the fish supper had been replaced with Chicken Chow Mein and the glass of milk had become a glass of cold white wine, but the thrill of it was just the same. She and Natalie would set the table as they waited for the Chinese delivery, and since Liam was still with them, he would squeeze in too and they would try to wring some money out of him in return.

"Any chance of a tenner, sis?" he asked, drumming his fingers on the small table they used for dining. "I'm going down to the pub quiz and I'm running a bit tight on the old financial front."

"No bloody wonder," said Natalie. "What excitement did you get up to today? See the Olsen twins walk straight past our door? Don't forget you've a flight to catch too. An overdue flight that is, so if I were you I'd be saving my pennies not spending them on pub quizzes."

"Ha fucking ha," said Liam as Cara handed him a crisp twenty-pound note. "At least I won't be eating your precious Chinese takeaway, you tight –"

"That's enough, Liam!" said Cara, wanting to reprimand Natalie too for taunting him.

"Thanks, Cara. You know I'll get it back to you when I can. Mum is sending me over some extra this week."

He stood up, kissed Cara on the cheek and made his way out through the front door. Cara avoided Natalie's eye. She knew what was coming and wasn't sure she was in the mood to take it.

"You are way too soft with that boy," said Natalie as she lifted the knife and fork she had originally laid out for Liam and put it back in the cutlery drawer. "If you don't stop giving him money he'll never get a job. And, more importantly, if you don't stop giving him money, he'll never go home and that won't do any of us any good."

Cara bit her tongue to stop herself lashing out. As much as she had loved Natalie since they met ten years ago when she was a fresh-faced student and Natalie had bagged her a job in the Student's Union, blood was thicker than water and even though she knew Liam was heading for Loser Land the longer he camped out on their apartment floor, he was her kid brother and she didn't like to hear anyone saying anything bad about him. She, however, could say whatever she liked about him but she didn't like to hear it from others. That's just the way it was.

"He won't be here for much longer," said Cara. "I promise. I just want to give Mum a break. She worries about him so much when he's at home but she knows he's safe here with me to watch over him. Give it another week or so and I'll give him a gentle nudge."

"You can't baby-sit him forever, Cara. And neither can I."

Cara knew Natalie had a point, but it didn't stop her words knifing her where it hurt. "I know."

The doorbell rang and Cara jumped to answer it. She knew if she sat on she would say more than she should, so she grabbed her purse and went to collect their dinner. Natalie knew only a snippet of Liam's antics and bothers at home and that was the way Cara wanted to keep it.

"Fourteen pounds altogether, please," said the delivery guy and Cara rummaged in her purse, unable to concentrate on counting out the correct change. She lifted her eyes and did a double take as she recognised the man at the door. She knew by the look on his face that he recognised her too.

"Em, yes, just a second." She closed the door slightly and took a deep breath, her heart thumping as she searched for pound coins amongst credit-card receipts and store-discount vouchers. Gathering two ten-pound notes in a ball, she passed them round the door and reached for the paper takeaway bag from the man who was whistling casually and looking around him.

"I know you from somewhere, don't I?" he said, looking right at her and trying to hold her gaze as he reluctantly let go of the bag.

Cara buried her chin into her chest and shook her head. "No, definitely not. I just moved in here. Never saw you before in my life. Mistaken identity. Keep the change."

She closed the door and stood up against it, realising how close she was to being made an utter fool of.

"Well, in that case you have a twin living at the other side of town. A very rich twin," said the man through the letterbox. "And gorgeous. Are you single?"

"No!" lied Cara. "Now, don't you have more deliveries to make? Bye!"

Cara felt like kicking the door, no, kicking herself actually for how stupid she had been. For the man who delivered the Chinese was the same person who had mistaken her for Sophia Brannigan earlier that day. The same person she had let *believe* she was Sophia Brannigan earlier that day. Delivering Chinese take-aways was obviously his evening job! She was skating on very thin ice and she knew she had got away from Summer Manor just before she made a total and utter fool of herself. Perhaps Sophia Brannigan had just done her a major favour by giving her the boot.

Dylan Summers arrived home from his evening two-mile sprint to see his girlfriend dressed down in all her finery. She greeted him at the door wearing a black silk and lace robe that skimmed her thighs and a pair of killer heels that made her half an inch taller than he was. Her nails matched her blood-red lips. She had all of the curtains pulled to give warmth to the huge home they shared and the soft sounds of their favourite love songs filled the background.

She led him into the dining room where a huge candelabrum glowed and a blazing fire scorched in the corner, creating a truly sensual atmosphere. Slowly, she poured him a glass of chilled champagne, then clinked her glass with his and pulled out a chair for him to take a seat.

"What's this all about?" he asked in surprise and, if the truth were told, a slight edge of fear. The last time Sophia had pulled out the stops like this was when Fulton had been promoted to the Premiership club a year ago but he couldn't remember having been treated this way since then. Not even on his birthday. Sophia normally preferred to dine out of the home where she would have a chance of being photographed by the tabloids or where she might accidentally on purpose bump into a celebrity whose fame grade was slightly higher than hers.

"I have good news, darling," she said and she scooped out some steaming Chicken Tikka Masala from a silver dish onto the plate in front of him, then added rice to the side. It looked delicious, but then so did she. "I know you don't normally like to eat such rich foods during training season but I hope you don't mind celebrating with me."

Somewhere beneath her jovial mood, Dylan sensed that for once in her life, Sophia was nervous and this was making him all the more so.

"Go on, then. Are you going to tell me?" he asked. "Are you pregnant?"

Sophia swallowed a sip of champagne and looked up at him from beneath her extra-long eyelashes.

"No, silly. You know babies aren't my thing. Not for a long time anyway and, even if they were, we'd need a bigger place than this."

Dylan pretended he didn't hear her last comment, but was relieved there were no tiny feet coming their way any time soon.

"So what is it then? Come on, tell me."

"I got the column! I got the column in *Fab!* mag!"

He held out a hand and squeezed hers tight. Fair play to Sophia. It was what she really wanted, but then she always did seem to get what she wanted.

"Fantastic. That's great news, love. I knew you would get the job." Dylan leaned over and gave his girlfriend a kiss on the cheek. "Congratulations! Now, what are you going to write about? Have you planned what to say?"

"Not exactly, but I'll manage."

There it was again, thought Dylan. She seemed unsure.

"Just the usual celebrity gossip, fashion tips, you know," she added, chasing a piece of chicken that had been killed in vain round her plate. It would never get as far as her stomach.

"Great stuff. Now, this looks great," said Dylan as he tucked into his Tikka. "And this place looks wonderful. You've really pulled out the stops with dinner."

"Mm," said Sophia, almost apologising for her lack of culinary skills. She knew it would have much more effect had she cooked it herself.

"Compliments to Cara, I suppose. This is fantastic. I must admit, Soph, you found a gem of a housekeeper this time."

Sophia's face fell. "Compliments to who?"

"Cara," said Dylan, then set down his knife and fork on noticing Sophia's reaction. "Oh no, don't tell me I got her name wrong again. I thought —"

"No, you didn't think at all, that's the problem. I just wonder why you supposed *she* made it and not me. I *can* cook, Dylan. I just don't have time. And Cara won't be cooking for us any more. I sacked her."

Dylan looked shocked. "Jesus, why? You said yourself she was perfect?"

"Yes, well, maybe that was the problem. Maybe she was too perfect. She was getting too cosy around here and I don't have time to baby-sit our housekeeper just the way I don't have time to do the work they are supposed to do. I need to strike a balance so I had to let her go. The little bitch was trying on my shoes. As if I have time to monitor that type of behaviour!"

Dylan smirked and held out his hand to Sophia who was wearing her pout to perfection.

"Don't be silly, babe. I know you don't have time. Shopping and monitoring Amanda Stewart's lifestyle is a full-time job. And now you'll have to write about it too."

Sophia stood up in a rage. "How dare you? How dare you belittle me like this? Why are you being so horrible, Dylan? What way is that to show your support? Would you rather that I slummed about here all day in rags like our housekeeper, just so you can be satisfied that you've a domestic goddess at home waiting for you on the sidelines of *your* hot-shot career?"

Dylan speared a piece of chicken on his fork. He hadn't intended to sound so mean, but all this obsession with celebrity was grating on his nerves and he had so much more important things he needed to talk to Sophia about. He didn't give a toss about other people's business. He had feelings and thoughts about things that were so far removed from Sophia's priorities.

"Sometimes I wish we could talk about stuff that

really matters, that's all. I'm sorry but I don't think it makes much difference to either of us if Emily Evans strips to her knickers at an awards ceremony, or if Amanda Stewart's baby burps in public. I just don't care any more, but it seems to be all you can talk about."

"But why does it always have to be about you? This is your house, your cars are parked at the doors, you pick the gardener, you pay the bills, you –"

"You picked the housekeeper."

"And, boy, do I regret that! I picked her because she was a frumpy little mousey girl who I'd hoped would go unnoticed around here, but Sam couldn't stop praising her and then you make me take her to a party and she gets more attention than I do and you drool over her cooking and then she broke my shoe and –"

Sophia stopped herself before she mentioned the fact that even Jake Johnston had chosen Cara's column over hers. The woman was taking over her life!

"Sophia, can you please listen to yourself? My father, who hasn't spoken to me in four years, is likely to drink himself to death any of these days and there is very little I can do about it and meanwhile, back at the ranch, the toughest thing you seem to have to deal with is a broken shoe! Admit it, Cara was great around here and you know it! She and Sam being here meant that you and I had nothing to do, only come and go as we pleased. Didn't you appreciate that at all? Give the girl a break."

"Oh, so you do think she is wonderful too, then? Well, then, tell her to keep her filthy paws to herself. One day my shoes, the next day she'll be setting her sights on you!"

"Please don't tell me you were jealous of our housekeeper, honey. You are paranoid beyond belief."

Sophia sat back down again and pushed some rice around her plate. She couldn't tell Dylan the truth about the column. She had made the right decision. After all, the longer Cara McCarthy spent around their home, the more of an influence she was having over their lives. She just had to go.

Cara flicked through the television channels and sighed in fatigue at how many reality shows dominated the box. The apartment was cold and with three of them sharing and only one now fit to pay their way, things were set to get tighter financially than she cared to admit. She pulled a throw from the back of the armchair and tucked it around her, then flicked again, hoping to come across something that might lift her mood or at least distract her for half an hour or so until she felt tired enough to sleep. Apart from the odd chat show, there was nothing else, only reality shows with Desperado Joe Publics or "celebrities" pushing for their fifteen minutes of fame by exposing themselves in any way they could. Surely there were less fickle people in the world to entertain us on a Friday night, she thought and took a gulp of her wine.

She hated drinking alone, so the same glass she had poured to drink with her Chinese had lasted over two hours. Natalie had gone to bed as the atmosphere was anything but civilised since Liam left and Cara was determined to wait up for her brother, feeling more protective than ever.

She checked the clock to see if it was too late to call her mother. For the first time in a few months, Cara felt homesick and she longed to hear her mother's lilting voice telling her not to be silly and that everything was going to be all right even if she did have a weird fetish for trying on other people's clothes and breaking their shoes etc.

She dialled the number and waited for her mum's friendly voice.

"Hello, Graceland Saloon Bar and Restaurant," said her dad.

"Oh, hiya, Dad! It's just me." Cara's father rarely answered the phone but when he did, he tended to exaggerate the level of establishment he was running. "There's no need to give the full title every time you answer the phone."

"But, admit it, it sounds great. I'll get your mother now. Everything okay?"

"Yes, fine."

"And Liam?"

"Good." Cara gulped. Just get Mum, she thought.

"Right, here she is then."

Cara could hear the clip-clop of her mother's shoes across the bar and she smiled already.

"Hello there, wee pet. How are things in the city of London?"

"Great, Mum. And how is everyone in the city of Kilshannon?" Cara tried her best to sound upbeat. The last thing she wanted was for her mother to sense she was feeling a bit down in the dumps.

"Oh, you know this place, full of excitement as always," said Margaret. "Actually, now that you mention it, I do have a bit of news. The post office was robbed on Thursday afternoon. Now, beat that if you can. Would you ever have thought? A robbery in Kilshannon? It even made the Big Newspapers in Belfast!"

Cara smiled as her mother paused for effect. She remembered how things like that were talked about for years and knew she'd have to gasp and condemn it outright.

"Gosh, that's terrible," she said in the most dramatic tone she could find. "Poor Minnie! Was she hurt?"

"No, the poor wee mite was badly shaken and sure you know she's not good with her nerves as it is. It won't do her any good, that's for sure. She was in here earlier and she downed two brandies. Two. They could rob the place dry tonight again and she wouldn't hear a thing."

Cara also recalled how a lot of people around Kilshannon weren't "Good With Their Nerves". She wondered who decided that and if the people knew that they weren't good with their nerves themselves, or if it was a diagnosis by neighbours that they were unaware of.

"So, any news with you?" continued Margaret McCarthy. "What about that son of mine? At least they can't blame him for the post office robbery when he's safe over there with you."

Now it was Cara's turn to pause. Not for effect though. She paused because she didn't really know how to answer.

"He's, um, well, he's still here obviously and I've told him he can stay for as long as he needs to but, you know, Mum, he'll have to go home and face the music at some stage."

"That's what I've been telling him," said Margaret and her voice began to shake. "I can't hold this from your father for much longer, Cara. I'm going to have to tell him."

"No, no, please don't, not yet. He'll collapse if he has to hear of another scandal in the family. Look, I think I hear the door. That'll be Liam back so I'd better go. Don't worry, Mum. I'll talk to him. Night night."

Cara hung up the phone and took a sip of her wine

which now tasted sour. So much for having a year of a stress-free lifestyle. So far, she couldn't even manage a Friday night in front of the box without watching Natalie take the huff and now her mother was upset.

She looked up at her baby brother who sat down on the couch opposite her and put his head in his hands. Over the past few weeks she had often wondered if Liam knew how his actions had affected those around him down the years, but as she watched him sob right now in the corner of her London apartment, Cara realised that he knew only too well.

"I'm scared, Cara," he said. "Don't tell anyone, but I'm really shit scared."

"It will be all right," she said and she joined him on the couch and pulled a throw over both of them. "It will be all right, you'll see."

9

Little Brother

Cara awoke on a bright sunny Monday morning to the usual sounds of Natalie blow-drying her hair and the blaring sound of GMTV from the sitting room. She had no plans for the day ahead whatsoever now that Summer Manor was as far from her life as it had been when she was back in Ireland.

Natalie called to her from the sitting room. "So do you want me to give Juicy John your number? It's not hard work and there's absolutely no chance of you breaking any of *his* shoes. He wears sandals or clogs most days."

Cara turned over on the bed and wondered if she should take on Natalie's generous, if uninviting offer.

"I'm not totally convinced, no offence," said Cara.

"But give me one day of daytime television and I'll probably be scrambling down to that mall begging Juicy John to let me squeeze some of his Jaffas."

Natalie strode into Cara's bedroom with a toothbrush in her right hand and a mouthful of froth.

"That's fine, but don't think we can keep this apartment afloat on one wage, Cara. I'm not slaving over smoothies and frozen yoghurt for you and Junior out there to leech off me like I'm the daddy of this whole operation."

Cara snuggled further under the duvet. "I think we'd make a lovely little family, Nat. I could be the perfect housewife – after all, look at all the practice I got at Summer Manor," she said, with just a tinge of sadness. "Oh, how the hell did I manage to screw that one up, eh?"

Natalie sat on the edge of the bed in sympathy. She totally agreed that Cara had let the job from heaven slip through her fingers.

"You'll land on your feet out of this, McCarthy," she said. "Wait and see, there's something better for you just around the corner. You might fall in love with John's Juicer and before you know it there'll be mini-Juicers all over the UK with you appearing in all those Women in Business journals boasting of how you made your first million using home-grown produce."

Cara shrugged. "You're too kind, Nat . . . but I will find something, I suppose. Or I could always go home?"

"Don't even think about it," said Natalie, and she left the room to put on her citrus-coloured uniform.

Cara decided to use her first day of unemployment as an opportunity to spend some quality time with her kid brother. Since Liam had arrived, she had been so busy mopping and mooching around Summer Manor she hadn't even had time to show him around but, as she'd correctly supposed, Liam had found his own bearings quite quickly and seemed to know London much better than she did.

"So, if we take the Piccadilly Line, we can get off at Knightsbridge and have a look around the posh end of town. You should feel right at home there after all the time you spent hanging out with celebrities," he said as they studied a map of the Tube.

"Are you sure it isn't the District Line we need to get first? And for the record I did not spend my time hanging out with celebrities, Liam. I was merely a housekeeper to two jumped-up arseholes who wouldn't recognise the real world if it jumped up and bit them on their pert little bottoms."

Liam led the way towards the Underground as Cara shuffled alongside him. For an older sister, she looked quite cute in her flat silver pumps and leggings. She really was a little poppet in the nicest possible way and Liam knew he was lucky to have someone like her on his side. His eldest sister back at home still wasn't speaking to him after all the stress he had caused his mother over the past few months, but then she was just trying to stay in mummy's good books while Cara had recently proved that she could stray on the dark side just like he did from time to time, if the Michael Bradley episode was anything to go by.

"All right, let's drop the subject. No more work chat. After all, I can hardly contribute to the conversation as I'm not the ideal employee any more, am I?" said Liam. "Not as soon as all my dodgy business gets out in the open."

Cara linked her brother's arm and marched alongside him, desperately trying to match his long strides. He had the McCarthy height, while she took after her mother's petite side of the family. She wondered briefly how onlookers would judge them as they walked through the streets of London. She was hardly a match for her brother's bleached Mohican hairstyle and torn jeans with her modest duffle jacket and dark hair. She might have learned a few fashion tips from Sophia but she had yet to apply them to her own wardrobe.

"Let's not go into that today, Liam. I was hoping you and I could have a good old-fashioned afternoon out with sightseeing, a little shopping and a good old slap-up lunch to top it all off. Let's pretend that neither of us have a care in the world."

"I can't run away from it forever, sis. I'm due in court soon and I'll have a criminal record."

Cara leaned her head against her brother's shoulder.

"Stealing a few hundred quid is hardly equivalent to murder, you know. I'm sure you'll live to tell the tale and at least you've learned from it all. Not so long ago I was the talk of the town and by the time you get home it will be someone else. Sure, didn't I tell you the post office was robbed yesterday? It was music to my ears to hear that you're not the only criminal in town. Now, enough of that chat and help me figure out our route once and for all."

The city centre of London gave Cara a rush of excitement every single time she climbed the steps of the Underground onto the hubbub of its busy streets. The black taxis, the anonymity, the cultural diversity, the sounds, the smells, all filled her senses and she knew this was just what she needed to spread her wings and discover who and what she wanted to be in life. Kilshannon was claustrophobic and Belfast was too close to Kilshannon but here she could be whoever she wanted to be. Here, she wasn't a publican's daughter from the back end of beyond with a funny accent – she was just a girl who came from Ireland with whatever story she wanted to have. She was no longer the odd one out in the glamorous industry in which she had made her name over the past few years. She was no longer labelled as the silly little office junior whose stupidity led her into the arms of Michael Bradley only to be let down by all his empty promises and clichéd dreams.

"So, what shall we do first?" asked Liam as he stared around Bond Street. "Visit the Queen? Lunch with the Lords? Check in on Gordon and the guys in Downing Street?"

"How about we have a wander around Harrods and pretend to be rich and famous and then buy the cheapest thing we can find, just to say we were shopping there?"

Liam's eyes widened. Celebrity-spotting was his favourite London pastime after all so pretending to be a celebrity was right up his street. "Sounds like a plan. Now, look important. Who do you want to be?"

Cara thought. "I'll be Catherine Zeta-Jones."

"Cool. I'll be Ronaldo."

"Excellent. Together we are totally unrelated but unbelievably minted. Now, let's window-shop. And keep your fucking hands to yourself."

Harrods was like a maze of aisles of beautifully presented variety. The smell of summer fruits made Cara gasp with thirst and Liam headed straight for the food aisle where his mouth watered at the range of cakes and treats layered upon the shelves.

"So, what shall we have for dessert, Catherine? Tiramisu?" he said to his sister who was waving oddly at him from behind a triangular mountain of pineapples.

"Ssh," signalled Cara, shaking her head and running her fingers along her lips to tell him to zip it. She pointed towards a selection of chocolate éclairs behind Liam and warned him to be quiet. It took a few seconds for him to realise that she was hiding from someone. Someone standing behind him.

"But I didn't touch anything," he said.

"Shut up!"

Liam froze as instructed and then casually browsed along the food aisle, admiring a range of meringue nests and avoiding eye contact with Cara who by now was superglued to the fruit she was standing beside. The look on her face told Liam she was concentrating totally on the conversation of the person she didn't want to see. He stole a glance in the direction Cara had pointed out and guessed the mystery shopper with a mobile phone stuck to the side of her head could be one person and one person only.

Sophia Brannigan.

"Oh, don't worry. I can redo it," she was saying. "Yes, I get it. Of course I understand. Some warmth, some more humour, I know. Yes, the first version was quite natural but I'm just under a little bit of pressure at the moment. No, it isn't a problem at all. I'll get you another version, just as good as the first one. By Wednesday? Yes, I can do that. No, I won't let you down. Goodbye now, goodbye!" Sophia hung up and shoved the phone into her bag. "*Bastards!*"

She slammed some strawberries into her basket and sighed as she strolled absent-mindedly up the aisle. She bumped into a fellow shopper whose food spilled out of her hands but, instead of apologising or helping the poor lady, she marched off in the opposite direction in a fluster. Liam ran to the shopper's assistance while Cara checked the coast was clear and then emerged into public view just as her mobile phone rang.

It was Sophia.

"Er, hello," said Cara, waving once again to get her brother's attention and pointing frantically this time to her phone. She covered the phone with her hand. "It's her!" she hissed.

"Cara. I'm sorry," said Sophia.

"You're what? Sorry?" said Cara. "You'll have to speak up, Sophia. I can't hear you very well. I'm in, er, Lidl. I mean, Tesco."

Cara looked ahead down the aisle of Harrods to see Sophia march up another aisle, her mobile phone as always to her ear and her other hand holding her hair in stressed-out mode.

"I said, I'm sorry! Look, I need your help, Cara. I'm sorry for sacking you so unfairly. Can we start again? Please?"

Cara stared at Sophia in disbelief and wondered how someone could get so stressed out over shopping for strawberries in Harrods. The woman was deranged and for a split second Cara almost felt sorry for her.

"I'm not so sure, Sophia. What if it happens again? I need job security as well as the next person. I need to know you won't get rid of me in a few days' time."

"Oh, believe me, I won't," said Sophia. "Can you come back tomorrow? Dylan would really be delighted. He really misses having you around and said only yesterday how he would love some of your roast chicken and chomp."

"Champ," said Cara. "It's called champ, not chomp."

Cara's heart swelled for a second until she noticed the cold look on Sophia's face in the distance. The lying bitch. Dylan and his chomp had shit all to do with this. This had got to be for Sophia's own benefit. It always was.

She quickly weighed up her options.

Cleaning at Summer Manor was a much more pleasant option than serving shoppers in the evenings at John's Juicer. She didn't really have a choice, plus she really missed her morning tea with Sam and she hadn't said a proper goodbye to him. She wouldn't give in that easily, though. Sophia seemed desperate and Cara decided to play her at her own game.

"I think we both know Dylan couldn't give a toss who you hire and fire, Sophia," said Cara, knowing that for some reason she was in a position to call the shots for once. "I'll think about it. You can call me again tomorrow."

"Okay, okay. Tomorrow," said Sophia and she walked out of the store, unaware of Cara and now Liam watching her every move. "But think about it seriously, won't you? We can negotiate."

"Yes," said Cara. "We can negotiate." And she hung up the phone.

"What's up?" asked Liam who was really enjoying all this cloak and dagger stuff.

"I need a plan, that's what's up," she said. "I need time to think, but not now. Now, let's go and get pissed."

"At this time of day?" he asked, a broad grin sweeping over his face. "You're on. No problem."

They chose a bar off Bond Street that was full of modern-day yuppies in business suits and briefcases who fought over who could talk the most about capital shares and investments.

Cara looked at Liam who took one glance around the place, shook his head and they both walked straight back out. In his torn jeans and bomber jacket, Liam wasn't exactly dressed for the environment they had chosen so they walked further down the street, turned off several side streets until they were greeted by a huge shamrock and a harp hanging from the side of a mock stone wall.

"Home!" said Liam and they almost raced each other inside to the cosy traditional Irish bar which had proper high stools and snugs and a warm, welcoming atmosphere.

With a half pint of Guinness each for tradition's sake, they settled into a corner and Liam lifted a daily newspaper from the empty seat behind him and began to scan it from back to front.

"There's *your* man, look, Cara," he said, pointing to a half-page item on Dylan Summers on the inside back pages. "Looks like he's up for a big transfer soon."

"Really? Let me see," said Cara. "And he is not my man, by any means, dear brother. He is merely the boyfriend of my ex-employer – but out of sheer nosiness, I'll have to read that article."

Cara scanned through the soccer gobbledygook until she came to the interesting bit.

"*Summers, 28, is rumoured to be attracting the attention of two of the Premiership's top clubs,*" she read aloud. "*Both Arsenal FC, who recently signed Summers' old team-mate Andrew Stewart, and northern legends Newcastle United are throwing in bids to see who can win over the man they call The Sunshine Kid. This is set to be the move of his career and one he will have to choose carefully.*"

"Wow!" said Liam. "Looks like Dylan is set to become even hotter property. And to think you once washed his underpants. Can I tell my friends? Please?"

Cara laughed at Liam's observations and realised again just how much she had enjoyed her time at Summer Manor. When Sophia wasn't around, which was most of the time, she truly spent her days surrounded by beauty and luxury. Her working day was over most days before Dylan arrived home and it was usually just her and Sam and her imagination to contend with. Perhaps she could give it another go.

"She asked me back today," she told Liam, who

took a sip of his half pint and left the froth around his mouth to savour the flavour.

"I hope you told her where to shove it. Doesn't she know you have a degree and years of experience working in one of Ireland's top –"

"No, of course she knows absolutely nothing about me and that's the way I want to keep it. I am tempted to go back, though. I mean, it was a really nice place to work and it was good money for having to keep the place clean and tidy and listen to Sophia throw the odd hissy fit."

Liam fiddled with his beer mat. "Just sleep on it, Cara. Let her sweat it out and have to pack the dishwasher herself for a day or two. Then she'll really miss you and beg you to come back."

Liam's advice triggered something in Cara's brain that made her realise something wasn't quite right.

"You know, there are plenty of people out there who can pack a dishwasher. I'm sure London is full of housekeepers with bags of experience working for so-called celebrities and sports people but for some reason, Sophia wants *me* in particular. Liam, I think I might be in a position to seriously *negotiate* with Miss Brannigan. And that was *her* word, not mine."

10

A Little Less Conversation

Dylan and Sophia were enjoying a long, leisurely breakfast the following morning when Sophia's cellphone rang. She tutted and shrugged her shoulders in apology at her boyfriend who was tucking into an extra-large fruit salad but was yearning for the bacon and eggs he could once in a while enjoy when the game was out of season.

"Miss Brannigan, this is Shelley from *Fab!* magazine," said a young voice whose owner was much too chirpy for such a ridiculously early time of the day. "Mr Johnston asked me to contact you this morning about your column. I hope it isn't a bad time."

"It's *Fab!* magazine," mouthed Sophia to Dylan who pretended he was impressed. "Yes, do go ahead, Shelley. How can I help you?"

Sophia stood up in delight, hoping that perhaps Jake had decided to do an "at home" feature with his new columnist or whisk her away to an exotic location for a swimwear photo shoot. Perhaps he had heard the rumours of Dylan's big transfer hopes and was going to beg the two of them to do a cover shoot for a ridiculous fee that they would of course donate to a trendy charity and perhaps be invited to become ambassadors. The world was her oyster at last.

"Em, I really hate to pile on the pressure," said Shelly, "but we have just been told that we are going to print a bit earlier this week in order to scoop the first pictures of the Stewart twins' second birthday party. We don't have an exclusive on it – Amanda and Andrew don't agree much to exclusives with us unfortunately – so we don't want to be pipped at the post by some smutty tabloid. I'm sure you know the score."

"Actually, no, I don't. Know the score," said Sophia, frustrated at the very mention of those darn Stewart twins and the fact that Amanda hadn't invited her to their stupid birthday party.

"Well, it means of course, Miss Brannigan, that we will need your column a little bit earlier. Like, tomorrow? As in Tuesday instead of the usual Wednesday submission deadline?"

"Not possible," snapped Sophia. Who did they think they were, issuing her orders like this? She would not pressurise herself just so that *Fab!* could work around Amanda bloody Stewart's children. And besides, she couldn't write the darn thing until that smartass little Irish girl came back to cook and clean for her. It was Cara's style that Johnston loved, not Sophia's.

"Oh, well, I will let Mr Johnston know that it's, er, that it's *not possible*," said Shelly. "I'm sure he'll be in touch with you. Very soon. That will be all. Have a nice –"

"Wait a minute, wait a minute, Kelly!" Sophia looked around the dining room for something that might resemble a brown-paper bag. She seriously feared she might have a panic attack.

"It's Shelley."

"Whatever. Look, I'll have it done. I promise. I will have the column to you by tomorrow close of business. Okay? Just tell me where to send it since it's so goddam urgent. Hold please so I can find a pen."

Sophia clicked her fingers at Dylan who passed her a piece of paper and a pen so she could write down the email address. She wrote "*Jumped-Up Bitch*" and held it up for him to read.

"Right, go ahead," she said.

"You can send it directly to Mr Johnston, Sophia," said Shelley. "He said it's important that he reads over everything of yours before it goes to print as your last attempt just wasn't up to scratch. Your first one was amazing but the last one seemed, well, rushed. Almost like it was written by a different person."

Ow! That hurt! Sophia held back a scream,

146

slammed down the phone and then opened her lungs and let out an unmerciful screech that almost moved the entire contents of the fitted kitchen.

"Holy smoke, is everything all right?" said Sam, who stumbled through the door. "I was just filling the wheel-barrow at the side of the house when I heard a scream. Have you hurt yourself, Sophia?"

"No, I have not hurt myself, and no, everything is not all right! Dylan, I'm going upstairs. Do not disturb me unless it is an extreme emergency."

"Okay, Soph," said Dylan and he pulled out a chair as Sophia disappeared. "Here, have a seat, Sam. I'm sure my girlfriend just gave you the fright of your life."

"It doesn't take much these days, Dylan. It doesn't take much."

"So, what are the big plans today?" asked Natalie as she stomped around the apartment in search of her new brown handbag. She was sure she had left it in the living room somewhere but it was impossible to find anything with the long legs of a platinum-haired delinquent taking up most the room. His guitar was in one corner and she vowed if she heard him try to play "Sweet Child of Mine" once more she would batter him stupid. She cagily lifted a pair of jeans from behind the sofa and dropped them on Liam's chest who spluttered out an expletive in response and turned in his sleep.

"I'm contemplating taking my old job back," said Cara as she munched her way through a bowl of cereal. "That's what my main plan is today."

"What? In Belfast? Don't tell me you're chickening out on me already!"

Cara waved her spoon as she swallowed her breakfast cereal. "No, not at home. At Summer Manor."

"Really?"

"Yes, I think so. Sophia phoned me yesterday out of the blue and asked me to come back. Liam and I were having a stroll around Harrods, as you do, and she was actually there at the time too but she didn't see us. It was quite funny, actually. She sounded desperate."

"Maybe she is," said Natalie. "People like Sophia don't like to lose their lady in waiting, unless they catch them in bed with their other half."

Cara rolled her eyes. "Touché!" she said. "I do smell a rat, though, but I think I'm going to play along to find out what she's up to. She said she's willing to negotiate terms with me which makes me think there might be more to it than meets the eye."

Natalie sighed in relief when she spotted her missing handbag peeking out at her from beneath a separate bundle of Liam's "stuff". She lifted it and gave a deep sigh.

"What's so weird about that? The girl is a spoilt princess who can't be arsed lifting her pretty little finger and you are an excellent cook who can keep a place clean and tidy and, most of the time, keep out of her way, so she wants you back. Simple as that, I say."

Natalie glanced over at Liam who was snoring even louder than normal and she resisted the urge to slap him over the head on her way out with her handbag. If only the McCarthy tidiness had rubbed off on the male of the family!

"Maybe you're right," said Cara. "Maybe it is my culinary skills she is after, but time will tell, Nat. Time will tell."

Sophia sat at her laptop, drumming her fingers off the desk in frustration. It can't be that difficult she told herself. Just write down a few funny anecdotes about living in the land of make-believe and Bob's your uncle. If some of those big-boobed glamour models and ex girl-band singers could do it in rival magazines, surely Sophia Brannigan who had passed every English exam she had sat could drum out a few paragraphs in the space of seven hours?

But Jake Johnston didn't want Sophia's honest or otherwise account of living the life that everyone wanted. Jake Johnston wanted "WAG Tales". He wanted – how did he put it? *"That unique voice, that style, that wit, that humour."* And that smug little bitch still hadn't phoned and Sophia was battling with her temper that she had the damn cheek to play hard to get. Should she call her again? No, definitely not. She didn't want to sound too needy and how she was going to address the column issue with her was another conundrum.

To rub salt in her wounds, news had just come her way that Emily Evans, the little tart, had signed a children's book deal for over a million pounds and her face was on every digital and printed medium going. That silly little bimbo could barely spell her own name and the public were being led to believe that she could actually tell a story. It was ludicrous and Sophia was insanely jealous. But she would do ludicrous too if the opportunity would only come her way.

She needed to take action on her career, big time. This column was proving much more difficult than she had anticipated. She hadn't been to any parties since the Stewarts' and the only invitation she had was to a foam party at a nightclub in town to celebrate Emily's book deal. If things went according to plan with Cara writing the column for her, or at least helping her out, she would need to drum up some more social invitations and more importantly, she would have to take the frumpy little cow to all the parties with her. Yuk!

Sophia lifted the phone to call her PR agency who were doing shit-all these days to help her cause and she was paying them good money to plunge her into the WAG A-list. At this moment in time she didn't even have a nightclub buddy to be photographed with and Kirsty and Avril, the only other WAGs who gave her the time of day, were avoiding her like the plague as they were papped left, right and centre.

"Good morning. Assets PR. Penny speaking. How can I help you?"

"Penny, this is Sophia Brannigan. As you may know, I have been invited to pen the new party column at *Fab!* magazine."

"Yes, Sophia," said the ever polite Penny. "I actually meant to call you to congratulate you. I was chatting to Jake the other day and he was so surprised at how witty you were in your sample column. I just can't wait to read it for myself and –"

"Okay, okay, but this is where I need you to come in."

Sophia didn't need to hear how wonderful her column was. It wasn't technically hers after all.

"Right, tell me more," said Penny.

"The thing is, I need more parties to write about," said Sophia. "I need a variety of people begging me to cover them in my column, so go and find me some. That's what I'm paying you for. Don't you realise my boyfriend is on the verge of being snapped up by one of England's highest-profile clubs and I want to maximise every PR opportunity we can find to make sure he is selected by the *right* one?"

Penny cleared her throat as her client got herself into a right old state on the other end of the line.

"Sophia, I'm not sure that football clubs select

players on the level of their celebrity. In fact, I'd say it's quite the opposite," she said, expecting a lash-back from her client. "Look, if your column is as clever as Jake says, the invitations will pour in and you won't have to worry about a party drought, but I'll send out a few feelers in the meantime to give you a head start, okay?"

"I suppose, but hurry," snapped Sophia. "I need my diary filled up pronto, no matter what it takes, do you hear? Pronto!"

11

Suspicious Times

Cara parked the Uno right outside the front door of Summer Manor, knowing fine well it would irritate the life out of Sophia, but she had asked her to come over immediately and Cara had obliged out of sheer nosiness. She was greeted by Buster the Labrador when she got out of the car and he wagged his tail and jumped up on her as she ruffled his ears.

"Did you miss me, Buster old buddy? Good doggy."

She lifted her hand to press the doorbell, but Sophia opened it before she got the chance and ushered her inside.

"Thanks for coming over so quickly," she smiled.

Cara felt just a tiny bit scared. "That's okay." Sophia was being nice to her. Sophia was never nice to her.

Then she let her character change slip ever so

slightly. "Shoo, you ugly mutt!" she said to Buster, then her painted smile was back. "So, Cara. Did you get your hair done? It looks different?"

Cara twiddled a strand of her hair in bewilderment. Was she now being sarcastic or just trying too hard to butter her up?

"No, I haven't. So you want me to come back then?" She wasn't going to stand for Sophia's sucking-up routine. "Really, you don't have to be so nice. As you said before, I'm just a cleaner. I can stay out of your way and obey the rules this time and we can all live happily ever after. It suits me just as much as it suits you."

They went into the drawing room where a small table was set in an immaculate fashion for coffee and Cara wondered how Sophia had laid it out so impressively.

"Sam did it," said Sophia, obviously sensing Cara's bewilderment. "He said you love cappuccino, so I got some cappuccino. I also got your favourite shortbread. Here, tuck in."

Cara sat down cagily and waited as Sophia poured her a steaming fresh hot cup and then she lifted the frothy liquid to her lips. Something was going on, just as she had suspected. Sophia was drinking cappuccino and she barely drank anything other than herbal tea that doubled up as a laxative. She was beating about the bush, big time.

"Okay, so let's cut to the chase, Sophia. You didn't call me over here to take me back as a cleaner, did you? What's up?"

"I did, I do want you back as a cleaner. We all missed you around here. Well, I did. And I need you back."

"You need me back, more than you want me back. That's what I thought."

"Darling, darling Cara. You see through me so well. I have to be honest with you as time isn't on my side, but believe me I will make this worth your while."

"Go on . . ."

Sophia straightened her back on her chair and flicked back her hair, then smiled as if she was the most sincere, honest person in the world.

"First of all, can we forget about the shoe incident?"

"Forget about it? After you sacked me and called me evil?"

"I know, I know, but I've been thinking about that. I have a million other pairs of shoes so let's put that all behind us and start again. I've been feeling so bad about how I treated you so I've been thinking about how I can make it up to you by tweaking your job description slightly. I'd like to give you more responsibility."

"Responsibility? Oh, so I'm allowed to take your calls *and* check your emails? Oh, the excitement!"

"I need a ghost writer."

"A what?"

"A ghost writer. I need you to accompany me to social events and then write about them for my column. You see, I have another few, let's say, opportunities to pursue and, while the column is so important, I don't exactly have the time to actually write it, so that's where you come in."

Cara felt a grin twitching across her face. Sophia had dressed this up quite nicely and, to be honest, it was practically her dream job to write for a living, but she knew she wasn't getting the big picture at all.

She decided to make Sophia sweat just another little bit. "You said you would make it worth my while. How?"

"Er, well, financially of course. I can give you a raise of a hundred a week —"

"Pah! Are you serious? A hundred quid for doing work you just can't be arsed doing? How about two hundred and fifty?"

Sophia raised an eyebrow. "Two fifty . . . oh Cara, if that's what you need then how could I refuse? Of course, your usual chores still stand and I'll expect just as high a standard around the house. Look on this as an additional extra."

Cara sensed she had just another little bit of mileage she could drag out of Sophia.

"I have a question," she said.

"Sure, fire away."

"These, er, social occasions, as you call them. They will be during the day, right?"

Sophia looked back at her and took a sip of her coffee. "Well, some of them will – for example, product launches and charity coffee mornings – but I would imagine there will be some cocktail parties and evening events as well. Dylan doesn't like to be seen at those so I'll need you to come with me and make mental notes for my – for our column."

"Mm," said Cara, fiddling deliberately with a frayed hole in the knee of her jeans. "So I need to look appropriate then. I wouldn't want to let you down."

"Oh, all right then. I could add on a clothing allowance, I suppose. And I could help you shop."

Cara's face broke into a grin. Bingo. This is just what she had hoped her boss would say.

"It's a deal," said Cara. "Now, where do I start? In the kitchen or on the column?"

"On the column," said Sophia, and she offered to shake Cara's hand, but Cara was already halfway up the stairs towards the office to start her first real version of "WAG Tales". What she would write about, she didn't exactly know, but she was fully confident that she could come up with something as sparkly as ever.

Dylan pushed himself to do extra sit-ups, knowing he was being watched carefully from the sidelines by the team selector. Ten, nine, eight . . . he battled with the pain barrier and then on "one" he lay back and stared up at the summer sunshine.

"Hey, kid, are you okay?" asked Paul Henderson as he offered a hand to pull Dylan to his feet. "You seem distracted again. Anything I can do?"

Dylan rose from the ground and took a gulp of water. "Just the usual, mate. Family stuff."

Paul shook his head. "Your dad?"

"Yip. Who else?"

"He's been on the sauce again, then?" said Paul. "That's shit. Maybe you should take some time out and get things sorted. Besides, you need to get your head into the game and it's anywhere but there at the moment."

Dylan and Paul did a warm-down as they spoke, knowing they would get their knuckles rapped for disrupting a training session. Dylan had already been fined £2000 the day before for taking a call from his brother ten minutes into training.

"I spoke to Mark yesterday and he seems to have it under control for now, but I just feel I should be doing more. It's like we live in a different world down here, away from all sense of reality."

"How about Sophia? Have you discussed any of this with her?" asked Paul. "If you're worried about your old man you need to talk it through with someone."

Dylan knew what Paul was thinking: that family problems weren't exactly Sophia's forte but he could at least give her a chance to help him through it.

"I did mention it briefly but you know Sophia almost as well as I do. I'll tell her the true extent of it all when I have to."

Paul shook his head. Dylan had a habit of bottling things up and it was beginning to put him under strain. A few days with his family might be just what the doctor ordered.

"Why don't we go for a run this evening? Let off a bit of steam and afterwards you can go home and have a good chat with Sophia, then plan to go and see your folks. It would do you good."

Dylan was about to respond when Joe Buchannan, his agent, signalled to him from the sideline. He jogged over to where the team selector was standing.

"Have you heard yet, kid?" asked Joe in between chewing ferociously on his tenth piece of gum that morning.

"No," said Dylan, sensing the worst. "But I hope you're going to tell me."

Joe put his hand on the younger man's shoulder as they walked towards the changing rooms.

"I'll tell you inside. There's nothing to be concerned about, though, so you can take that look of dread off your face," he said and stayed back to talk to Fulton's manager.

The smell of Deep Heat met Dylan at the doors of the changing room and he leaned down to unlace his boots.

"Well done, big lad," said another team–mate and Dylan looked up in surprise.

"What for? What's going on?" he asked the young player.

"They love you so much here they want to keep you," said the boy and he began to untie his own boots.

"What? Are you sure?"

"Sure I'm sure. So does this mean you won't be leaving the city after all?"

Dylan stood frozen in shock, not sure what way to react until he heard the news officially.

Joe Buchannan came towards him with a hearty laugh.

"I take it Rubber Gob there has let the cat out of the bag before I could tell you, Dylan. Looks like you are staying on this turf for another while. I've negotiated a good deal for you to stay here for the first few months of the season and then they might let you go on the January transfers."

"Oh," said Dylan, and he stripped off his gear and headed to the showers.

"Hey! You don't seem too happy about it," said Joe, following his prodigy into the steamy shower room. "I thought you were happy here?"

"I am. I had just geared myself up for some big changes, that's all."

"I see," said Joe, and he left Dylan in peace, not sure whether the changes the young man referred to were entirely football-related.

12

I Just Can't Help Make-Believin'

Cara pressed the send button on Sophia's computer and chuckled to herself at the very idea of ghost writing for a celebrity magazine. This was much more exciting than she had ever hoped for and since it was integrated into her daily job at Summer Manor, no one need ever know it was she and not Sophia who penned "WAG Tales".

Sophia had read over the column and barely reacted, whereas Cara herself was delighted at her account of the happenings in the celebrity world of footballer's wives. She wrote a sarcastic account of Emily's forthcoming book launch and a respectable feature on the first two years of the Stewart twins' lives, as well as a humorous prediction of what the future might hold for Britain's most adored toddlers. Sophia had sniffed slightly at the fact they were being mentioned at all, but Cara had convinced her that the public, whether she liked it or not, were obsessed with Amanda and her girls and it would draw even the most cynical reader towards the column.

"I'm off now," said Sophia, once the column was written and an email receipt came through to prove it had been received on time by Jake Johnston.

"Do you like it?" asked Cara.

"Like what?"

"The column. Do you like it?" Cara was a tad surprised at Sophia's indifference to what the column actually contained and felt it would be much more beneficial to her if she actually read the darn thing through in case she was questioned about it.

Sophia ran her fingers through her hair and smacked her lipstick, then pouted.

"Cara, I don't really care what it details, as long as Jake Johnston likes it. He owns *Fab!* magazine and a million others so he is the one to please, not me. He's the one who really matters, so let's wait and see, eh? Just go easy on the Amanda Stewart stories. She doesn't exactly need the publicity, does she?"

Cara rolled her eyes and lifted her apron from where it lay across the back of the computer chair. She had just a few bits and pieces to do around the house and then she could go home. No doubt Natalie would give her a tongue-lashing for going back to work for

Sophia again after the way she had been treated, but then Natalie didn't know that Cara was now working under very different terms.

It would be strange seeing her own writing in print again. Apart from writing the column for Sophia, it had been ages since she'd last put pen to paper. In the meantime she had satisfied herself with the odd diary entry but would always end up tearing it up in case anyone ever read her deepest darkest secrets. Sometimes she wrote letters to Michael and then binned them without sending them, questioning him on why he had let her down so badly, why he had made such a fool of her in front of her colleagues and more importantly, her family.

Then she would blame herself for what happened in other ways. Just who did she think she was anyhow? Why would she have ever believed that a highly successful, handsome, married man like Michael Bradley would ever leave his cosy lifestyle where he had the best of both worlds – a glamorous wife and an obedient, if impatient mistress – just to be with her and her alone? Plus, as it turned out, Michael liked to trade in his mistresses as often as he traded in his cars.

Cara couldn't get a man of her own, Michael's wife had said quite publicly. Cara "Plain Jane" McCarthy had to try and steal someone else's man because she wasn't pretty enough to get herself a boyfriend. Cara's poor father was disgusted as his bar-room buddies took the mick out of him as to how it was the quiet ones in the family you had to watch and he still could barely look his daughter in the eye.

Her sister Olivia had travelled to Belfast with a bottle of wine and ran her a long bubble bath when the news broke, and Liam offered to smash Michael's windows in or he could arrange a hijacking if she wanted. Cara thanked her brother for his kindness and support, but opted for a twelve-month career-break application which Michael had signed off in an instant.

Now, only months into her career break and her new life in London, Cara had found the opportunity to write and no one, not even Natalie or Liam needed to know she was doing it. It was almost too good to be true.

"You're back," said Sam with a huge grin as Cara entered the kitchen. "I saw your wee car there and I just hoped you would say yes when Sophia asked you to come back to us."

"Oh shit, I didn't park it at the back. I'll go and do it now," said Cara.

"Don't be silly. I'll move it for you. We missed you, hen. Come here till I give you a hug!"

Sam stretched out his arms and Cara gave him a gentle cuddle. He winced ever so slightly and Cara looked at him with concern.

"How have you been feeling, Sam? You look a bit tired."

Sam brushed off the comment and threw up his eyes. "Oh, I've just been overdoing it a bit, I suppose. These grounds are a lot to get around at this time of year. I'll be fine."

Cara shook her head and flicked the switch on the kettle. "Typical man, Sam, as my mother would say. You should slow down a bit before you really do overdo it. Now, sit down and get comfortable and let me make you a cup of tea."

Sam shuffled over to the far side of the kitchen and sank into the soft leather sofa. He lifted a newspaper and scanned the back pages, looking for any news on Dylan's team as it always made him feel so proud.

"Do you follow football at all, Cara?" he asked as he flicked through the pages.

"Not really, but my brother is a fanatic since he was knee high," she laughed. "I can bring myself to watch a game on telly and I do know my Ronaldo from my Ronaldinho, believe it or not."

"Gosh, that's not too bad at all. So who does your brother support?" asked Sam.

"Manchester United all the way," she replied. "They have a huge following back at home and, until he fell in with the wrong crowd, Liam was actually showing fine potential on the field. Such a shame, really. Oh, speaking of superstars, looks like Dylan has just arrived. I'll put out an extra cup, shall I? Give you two a chance to talk."

Cara set out a plate of sliced wheaten bread she had brought with her that afternoon but had abandoned when she saw the effort Sophia had already gone to, and sliced some cheese and tomato onto some side plates. She filled a pot of tea and then brought it over to the coffee table where Sam sat, as Dylan made his way into the room.

He stopped and did a double take when he saw Cara serving the tea, like he had just witnessed an apparition.

"Er, hello, Cara. I didn't realise you were due to visit," he said, glancing over at Sam who wore a contented smile as he tucked in to Cara's small feast.

"Oh no, Mr Summers —"

"Dylan."

"Dylan, sorry. No, I'm not here to visit at all, Dylan. I'm back to work here. If that's okay with you? Can I get you some tea? Coffee?"

"Tea would be great," said Dylan and he sat down to join Sam.

Cara poured a cup of tea for him but then remained standing. There was no way in the world she would be so presumptuous as to sit with this man who she barely knew.

"Didn't Sophia say I was coming back?" she asked.

"No, she didn't, but it's good that you're back. Great, in fact," said Dylan and he pulled out a chair and nodded at Cara.

She sat down obediently and urged herself to relax. This time last year she would have given her left kidney to have interviewed a public figure to make her name and impress Michael Bradley, and now here she was having afternoon tea with Dylan Summers and she wasn't even on official business. She would just have to pretend she was as calm as Dylan expected her to be. She had barely been in his company before without Sophia's interference and demands and she was determined to let him see that she was actually a fun person beneath her apron and rubber gloves.

She took in his toned physique under his loose sports wear and tried not to swoon. The man was so damn hot she couldn't help but stare.

"Isn't it great to have Cara back, eh, Dylan?" said Sam. "I really missed my wee morning chats with her and it's good to know there's someone trustworthy in the house when you and Sophia are away so much during the day. An old man like me tends to get very lonesome in a big place like this."

"I don't quite understand why she had to go in the first place," said Dylan, looking directly at Cara as he spoke. "Apart from the shoe. It was all about the shoe." Dylan leaned forward, his elbows resting on his knees.

"Well, I should have obeyed the rules. Don't touch what you can't afford and all that." Cara gave a wry smile.

"Oh come on love, it was hardly a crime," chuckled

Sam. "But, anyhow, it's a joy to see you again. Just stay away from the shoes."

"I will," said Cara, but she still felt awkward and out of her depth in Dylan's company.

"So, apart from your bid to break shoes and cook us fine meals, what else brought you to London, Cara?" asked Dylan.

"Em," said Cara, searching for an answer. She couldn't lie to him. But she had to. "Well, this and that. I'd been temping here and there for a long time, waitressing, helping out at Graceland. I just fancied a change of scenery, really."

"Graceland?"

"Oh, it's our family pub back in Donegal. It's nothing fancy but in a few years' time I plan to give it a good old face-lift. It's on a central tourist route and has great potential, but no one has the resources to give it the TLC it needs at the moment. We have some fine characters who call in full of stories and their own versions of the King of Rock 'n' Roll."

Dylan sat back on his seat, intrigued. He could picture exactly what Cara was describing. The idea of modernising a small, rundown pub with a fine reputation and loads of potential to become a real gem on the tourist map was something he could get really into.

"So why is it called Graceland?" he asked. "Are there any connections to the man himself?"

"Absolutely nothing at all, except that my father

once won a talent contest in Donegal town when he was just married and the fame went to his head." Cara relaxed slightly when Dylan laughed at her explanation and she continued. "It was originally called just plain old McCarthy's, but before my mother could say 'Blue Suede Shoes' he had changed the name and decorated the place with framed photos of Elvis down the years. He says he opened it on the day Elvis died, but sure if you believe that, you'd believe anything."

Sam thought of how refreshing it was to watch Dylan smile again after seeing him so miserable over the past few days. While he knew there was a lot going on in Dylan's head, he only wished he could do more to help him sort things out with his father. Deep down he feared that things had already gone too far. Dave was fast becoming a lost cause and there was very little anyone could do about it.

"It sounds like my type of place, Cara," said Dylan. "We'll definitely have to make a trip to Graceland then, Sam. What do you think?"

"Some day," said Sam. "Some day."

The jovial mood was interrupted when Sophia breezed in, laden with shopping bags and talking as usual on her phone. She paused when she observed the cosy set-up and sneered.

"What's this? *Jacka-flippin-nory*? Sorry to break up your story time, folks, but I need Cara to come with me. I'll be upstairs. In my office."

Sam looked at Dylan who smiled awkwardly at how rude Sophia was, issuing her demands as soon as she arrived. Cara stood up and she sensed that Dylan was swallowing hard so as to not speak his mind.

"I'll pop those cups in the dishwasher in a second," she said.

"No. That's okay. I can do it," said Dylan and he took her cup from her. "Why don't you go and see what life or death situation my girlfriend is in as she seems to need your presence so urgently."

As she left the kitchen, Cara was almost sure she could sense Dylan's mood taking a nosedive already.

13

Rubberneckin'

By Saturday afternoon, Dylan Summers was on every back page of every daily newspaper in Britain while his girlfriend graced at least one of the five front pages of the *Star*, the *Mirror* and the *Daily Mail*. News of Dylan's removal from the transfer window was the top story on every football fan's lips and rave reviews of Sophia's hot new column whistled through the media like wildfire.

"*Gossip with a bite – this girl can write!*" said the *Sun*.

"*It's a Home Goal for Summers and Fab! for his Girl*" said the *Mirror*, featuring a photo of Sophia leaving *Fab!* Towers with a copy of the magazine under her arm.

On eyeing all the coverage, Sophia was like a child at Christmas and she gathered all the clippings together on the kitchen table. She wondered would it be acceptable for her to start a scrapbook of all her coverage to date? Perhaps she should drop a casual hint to Cara to set up a clippings system so that she wasn't seen to be too big-headed. Yes, she would do that.

"Good luck for today, babe," she said to Dylan, her head buried in the latest issue as she read her column for the fourth time. It looked so much more exciting when it was laid out in the magazine with its racy colours and playful fonts, not to mention the huge photo of her in the top right corner. Maybe she should get an extra shot of Botox above her left eyebrow, she thought, and made a mental note to do so the next time she visited her surgeon.

"You mean you're not coming to the game today?" asked Dylan. He stopped in his tracks on his way through the room and realised his girlfriend wasn't dressed for outdoors. Besides, she hadn't taken her nose out of the newspapers all morning and he'd had breakfast staring across at red-top tabloids with barely a grunt from behind them.

"Er, no, actually," she said.

"Are you serious? You're joking, right?"

Sophia hadn't missed a game since she had met him over a year ago and had almost choked with excitement when she saw Colleen McLoughlin at a recent Premiership clash with Man U. Whether or not she watched the game was a different story, but Dylan liked having her there to support him. Apart from Sam, she was the closest to family he had at home games and it was a real boost to know you had someone who cared in the terraces on a big day like today.

"Oh, didn't I tell you, babe? I can't go today. I promised Jake I'd meet him for coffee to discuss ideas for next week. He says the party invitations are pouring in and I have to sift through which ones I'm going to attend this week. He reckons I'm the talk of the trade at the moment so we have to strike while the iron's hot. Can you believe it?"

Dylan looked around him in disbelief and hurt. "You aren't coming then? You *are* serious? Come on, Sophia, don't do this to me!"

Sophia lifted her head from the magazine and cocked her head to the side. "Ah honey, don't look at me like that. You know how important this is to me and I've never missed a game since we met. Missing one game won't hurt, will it?"

"But it's the season opener and I might only have a few more games with Fulton before the next transfer window opens. It would be nice to show your support after how good they have been to us over at the club. And it's a home game."

"And that's another thing we have to discuss, Dylan," said Sophia, standing up and making her way towards her boyfriend. "How can I attend all these parties and events Jake wants me to if you are eventually transferred? I can't possibly keep on top of this by commuting from some remote corner of the country into London. It just wouldn't work. Have you even thought about me in all of this?"

Dylan held out his hands in frustration. "Sophia! Can you please put this all in perspective? I'm delighted you have got this column, really I am, but for Christ's sake this is the move of my career we're talking about and it's a few months away –"

"Oh, it's all about *your* career, isn't it? Well, what about mine? I am finally making a name for myself and you can't stand it, can you? As long as you get to follow your dreams, who cares about mine!"

"No, Sophia, it's not like that, but please listen to yourself. It's football that keeps a roof over our heads and it's football that gives you all the trimmings you've become accustomed to, not a column you have only written for a week or two! Surely if it's so important for them to keep you on, you can write it from anywhere?"

Sophia took a deep breath and sat back down again. "I do not want to fight with you over this, Dylan, really I don't, but I am so excited about where this could lead and I need to give it my best shot. I hoped you would understand. I mean, I made page 3 of most papers today. Page 3! And not a boob in sight! Do you know what some people would give to be on page 3 of the *Sun* without having to get their kit off?"

She reached for a random copy of a tabloid from the pile she'd had delivered that day, opened it at the page where her photo and caption was placed to show him.

Then she looked up for his response, but Dylan was already gone.

The Coat of Arms was packed to capacity for the big game and Cara and Natalie could barely find a seat. Fans wearing both teams' replica jerseys and scarves squeezed in amongst neutral football followers and those like Cara who really couldn't give a toss but felt it was better than sitting in a freezing flat where the heating had packed in.

Liam waved to them from a corner and pointed to where he had saved them two seats beside him.

"See, he's not all bad," said Cara and she nudged her friend playfully. "He does have a wee heart in there somewhere."

"Huh," said Natalie. "I suppose I'll give you this one. At long last he's good for something."

They brought three pints of lager to the table to keep with the spirit of the game and joined Liam who was bubbling with excitement as the first match of the Premiership was about to begin.

"I know Summers is going to play a stormer today, Cara," he said. "He'll want to go out with a bang in January and Fulton have shown him so much respect asking him to stay to see the first half of the season out. Did he seem nervous yesterday?"

"What would I know, Liam?" said Cara and she and Natalie laughed. "I honestly don't have a clue. It's not like I'm his best friend."

"He's going to be huge, mark my words," said Liam and he launched into a rendition of "Summer Time" with a group of Fulton fans who were sitting at the adjoining table.

"Summers is a wanker!" shouted a leery lout in response from the middle of the bar and the crowd roared, with some throwing beer mats at him and telling him to sit down, while others cheered him on. "Summers is a WANKER!" shouted the man even louder.

Natalie looked at Cara and then burst out laughing. "Oh my word, I wish I had brought my camera," she said.

"What?" asked Cara, her eyes fixed on the group of men who were putting together a derogatory chant about Dylan.

"You look like you are about to blow a fuse. What are you, his mother?"

"What? Oh, right, gosh, am I that obvious? Wow, I don't really like them saying that about him, though. It's just because I sort of work for him. Well, not for him. For Sophia. But still. Maybe I'm being a little bit over-protective."

The game began and Cara found herself engrossed, cheering with Fulton as its players charged against a stronger opposition. Natalie was much more interested in talent-spotting and had her eye on a red-haired man at the end of the bar. She would wait until half time and then casually bump into him as he too seemed to be wrapped up in the game like everyone else around her.

"Offside!" shouted Liam and the linesman raised his flag as the pub audience cheered.

"Yeah, offside," said Cara and then, catching Natalie's eye, she laughed as neither of them had any idea what the offside rule entailed.

"Hey, gorgeous, what does offside mean?" said a voice from the group of "neutrals" from the next table.

Cara and Natalie looked at each other, then looked back at the boys and shook their heads.

"Say what?" asked Cara.

"Offside. What does the offside rule mean?" asked one with a cheeky grin. "I've never met a girl who understands it yet."

The crowd of men let out an *ooooh* sound and stared at Cara who was scrambling for a smart answer.

Liam leaned in with his back to the "neutrals" and whispered to his sister: "When a player is nearer the opponent's goal line . . ."

"Basically, it's when a player is nearer the opponent's goal line . . ." said Cara, urging herself not to laugh.

". . . than the second last opponent . . ." said Liam.

". . . than the second last opponent . . ." she repeated. "I could show you, but I'm wearing the wrong shoes and I left my football at home."

The group cheered, some knowing Cara had been given a little help with her vague explanation but impressed nonetheless at her banter.

"Wow, that was as clear as mud!" said the young man who had posed the question and he winked at Cara who blushed under his gaze.

Their moment was interrupted as just before the half-time whistle blew, Dylan Summers knocked the ball into the top left corner, equalising the game, and Cara watched as his face filled the screen, his gorgeous smile beaming out at her as he raced towards the fans in the stands. Cara glanced across to where her new admirer was taking in her every move.

"Ooh, looks like Summers mightn't be the only one who scores today," said Natalie when she noticed the connection. "Good work, Liam."

"Ha ha," said Cara but her response was cut short when she saw her aficionado pull his stool over to their table. Cara reached out her foot and clamped it down on Natalie's toe, a signal they had used for years when they were nervous or excited at a man's approach. For the first time in her life, Natalie was glad her best friend wore flat shoes.

"I'm Tom," said the young man and he blatantly

ignored the other two at the table, not taking his eyes off Cara.

"Cara," she replied.

"Irish?" he asked.

"Correct," she said.

"For 'friend'?" he asked.

"Yes. Now, *I'm* impressed," she said back, and looked at her brother and her friend in shock.

"Charming bastard," whispered Liam and Natalie gave him a sharp dig in the ribs. Even she was caught up in the romance of the moment.

He stood up and took Cara's hand, then pulled her to her feet. "I think that attempt at an offside explanation deserves a drink," he said and he led her by the hand to the bar.

She looked back at Natalie who held her hands to her face with delight. Cara had pulled a man. A nice, decent, pleasant man. At long, long last.

"Just what the doctor ordered," said Natalie. "I hope to God he's single."

"I'll drink to that," said Liam, and he clinked glasses with Natalie then tuned in to the half-time commentary as Natalie excused herself to try her arm with the ginger man at the bar.

14

Love Me Tender

"You look like the cat that got the cream," said Sophia to Cara on Monday morning. "Good weekend?"

"You could say that," said Cara, trying not to think too hard about Tom, but his face wouldn't leave her mind. They'd had such fun on Saturday and had ended up celebrating Fulton's big win into the wee small hours. Tom had walked her home, taken her number and, after they shared a light snog at her front door, promised to call her very soon. Cara had been so tempted to tell Tom and his friends that she washed Dylan Summers' training kit for a living but instead she stuck to the PR for Animals story she had come up with at Amanda Stewart's party.

She was glad she had kept her business to herself for now when Tom told her he was on the production team of a well-known daytime chat show. It was early days to open up to anyone about her working life, past or present.

"Well, I'm afraid there is no time to dwell on love's young dream," said Sophia. "This morning I will attend my first event of the week."

"*You* will attend. You mean *I* am not going. That was a short and sweet arrangement −"

"Let me finish, Cara," said Sophia and Cara wanted to punch her when she clicked her fingers in the air. "*I* will attend the opening of an art gallery near Hyde Park but it clashes with a kiddies' picnic in the park. I promised Jake I would cover both events since geographically they are so close but the very thought of a pack of spoilt brats in designer clothing is enough to make my stomach sour. So I figured you could cover that better than I could, okay?"

"Okay." Cara took off her coat and hung it in the usual place in the cloakroom and followed Sophia into the drawing room, her notebook and pen poised to take notes.

"And what do you think you're doing?" asked Sophia.

"Well, I need more information so I hoped we could talk it through over coffee. You know, research info like who is going to be there? What do I say to gain entry to the picnic since I have no official business there as far as *Fab!* magazine or the party organisers are

182

concerned? What is the dress code? Do I need to know children's nursery rhymes 'cos it's been a long time . . . you know!"

"No, darling, I don't know," said Sophia as she marched out of the drawing room and up the stairs with Cara on her tail. "I don't know any of that. I will obviously be using the 'WAG Tales' card and of course by now I am on the guest list for both events but you can't possibly pretend to be me, so figure it out on the way."

"But . . ."

"No time for buts. Come on now. Get your coat back on and hurry up. They both begin at eleven and it's a long trek across town at this hour. I'm going to change my dress. I've already been papped in this one. I'll meet you at the car."

Cara got out of Sophia's sports car and closed the door sheepishly. The sheer size of Hyde Park made parks in Belfast look like someone's garden and she had no idea where she was supposed to go and what this bloody picnic was all in aid of.

"Oh, do give over, Cara. Just look out for a bunch of squabbling terrorists dressed as toddlers and you can't be far off. You might even recognise some of the yummy mummies but try and stay out of their way. You don't want to be mistaken for a kidnapper, do you?"

"My God, do I really look that scary?" asked Cara, fixing herself in the window of the car.

"Mm, I won't answer that, though if I went there myself I'd be sorely tempted to dispose of a few of their little bundles of joy. Maternal I am not."

Sophia put on a pair of huge sunglasses and wrapped a light shawl around her shoulders. She was effortlessly glamorous and Cara felt like a prize donkey beside her in her cropped white jeans and plimsolls. At least her hair was tied neatly back and she had become used to applying some light foundation, eye make-up and lip-gloss on a regular basis, plus Natalie had cut her a deal on a weekly spray-tan. Compared to how she looked a fortnight before, she was like a supermodel.

"So, did you say we'll meet up at twelve noon then?" said Cara. "It's just, well, it really doesn't give me much time to find the party and take enough in to write about it."

"Yes, twelve noon," said Sophia, ignoring Cara's concerns. "And for goodness' sake, don't be late. I hate art galleries and it will be all I can bear to stick it out for a full sixty minutes. All I need to know is who is there, who isn't and the rest is up to you. Now go mingle with the mummies."

Cara made her way through the gates of Hyde Park, dodging joggers and skaters and people walking dogs of all shapes and sizes on leads in all directions. She kept her eyes peeled for any signs of children's activities and then remembered the sheer size of Hyde Park. She could be miles away from the picnic.

Then, far in the distance, she saw what she thought was a bouncy castle and she made a run for it. It was already eleven fifteen and it would take her a good ten minutes to get there, plus another ten to think of how she was going to gain access to the party without being arrested.

As she ran, she chanted all the names of the Mummy WAGs she could remember – there was Amanda Stewart and the twins, Abigail and Meg, who wouldn't be there as they were off to visit Amanda's parents who had retired to Italy according to the *Daily Mirror*. Emily Evans might be there with her two children, Tilly and Rocco, who were born to different footballer fathers and rumour had it she was expecting a third to another footballer. Then there was Paul Henderson's lovely girlfriend Chantelle, who seemed quite down-to-earth and who was the face of a make-up brand, and their little son Adam. And she was sure she would recognise a sprinkling of others who might or might not merit a mention in "WAG Tales" if they bore any interest for the public at all.

Eventually, Cara found her way to the hive of activity and she knew she was at the right place when she saw a young busty blonde with a size-zero figure holding a newborn clad in Burberry. There was no one in the real world who could deflate like that after giving birth.

A fussy lady in her early fifties wearing a red T-shirt that said "*Klobber For Kids*" with a smiley-faced logo beneath it approached Cara with a clipboard.

"Now, *you* must be . . ." she said, running her pen down a list of names that wouldn't have been out of place on a guest list in any London nightclub.

"Er, well, you see . . ."

"Sara! Is that you?"

Cara's heart stopped when she saw Amanda Stewart come bounding towards her, all smiles and perfect porcelain teeth. Cara thought she was going to be sick.

"Hi, Amanda! Gosh, I didn't expect to see you here."

"Likewise. This is Sara, she works in PR," Amanda said to the lady with the funny T-shirt. "Thank you so much for coming, Sara."

They both stood staring at each other before Amanda linked Cara's arm and led her towards the picnic area which was heavily branded with the charity's logo and was filled with lots of children's entertainment.

"I can't believe you're here. It's great to see you again," said Amanda.

"You too," said Cara in horror at being recognised, but at least Amanda had sashayed her through the Red-T-shirt security.

"Oh, I couldn't possibly miss this picnic with Andrew being patron of the charity and when I heard it clashed with our trip to Italy I just had to change my dates," said Amanda. "Whatever brings you here? I thought you'd be back in Ireland by now?"

Cara's tummy did a somersault and she could feel her face flush as she prepared to tell a few white lies. "I got the opportunity to, er, well, get some work experience this side of the pond, and I thought, well, with having no real ties in my personal life as yet, that I might as well give it a go for a while."

"And what's your role here today, then?"

"I, well, I was actually at another function here in the park where they were racing pigeons and I'm investigating the possibility of an article on pigeon racing in, um, *The Pigeon Racer*. It's a new magazine, for, um, pigeon-racing lovers. Then I spotted the bouncy castle. I'm a sucker for bouncy castles."

"Me too," said Amanda and she squeezed Cara's arm. "Meg, let go of your sister's hair. Oh do excuse me, Sara. Actually, why don't you come and join me and the girls. I always feel like a sore thumb at these events but this one is so close to my heart."

Cara stumbled along behind Amanda, wondering how on earth the girl managed the grassy park beneath her in her six-inch stilettos, especially with two toddlers in tow. One of her daughters had her hands covered in ice cream and Amanda expertly whisked out a couple of baby wipes and wiped each of their cherub faces and their hands clean as they giggled at each other.

"Are you sure you don't mind me tagging along? I

really don't want to get in the way," said Cara, feeling ever so guilty for telling porkies about her PR career in the first place. If Amanda brought it up again she would vomit.

"No, not at all. In fact I'm glad to see a friendly face. Between you and me, the other girls are all really lovely but, apart from the next soccer game or fashion crap, I don't have a clue what to talk to them about."

Cara looked around at the sea of little people around her and the ultra-glam, way-too-young mothers who accompanied them. "Don't they talk about their kids too?"

Amanda laughed. "Oh Sara, you are so sweet! No, they all bring their nannies to these events so there is no point talking to any of them about children. It bores most of them to tears."

Cara took a seat on a picnic rug beside Amanda and absorbed her surroundings. Most of the girls were about twenty-three years old and each of them looked slightly out of their depth, hiding behind their nannies or pretending to be entertained by the kiddies' activities.

"Most of them look young enough to have nannies to look after *them*, never mind their children," said Cara and Amanda nodded in agreement. "So what's this all about, if you don't mind me asking?"

"Well, most of these girls are either daughters of famous faces, hoteliers, or big-time bankers. The odd one is married to a very rich sugar daddy and then there's a scattering of footballers' wives or girlfriends – and then there's Emily who can't decide which of the above she wants to be. The children are mostly accessories they have to have when they grow tired of their pet poodle. This event is their way of appearing charitable. Especially Emily." Amanda paused in distaste when she said the glamour girl's name.

"Klobber for Kids?"

"That's it. Basically all the mummies bring clothes their little ones have outgrown and the charity sells them off on the cheap or some of them are given away to the needy."

"Sounds good," said Cara. That explained the rainbow-coloured lorry with a mountain of black bags stuffed with clothes in the back.

"It's a fantastic concept," said Amanda. "Plus it gives us a great chance to clear out a few wardrobes. I swear, it's embarrassing but I have brought at least sixty outfits I bought for the twins that they never got to wear. They still have the labels on them. It's disgusting really, but no matter how many times I told myself I wouldn't, I just had to buy every outfit in sight. Then there was all the sponsorship clothing they received as gifts as well."

"Wow," said Cara and she took a sip of the flavoured water she had been handed by a charity worker. "So, is Emily involved here too? She seems to be organising something over there or is she just one of those people who would be in the crib at Christmas if she got the chance?"

Cara thought Amanda was going to explode she laughed so much.

"You can bet your last penny she'd be at the opening of an envelope," said Amanda. "There's something about that girl that screams desperation. She really does push herself to the front of everything. You have her measured up just right."

Like Sophia, thought Cara and she knew Amanda was thinking the same.

"So, tell me. Have you seen our mutual friend?" asked Amanda, handing her girls a small bunch of grapes each as she spoke. "I see she got her column after all."

Cara knew this conversation was inevitably going to come up but she still wasn't quite sure how to handle it. "Oh, well, she's fine. She's great. Fine, really."

"Well, as much as it pains me to say it, I did read her column," whispered Amanda.

"And?" asked Cara as her heart began to race. "What did you think of it?"

"It has definitely got her to where she wants to be, that's for sure. In every tabloid imaginable. She's been plastered all over the press this week, or so I'm told. I don't read that rubbish any more."

"So you don't rate the column then?"

"Sara," said Amanda, "I do still read *Fab!* as I'm so involved with them and it's better to keep them on side.

To tell you the truth, I think Sophia's column is amazing."

"Amazing?" Cara wasn't sure she'd heard her properly.

"Amazing. I used to work in the publishing trade myself when I was younger and I can tell you, if that girl can write as well as I'm sensing from her column, she doesn't need to suck up so much to Jake Johnston. She is selling herself short."

Cara tried not to burst with excitement. "Really? Oh, I'm – I mean, Sophia would be delighted to hear that. You honestly think she could do even better?"

Amanda looked around before she replied. "You bet," she said. "And I have heard from a very reliable source that Jake will do anything to hold onto her. He is quaking in his boots that she will be snapped up by a rival magazine, so don't be surprised if your old friend Sophia gets a mega-bucks promotion very soon. He will keep her on her toes though by making her feel a little insecure, but that will be his idea of playing the game. In baby steps, Jake will tie Sophia into a knot with him that she'll find it impossible to get out of. I've seen it all before."

Cara gulped and tried to let Amanda's comments sink in. She didn't care how Jake treated Sophia as she was well fit for him, but were her own efforts really so good? She knew she could write, but could this be real? Maybe her career as a ghost writer was a shadow of what she could really achieve, if she was in the right place at the right time. Her watch bleeped on the hour, waking her out of a dream where she was rubbing shoulders with JK Rowling.

"Oh, look, is that the time? Gosh, it was great to catch up with you, Amanda, but I'm really going to have to dash."

"Oh, why so soon? We were just getting started."

"I know, I'm really sorry. I'm supposed to meet a journo from the *Horse and Hound* magazine at noon. Bye, girls!" Cara grabbed her bag and waved a friendly goodbye to the two little girls who she had only ever seen before in magazines. She would have asked them for their autographs only they were too young to hold a pen properly. "Lovely to see you again, Amanda. I really enjoyed the chat."

"You too, Sara." Amanda stood up and pushed her sunglasses off her face to say her farewells. "Oh, and by the way, if you're ever around town again, maybe we could catch up properly over a coffee. I do enjoy your company."

"That would be lovely," said Cara, feeling like such a cheat. "Coffee sounds really good."

"Great! Here's my number," said Amanda and she scribbled her mobile contact down on the back of a sweetie wrapper. "Sorry, I never thought to bring any proper cards. I hope you can make out my scrawl."

Cara took the piece of paper in her hand and read it back to Amanda who by now had a two-year-old toddler on each hip.

"Looks like I can read your scrawl. And many thanks for making me feel so welcome. I do hope we can meet up again."

Cara raced across Hyde Park as soon as she was out of sight of the posh kids' picnic and by the time she reached Sophia's car she was out of breath. Amanda was so refreshing and honest and yet here she was fooling the girl into believing they could be friends when she had given her a false name and background. She checked her watch again. It was ten past twelve and there was no sign of Sophia at all.

Soon it was twenty past, then twelve thirty and by quarter to one Cara felt panicky. Had she made a mistake? Was she in the wrong meeting place? Sophia had warned her not to be late and yet she was forty-five minutes late herself.

Eventually Sophia appeared in the distance, walking as quickly as she could in her sky-scraper heels. On arrival, she clicked open the car door without one word of apology.

"So, how did the brat feast go?" she asked as she started the car.

"Good. And the arty farty gallery?"

"Wonderful," said Sophia with a wry smile. "Just wonderful. And I am being totally serious."

15

Promised Brand

Later that afternoon, Cara was cleaning the downstairs bathroom when the landline at Summer Manor rang. She made a dash for it, taking off her rubber gloves as she ran, and grabbed it just before it rang off.

"Really, Cara, what takes you so long? I was beginning to think you weren't there," said Sophia.

"Well, I *am* here," said Cara. "I just happened to have my hand shoved down your toilet. What's up? Do you have another yummy-mummy gathering for me to attend to make me feel even more frumpy?"

"No, no, not at all. In fact, on the contrary, I need you to stay exactly where you are. I'm on my way to meet Jake and I need you to man the phone in case I need to speak to you urgently – you know, in case he asks any difficult questions."

Cara swung her rubber gloves around as Sophia spoke. She was fast turning into Sophia's beck-and-call girl. "Didn't you say he turned up at the art gallery today already to tell you how wonderful you are?" She could almost feel the beam on Sophia's face from the other end of the telephone.

"Yes, he did, but he needs to go through another few ideas over a quick coffee. Oh, and if Dylan comes home, please don't mention Jake. I don't want my baby to be jealous."

Cara hung up the phone, put her rubber gloves back on and made her way back to the bathroom. Cleaning her toilet, writing her column, cooking her favourite meals were all fine and dandy, but lying to Sophia's boyfriend? Cara didn't remember that particular part of the agreement and it was an area she was determined to avoid at all costs.

"Sophia, darling. You look radiant," said Jake Johnston as he pulled out a chair for his favourite columnist. "So fashionable as always and I adore your scarf."

"Oh, this old thing," said Sophia as she twiddled with the soft black chiffon around her neck. "Yes, I suppose it is sort of new. It's Gaultier."

"Thought so. Now, Miss Brannigan," he said and looked at her seductively, "have I got news for you?"

"News?" said Sophia with a flirtatious giggle. "But I thought we were here to discuss the content of next week's column. What sort of news do you have for me, Jake?"

Jake threw his eyes up and then leaned across the table to where he invaded Sophia's space but she didn't care. The man was showing signs of being besotted with her and she was quite happy to lap it up if it meant more public admiration.

"Do you know what I admire the most about you, Soph?"

He called her *Soph*. No one but Dylan had ever been allowed to shorten her name but on this occasion she was prepared to let it go.

"Go on," she cooed.

"Your modesty. It is just so damn endearing. Do you have any idea how talented you are? I don't think you do."

Sophia shook her head and could feel her earrings swing and her hair brush across her face as she spoke. The man was like jelly on a plate where she was concerned.

"I have no idea where you are coming from. *Me*, modest? In what way?"

Jake rested his hand on hers. "Sophia, have you read what the tabloids are saying about you? You have every columnist in the country trying to keep up with you. They call you 'Vain with a Brain', 'the sassiest writer we have seen in a weekly magazine in years', 'the voice of the season' . . . I could go on." He paused for effect.

"I want to look at your contract again. I want you to . . . I want you to write *features* for my magazines."

"Features?" Sophia gulped. She had no idea what he was on about.

"Yes, features. I have six magazines in my company, Sophia. *Six*. I could offer you a hefty salary if you could write me just one feature a week for at least two of them. If they're a success, I have a television company waiting in the wings for a series."

But Sophia's reaction was not what Jake had expected. She looked frightened and confused.

"I'm not sure what you mean, Jake. Television sounds just absolutely incredible but isn't it a bit soon to expand the column into features? Features on *what* exactly?"

"Oh, 'WAG Tales' will stay as a column but the features are extras. They can be on anything you want. *You* are the creative genius, I'm the business head. Together we could whip the butts of every other magazine in the UK if we play our cards right. We need a catchy name and soon you'll be on network television in association with *Fab!*. What do you say?"

Sophia didn't say anything at first. She looked frozen, like a mannequin version of herself.

"Can you excuse me for a second?" she asked, grabbing her purse and phone. "I've just remembered I have to make an urgent phone call. To my, er, mother."

Jake laughed and raised his hands. "Of course, of course. Mother knows best and all that. I can wait until you ask your mum for advice. I have to admit I do the same myself sometimes."

Sophia scrambled away from him and Jake shrugged as she headed towards the bathroom. A strange place to go to make a phone call but she could call the Queen right now for all he cared, as long as she came back with a yes to his suggestion.

Not knowing if what she had heard was the career move she had been waiting for, or the straw that would break the camel's back and expose her as a fake to all at *Fab!* and further afield, Sophia locked herself in a cubicle and rang Cara back at Summer Manor. She needed to know if Jake's proposal was at all possible. Television? She thought she was going to be sick with nerves and excitement.

"*Features!*" she said before Cara could even say hello. "Can you write features and pretend they are written by me?"

Cara was scrubbing the shower with one hand and holding the phone with the other. "What sort of features?"

"*You* tell *me*, Miss Brainbox. How am I supposed to know what sort of features you can write? *You* are the creative genius and I am the business head behind this operation," she said, blatantly quoting what Jake had just said to her.

"Em, well, let me think . . ."

"Cara! I am locked in a bathroom cubicle in a coffee shop. I don't have time for you to think!"

"And I am locked in your downstairs bathroom cleaning your shower! Look, I suppose I could write a feature about living the dream, you know, how different your life is now to what it was before."

"Go on, I need more ideas than that – think, quick!"

"Maybe a feature on your fashion sense and where you inherited it from?"

"Yes, yes, now I'm getting it," said Sophia, her eyes widening as she tried to remember what Cara was telling her.

"Your love of fast cars, of fine foods, your favourite restaurants, your fashion designers, your best holiday destinations –"

A knock on the bathroom door made Cara jump.

"Are you all right in there, wee hen?" asked Sam as he made his way past the downstairs bathroom which was en route to the kitchen where he was heading for his afternoon tea.

"Fine, Sam, fine. Just put the kettle on and I'll be with you in a second."

"Hurry up, Cara. Is that it?" said Sophia. "Do you think that's enough to convince him we have what it takes to pull this off?"

"Wait, wait, we need a name for it," said Cara. "For the features to keep them all consistent, to brand them . . .

how about, um, how about – I know! *So Sophia*? Yes, that's it! *So Sophia*. I can feature your best restaurants, best bands, best nightclubs, you get it now?"

"Yes, yes, yes! That is so *good*!" said Sophia and she opened the cubicle door to where an elderly lady stared at her. "Yes, yes! You are the best!"

She ignored the woman's glances and waltzed with confidence back into the coffee bar where she sat back down to talk business with Jake Johnston.

16

Can't Help Falling In Love

Dylan Summers entered the south-side café, knowing he was attracting stares from every corner of the room. A photographer snapped him just as he crossed the threshold and he gave a light smile, then looked around for his brother. His career was soaring at lightning speed with two top Premiership clubs now expressing a serious interest in signing him up after his performance at the weekend, yet his personal life was plummeting out of control.

Far in the corner, Mark sat with his nose in a bestseller, his forehead crinkled into a frown that Dylan recognised as almost identical to his own.

"Good choice on the seats, Marko. Do I have ketchup on my face? Everyone is staring."

Mark stood up and gave his brother a friendly pat on the back.

"Hey, kid, it's so good to see you and, from what I hear, you'd better get used to being recognised in the streets. Fulton is a great club, but now the public has got a sniff that the big ones are showing an interest, you're going from soup of the day to catch of the day."

Dylan sat down and lifted the book his brother was reading. "Hey, when did you turn into a literary buff? This is pretty heavy stuff and a bit of a step up from your old Marvel collection," he said as he flicked through the Pulitzer Prize-winning novel.

"I'm trying to widen my horizons, bro'. It's called the influence of a good woman."

"Excellent," said Dylan, and without meeting his brother's eyes, he lifted the coffee menu and scanned down its listings but the words blurred into one another. He couldn't even concentrate on a damn coffee menu these days. His head was a muddle.

"Why the long face, Dylan? I thought we could go and catch a movie or something while I'm in town, but you look like you just murdered someone. What's up?"

"I dunno, Mark, and that's the truth. Pressure? The future? I don't know."

The boys fell silent as the waiter approached their table and they ordered a large coffee each. Like the customers surrounding the two, the waiter did a double take when he served the drinks and raced back to tell the kitchen staff they had a star in their midst.

Mark fiddled with his coffee spoon and then looked his brother in the eye. "Hey, what do you say we ditch the movie and you drive me out to that home of yours so I can whip your butt on the tennis court?"

"Okay, okay, I suppose. I don't think I could concentrate on a movie. Drink up and we'll go and imitate McEnroe and Agassi."

"I'm Agassi," said Mark with a grin.

"Not a chance," said Dylan and he took a long drink of his coffee. "I'm Agassi."

"Okay, you win. It's your tennis court," said Mark, not realising just how much seeing him again had lifted Dylan's spirits already.

Sophia's car was absent when the Summers brothers arrived at Dylan's home and like every day for a number of weeks, he had no idea where she was.

"Did you ever in your wildest dreams think you would one day own a place like this?" said Mark as they approached the gates. "This is the same size as the entire apartment block we were brought up in."

Dylan laughed and put down the window to wave at Sam who was, as usual, in the garden. Today he seemed to be sieving out the pond with the ever-faithful Buster by his side.

"I know, it's so amazing, sometimes I think I'll wake up and it will all be a dream and I'll be working as an electrician as I'd planned to in Newcastle, maybe struggling to make ends meet when the going gets tough."

"Like me," said Mark. "No, whoah! I didn't mean it like that."

Dylan sighed and pulled the car into its place at the side of the house. "Sure you did."

"Really, Dylan, I am so proud of you and all that you've achieved as a footballer. It's every boy's dream for Christ's sake, and I'm not exactly struggling. Far from it, actually, and Fiona works hard too. We're doing fine, just fine."

They got out of the car and Mark couldn't help but stare at the impressive Summer Manor. If only his parents would swallow their pride they could enjoy all of their son's fine lifestyle as any parent deserved. At least Sam had stuck by Dylan through thick and thin. He would have to have a good chat with the old boy before he headed back up North again.

"Let's go inside and get some cold drinks," said Dylan. "Then I'll show you what for on the tennis court."

"Sounds good to me," said Mark.

Inside, he took a seat at the breakfast bar while Dylan went to change his clothes.

Dylan sauntered down the corridor towards the

stairs and wondered where Sophia was. He would have loved if she could have spent some time with his brother. This column had really taken over her life, as much as she denied it, and the way she was being so secretive and defensive about the whole thing was turning her into a different person. It had gone from a minor obsession with celebrity to an out-and-out compulsive obsession and it was freaking him out. He had seen what it was like to live your personal life in the public eye with some of his former team-mates and as Andy Stewart had once told him, when magazines were knocking on his door wanting to know every move he and his family made, the worst thing about living in a bubble is that some day, when you think you are invincible, the bubble will burst.

As Dylan turned towards the staircase he stopped and listened. He could hear something from the piano room that he hadn't heard since he had left home many years ago – the sound of someone playing an old Elvis song. He approached the door carefully, not wanting to disturb the music but curious as to who was on the other side of the door. Sophia didn't play – she had insisted that he bought the instrument because it looked good – and the only music Sam could make was with the bagpipes and that was many moons ago. It had to be . . .

"Cara!"

Cara jumped and held her hand to her chest. "Oh,

I am so, so sorry," she said, lurching to her feet and knocking over a vase of flowers that sat on top of the piano. She quickly righted the vase and then rooted a cloth out of her apron pocket to wipe up the water before it did any damage. "I just couldn't resist. I didn't know you were home."

"No, *I'm* sorry for disturbing you," said Dylan, racing to her aid and wiping up the rest of the water with the end of his T-shirt. "Here, let me help. Which Elvis song was that? You played it really well."

"Er, 'Always On My Mind'," she said, wishing she had chosen something a bit more upbeat. She gathered up the flowers and stuck them back in the vase. "I'll go and fix this up." Then she looked at him and began to laugh.

"What?" he asked in surprise.

"Your T-shirt. It's soaking," she said. "Why on earth did you try to mop the water up with your T-shirt?"

He looked down and shrugged, then lifted the bottom of his T-shirt to take it off and Cara grabbed the vase of flowers and turned on her heel.

"I was going to change it anyway," he said, still laughing, more now at her reaction when he went to remove his shirt so casually. It was something he did every day on the pitch, but he supposed it was a bit strange in these surroundings. Cara averted her eyes but his muscular torso drew her eye like a magnet. The man was solid as a rock! A fine line of hair ran down the centre of his tanned, washboard stomach and continued down below his jeans . . .

Dylan crossed the room and held the door open for her. Her heart was thumping so hard she was afraid he might hear it as she passed.

"Oh, and you can play the piano anytime," he said as he followed her out of the room. "You're very talented. I could listen to you forever."

"Really?" She turned back to him.

Dylan nodded in earnest and smiled warmly. "I'm a big Elvis fan. Secretly of course. Next you'll tell me you're an undercover journalist and you're going to tell the world of my guilty pleasures."

Cara gave a nervous laugh. What did he just say? Was he joking or did he know more about her than she thought he did? "Of course not. Your secret's safe with me."

"Good. I believe you," he laughed.

Cara looked at his mouth, so full, and his teeth so perfectly white. When he smiled at her and stared at her like that, she really felt like she was floating. He was just so damn perfect. And so damn attached. To her boss, she reminded herself.

"I was reared on Elvis Presley," she said, determined to stay focused on talking about music and not on the fact that she was having a one-on-one, friendly conversation about Elvis with a drop-dead-gorgeous Premiership soccer star. A *shirtless* drop-dead-gorgeous

Premiership soccer star at that! "I've had years of listening to my dad and being forced to entertain locals as they sipped pints. I know it's not exactly hip these days, but I like it."

"Well, we'll let this be our little secret," whispered Dylan and he touched her arm. "I won't tell anyone about your tendency to play Elvis when you see a piano if you don't tell anyone about my love of the King."

"It's a deal," said Cara and she looked up at him, and then glanced away when she encountered his green eyes. She could swim in those eyes. She wondered if she was dreaming or if this was really happening. "Well, I'd better go and replace the water for these flowers. Let me have your T-shirt."

He handed it over. "Thanks. Hey, I might ask you to play again for me sometime, if you don't mind."

"No," said Cara. "I don't mind at all." She smiled and blushed again, then made her way to the utility room. She closed the door behind her and held his shirt to her face, inhaling his manly scent.

"Stop this. Stop this now!" she muttered and reached for the washing powder. She couldn't afford to let this happen to her again.

"Cute housekeeper," said Mark as he served the ball on court a few minutes later.

"Cara? When did you see her?" asked Dylan,

whacking the ball in return. The way Cara had looked at him was still on his mind, and more importantly, the way he had held her gaze so deliberately was making him think and making it very difficult to concentrate on the game.

"In the kitchen earlier when you were changing into your tennis gear."

"Yeah," said Dylan. "She's a great girl. In every way. Shit! Fifteen love."

"So much for whipping my butt," said Mark and he served again. "Oh, there's your little Irish girl now. Looks like she's pretty desperate to get your attention."

"What? Where?" said Dylan, and he missed Mark's serve.

Dylan looked behind him to see Cara at the far gable of the house. Buster was by her side, barking loudly.

"Dylan, come quick!" shouted Cara. "Please come quickly! It's Sam. Hurry!"

Dylan and Mark dropped their tennis racquets and raced across the lawns to where Cara stood, shaking and pointing towards the side of the pond where the boys had passed Sam only a little while before. Sam lay by the pond, his hand clutched to his chest, Buster alongside him now, his head on his paws.

Cara ran to him, leaned down and stroked his brow. "Don't worry, Sam. The ambulance is on its way. We'll have you up and about in no time."

"Maybe it would be quicker to drive him to hospital?" said Dylan, fearing the worst. "It will take an ambulance ages finding this place."

"Are you crazy?" said Mark. "We'd never get through the lunchtime traffic. That's what sirens are for. We'll keep him comfortable till the ambulance gets here."

Sam looked around in bewilderment, frightened and confused, his eyes glazed over.

"It's probably just a fall," he mumbled. "Don't fuss. I'll be fine. I'll be fine."

"Of course you will, Sam," said Cara.

With Sam safely in hospital for observation, Mark said his farewells to his brother and set off for Newcastle with a hope in his heart that he had witnessed enough drama for one day. The last thing he needed was to arrive home to another drama with his parents.

"Do you think Sam will be all right?" asked Cara as she put on her coat.

Dylan walked her to the door, realising that once she left he would be alone in his house for the first time since Sophia moved in. With Sam in the gatehouse, there was always activity around Summer Manor and since Cara had come, he had grown used to the company.

"I think it was a scare that was long overdue," he said. "Perhaps I should be more strict with him as well. He does far too much around here."

Tell that to your girlfriend, thought Cara but she bit her tongue.

"Well, I'll be off then," said Cara. "Goodbye, Dylan."

Dylan stood at the door as Cara got into her Fiat Uno.

"Oh, and thanks for all your help, of course," said Dylan. "If it wasn't for you today, Mark and I would still be pretending to be on Wimbledon and poor old Sam mightn't have been so lucky."

"Buster helped. If he hadn't barked so much at the time I would never have noticed Sam in distress," she said, waving off his thanks, praying he would go back inside so she could fight with the ancient automobile as it choked and spat before it took her home.

She turned the ignition and, as usual, the car gave a splutter and then died. Please, please, don't let him see this, she thought. She looked in the mirror to check if he had gone but he was still there. She gave an unconcerned wave and a smile as a signal for him to go and then turned the key the second time.

Nothing. Not a spark.

Cara was absolutely dismayed. If the car didn't go on the second turn, it wouldn't go at all. She was stuck and she knew it.

"What's wrong? Has it given up the ghost?"

Cara looked out to see Dylan, standing in his shorts and T-shirt beside her. "It's just a wee bit temperamental," she joked and turned the key again but there wasn't an ounce of life in the old car at all.

Cara looked at Dylan with a plea in her eye for pity at her misfortune but when she caught his eye they both laughed.

"That's one way of describing it," said Dylan and he lifted the bonnet while Cara got out of the car and kicked the tyre as hard as she could.

"Stupid pile of rust!" she said.

"Cara McCarthy, I don't think I've seen a car as out of breath in a very long time! Come on. Let me drive you home and I'll have someone come and look at it tomorrow."

"Okay," said Cara and she didn't know which had pleased her more: the fact that Dylan Summers was going to take her home, or that he had not only remembered her first name, but had somehow found out and remembered her surname too.

17

Always On My Mind

Cara wondered if she was talking too much. They had only hit the motorway and already she had told Dylan Summers the guts of her life story. She knew she should maintain a level of distance as far as her personal life was concerned but Dylan seemed genuinely interested and she had found herself talking about Liam.

"Family can be hard work, eh?" he said. "If you even knew half of what I have going on right now with my lot it would make your brother seem like the Angel Gabriel."

Cara knew her place and wouldn't dare pry unless Dylan wanted to talk.

"I can only imagine how stressed you are," he went on. "Actually, I can *really* imagine how stressed you are if your family issues are as complicated as mine are at the minute."

Cara looked at Dylan's strong arms as they held the steering wheel of the huge jeep he was driving. She felt like she was sitting in a private jet with its bulky exterior and cosy, protective frame surrounding her.

"It's pretty tough at the moment, Cara, I have to admit so forgive me if I've been distant and moody," he said, his eyes fixed on the road. "I feel I wasn't very nice to you all along. Well, maybe 'nice' isn't the right word. I wasn't very . . . I didn't really pay you any attention. I must seem very ungrateful for all you do around the house and with Sam."

Cara looked at him, puzzled. "I didn't notice you not paying me any attention. And I love spending time with Sam. Oh I do hope he's okay!"

"Of course he is," said Dylan, wondering why he felt the need to apologise in the first place. "Seeing how much you cared for Sam this afternoon, it just made me realise that I should have, I don't know, talked to you more?"

"Well, we are sure making up for it now."

Dylan flashed a smile in Cara's direction that would have made any other woman in the country melt or faint at his feet, but Cara didn't see that any more. Instead she saw a man who had been thrust into a very public life he wasn't very comfortable with. Deep down he was just as grounded as everyone else. Gorgeous, gifted, but very grounded.

He turned up the radio when an Elvis song came on. It was "Always On My Mind".

"Gosh, that song seems to be following us today," he said.

"So it does," said Cara, feeling the hair on the back of her neck stand up as Dylan hummed along.

Neither of them spoke until the song had finished.

"So, enough about me," said Cara. "I feel like I've been rambling on."

Dylan turned the radio down again. "It's fine. Tell me, how did you enjoy the party at Amanda's house that night? Was it, excuse the pun, *fab*?"

He laughed at his own joke and Cara joined in.

"Truly amazing," she said in a sarcastic tone.

"Was everyone gorgeous?"

"Beautiful. I can't wait to go to another one."

"Well, please do, because it saves me from standing like a prune in the corner while Sophia does her thing. So I take it you weren't really impressed then?"

Cara thought before she spoke. It would be a lie to say she wasn't impressed.

"Oh, it's a wonderful lifestyle, don't get me wrong, and once a month or so it would be nice to get dressed up and sip champagne in such lavish surroundings, having your photo taken and being fussed over. But as far as a general night out is concerned, I'd much rather have a nice meal in my favourite restaurant and then go somewhere I can let my hair down without worrying constantly about who is watching and where my picture will end up."

Dylan nodded. "I couldn't agree more."

Cara's mobile phone rang from her handbag and she wasn't sure what to do. If she answered it and it was Natalie and she said she was in Dylan Summers' car it could be highly embarrassing. He was sure to hear her hyena-like squeal of excitement from where he was sitting.

"Aren't you going to take that?" he asked. "Go ahead. I won't listen in to your intimate chats with your boyfriend."

The phone stopped ringing and Cara breathed again.

"No worries, he'll ring back," she said. "In fact, George rings me around this time every day. He's very protective and he does get jealous so it's best not to upset him."

Dylan drummed his fingers on the steering wheel. "I'd say he does. So is George the love of your life?"

"Dunno," said Cara. "It's a toss up between him and my other guy. I'm just trying to decide which I like best. Cara Clooney or Cara Pitt. What do you think?"

Dylan smirked and played along. "Oh, I'd go for Clooney. No baggage. That other guy has too many other commitments, from what I hear. He's big into adoption."

Cara's phone did ring again and this time she knew

she shouldn't ignore it. She looked at the caller display and her heart skipped a beat. It was Tom, the football fan from the pub on Saturday. At long flippin' last. She had almost given up on him.

"Do you mind?" she asked Dylan and he shook his head.

"No, go for it."

"Hi, Tom," she said. "How are you?"

"I'm great. Just wondering if you'd like to catch a movie tomorrow night since there's no football on telly, what with you being such an expert on the subject?"

If Dylan could hear what Tom was saying, he pretended not to.

"Sure, that would be really nice. I'm almost home now and I'll give you a call when I get there."

"Oh, sorry, are you driving?"

Cara couldn't lie again. She had been forced into too many white lies lately.

"Er, no, but my, er, my boss's boyfriend was kind enough to give me a ride home when my car broke down. I'll chat to you later, okay?"

When Cara hung up Dylan felt the time was right to turn the radio back up again. He didn't want her to feel she had to explain her plans for the evening following her phone call. He was after all, as she put it, her "boss's boyfriend".

"So have you decided yet?" he asked over the music. "Which man to choose?"

"Oh, between Clooney or Pitt?"

"Uh huh."

"No way. I think I'll leave them hanging for another while," she said and she rested back on the headrest.

They drove further into the summer evening in a comfortable silence, both lost in thought of the haze of activity that was going on in each of their lives.

Cara glowed inwardly at the thought of her forth-coming movie date with Tom. He had been quite the gentleman on their first encounter, laughing at her lame jokes and taking the time to converse with Natalie and Liam, so much so that by the end of the evening he had all three of them eating out of his hands.

Natalie, being her cynical self, had commented on how he was almost too good to be true. Good fun, check. Good job, check. Good looking, double check. Not married, not in a relationship, not gay, triple check. Yes, Tom had been elevated swiftly to potential new boyfriend status by the end of the evening and Cara was delighted to have progressed to step two of their budding relationship. A date. Yet, somewhere in the back of her mind a warning signal was threatening to erupt to take her back into the "all men are bastards" zone that she had been plummeted into after her encounter with Michael "Boss Man" Bradley.

"You hungry?" asked Dylan, bringing Cara back into the real world, where she was sitting beside a top

Premiership footballer in his state-of-the-art vehicle which was practically driving them by itself to her modest quarters with its high-tech Sat Nav system. Was she hungry? She could eat the hind leg off a donkey.

"Um, well, I suppose, not really. Sort of. Why?"

Dylan didn't answer at first and Cara noticed he was smirking slightly.

"You suppose, not really, sort of, why?" he said. "I'll take that as a yes."

"Er, okay."

"Would you mind if we stopped somewhere to grab a quick bite? I'm pretty famished but if you're in a hurry home it doesn't matter."

"Oh, no, of course not. I'm in no hurry. I wouldn't want to get between any man and his stomach. I have a brother so I know it's not a pretty place to be."

Dylan Summers was driving her home and he was hungry. He wanted to stop for something to eat. Who the hell was she to refuse?

"So, where do you recommend around these parts? It doesn't have to be anything fancy," he said. "Just a quick pizza or sandwich bar will be fine."

Cara looked out of the window and recognised where she was. There were a few shabby-looking eateries scattered amongst newsagents and takeaways, but she knew that further down the road there were one or two places that shouldn't involve the risk of poisoning a soccer star.

"I'd love some toasted soda bread," she said for a laugh, knowing it would confuse him.

"Soda what?"

"It's an Irish bread. I've been craving it since I first arrived here. Seriously though, where to eat around here depends on whether your stomach is made of iron, really. Most of these places belong in Cholesterol City but I do know of a quiet little pizzeria about a mile or so from here that just might pass the taste test. It's a family-run, genuine Italian-café-style place, or so they say."

"Sounds spot on to me," said Dylan.

They parked under a lamppost in view of Paolo's Pizzeria and Dylan grabbed a baseball cap from the back seat of the car. He wore a faint stubble that was very becoming and Cara wondered if she could run the risk of sending Natalie a quick text to say that Dylan had finally decided to leave his model girlfriend for her and that she would be around shortly to pack her bags and move into the home with him.

She noticed how he walked just a slight pace in front of her and kept his head down all the way into the café. No one on the street gave him a second glance and Cara was pleased at his anonymity. He chose a table at the side of the room, away from the window and any prying eyes that might realise who and what he was.

"Do they teach you how to do that?" she asked him when they had settled into their seats.

"Teach you what?"

"You know, how to fit into the world of Joe Public when you spontaneously decide to grab a quick pizza in a different end of town? I'm just surprised that you aren't recognised more, that's all."

Dylan glanced over the huge laminated menu towards her and then averted his gaze back to the list of pasta and pizza dishes.

"Despite what you think, I don't tend to be recognised a lot once I leave the football grounds. Unless I am with Sophia, of course, as nowadays she is the one who is more likely to be noticed in public." Dylan shrugged to indicate his indifference to it all.

"You really don't like any fuss, do you?" said Cara.

"Am I that obvious?" he smiled. "Don't get me wrong, I know part of it comes with the job as far as football fans are concerned, but I don't think that all footballers have to or want to be a celebrity, that's all. Sophia has other notions and, as I'm sure you gathered, that's where we clash."

He looked up at Cara again and she shifted in her seat. The whole situation, sitting here with him in such personal surroundings was enveloping her and she didn't want to talk about his relationship with Sophia. Every time she looked across the table she discovered something new about his appearance, like the way his hair was cut tightly into the side of his face, the way the stubble from earlier that day had darkened slightly, the way his eyes creased up when he laughed and his arms as they leaned on the table . . . Stop it now, she told herself. There was no way in the world she could allow herself to start fancying Dylan Summers. It was too typical, too fairytale and too much like a road to nowhere. It was time to change the subject. Fast.

"Tell me this," she said. "Do you think that Paolo who owns this place has any connections whatsoever with Italy or is he really a relative of Grant Mitchell's who would be much better suited down The Vic?"

Dylan looked around as staff milled past tables. The setting was a fair stab at real Italy, with plenty of green, white and red and chequered tablecloths and a warm, cosy atmosphere. The menu was bilingual and a stout, dark-haired man was in command, greeting customers with a perfect "*ciao*" and "*grazie*" and then Dylan noticed his name badge which said *Paolo De Marco – Restaurateur*. He looked Italian. He sounded Italian.

"First cousin of Phil and Grant Mitchell from *EastEnders* for definite," he said. "Pure Cockney. In fact, I would swear that I just heard him tell one of the waiters to go 'up the apples and pears' and fetch some ravioli."

Cara laughed in agreement and soon they were tucked into a large *Mexicano* special pizza with lots of spicy meats and peppers, served by Paolo himself. Cara's intention to nibble like a waif went out the window as she wolfed down a second slice washed down with a glass of rich, red wine. She was relaxed now and was surprised at how easy she found Dylan's company.

"Good job you weren't hungry," he grinned as she picked a stray mushroom from the side of her plate. "I just knew you were starving after all the drama with Sam today but you didn't like to say."

"I was, to be honest. Oh, I can't stop thinking about poor Sam," said Cara. "You will give him my love, won't you? I dread to think of him all alone and worrying in hospital. He got quite a scare this afternoon."

Dylan signalled to the waiter to fetch the bill.

"I know. I think I'll pop across and see him when I drop you off. You and he seem to have really gelled. I think, if he could, he would have you move in and look after us all of the time."

Paolo the owner made his way back over to the table and Cara's eyes widened, knowing that Dylan was thinking the same thing as Paolo began to speak. She felt like a child in church who was told not to laugh and the more she tried to keep it in, the harder it became. Now was the time to see if Paolo passed the Italian test but Cara was too giddy to challenge him.

"*Prego, Signore, Signora.* Deed you 'ave a nice meal?" asked Paolo, and Cara pretended she couldn't find her handbag to avoid meeting the man's eye.

"It was delicious. Wonderful, sir," said Dylan in an award-winning voice of sincerity. "I will most definitely come back to your pizzeria in future."

"Christ!" said Paolo in a strong East London accent. "If it isn't . . . what's your name again, son?"

"Er, Summers. Dylan Summers."

"That's right. Good luck for the game next week, young Summers. Fulton were right to hold on to you for another while. What do you think of Larssen's move to . . ."

Cara stared at Dylan, who was on the verge of being lured into a debate on the state of European football and then excused herself from the table. She was going to explode into a fit of giggles and she couldn't hold it back any longer.

"Cheers, mate. Keep the change," said Dylan quickly and he followed Cara out onto the street.

"If you only had seen the expression on your face when he recognised you! We were right! He's as Italian as the Queen Mother!" she said, wishing she could capture the look on Dylan's face and keep it forever. She had never seen him grin so much in all the time she had known him.

"He's as Italian as the Rovers Return," he said, as they walked towards his car in great joviality.

18

Treat Me Nice

"If you don't kill him, I will," said Natalie, as she whizzed past Cara in the hallway of the apartment the next morning. "I swear, if I trip over one more pair of size 11 Doctor Marten boots I am suing him for damages. This place wasn't built for three."

Cara watched as Natalie scuttled towards her bedroom with a white fluffy towel wrapped round her body and another round her head. As always, she was bang up to date with her beauty regime with her bronzed pins and painted toenails – even the floral tattoo around her ankle looked pretty, while Cara sensed that on anyone else it would look either tarty or hippy.

"Give over, would you, Natalie? And where are you going anyhow at this time of the morning? I thought you weren't working till noon today?"

"I have a date."

"At nine thirty in the morning?"

Liam lifted his head from the couch and pulled a face. He had long ago decided that, if Natalie hated having him around so much, he would lash out the insults even more. She looked so hot when she was angry.

"You're going on a date?" he said. "Oh, the poor guy whoever he is – imagine having ice for breakfast. *Brrr!*"

"Shut your face, loser! I actually have arranged to meet Juicy John's brother for elevenses and, believe me, he is even more luscious than the strawberries I squeeze on a daily basis and, if I am made of ice, he can melt me any time."

"But I never heard you mention that anyone belonging to Juicy John was luscious. You said Juicy John wears sandals and clogs," said Cara.

Natalie sat on the edge of the sofa and put one elegant foot on the coffee table, then topped up her nail polish. She hadn't got around to putting her face on as yet, but she still looked passable even at such an early hour.

"He does. And you know, I could almost see past the dodgy footwear, but how could you fancy a man who says things like 'delightful' and 'exquisite' when he is describing a pear or a banana? It's just not normal. His brother, on the other hand, is exactly my type. Tall, dark and *loaded*."

"You're so fickle, Natalie," said Liam and Natalie fired a cup between his legs.

"You're so useless," she replied. "Now, get up and do something, you lazy wee shit! At least I have a date. You couldn't pull a pint, let alone a good-looking woman."

Liam rose to her challenge. "I bet I could. I know *you* fancy me, Natalie, even though I wouldn't class you as good-looking. You always have. Admit it. You like me."

Natalie looked around for another weapon and then gave up. "Yeah, you're absolutely right. I do. Not!"

"Children!" said Cara, applying a new shade of red lipstick in the hallway mirror. It complemented her light tan and dark hair and made her feel instantly glamorous. She was getting quite used to her morning beauty routine now, and today she had chosen her outfit carefully – a black cotton shirt-dress that hugged her hips and skimmed her knees, and a pair of red kitten heels to match her lips and the red clutch bag she had found at the bottom of Natalie's wardrobe.

She had developed some self-pride but, as well as this, she had an important event to attend this morning and she had to look well enough to blend in with the other guests, yet subtle enough to fade into the background.

"Where the hell are you cleaning today, Cara?" asked Liam. "The Ritz?"

"Nowhere important."

"I didn't know Mrs Mop wore heels and lipstick?" he said.

"And who said I was being Mrs Mop today? There is more to me than meets the eye," she teased and gave her eyelashes a generous sweep of black mascara.

"Well then, you must be out to impress the man of the house," said Natalie. "Remember, he is taken, Cara, and once bitten, twice shy. Be careful."

Cara paused in disgust at her friend's tendency to remind her of her previous mistakes.

"Shut up, Natalie. For your information I am meeting Tom after work and we are going to the cinema. That is why I am making such an effort."

Natalie scrunched her face in apology. "Oh, that's wonderful. I'm sorry. I didn't mean to upset you. I just thought that after your rendezvous with Dylan yesterday evening you were beginning to set your sights on forbidden fruit again."

"Oh for crying out loud! It seems like I just can't win," said Cara. "One minute you are waxing and spraying me and fixing my hair and then when I finally get into the habit of not looking like Attila the Hun, you accuse me of moving in on another woman's man. Again. There I said it! Again!"

Natalie held her hands up in defeat. "You shared a pizza with him last night – and that's perfectly fine – but I'd say, if you surveyed one hundred red-blooded females the length and breadth of this country, you'd be in the minority if you didn't at least try to —"

Natalie didn't get to finish her sentence as Cara grabbed her purse and coat and slammed the apartment door behind her.

"You are such an insensitive gob," said Liam, enjoying the moment as Natalie's words bounced around the room into nowhere. "What the hell did you have to go and say that for?"

Sophia looked at her watch. She would just have to go inside by herself if Cara didn't hurry up. The invitation said the function began at ten thirty with brunch and, though Sophia didn't have any interest in food, she wanted to watch how some of the other socialites nibbled on grapes and olives then discreetly spat out the contents into a napkin pretending they had discovered a pip.

Besides, she had already eaten half a cracker for breakfast and the herbal tea which guaranteed weight loss was most definitely living up to its reputation as an internal cleanser as every morsel she put into her mouth made a swift return out of her body as if it had taken a ride on a rapido slide. Eating in public was a risk she simply couldn't take.

Then she finally spotted Cara charging along the footpath from the nearby Tube station.

"There you are," she said from the front seat of her

car as Cara drew level. "At long last. There are two things I cannot stand in life, Cara. Lipstick on my teeth and people who are late!"

"I'm so sorry, but I'm sure Dylan told you about my car trouble yesterday evening. I'm going to have to make other travel arrangements until it's fixed as taking the Tube in the morning is like travelling in a sardine tin. Any word on Sam? How was he last night?"

"He'll live," said Sophia and she got out of the car, flipped her sunglasses down from their perch on her new blonde mane and marched ahead of Cara towards the boat club that was the starting point for the perfume launch of a reality television star.

"I hardly recognised you with your new hairstyle. It's quite, em, different," said Cara, hiding a chuckle at her boss's new platinum do. It certainly was a head-turner.

"Well, you have to move with the times or the media loses interest," said Sophia. "I hope to steal this little untalented wannabe's limelight today by attracting some of the paps to come my way. Remember that guy Bryan who you were blatantly chatting up at Amanda's party?"

"I was so not chatting him up. He was chatting me up."

"Dream on. Anyhow, he made so much money out of my pictures on that occasion that he is now quite the little stalker – so if he's here I'm sure to wipe little

Miss Sailor's eye with my column inches in tomorrow's news."

Cara tried to figure out the occasion of today's outing but as usual Sophia's information via text message had been so scant there was no way she could have interpreted its cryptic clues.

"Any advice from Jake on what angle we should cover today?" she hinted, hoping for some information to get her creativity flowing.

"Oh, just get the name of the perfume, what's-her-face's name and a brief who's who in attendance. Say the yacht trip was fab, blah, blah and weave your usual magic around it. Easy peasy to a genius like you." Sophia almost snarled as the sarcasm dripped off her tongue.

She pulled her nautical navy and white striped top off her shoulders to reveal bony but brown flesh and opened her matching handbag to reveal a cute sailor-style hat which she placed to perfection on her head. Her skinny hips were squeezed into a pair of wide-leg white-cotton trousers to show off her best assets and the outfit was finished off with a pair of navy wedges which were as close to flat shoes as Sophia would ever put her tootsies into.

"Did you just say there is a yacht trip?" asked Cara in horror. "You didn't tell me we were going on a boat!" Suddenly her black shirt-dress with red accessories felt wintry and dark and out of sync compared to

231

Sophia's bright sunny ensemble, not to mention her new brassy stand-out-from-the-crowd hair style.

"Didn't I? Whoops! Then I suppose I didn't mention the dress code either? Oh don't worry, just say you forgot. I'm sure Cindy won't mind if you ignored her 'Blue Ocean' theme. She'll get over it when she's stacking shelves in Tesco once her fifteen minutes of fame is over."

Bitch, thought Cara. Hateful, spiteful bitch.

"I'm not going in," she said, and she stopped dead only yards from the entrance to the upper-class venue which looked more like a country club than a boat club.

"Oh, yes, you are going in, Cara."

"Oh, no, I am not."

"But you have to."

"Actually, that's where you're wrong, Sophia. I don't have to. I can walk away right now and you would be in shit right up to your tits. Write your fucking column yourself!"

"Are you threatening me?" asked Sophia and she gave her trademark nasty cackle. "Don't threaten me, brainy, because I know more about you than you care to think and I could make your life a misery. Now, come inside, make a few mental notes and then we'll go back to my place and –"

"Oh, so *you* are threatening me now, are you?" said Cara. "And what could you possibly know about me that would even measure up to the fact that without me you will slide right back down the celebrity alphabet to become the nobody that you were until I started writing your column? You're a fake and you know it! A pathetic Z-list *fake!*"

Sophia put a hand on her hip and grimaced. She knew Cara was telling the truth, but where did the jumped-up little bitch get all her courage from? Sophia had nothing on her at all. Not yet, but all that would change sooner or later. She had her feelers out. There had to be some juice she could bribe Cara with. She had anticipated that she would get on her high horse now she had a few columns under her belt.

"Okay, okay. Let's just calm down for a second," she said. "You *know* we have to go in. It's my job, well, it's not just my job, it's your job too and Jake really wants this launch covered. He pays me, I pay you. Now, there has to be a way around this." Sophia's eyes brightened as if she had come up with the ultimate solution to their conundrum. "I know! How about if you stand at the back? No one will even know you are there and you'll have a bird's-eye view. You can stand at the back!"

Cara matched Sophia's stance by folding her arms.

"Stand at the back? At the back of a boat? What the hell difference will standing at the back of a boat make? Everyone else will still be dressed like Popeye's cute little sister while I look like, what do you call him again, the fat baddie man."

"Bluto. His name was Bluto. And now that you say it —"

"Shut up!" Cara recoiled as a host of skinny starlets made their way into the party with ditzy designer sailor outfits that they had obviously spent weeks planning.

"But that's a great idea," said Sophia. "Should anyone ask you about the dress code, say you came as Bluto. They will think you are so original and creative, rather than simply following the pack and —"

"Then swap."

"What?!"

"Swap outfits," said Cara. "Go on. If you are so convinced it's original and creative to go as Bluto, then let's go back to the car and you can wear my clothes and I will wear yours. Then we'll go inside, take a spin on the boat, go back to the house and I'll write up the column and Bob's your uncle!"

"Now, that is utterly ridiculous. There is no way I am giving up my new outfit for you."

"Well, then there is no way I am going to write a column any more for you."

They stood glaring at each other, both locked in a stubborn stance and neither wanting to give in.

"Cara. I have to write up this event. I mean, *you* have to write up this event. Jake isn't as much of a pussycat as I once thought and no matter how successful 'WAG Tales' is, he knows he can keep me on my toes by mentioning Emily Evans' name at every opportunity and it's making me quite shaky. Now, let's be sensible here. For once. No one has any idea who you are so if you ignore the dress code, they won't notice."

"Bollocks. If I am wearing a sailor-style outfit like everyone else, I will blend in with the crowd. If I, on the other hand, am dressed differently, then I will stand out like a sore thumb. People will ask questions, mainly *who the hell is she?* On the other hand, you might just steal the thunder of the party girl if you blatantly ignore the dress code, no? Am I making sense?"

Sophia tapped her toe on the sidewalk, contemplating what Cara had just said. She did have a very good point. Sophia's aim after all was to be noticed. She hated blending in with the crowd, but could she be so blatantly cheeky as to ignore the dress code and march into a party dressed totally different to everyone else?

"Right, where do we get changed?" she said. To hell with the dress code. No one told Sophia Brannigan what to wear.

"In the car?"

"Let's go," said Sophia. "Before I change my mind. I'll wear black but I have a feeling I will either be crucified or congratulated for doing so. And for your sake it better be the latter."

The first person to comment on Sophia's defiance of the dress code was an unfortunate waiter who was serving a selection of seafood canapés beside a table of champagne at the entrance to the yacht club.

"Oh, you must be at the wrong event, darling," he said quietly to a stony-faced Sophia. He took her arm and said in a low voice, "The funeral boat is just along the pier. I think they're just about to begin the service. Such a tragedy. So sad."

"The *what*?"

"The funeral boat?" said the boy and he winced as Sophia pushed his hand off her arm. "As opposed to the Blue Ocean perfume launch in here? You know, I'd like to have my ashes strewn into the river too when I depart. There's something poetic about it, don't you think?"

Sophia swallowed hard, then lifted a mussel filled with tomato sauce and blatantly spilled it down the hapless waiter's crisp white sailor suit.

Cara gasped and apologised on her behalf immediately. She truly thought the boy was about to cry.

"I'm so sorry, sir," she said, lifting two glasses of plonk and glaring at a defiant Sophia as she spoke. "It's just that I found her skulking around on shore and she seemed so lost and lonely, so I hope you don't mind if she tags along with me? She's still grieving, I suppose. She was very close to the deceased."

The waiter nodded his head and shooed them on inside the club, afraid that the scary platinum lady in the black dress would attack him with more fish if he refused. He laid down his platter and ran off in search of a clean shirt before the main event began or, worse, before he got the sack.

"One more time," hissed Sophia, as they mingled through the crowd towards the back of the yacht club's sprawling interior. "One more time and I am out of here! Funeral boat! Huh! If he insults me like that again he'll see his ashes scattered sooner than he'd planned, the cheeky pup! Or anyone else for that matter!"

Cara couldn't help but laugh and she pointed out some seats in the corner. By then she realised that keeping Sophia out of the way was definitely the sensible thing to do.

"Oh, come on," she said as they took their seats. "How was he to know you are trying your best to deliberately stand out from the crowd? And he probably made a genuine mistake if there really is a funeral boat over there. In any case I'm sure he's under strict instructions from some PR person to make sure all of the guests adhere to the dress code. It's hardly *his* fault and now he has to change his shirt, poor mite. And he'll probably get a bollocking for it. That really was mean, Sophia."

Sophia sat up straight and sniffed into the air. "Well, Sophia Brannigan doesn't do dress codes. Not any more, even if I do resemble a Merry Widow in this hideous dress of yours. Now, get me a glass of champagne or something else alcoholic quickly. To hell with driving home, I'm parched. And I hope you're taking notes!

This outing is for the column, you know, not for your own warped pleasure so you can stick to the orange juice and stop guzzling back champagne!"

Guzzling back champagne? She'd had half a glass! Cara's lips tightened but she didn't retort. Instead, she stood up and eyed the room for a server – and then she spotted him – the mussel man – far across the crowd in his new, clean uniform. She made her way over to him.

"Hi, there!" she said, tapping his shoulder from behind.

The boy looked back at her like a rabbit caught in headlights.

"I just wanted to apologise again for my new friend's rudeness. I mean, to blatantly spill tomato sauce down your shirt was just appalling and you were only trying to help her."

"It was appalling," whispered the waiter. "And now I am wearing a spare shirt that the events company luckily happened to have with them."

"Luckily," said Cara.

"But the thing is, it's three sizes too bloody big. I feel like a pea in an oversized pod. I must look like a clown!"

Cara took a step back and observed his new attire. "Oh, I can see why! It does sort of resemble a parachute . . ."

"And the worst thing is," he continued, "we were

told that the catering staff would take part in a photo-shoot to promote the new Ocean Blue perfume but now I've been told to stay in the background and keep out of all official photos. I'm mortified. I've been totally outcast."

Cara glanced back at Sophia who was preening herself like a peacock, smiling in the face of adversity as navy-and-white-clad guests stared at her black attire in disgust.

"Terrible," said Cara, nodding in Sophia's direction, "but you see, the poor girl's had quite a shock with the death of her, er, second cousin twice removed and I think she needs a good, stiff drink if you know what I mean. A really strong drink to numb her pain a little."

The waiter paused for a second and then, noticing the light smirk on Cara's face, he caught her drift.

"Ah ha!" he said. "Something really strong? I think I might have just the very thing. I'll be back with you in a second."

He returned moments later with a long flute containing a concoction he referred to only as "Ocean Enigma"– a strange blue-coloured cocktail with a frosted top and a dolphin-shaped stirrer resting on the side of the glass. Cara took it, sniffed it and smiled. It was perfect.

"I gave her an extra shot of vodka just, you know, to help her through the pain," he winked and he walked off with an all-new confidence in his step. "I think you are all being called onto the boat now."

Cara saw Sophia wave across at her frantically to hurry and she quickened her step, being extra careful not to drop any of the delicious Ocean Enigma. Natalie would be salivating at the thought of all that alcohol in such a pretty glass. She made a mental note to ask her new waiter friend the ingredients before she left – the original version though, not the "grieving mourner" version.

"Ooh, what's this?" asked Sophia as she clawed the glass and sucked a long drink through the pale blue straw.

"Ocean Enigma. It's a cocktail, but go easy, it's pretty strong."

By the time they were on the deck of the yacht and the formalities were underway, Sophia had downed another three Ocean Enigmas from the mussel–man waiter who was taking great delight in serving them up to her.

"Really, Sophia, you've had far too many of those. You were only supposed to have one," said Cara as the party's hostess cooed over her new perfume from a podium at the bow of the boat, thanking everyone on board for supporting her and her new exciting venture.

"Jush one more," said Sophia. "They're delishus!"

Cara shook her head and the wind swept her hair back as they sailed past the Tower of London on the left and the ITV studios on the right. She wished she had more freedom to look around the boat which was just as luxurious as she had hoped it would be, despite Sophia's insistence that it was like Popeye's ship. The more Ocean Enigmas she drank, the louder she sang the Popeye theme tune and Cara sensed it was just a matter of time until she would be asked to leave. As much as Sophia irritated her at times, that was something she really didn't want to see happen.

But she needn't have worried as then Sophia dropped a bombshell.

"Cara, Cara, Cara," said Sophia. "I can see three Caras. *Three* Caras! One is enough but I can see *three*!" Sophia laughed as she spoke but Cara knew what was coming next when her boss burped, then heaved, then . . . "Cara, oh no, Cara I'm going to be . . ."

Cara hoisted Sophia by the elbow as discreetly as she could and pulled her towards the back of the boat where Sophia was sick enough to make sure the pigeons of London had a helping of Ocean Enigma.

Her new blonde hair just didn't have the same glamour to it when it reeked of vomit. Cara looked behind her to see her little waiter friend in his parachute shirt, who glanced over with just the slightest, almost smug, smile on his face.

19

Wooden Heart

Tom was standing outside the cinema puffing on a cigarette when Cara raced down towards him later that evening. She had just spent two hours on the phone to her mother, reassuring her that Liam was in no way doing drugs in London and when she finally got away from the telephone, her biggest fear, apart from being late on her first proper date in years, was that she wouldn't remember what Tom looked like.

By the time she'd got Sophia home and tucked into bed without Dylan or Sam noticing the state she was in, got her black dress which was covered in sick put through a wash and changed out of her own sailor attire into a pair of Sophia's jeans and a clean top, talking on the phone for hours was the last thing she wanted to do but her mother needed an ear and how could she refuse?

She recalled how she and Tom had ended their initial evening at the pub with quite blurry vision and she worried that she had viewed Tom's handsome good looks through beer goggles and mistaken his humour for giddiness through copious amounts of gin and tonic.

"Hi there. You look scared," said Tom when he spotted the glare on Cara's face.

"Oh, hello. How are you?" said Cara and she could feel her hands shaking. He looked a lot better than she expected. His hair was lighter in the evening sun and he wore a blue Gorillaz T-shirt over trendy faded denims. So far, so good and not quite the Herman the Monster she had feared.

"I'm good. Better now, actually. I was beginning to think you had stood me up," said Tom, taking Cara's hand and leading her inside the cinema. "Have you had a good day?"

"Oh yeah. Just work. Nothing exciting," said Cara, regretting having brought up the subject. Why had she lied about her job in the first place when she had met Tom? Just because he was a football fanatic didn't mean he would judge her differently because she had a direct line to Dylan Summers. "How about you?"

Oh Christ, she thought. I sound like a bloody puppet. *Hello. Hi. How are you? Good. How are you?* Riveting conversation it wasn't.

"Let's not talk about work," he said. "There are

much, much more exciting things to talk about and I have to get to know all about you. Now, which movie would you like to see? Gory horror movie, action thriller or weepy chick flick? Since it's a first date, and I hope it's the first of many, it's your choice. After tonight, I will argue black and blue if you try to make me watch something that involves going through the crucifying pain of a weepie for almost two hours."

Cara was delighted to have ruled out work as a topic of conversation and equally so that she was given free rein to choose a movie. She quite fancied something to get her pulse rate down after the hectic day she'd had on a boat with Sophia.

"I'll go for the chick flick as I'm sure it will be the only time I will ever be allowed to choose one of those on any date in my life," said Cara and Tom shrugged in agreement.

"I can second that, if it has anything to do with me," he laughed.

The movie was as predictable as they both anticipated but it was easy viewing and just the right blend of romance and comedy to have lifted Cara's mood when they emerged from the cinema almost two hours later.

"So, do you fancy a quick drink before I take you home?" asked Tom. "I could murder a pint of orange juice."

"Ooh, tempting. Though I think I would be much

more inclined to go the whole hog and kill off a double gin and tonic if you don't mind," said Cara. She needed a drink after the rollercoaster of a day she'd had and she couldn't tell anyone how afraid she was that Sophia was going to get a bollocking in the press the next day for ruining the perfume launch by ignoring the Blue Ocean theme and by puking into the Thames. Still, it could have been worse. It could have been Cara and then tongues would really have wagged.

They went back to the bar where they had met and it instantly put both of them at ease. Tom was as ever the gentleman, seeing to Cara's every need and when they had settled into a quiet booth with their drinks, the conversation began to slowly take shape.

"First dates are shit," said Tom. "I mean, here I am, wondering what you are thinking or if I'm trying too hard to impress you and you are probably wrecking your head trying to come up with the next conversation topic. It sucks, doesn't it?"

Cara stirred her gin and tonic and looked at her date. She really had come a long way in her talent-pulling tactics since she was last invited out to the cinema or for a drink. Normally, her companion was a nerdy computer-games whiz-kid or a psychotic movie buff or a married man who fed her full of shit. Now, here she was, in her new, temporary life in London and she had managed to find possibly the cutest guy she had ever been out with in her life. And, as a bonus – and for Cara it truly was a bonus after the Michael Bradley fiasco – Tom was single. Result!

"I have an idea," she said. "Why don't we cut the first date fears as technically we have actually been in here together before? After all, we know already that we're both football experts and I can choose a predictable but feel-good movie and you can choose a good pub. And we both hate work talk. So, already we're over the first-date fears."

"I like your style," said Tom, already showing relief. "Now, I know. Let's ask each other random questions. Ask me the first thing that comes into your head."

"Oh, okay. Let me think. Okay. That group of soccer yobs you were with on Saturday. Which of them do you live with?"

It was a strange first question but she wanted to find out if he was a mummy's boy who still lived at home, a lone bachelor boy or an apartment-sharing wild boy. He stalled as if he was pondering his answer. Perhaps he sensed it was a question with an ulterior purpose.

"Um, well, all of them."

"What? Do you live in a mansion? There must have been seven of you here the other night."

Again Tom stalled. Gosh, it really wasn't that difficult, was it?

"Well, there are . . . there are six of us," he said eventually. "We have rented out a pretty cool place about two miles from here. It was our first time in this bar on Saturday and we only came because of the big screen and to watch the footie. And then I met you. Serendipity or what?"

"I know, and you didn't realise I was such an expert in your favourite sport, did you? Fancy that."

Tom was easy company, so far. Then it was his turn to ask a question.

"Right. If you could ask God one question, what would it be?"

Cara thought for a second. Should she be deep and meaningful in her answer, or try to be funny? It could say a lot about her personality if she went the wrong way about it.

"I would ask him . . . why isn't fake tan permanent? It took me a long, long time to discover its essential purpose and now it pains me to have to keep reapplying. Or I would ask him, are you really –"

"Ah! One question, I said. Now, your turn again. Ask me anything."

Over the course of an hour, Cara found out that Tom's first pet was a sheepdog called Sheep, he had a brother who was named after Les Dennis and then, just as she thought she had died and gone to heaven with a man who had absolutely no commitments whatsoever in life apart from making it to work on time and planning his weekend around the next football match, he dropped a bombshell. Not a bomb, by any means, but a bombshell that admittedly knocked Cara back just a step or two. Or three.

It was just after they had cagily kissed goodnight in the car outside her apartment when Cara took the bull by the horns and did something she had vowed she would never do again in her life since she almost threw herself at Michael Bradley. She asked to see him again.

"So, what are your plans for the weekend? Would you like to hear round two of my extensive football knowledge over a pint in front of the big screen, or do you have another girl to take to see a soppy film that I don't know about?"

Tom looked a tiny bit reluctant to answer and Cara felt like kicking herself in each shin, one at a time for letting off the "too keen" alarm. The look on his face resembled the one time she asked Michael Bradley if he would ever leave his wife for her. Shit!

"Actually, I can't this weekend. I have other plans."

"Forget I even asked. I'm not normally be so forward, it's just – I had such a lovely evening and it was so refreshing to go out with someone who was as footloose and carefree as I am – but forget about it. Just give me a call when it suits you."

Tom held Cara's arm lightly and shook his head. "Don't be silly. I would love to spend some time with you at the weekend but . . . I wasn't going to tell you this on our first night out but I have two children and this is my weekend to see them, hence the Tuesday-night date at the movies."

Cara automatically drew back. "Okay," she said. "That's nice."

She knew there was a huge flashing in her brain that said "Baggage Alert" but she tried her best to ignore it. He was still single, just not as footloose and carefree as she had just said he was. Now she felt really stupid.

"That's put you off now, hasn't it?" said Tom and he turned the ignition in his car. "I can see it in your face. Don't worry. I'm used to it."

"No, no, it's not like that at all. Oh, I'm sorry, Tom, it's just not something I was prepared for – but it's no big deal. Really. I love kids. Let's just see what happens, eh?"

She got out of the car and Tom nodded and wished her goodnight, then he called to her.

"No pressure," he said. "A lot of women don't understand when their fella isn't available on tap."

"Oh, I do understand, Tom. Believe me, I do." She paused, then gave him a light smile. "So, what are their names?"

"Sorry?"

"Your children? What are their names?" Cara figured that since she'd had such a good night with Tom that it would be unfair to be blinkered just because he had a past. Everyone has a past she told herself. It wasn't like Michael Bradley again, she reassured herself. There was no wedding ring after all.

"Tom, after me and . . ." he said and his eyes darted around him.

She felt for him, wondering if it was the first time a woman had shown the interest to ask. "Ah, very nice. And . . ."

"And . . . a girl," he said. "A beautiful little girl called Sophia."

His eyes brightened and Cara felt her heart warm, then realised the irony of it all.

"Sophia?" she said, barely unable to hide the irony of it all. "How lovely. I'll see you again soon, Tom. Thank you so much. Goodnight."

When she opened the front door of her apartment, Cara was met with a thick cloud of smoke and the strum of a guitar accompanied by a wailing screech of someone attempting to sing what vaguely sounded like "You're So Vain" by Carly Simon.

"Keep up, Liam," said Natalie as Liam strummed for all he was worth. "I bet Carly Simon didn't have to shout at *her* guitarist."

"I bet Slash didn't have to take this shit from Axel either," slurred Liam in return and he strummed his strings all the harder.

Natalie waved a glass of red wine in her hand as she "sang" the lyrics with venom. Her lips were black, her teeth were a charcoal shade of grey and she had developed two purple-coloured stains at each side of her mouth – known as "Red Wine Devil Horns" in their circle of friends back in Belfast. Liam lay bare-chested on the couch, clutching his guitar, his bleached Mohican lopsided, in his uniform ripped jeans and two different socks. He and Natalie made a very attractive pair – or so they thought as they roared out their duet.

"Is this a private party or can anyone join in?" asked Cara, pouring herself a glass of Natalie's wine and ignoring the evil looks she was getting from her friend in the process. "And Liam, excuse me for asking, but why are you smoking?"

"The devil made me do it," he said and he interrupted his Grammy Award-winning performance to point across the room at Natalie.

"What?" asked Natalie as Cara glared at her. "Who the feck is the devil around here? Me?"

She waited for their response in bewilderment and then realised what Liam was referring to. "What? Oh, do I have Red Wine Devil Horns? Omigod I do! Liam, you should have said!" She wiped the stains from the side of her mouth and moved over to let Cara sit down beside her. "Sooo?"

"Sooo," repeated Cara.

"Sooo, how was the lovely Tom? Are you in lusssst?"

Cara wondered whether it was worth while divulging the detail of her date as both her friend and her brother seemed to be on a slightly different level of alcoholic bliss than she was. She had a feeling she would have to tell the whole story over again tomorrow as they were highly unlikely to remember the finer detail of her first legal, un-adulterous date in years.

"He was very nice."

"Very nice?" said Natalie. "Is that it? Very nice is sooo boring. Snore City. I'm asleep already."

"No, it isn't boring. It's nice."

"Did he try to get you into bed?" asked Liam. "Or was he too nice for that too?"

"No, of course he didn't try to get me into bed! It was our first date!"

"He's gay!" they both chorused and then pointed at each other in a mimed laugh.

"Oh, you two were made for each other," said Cara in disgust. Having a sensible conversation with them was evidently out of the question when they were in Silly Land. "So, what's the occasion? Why are you drinking, smoking and singing on a Tuesday night? I thought such activities were only for Saturday evenings after *X Factor*?"

"Because," said Liam and he raised a glass in Natalie's direction, "Natalie slept with Juicy John's brother. Unlike you, big sister, Natalie got the ride."

"You dirty bitch, you did not!" said Cara and she looked at her friend in disbelief. She had just broken the NOAFD rule. Never On A First Date. It was golden and precious and never, ever to be broken. Ever.

"Did so," said Natalie. "And, in the words of that old philosopher Tony the Tiger, it was *Grrrreeeaattt*! Your brother and I are celebrating the fact that my celibacy in London is over."

"But Natalie, you don't even know Juicy John's brother."

"I do now," she said and gave a dirty cackle.

"But he might be a secret clog-lover."

"Maybe so, but at least he's not just *very nice*," said Natalie in a squeaky voice. "Go on, be honest, *very nice* means *boring*."

"I didn't say Tom was boring. He was nice. What's wrong with being nice? Just because he wasn't a horny creep who got me drunk and took me to bed, doesn't mean he isn't a nice guy."

"There! You said it again! *Nice*! Cara McCarthy, you have earned yourself a Master's degree in Bad Judgement. Nice equals boring."

Cara feared she was liable to hear that same statement at least ten more times but Natalie ranted on.

"We didn't come to London to do boring things, did we? We came to let our hair down, to celebrate being single. To do *baaadd* things."

"Speak for yourself. I got up to enough man trouble when I was at home, so if nice equals boring,

I'm all on for that."

Natalie threw her eyes up. "Look, I don't know what you're up to these days, but all you want to do is work, work, work and you are becoming a little bit dull, dull, dull. Are you up to something? I have a feeling you're hiding something from me. It's almost like the early days when you were sneaking around seeing –"

"Don't say it!"

Cara stood up, realising at last that the longer she stayed in the present company, the greater the likelihood one of them would say something they sorely regretted. She handed Natalie her half-full glass of wine and made her way to bed.

20

Her Latest Flame

"Jake, can I be honest with you?" asked Sophia, scurrying behind him into his top-floor office at *Fab!* Towers the next morning. A tall, willowy girl offered him some breakfast but he refused and didn't extend the offer to Sophia.

"Please do be honest," he said, indicating for Sophia to have a seat. He closed the door behind him but didn't close the Venetian blinds for privacy. He used to always close the blinds for privacy when Sophia was around.

"I feel it is best that I just come out with how I'm feeling at the moment about the column and the TV show we talked about," said Sophia.

Before she could continue, Jake's landline rang and he glanced at the caller display. "Oh, do excuse me, I have to take this call."

Sophia crossed her legs impatiently and ran her hands across her velvet thighs. She had chosen a stylish shift dress similar to one she had seen on Victoria Beckham a few weeks ago when she attended an LA movie premiere and if it was good enough for Posh, it was good enough for her.

She looked amazing and she knew it, but for the first time since she had met him, Jake had not even commented on her appearance and she deeply feared that she was slowly moving from pole position.

"Yes. Yes," he said, staring at his desk. He fiddled with a pen and then laughed and then turned serious again. "Well, it's not the most *ridiculous* suggestion I've heard, no. It just might work. Go on . . ."

She tried not to listen in to his phone call but he spoke so loudly she couldn't ignore him. He was so damn arrogant, sitting there in his swingy chair with his silver-flecked hair and Barbados tan and his open shirt that revealed just enough chest hair to make a woman wonder what else there was to see. Plus, he smelled so good – a rich, manly smell. Not the "just out of the shower" sporty smell that she once found irresistible with Dylan. No, Jake Johnston was on a totally different level.

At only thirty-nine years old, he was hotly tipped as the next big media tycoon that would soon give Simon Cowell a run for his money with his range of weekly and monthly glossy magazines, a production company that specialised in television chat shows and the soon to be launch *Fab!* network TV channel. And Sophia wanted some more of it. Now.

"Sorry about that, Sophia," he said eventually with a capped-toothed smile. "That little minx Emily Evans is determined to release a record and she wants me to push a few buttons for her in the industry. She is so damned ambitious. Just where does she get the energy from?"

Sophia flinched and she feared her face was turning a seaweed shade of green. A *record*? "But she has just launched her book and she's bloody pregnant again. That is outrageous. What did you tell her?"

"Oh, Emily is too clever to negotiate with me directly. I deal only with her agent. He's one of my best pals so I said I'd make a few calls. I'll do what I can. Said I might get her on to one of my chat shows. That should keep her quiet till I get a call for her into BMG. You know, pull in a few favours. Like they say, it's all about *who* you know, not *what* you know."

Sophia's eyes widened and then formed into two narrow slits as she pictured Emily Evans lip-synching to some dodgy Samantha Fox cover. How the hell was she supposed to keep up with all this? She had been promised the sun, moon and stars when she had first launched "WAG Tales" and there wasn't a word in weeks about her *So Sophia* television show, even though the features were making the magazine fly off the shelves. It was a dog-eat-dog world out there and it was time she got a piece of the action.

"Jakie," she said, in a purr, "don't mind me. I am just a bit anxious and I like to get what I want, when I want it. Perhaps I'm just a tad impatient."

If he thought that pneumatic bimbo Evans was ambitious, he hadn't seen Sophia Brannigan in full flight. She would show that little tart up in no time.

"Of course you are keen to move things on, Soph, but all in due course," said Jake, leaning back in his chair and raising his hands behind his head. "I am working really hard to launch the *Fab!* channel and I have a team of writers working on *So Sophia,* but let's just say I'm finding it hard to get the sparkle I want into it. Won't you consider meeting with them and telling them exactly why I love your style so much and how to recreate it in a TV chat show over a twelve-week series? It could move things along so much quicker."

Shit! This was not the angle she wanted at all. Cara was the genius of sparkle he needed, but of course she could never admit to that and she couldn't exactly bring *her* in to meet writers.

"No! I just don't work well in groups, Jake, that's all. It gives me writer's block. Believe it or not, I'm quite shy about discussing my work with others. Especially other writers."

"Well, then, you will just have to be patient until they work it out for themselves," said Jake and he pressed the loudspeaker on his telephone. "Cindy, get me BMG on the phone. No, Cowell himself. Tell him I have an idea how we can hit the Number One spot again together."

Sophia's face broke into a grin. "You want me to make a record?" she said. "Well, to be honest, I can't really sing but with all of the technology nowadays –"

"No, don't be silly, Sophia. I don't want you to make a record. I'm phoning about Emily. Look, I'll be in touch with you when I know more about the series. Now, just keep doing what you do best in the meantime."

"Which is?"

"Writing," he said and glanced towards the door, indicating that her time was up.

Sophia sat in a frozen pose. "Well, okay, fine, fine," she said. "Maybe I *could* have another think about brain-storming with your writers. Perhaps I could spare an afternoon session with them after all."

"You do that."

"I will," she said and stood up, pulling her skirt back down on her way towards the door.

"Oh, and Sophia?" he said, looking up as he rested the phone handset between his head and his shoulder.

"Yes, Jakie?"

"Lose the platinum-blonde look, darling. It really doesn't suit you and it would never work on TV."

Sophia breathed in deeply through her nose and slammed the glass door behind her.

"Bastard!" she said in a high-pitched voice with such force that Cindy the secretary knocked over a plant in shock.

Cara checked her watch and hoked and poked through her CD collection until she found what she was looking for. She flipped the CD from its case and scanned down the list of songs, then selected the number on the player – "You're So Vain" – and woofed up the volume.

"Good morning, campers!" she shouted at the top of her voice.

"Jesus, what the hell?" said Liam and he sprang up from his makeshift bed on the couch.

Two empty wine bottles sat on the coffee table and an overflowing ashtray threatened to grow legs and make its own way to the bin along with a sticky bowl of nachos that looked like they belonged at the bottom of a toilet bowl.

"It's your song," said Cara. "I thought I'd play it for you both this morning as a wake-up call. Carly Simon at her very best. Now get up and get this place cleaned before our visitor arrives."

"What visitor?" asked Liam, removing the odd socks he had slept in and tucking his sleeping bag around his waist. "We never have visitors. We are strangers, nomads and no one knows we live here. I'm an Irish Man in London. Here, give me my guitar, I feel a song coming on."

"Correction, my dear brother. No one knows *you* live here. People *do* know I live here and this morning my car is being delivered back in what I hope is full working order so I can get to work at some stage of the day."

"Shit, would you turn that racket down," said a pasty-faced Natalie who emerged in a mismatched pair of cotton pyjamas which had made their way to London in Cara's suitcase. Mickey Mouse on top, and Donald Duck bottoms. The proper match to each was still back in a drawer of unwanted items somewhere in the McCarthy household in Kilshannon, and no doubt had by now been used as rags to wash the windows of Graceland by her OCD-suffering mother.

"It's almost ten in the morning, Karaoke Queen," said Cara. "Don't you have a job to go to today?"

Cara fixed her hair in the mirror over the mock fireplace and kicked a few crisp bags closer towards the wastepaper basket. The mechanic had texted her to say her car would be delivered by ten thirty and Cara was well impressed with the swift service, not to mention the door-to-door delivery. She wondered would she have to drive him back to the garage and hoped she wouldn't as she had to pen this week's column and liked to spend as much time on it as she could.

"Oh man," said Natalie, observing the mess, "did we really drink all that wine last night?"

Emma Heatherington

"No," said Liam, reaching for his discarded jeans and then realising he still had them on. "*You* drank all of that wine. I have my own collection of beer cans in here somewhere. Yes, here they are."

He lifted his sleeping bag to reveal almost eight cans of cheap lager with cigarette ash nesting around the rims and on seeing them he turned a deathly shade of grey while Natalie buried her face in her hands.

"Oh, holy shit, I'm having flashbacks," she squealed. "Oh, holy crap, I slept with Juicy John's brother, didn't I?"

"Yes," said Cara, enjoying her once-in-a-lifetime pious moment.

"I am such a tart."

"You said it," said Liam and then guarded his face, knowing he was due a missile in his direction.

"Oh man!"

"Well, *I* do have work to go to and I have to say, it's just wonderful to have such a clear head and a clear conscience on a Wednesday morning," sang Cara. "What was it you called my date last night? Boring? Well, at least my nether regions are as intact today as they were when I left Belfast in June. Now, where did I put my hair-straighteners?"

Cara couldn't hide her smug non-hangover state as she beautified herself whilst the living dead around her cagily picked up their debris from the floor. Then she remembered Tom's extra commitments in life and

262

her self-satisfaction diminished as quickly as it had come over her. Maybe she did have a qualification in bad judgement after all. She couldn't spot an unattached man in a rugby squad.

"Have you seen my phone anywhere, sis? I need to call Mum," said Liam in a mumble that indicated he felt restless and needed reassurance to soothe his hangover.

"It's in the bathroom, where you left it last night. And I'm sure your old friend Julie back at home was very pleased to receive your call at silly o'clock this morning as you went to the loo. She must be so into you now, more than ever, especially since you serenaded her with Westlife songs as you peed."

"Westlife! You liar!"

"Right, that's it," said Natalie, laden with her two empty bottles, one in each hand. "No more post mortems, Cara. You'd think to hear you that you never made drunken middle-of-the-night phone calls. Give the lad a break."

Cara looked around the room. No, she wasn't imagining things. Natalie had just stood up for Liam. So miracles did happen. She was just about to respond when the doorbell rang.

"That will be Mr Mechanic with the little green shuttle, all ready to take me on my travels while you two wallow in your hazy world of self-pity and cringes. Have a nice day. Shit, where is my purse?"

"I'll get the door then, Cara," said Liam and he made his way through the mess while Cara grabbed her purse, then slipped on her kitten-heel shoes that set off her newly acquired Diesel jeans.

"Shit," said Liam. "Jesus!" He came running through the hallway again like he'd seen a ghost.

"What the hell?" said Cara. "Who is it? Isn't it the mechanic with my car? Is it Mum and Dad?"

"No," said Liam. "It's fucking Dylan Summers! I swear, Cara. It is."

"Liam, I have had enough of your stupid celebrity false alarms," said Cara and she pushed her way past her brother to the doorway. But when she got there, she thought she was sleepwalking. Rather, she hoped she was sleepwalking and she thanked the Lord for such divine inventions like eyeliner and mascara.

"Good morning. One set of keys personally delivered to your door, madam."

"Oh Mummy!" squealed Natalie, still clad in the Mickey/Donald combo and she raced across the sitting room, whacking her toe on Liam's guitar on the way through.

"Dylan!" said Cara. "You really needn't have gone to all this bother. I was expecting the mechanic would drop the car off, not you."

She had no option but to stand back and let Dylan in to survey the bombsite that was her humble abode. Then she caught a glimpse of Natalie in a Disney mirage, hobbling towards the bathroom as fast as her long legs could carry her and she felt like Grace Kelly in comparison.

"He did. But since I was coming this way, sort of, I thought I'd save you a trip so I dropped him back to the garage and then brought your keys here. Oh my God, were you burgled?"

Cara looked at the mess which was ten times better than it had been ten minutes before. She opened a few windows and lifted Liam's sleeping bag from the floor, then gave her brother a dirty look which urged him to explain his mess for himself. There was no way she was taking any credit for turning her normally spic and span home into a landfill site.

"I'm Liam. Cara's brother. The delinquent. This is all my doing, I'm afraid. But Natalie helped me."

Natalie appeared at the doorway with a towel wrapped into a turban on her head, even though her hair was dry underneath, and wearing a virgin-white bathrobe. She had given her face a quick scrub and there wasn't a trace of a Red Wine Horn to be found around her mouth. Apart from her bloodshot eyes, she looked the picture of health.

"I'm Cara's roommate," she cooed. "Natalie. I'm a beautician."

Dylan shook her hand and Cara was sure Natalie was on the verge of fainting. The body heat of a severe hangover and the shock of a dishy soccer star in your

apartment was a sure-fire recipe for a collapse of some
sort.

"Lovely to meet you both," said Dylan and he
stepped over Liam's guitar to shake his hand. Natalie
took a step and mouthed "fucking babe" at Cara who
pretended she didn't see her.

"Well, we'd better get going," said Cara. "I'm sure
you have a busy schedule and I don't want Sophia to
think I'm taking the mick by using the car as an excuse
for being too late."

"Oh, she'll be fine. Nice to meet you, Liam the
Delinquent and Natalie the Beautician," said Dylan
and Natalie tried to cool herself off by fanning her
face with the phone book while Liam looked smug at
having spotted a real-life celebrity with two witnesses
at hand.

Dylan walked back into the hallway and Cara
turned to her associates and said under her breath,
"I will murder you two after this. You two are dead
meat. You two are *so* dead when I get home. You are
shameless!"

She walked outside and with Dylan safely a few
steps in front of her, she slammed the door as hard as
she could while the two indoors screamed and danced
around the living room in delight.

"I should have called you in advance," said Dylan
when they got to the street. "I didn't mean to spring an
appearance on to you like that but I thought you'd be

keen to get your wheels back. Public transport is no fun at this hour."

As angry as she was with Natalie and Liam, Cara was flabbergasted at Dylan's act of generosity and was highly relieved that he hadn't called half an hour earlier when she too would have passed as a member of the Addams Family.

"I really appreciate you doing this, Dylan, but you have to know, I don't really live with two piglets. My friend and my brother, for some wacky reason justifiable only to themselves, decided to get pissed last night and you were unfortunate enough to witness the fallout just now. It's not our normal routine by any means for a Wednesday morning to have our place looking like a crime scene."

Dylan pressed his key card to open his car door from over twenty feet away and Cara fiddled with her weighty set of Iron Age keys in her hand.

"Oh, don't worry. I just wish I could do the same more often," he said. "We footballers are known to get ourselves into very sticky situations sometimes when we let our hair down. We all like to blow off some steam every now and then."

He winked at her and she blushed deeply.

"But not you," she said. "Somehow I don't think you're the type to take girls back for wild parties to your hotel room at away games."

"No. I like to keep my private life just that. Private."

They held each other's gaze for a few seconds and then both went to speak at the same time.

"Anyway –"

"Anyway," said Dylan. "I'd better shoot as I have to pick Sam up at the hospital. He's being discharged from hospital today and is looking forward to seeing you."

Cara's mind switched back from imagining Dylan surrounded by drunken athletes and lithe-limbed bimbos.

"Ah, that is great news. Will he have medical care for a while at home?"

"I'll make sure he gets the very best of care, and he will need to take it very easy but, if I know Sam, that will be easier said than done."

21

Pound Dog

The final weeks of summer raced by with Sophia's irritation growing like a rash at Jake Johnston's ability to blow hot and cold with her regarding her television opportunities. Emily Evans was constantly nudging in front of her, threatening all the time to swipe Sophia's special place in Jake's pecking order with her constant bursts of ideas on how to brand herself as a model with musical ability. Sophia feared it was just a matter of time before she elbowed her right off the slippery slope of celebrity and back into the valley of flash-in-the-pan wannabes.

When news of Amanda Stewart's latest conquest as Yummy Mummy of the Year broke, Sophia's urge to hit the panic button on her career reached new limits. She knew she had only one way of keeping up with Amanda's maternal reputation, and one way only and it didn't involve dirty nappies, night feeds or Caesarean section.

She burst into the conservatory of Summer Manor where Dylan was reading the morning paper and dropped a white ball of fur into his lap.

"What the . . . ? Sophia what are you up to now?" he said, realising now that the ball of fur was moving and making high-pitched yelping noises.

"The silly little bitch pissed on me," said Sophia, reaching for a tissue from the sideboard and sneezing uncontrollably. "Plus, I'm allergic. How typical is that!"

"Which silly little bitch would that be now – Amanda or Emily?" he asked.

"Ha fucking ha. The dog! Look, you obviously have no idea – or is it no *interest* on how much I'm struggling at the moment to keep up with those two? They are always pictured looking oh-so-maternal with their two-point-four children so I figured it was time to get every woman's baby substitute since I have absolutely no intention of pushing out a sprog of my own within the next ten years. Her name is Lola."

"Is she a show girl?" laughed Dylan, rubbing the puppy's ears. "She's quite a cutie. A poodle, isn't she?"

"No, she's a Bichon Frisé. Very 'in' at the moment."

"Well, I'd say she's worth at least a one-line mention from the 3am Girls."

"Let's fucking hope so. Jake is really cooling off on me and I'm conscious I need to make more of an effort if I'm to keep up with Tweedledum and Tweedledee with their bloody awards and multi-careers. But I have this fantastic idea. All I have to do is pull some adoring pictures out of oblivion of me coo-cooing over little Lola, then I'll stage her kidnapping and be all teary-eyed and then we will have this very emotional reunion and –"

"I could have let you have Buster for the day."

"Buster is a monster. Lola may be a pain in the arse as she pisses over the person who feeds her, but she looks good."

Dylan wondered why that phrase sounded very familiar. "Don't tell me: then when she's served her purpose you'll hand her over, *publicly* of course, to some children's refuge as a sacrifice for the cosy life you have now in comparison to your upbringing in the slums of Liverpool as the daughter of a drug-dealing mother who gave you heroin when you were five."

Sophia paused. "I was going to say she would go straight to the pound but yours is a much, much more clever idea. Good one, Dylan. I like the heroin bit. I'll call my mum and explain it's just tabloid hype. It's great to finally have your support on my brand-building campaign. They definitely broke the mould when they made you."

Dylan stroked the tiny animal who looked up at Sophia with the fear of God in her eyes. "And which mould would that be, darling?"

Emma Heatherington

"The one that says 'all brawn, no brain'. You know. A footballer's mould. Speaking of brains, where is Cara? I think I'll ask her to take Lola for a walk. She can piss all over her for a change."

Dylan threw his eyes up at his girlfriend's attitude. "I think she's with Sam in the cottage," he said. "She brought him some Irish Stew over for his dinner. He's had a rough time over the past few weeks in case you didn't notice."

"Huh. And Irish Stew is the latest cure for a heart attack, is it?"

Sophia hated hearing such stories of how Cara could turn into Florence Nightingale at the drop of a hat and then be a whiz-kid at churning out 'sparkly' columns for *Fab!* in the next breath. Plus, Cara had really grown into her new image and was dressing somewhat normally these days and was looking, well, fantastic. People actually went out of their way to speak to her at parties now and admire her clothes and make-up. Sophia sorely regretted teaching her the basics of fashion and feared it was only a matter of time before Cara let the column cat out of the bag.

"Well, Sam needs someone to look after him and I suppose it's about time we looked into finding someone to help out round the gardens over the next few months," said Dylan. "With the weather so bad these days and his fragile health, we don't want to put any extra pressure on him."

"So, you're saying we need a new gardener? At long last," said Sophia, picturing a young, svelte, toned Jesse Metcalfe look-alike. "I'll ask around, see if there's anyone that meets the criteria. In fact, I may have a few contacts I could use to find us the right guy."

"Actually, Soph, leave this one to me. I should be able to draft someone in pretty quickly."

"Oh, suit yourself," said Sophia, cagily lifting Lola and holding her at arm's length with her face twisted into a scowl. "Now, Lola, you little piss-pot, let's go and see if Cara's wonderful nurturing side extends to animals because frankly you do nothing for my emotional needs at all. Then it's straight down to the shops for you and me, where hopefully I will earn back the ridiculous amounts of money you cost me by being snapped by the paps. I'll get Cara to give them a call as a tip-off."

Cara was clearing out the tumble dryer when she heard Lola yelp for the first time. She was down on her hunkers, folding towels as they came out of the heat and she mistook the noise from the tiny dog for a fault in the washing machine. Then a rub of fur caught her ankle and she squealed so hard she fell backwards until an ironing board broke her fall.

"Oh hello there," she said, sitting on the floor now as the gorgeous little white furball looked up at her with massive dark eyes and her head tilted to the side. She wore a hideous lemon bow which made her look like a Paris Hilton accessory and her tiny curly tail wagged at the sound of Cara's friendly voice.

"So who might you be?" she asked and reached out for the puppy to study the engraving on a platinum medal that hung around her neck. "'*My name is Lola. If I am kidnapped, please return to my sorrowful owner Sophia Brannigan, c/o Summer Manor, Wimbledon, London.*' Oh for Christ's sake!"

Cara couldn't believe Sophia had stooped to this! She had spent a fortune on this poor hapless animal and was planning to use her as a publicity pawn! The girl was deranged!

"You poor, poor little puppy," she said, nuzzling into Lola's cotton-wool neck. "Don't worry, I won't let anything happen to you!"

The laundry door opened and Cara's eyes caught the sight of Sophia's black stiletto-clad feet. She drew her eyes upwards and squinted at her boss.

"Well, if it isn't Cruella De Vil!" she said. "Look, Lola. Bad. Bad."

Sophia couldn't help but laugh. She couldn't deny it. She had as much feeling for the dog as she had for fake designer wear. None.

"It's all part of the game, Cara," she hissed. "A game that I employ you to play. Now as you two get acquainted, I'm going to get ready for my next bite of the media cherry. Amanda Stewart will never, ever top my puppy-kidnapping story! You'd better get used to pawing round little Lola there 'cos I'm only holding her for a photo – after that, she's all yours until we announce her kidnap, I turn on the waterworks for the cameras, we are gloriously reunited and I donate her as a gift to a needy orphan. Priceless."

And with that she exited.

Cara rubbed Lola's head as she whimpered and she snuggled her closer, then clambered up off the floor. "Don't worry, little girl. Orphan Annie will treat you better than Sophia would any day, but in the meantime you and I will have fun, do you hear? Yes, we will have fun."

Sophia's driver arrived within half an hour and she emerged at the front of the house in a Juicy Couture tracksuit – lemon, of course, to match Lola's bow – a pair of Ugg boots and her hair tied oh-so-casually-on-purpose into a pony-tail. Her make-up was as minimal as she would ever allow it to be and her new blonde tresses looked a lot softer now. Yes, thought Cara, Sophia could carry the blonde look off to a tee.

"Get into the car, quick!" Sophia told Cara. "And keep that mutt away from me. If I get as much as one dog hair within a metre radius of me I will scream."

Cara sauntered to the car and got in, cradling Lola in a new Fendi bag which she had no doubt would go straight to the bin once the photo-shoot was done. She patted the dog who still looked scared at the very sound of Sophia's high-pitched voice. "So what's the plan, Soph?"

"Soph?"

"Fia?"

"Familiarity breeds contempt, my dear. Let's not get too familiar. The plan is to get me in the papers. Same shit, different day. Now," she said as the driver zoomed off. "On my cue, you will hand me little snotter-face out of the car, in the Fendi bag, and as soon as Bryan gets his pic, I will throw her back to you, we will zip back to Summer Manor and Assets can write up a press release that Lola has been stolen from me. *Comprendez*?"

"*Oui*," said Cara.

Sounded simple enough. But of course it wasn't.

Kensington was buzzing with shoppers and, as soon as Sophia stepped out of the limo – her new shades perched on her crown, her trackie bottoms slumped on her slinky hips – and posed with the puppy-laden Fendi bag, Lola decided it was time for pee-pees. Sophia dropped the bag, Bryan was in hysterics and Cara felt like giving her new best friend a massive high five, paw to hand. Never work with children or animals – it was the oldest saying in the book. But then Sophia would never have thought of that.

Cara arrived back at Summer Manor that afternoon feeling exhausted, both physically and mentally, and

276

her working day had only really begun. But somewhere she found the strength to focus on her next task.

"What's the dress code tonight, Sophia?" she asked, her eyes burning with too many late nights at different parties where the same people hung out with the same motive in mind – to notice and be noticed, to see and be seen. Lola was in the care of a giant teddy bear in the laundry room, much to Sophia's disgust, but Assets were drumming up the said "kidnapping" press release as they spoke. Tonight's bash was a much more glamorous affair and, if she wasn't so wiped out, Cara would actually have looked forward to it.

"Glitzy and glam, and I *mean* glam," said Sophia. "There is no way I can be seen in any guise but my very best tonight."

Cara found it in herself to feel excited. "I've heard about this place. It sounds great."

"Well, yes I suppose it is. It's a really special venue and I want to make exactly the right impression," said Sophia. "Also, Jake is going to be there so I need you to stay very much in the background. In fact, maybe you should give tonight a miss after all. I don't want people to start asking questions."

Cara shrugged. As much as she would have loved to have seen the Crystal Club on Wells Street, she was truly wiped after three nights out on the trot at Sophia's beck and call, not to mention making notes for the column which was now extended to a double-page spread, tending to Sam who was still under doctor's orders to rest and looking after a fluffy dog that consistently used her leg as a toilet.

"That suits me fine," she said, picturing her favourite pyjamas, a good book and a steaming mug of hot chocolate. "Just make sure you get a chat with the happy couple, get a good look at her engagement ring and see what you can find out about whether or not they've set a date for their wedding. I'd like to get a real scoop on this one as it ties in nicely with *Fab!*'s publication date."

"Oh, I should be able to manage that. Plus, Jake has such respect from everyone in showbiz that I can't fail if I can manage to stay in his company. Do you think I would sound pushy if I called him and asked if I could accompany him, as in a business arrangement? He is my boss, after all."

Cara knew that Sophia wasn't asking for her opinion. If she told her the truth – that it would be very pushy or somewhat desperate or that it might give Jake Johnston the wrong impression – Sophia would throw a strop and then insist that Cara accompany her after all, so she merely nodded in agreement.

"Yes, it sounds like a perfectly professional arrangement to me," she said. "As you say, it's business, not pleasure."

"Great. I'll say that Dylan has a big training session in the morning and can't go, and if I can't go in Jake's company, then I can't go at all. Then I will make sure, no matter what I have to do to prove it, that Jake Johnston knows that Sophia Brannigan means business with a capital B and it's about time he realised it."

With Sophia gone to the hairdresser's in London to prepare for her big night, Cara took the opportunity of leaving Summer Manor early that evening in lieu of the extra canine activities she'd had to pursue earlier in Kensington. She found Dylan lounging in the sunroom. He had spent the afternoon relaxing in preparation for a weekend away-clash with top of the league Man. United.

"I'm off now," she called to him from the door.

"Oh, Cara, before you go!" he shouted back. "Can I have a quick word?"

Cara made her way into the sun-room which Dylan had turned into the ultimate chill-out zone with DVDs and books strewn around him. She sat down on the cream leather bucket chair opposite him and tried to ignore his state of semi-nakedness as he lay with his shirt open to reveal a tanned, toned chest with a sprinkling of dark hair to match the stubble on his face.

"Hi," she said.

"Hi. Sorry, are you in a hurry?"

"No, not really."

"I don't want to hold you back. I know you're on duty once again tonight."

"No, it's fine. I'm off the hook tonight. What can I

do for you?" she asked. She could feel her palms sweating and her heart thumping in her chest and her instincts told her to make this conversation short and sweet. "Is it Sam? Do you need me to help out with him more?"

"No, no, Sam has plenty of care and you've been such a great help to him. It's actually, well, you said your brother was looking for work now that he's decided to stay in London with you for another while?"

"Yes, now that he and Natalie can walk past each other without thumping each other, we have come to an arrangement that he can stay if he gets a job. Nat even got him a start on the Juicer stall – if you ask me, that Juicy John man must be desperate because he'd employ anyone."

Dylan sat up and leaned forward, his hands clasped and his elbows resting on his knees. "Well, that answers my question, then. You see, I was hoping Liam could have helped out around here for a while."

"Oh . . . around *here*? Are you sure?"

"Just for a few hours a week until Sam gets back on his feet. I don't want to give Sam the wrong idea by drafting in a whole ground force just yet, but someone like Liam would have been perfect to keep things ticking over by keeping the place tidy. It doesn't matter, though. I'll find someone else, but I'd have liked to have given him a chance."

Cara stood up and felt tears prick her eyes. Dylan

knew Liam had major problems and he was still willing to give him a start. She was tired and emotional already today, and now his act of kindness hit her like a bolt out of the blue and she felt the waterworks coming on.

"That's really, really nice of you to think of Liam, Dylan. I'll have a chat with him tonight when he's finished his shift and see what he says. Let me come back to you tomorrow, okay?"

"That's fine, Cara. No pressure," he said. "Hey, are *you* okay?"

Cara sniffled a bit, then swiftly wished she could magic herself away as she felt an uncontrollable urge to hug Dylan and snuggle up against him and never let him go.

"I'm – I'm really in a hurry. Thanks, Dylan. Thank you so much. You don't know how much this means to me."

She scurried across the sitting room floor, through the hallway and outside into the car which – since Dylan had it serviced for her it had learned how to start on its first go – and she allowed herself to cry all the way home.

22

My Boy

"You are totally pissing me!" said Liam when Cara told him of his job offer at Summer Manor. "Can I phone some of the guys at home and tell them? Bonzo is a huge Fulton fan and he'd be like totally over here in a flash if he thought I was working for Summers, not to mention that fox he is engaged to."

"Number one," said Cara, "the very notion of Bonzo or Gonzo arriving at my door is exactly why you are *totally forbidden* to tell any of your so-called friends back at home – and number two, Dylan and Sophia are not engaged."

"Irrelevant. They're shacked up together. Same difference. So, what do I have to do exactly? And more importantly, what do I get paid?"

Cara glanced at Natalie who was plucking her eyebrows in an illuminated mirror and sighed in despair. She was beginning to wish she hadn't even mentioned the job to Liam who was now faking soccer moves and headers around the tiny living area.

"I'll talk all of the finer detail through with him but, remember, it's just a temporary arrangement and all you have to do is keep the grounds tidy. There's no need to go into Alan Titchmarsh mode."

"Speaking of Alan Titchmarsh, guess who I saw today at Piccadilly on my way to get a top-up for my phone?"

"Shuttup!" chorused Cara and Natalie at the same time.

"Fine then, I won't say," he said and continued with his headers and keepy-uppy mime game.

"Don't bother," said Cara.

"Not worried," said Natalie.

"Daniel Craig," said Liam with a smug grin. "He was walking along –"

"Yeah, yeah, chatting on his phone and he was carrying shopping bags from M&S and had a girl with him who was the spit of Lily O'Brien who was in your class at school and who used to be a real dog but now is a real babe –"

"No, that was Hugh Grant," said Liam. "Don't believe me, then. You won't dismiss my talent for celebrity-spotting when I'm best friends with Dylan Summers and am hanging out with all the Premiership stars and I bag a WAG of my own."

Natalie shrugged at Cara who was running out of answers for her brother's Celebrity Diary claims. He could now claim to having spotted two television chefs, three Hollywood movie stars, a few *EastEnders* kids and too many footballers to mention.

"So what about the Juicer, Liam? Have I been dumped already? You are such a user, McCarthy," said Natalie. "Why do I get the feeling I pulled the short straw in this whole gap year, plus I now have to time my shifts around avoiding Juicy John's brother who somehow has transformed from having movie star good looks to resembling a greasy pervert who lies about his age."

"Yuk," said Cara. "And you had the cheek to say I have bad judgement."

"Well, you still won't tell us what happened with the very nice Tom the Football Fan, plus he hasn't been seen in the pub since your date. You must have scared him away."

Cara's stomach did a somersault when she thought of Tom and how she had resisted the urge to take his calls. She was in London for a break, not to fall into a situation that would potentially leave her heartbroken again.

"Let's just say I'm not looking for a relationship at the moment," she said. "As you continuously remind me, Natalie, once bitten, twice shy."

Natalie stood up and rubbed a sweep of Vaseline across her newly arched eyebrows.

"But who the hell mentioned anything about having a relationship?" she said. "Not every snog has to lead to happily ever after. It would be no fun if it did."

Cara shrugged. "I suppose it wouldn't. Ah well, I can always take up the offer from old Freddie McCormack back at home. He said if I was still barren and desperate by the time I was thirty-five he'd give me a turn. Now, there's something worth waiting on, I can tell you."

Natalie burst out laughing. "Is that the old guy with no teeth who wears the Elvis jumpsuit and says 'The King is Dead' every hour on the hour when he's knocking back whiskey in Graceland?"

"That's the very one. Drop dead gorgeous he is too. He's had his eye on me since I first served him a hot toddy on Christmas Day when I was about sixteen."

"Well, then you're all sorted," said Natalie. "I heard someone say he had property abroad and a big farm of land in Donegal. Think about it. In a few years' time when you hit thirty-five, you could do a lot worse. I wonder, does he have any sons?"

On the way out of the city, on Liam's first day on the job, Cara began her list of commandments of what and what not to do during his brief stint of employment to come.

"Number one, don't ever, ever repeat anything you see or hear when you're around the house," she said, thinking about her tendency to dress up to accompany Sophia to social gatherings. "Confidentiality is key and I mean that, Rubber Gob. If I hear you telling even Natalie any of the Summers' business I will chop your head off, Mohican and all."

Liam stared out through the passenger window and nodded like a dog, taking in only tit-bits of his older sister's orders.

"Well, does being a rubber gob, as you so fondly called me, stretch to the standard of, say, you calling Sophia an evil, vain, selfish bitch the other day when you nearly took our apartment door off its hinges?" he asked. "I'd say I can match those high standards, yes. Mum's the word."

"Which leads me swiftly to my next point, dear brother. Number two. Never, ever repeat any of *our* business to Sophia, Dylan or even Sam. I have told them all as much as they need to know. Remember, they live in a very different world than we do. Especially Sophia."

Liam's ears pricked up at the sound of this. It seemed like Cara had developed quite a little second life over at Summer Manor but was keeping her fleshy skeletons well and truly hidden in their crampy closet.

"Well, well, Miss Marple. What exactly have you been hiding from them, then? I need to know my boundaries so that I don't spill the beans on your exhilarating past."

"All I am saying is, in the unlikely event of Dylan or Sophia taking notice of you, do *not* tell them anything about my life in Ireland," she said. "For example, you should withhold the fact that I had a very publicised fling with a high-profile married man and almost lost my job over it which is the only feckin' reason I am over here in the first place. I'd appreciate your silence on that particular incident in my life, if you don't mind."

Cara let out a deep sigh that came from the tips of her toenails and the fear of God ran up her spine at the thought of anyone at Summer Manor finding out her seedy past. (Well, it was seedy as the Irish Sunday tabloids made it out to be, but in reality and in hindsight it was as boring as hell and not worth half the hassle.)

"All right – I think I've got all of that loud and clear. But they do know you worked as –"

"Jesus Christ, Liam, no! Oh, this is a mistake. I just know you're going to get me into trouble for the sake of sweeping up a few leaves and putting the bins out till Sam gets better. Please, just think before you speak, that's all I'm asking, okay?"

"Okay, okay, I get it. I'll keep my gob well and truly shut."

They drove another few miles in silence, and then Liam picked up on the subject again. After all, for any new job, you are entitled to ask a few questions.

"So, I take it they don't know about my past then?" he said.

"How do you mean?" asked Cara, turning up the radio ever so slightly and wondering if that meant she could pretend she didn't hear him.

"Where do I start?" asked Liam. "Let's see. Anti-social behaviour, a neat little petty-criminal record, or my gang of druggy friends who I was sent over here to get away from? That would really let the side down, now, wouldn't it?"

Cara didn't answer. She gave a light cough and then sang along to the new Kylie song on the radio.

"Huh! You did tell them!" said Liam. "I don't believe this! You told them absolutely nothing about *your* past, and yet you raked up *my* past shit and spread it all over the place. Thanks a million, sis! That's really boosted my confidence, that has! I can't wait to get there now. In fact, I bet they're stocking up on surveillance cameras as we speak! If we get there soon enough, I'll be able to give them a hand!"

"Look, I didn't tell all of them," said Cara, quickly backtracking. "I told Sam because we talk about these things. And yes, Sam knows all about me too if you must know, but I can trust him."

"And Dylan? Please tell me Dylan Summers doesn't think I'm some coke-dabbling thief because from where he is standing it wouldn't exactly get me on his Christmas-card list!"

"Calm down, will you! I might have told Dylan a bit about you but only because he is having problems within his own family and I wanted to make him feel better. To show that we all have our ups and downs but that there's light at the end of the tunnel. Look at you – you're doing fine now."

Liam clenched his hands in foul temper. He didn't know if he was more angry or disappointed with Cara. He had been so excited about hanging out at a real life "crib" for a few weeks and now he was ashamed of himself.

"Christ, Cara what the hell did you do that for? And I was all out to impress him, too. Shit!"

"Believe me, Liam. I get the impression that Dylan has too much on his plate to be worrying about you or me."

Liam thought for a moment. "Does he really have family troubles of his own?"

"Oh yeah," said Cara, turning a corner.

"So why bother with me? Why the hell would he do that? Most people wouldn't give me the time of day back at home, so why does Dylan Summers, who doesn't even know me and who has his own family to worry about, want to give me a chance?"

Cara shrugged and gave a light smile. "Because, Liam, that's just the type of guy Dylan Summers is."

"So, how did you get on at the Crystal Club, Sophia?

289

Did you manage to make mental notes to help me write up this week's column?"

Cara was suffering a rare case of writer's block as she stared at the computer screen in Sophia's office. She was worried sick since Liam almost fell at Dylan's feet on his introduction, despite having met him once before and all his claims of being unaffected by famous people since he had already spotted half of Hollywood in and around London's city centre. When he said "wow" for the tenth time as Dylan showed him around the house and some of the grounds, Cara pulled him to the side and warned him to stop acting like Bart Simpson or she would make him take Lola the Kid-Dog for a walk.

Now, Sophia was being unusually silent about her big night out and had next to nothing to offer for the column apart from how Lola was such a delight and was fulfilling all of her maternal instincts until such time as she had a perfect family of twin boys following her perfect wedding (despite the fact that Dylan had not as yet proposed).

"Change 'twins' to 'triplets' and make them three girls, please," had been her only comment in the past half hour. "I want readers to think I love kids. Pah!"

Cara had reluctantly changed her gushing baby paragraph, knowing that the world would know by looking at Sophia Brannigan and hearing her comments on everything from Botox to Britney that she would rather eat tinfoil for breakfast than go through the pain of giving birth to one child, never mind three at the same time.

"I really need to know some gossip from last night if I'm to fill this thing, Sophia. How about Emily? Did she do anything spectacular?"

"No."

"Er, how about the happy couple who got engaged – what was the ring like? Any wedding plans? You've got to know something!"

"Oh, make it up! I'm really not in the mood to talk about last night, if you don't mind, Cara. I'm tired and emotional and feeling a bit stressed to say the least."

She sulked and strutted back and forth across the floor, muttering what Cara interpreted as "fuck" and "Jake" and "Emily" and "Number One my arse" in sporadic outbursts.

"Anything?" said Cara, her fingers poised at the keyboard. If Sophia thought she was going to make her life difficult, just because she was losing her grip on Jake Johnston, she could think again. Putting up with her constant mood swings was becoming as exciting as trapping her fingers in the door.

"I think they're getting married in a castle in Ireland," said Sophia eventually. "I mean, how bloody original, and the ring is the size of the Rock of Gibraltar and is as tasteful as chewing a cardboard box. Is that enough?"

"It's a start. I'll get a Paul McCartney angle in, I suppose. Didn't he get married in an Irish castle?"

"Wait a minute!" squealed Sophia. "Intruder alert! Intruder alert! Who on this earth is that in my garden?"

Cara looked out the window to see her brother practising his kick-ups beside a mountain of autumn leaves. Oh my god, she was so going to kill him.

"Em, it's the new Sam-type person. You know, just a helper to do what Sam does until the real Sam gets better."

"The new Sam-type person? But he's playing football! And he looks like a thug! Sam doesn't play football! Where is Dylan? He will really give that scruffy-looking delinquent the sack when he sees what he is up to in his working hours. And right in front of my nose, too!"

"He's not scruffy. A delinquent, maybe, but not scruffy," said Cara in an outburst of defence in a "*he ain't heavy he's my brother*" type of way. She winced at the thought of explaining to Sophia that the new Sam was actually her brother who thought she was a "fox" and who was awaiting a court date for petty crime back in Ireland.

"He has a Mohican. He is scruffy. Quite good-looking, though," she said, craning her neck so she got a proper look at Liam.

"You should see his sister," said Cara. She couldn't resist it. "She's gorgeous."

"Huh?" said Sophia. She wasn't listening.

"Anyhow, I'm sure Dylan will be able to handle him." Cara watched Liam with affection and vowed to ensure that Sophia's snobbery didn't insult him to his face when his confidence was already at rock bottom. "Actually, Sophia. Dylan is playing football *with* him."

"What? Where?"

As Cara's heart went fuzzy and warm at how happy Liam looked, Sophia squinted in horror as her boyfriend engaged in a friendly kick-about with the new caretaker.

"I really must set new boundaries to improve etiquette and protocol here at Summer Manor," she said in a glassy tone. "It seems everything in my life is hurtling out of control and I have no hope of catching up with it. Now, there's a subject matter for your column!"

23

She's Not You

Sophia dabbed beneath her eyes with a cotton bud, careful not to smear her make-up. She had the house to herself for once, and had spent the past few hours feeling terribly sorry for herself. The Crystal Club itself had been a dream, but the evening was a disaster. Everyone was in high spirits to begin with, mingling with her when she was with Jake's posse, admiring her column (she was so tired of that now) and asking if she had any other projects in the pipeline. Amanda and Andy Stewart were there – together, as always. Even Emily's boyfriend was in the vicinity for once and seemed to be oblivious to Jake Johnston's lingering looks of admiration at the two of them. But as the evening went on, Jake and the *Fab!* team dispersed to speak to more interesting people and in comparison

Sophia felt as popular as a traffic warden in a town centre.

Even Dylan hardly noticed her these days, preferring to absorb himself in all things Fulton-FC-orientated and spending his free time fussing over Sam down at the cottage, or hanging out with that ghastly kid who apparently was a great help around the grounds when he wasn't pretending to be the next Kevin Keegan. Dylan had even taken him to training with him one day which apparently had boosted the boy's spirits no end.

She simply had to find a way of gaining her life back. Dylan she could win over in a heartbeat, but Jake Johnston and a few career moves were another story. It was almost November now and all she had was a measly column and weekly feature in *Fab!* magazine whilst her rival WAGs were enjoying a blaze of pre-publicity for their Christmas range of perfumes or hardback versions of their autobiographies.

Even her staged kidnapping of Lola had gone unnoticed despite Bryan the photographer's "photo-shopping" efforts to make her look distraught and heartbroken. Then their glorious reunion hardly rated a mention. The whole thing was such a flop, she hadn't even bothered to stage the "gift of a puppy to an orphan" part. She'd get Cara to pop her into the pound after all. Come to think of it, she had almost forgotten about the little mutt these past few days since she put

her outside for a wee and had forgotten to take her
back in again. Ah well, hopefully she had done a runner
for real.

Over dinner that evening Dylan seemed extra
jovial which added more to Sophia's sullen mood as
no matter how much she pouted and puffed, he was
absolutely oblivious. He had a spring in his step and a
smile on his face that she hadn't seen for months now,
and then, in a bolt of realisation, Sophia guessed that
he had something exciting to share with her. Perhaps
he was going to be transferred to Arsenal in the New
Year and was waiting to surprise her! Now, that would
boost her popularity no end!

"I have good news, Soph," he said eventually, over
a mountain of salad leaves and Sophia's heart soared.
She made a mental note to say a prayer of thanks later
as she had resorted to asking God why she was so
unlucky, but fair play to the Man Upstairs, he seemed
to have acted extra quickly.

"Go on," she said, preparing herself for his
announcement. She would have to appear surprised
when he said it as it would be unfair to let him see she
had already guessed so she took a large gulp of wine
to help with her acting abilities.

"As you know, my brother and I have been working
really hard lately to get my dad's life back on track."

"Yes, I do recall you mentioning that," said Sophia.
How this related to a transfer to a top London club

was anyone's guess, but she was happy to hear him out.

"Well, Dad's been sober for a while now and Mark has talked him round to coming here to visit over Hallowe'en. Isn't that great? I haven't seen my dad in ages and now he's prepared to make an effort at last. I can't tell you how thrilled I am, Soph."

Sophia's face twitched. *Thrilled? Great?* In her book, "great" was soaring to an A-List capacity with a lifestyle like the Stewarts', "Thrilled" was to be adored by the public, like Amanda, and have an agent who had to turn down offer after offer from every brand of every cosmetic and clothing range from every corner of the globe. But a long-lost parent coming to visit? That was just okay. Just about. No, not great at all.

"I'm delighted for you, honey," she said, and touched his chin. "That's something to really look forward to."

"I knew you'd be pleased," said Dylan. "I've been so concerned about the way his life was spiralling into the gutter and even though we haven't always seen eye to eye, this feels like a second chance and I for one am prepared to forgive and forget."

As he spoke, Sophia's brain was already hurtling in the opposite direction. Dylan's ex-girlfriend, the infamous Davina, had gone the wrong way about making headlines with Dylan with her sordid tales about his father's alcoholism, but she was much cleverer than that. She had an idea of how she could make this little episode worth her while but first she had to find out a bit of history and then let the whole thing fall neatly into place. Dylan's father was his Achilles' heel and Sophia was determined to make it work for her.

Cara hadn't seen Liam so settled since he first set foot in London and all he could talk about was who he had seen when Dylan took him to watch a training session at Fulton's home grounds.

"I have photographic evidence to prove it," she heard him say to Natalie who was winding him up as usual on his celebrity-spotting antics. "Dylan was like, so cool, and he even let me have a kick-about on the pitch afterwards. The coach said in a different life I could have made the game myself."

Cara and Natalie both looked at him in disbelief when he made his latest claim.

"Okay, okay, I'm exaggerating slightly, but he said I wasn't bad. Now, from him, I would take that to mean I'm close to awesome."

The girls shrugged, deciding for once to let Liam live in his little bubble of self-importance as it took him out of their hair for a while, and they cracked open a bottle of wine in the kitchen as a nightcap. Thursday was as good as a Friday for a glass of wine in their book.

"I can't tell you how pleased I am that Dylan has given Liam such a new lease of life, Nat. Even if it only lasts for another week or two, this is just what Liam needed to get his feet back on the ground."

"I know what you mean," said Nat, pouring two hefty measures and setting them on the table. "Anything is better than the crap he was caught up with back at home. Have you told your mum how well he's getting on?"

"Yeah and she's thrilled. She reckons it will give him the courage to get on with his life without those yobs and, if he decides to go back home, he can leave them behind and start again."

They sat in comfortable silence for a few moments.

"Cara, can I ask you something and please don't eat the head off me for doing so?"

"Go on . . ."

"Do you think Dylan Summers likes you more than he should?"

Cara's face froze and she felt a stutter rap coming over her. She tried to speak but the words wouldn't come out, a range of defence mechanisms hurtling from her brain but unable to get past her tongue.

"What? Why? Don't be so ridiculous. As if!"

"It's just that, well, you know when he arrived around here that morning with your car? I saw how he looked at you like as if . . . as if he really cared. And now, taking Liam under his wing when he knew how concerned you were over him. To me it all adds up. And I think you feel the same way, don't you?"

Again, Cara could think of a range of answers to defend herself but they were mumbled in her mouth and all she could muster was an emphatic "no".

"*No!*"

"Is that it? No?"

"Yes. I mean, no, I don't have feelings for him and no, I don't think he thinks of me in that way either. He just, well, I think he's so far removed from the lifestyle Sophia has moulded into and, while they drift apart, I just happen to be there to talk to on occasion. That's why he tells me things."

Natalie clinked the side of her glass with a spoon for attention, much to Cara's frustration.

"So, he tells you things? What type of things?"

"Natalie, will you stop! Just things – like family things. Like, about his father who he hasn't spoken to in years, since he took really bad on the drink and changed from someone Dylan loved and admired into a horrible man he didn't recognise. Then the whole scandal with Davina and how it scared the heart out of him."

"Does he talk to Sophia about these things too?"

Cara sat up straight in the chair. Natalie was jumping to conclusions and she would prove it so. "How am I supposed to know? I'm not there twenty-four hours a day and to be honest, I don't see a lot of Dylan. Not as much as you seem to think I do, anyhow."

Liam entered the kitchen and grabbed a beer from the fridge.

"What's up? You two look like you are having as Mum would say, a 'healthy debate'. Can I join in?"

"It's called bitchin' in the kitchen," said Cara. "And Natalie is simply in one of her 'jumping to conclusion' modes and now she realises she has absolutely no case."

"Oh well, I'll go back to watching *Lost* then," said Liam and he left them to it.

"Here is my case so far," said Natalie when Liam was out of earshot. "The long ride home when he bought you pizza, the personal delivery of your car, the confiding in you about his family problems and now all of this effort with Liam? Why don't you open your eyes and ears a bit more when he's around and I think you just might see for yourself that there's more than a hint of chemistry between you. And you can't deny it."

Cara didn't speak.

"Case closed?"

"Case adjourned," said Cara. "Case most definitely adjourned."

24

Trouble

Despite her best intentions to stay out of his way, Dylan Summers was the first person Cara met the following morning when she arrived at her workplace. It was a fresh, crisp autumn morning and Summer Manor looked even more picturesque than it did in the warmer months. The golden colours gave the house a totally new look and framed it like a halo in the morning sunshine.

Cara parked her car and noticed that Sophia had already gone to her morning exercise class with her new trainer, who she had hired in a bid to lose the last few invisible pounds she wanted to shed for the Christmas party season.

Normally, Dylan had already gone to his training session by the time Cara got there each morning but today he was in the yard polishing his car, wrapped up in a warm jacket and jeans, giving him a brand new image from the sportswear he normally donned during the day.

Cara felt slightly nervous after her conversation with Natalie the night before, but she was determined to be strictly business-like with Dylan so as to rule out any further ridiculous accusations of chemistry from her best friend.

"Cara, hi! How are things?" said Dylan with a more enthusiastic smile than normal. He stopped what he was doing and made his way towards her and her heart began to race. "I've been waiting to tell you some great news."

That was it. Cara felt like she'd been hit on the head with a sledgehammer. He had been waiting for her? Could Natalie be right?

"You've been waiting around for *me*?" she said.

He looked at her like she was on a different wavelength and then laughed. "No, I haven't been literally waiting around, not like that. I've got a day off today and when I say I was *waiting*, I wasn't actually waiting, if you know what I mean."

Cara felt herself flush with embarrassment and ducked her head to conceal it.

"Let me start again," said Dylan. "I was looking forward to telling you some great news."

Cara forgot her embarrassment and her smile

matched his as she realised it had to be only one thing.

"Don't tell me! Your dad? It's your dad, isn't it? I know by the look on your face."

He nodded and Cara could see the sheer excitement in his eyes. This was something he had wanted for so long.

"Hey, looks like you know me too well, Cara. My dad is coming to visit in a few weeks' time. For Hallowe'en. Can you believe it?"

Cara felt her heart was going to burst with delight for Dylan. He seemed like a totally different person now and she realised that the weight of worry about his father had been affecting him much, much more than he had ever admitted to anyone.

"Oh, Dylan, that is just the best news ever!" She felt her eyes fill up with happiness for him and hoped and prayed he didn't notice her display of raw emotion. She drew her hands up to her mouth and tried to fight back showing her heart on her sleeve. "I know how much you have wanted this to happen. You're a great person. You deserve this so much."

She looked up at him with tears in her eyes and before she knew it, he had his arms locked around her and her cheek was pressed against his strong, muscular chest. She could hear him breathe in and out as he held her close and she buried her face, feeling his warmth and his tight grip around her shoulders. What lasted seconds seemed like an eternity to Cara and then they parted again, leaving her stuck in a hazy daze of wonder and confusion.

"Thanks, Cara. You've been a great friend to me. Now, how about I fix us some hot chocolate and you can help me plan what the hell I am going to say to my old man without making a fool out of myself?"

They went into the kitchen. There was a brandy and a whiskey bottle on the table, presumably from the night before. Cara grabbed them and hurried off to replace them in the drinks cabinet in the living-room. She just wanted to get out of the room to recover her composure. She felt dizzy and light-headed after what had just happened. He said she had been a great friend. There, that was the proof of everything she had believed all along. He was happy, she was happy for him. End of story. Yet, why did she feel in the pit of her stomach that if the opportunity arose again, she wouldn't let go of him so quickly?

"Hiya, Lola," she said to the puppy who was being treated to sometime in the big house, now that Sophia was out of sight, and was loving every second of it. Dylan carried her about like a baby at every opportunity and even Buster had taken her under his wing, allowing her to invade his space in front of the huge fire that dominated the kitchen at Summer Manor.

"This really is a wonderful home you have, Dylan.

I love an open fire. It reminds me of Christmas at home."

"Same here," said Dylan. "When Sophia decided to call this place Summer Manor I wasn't at all pleased. She meant well, of course, having taken the title from my name, but this is a house for all seasons. I like it at this time of year best."

"Yeah, I can see why." She hunkered down to pay Buster some attention. "Christmas is my favourite. I can't wait."

"I think we're all the same," said Dylan. He knelt down beside her and scooped Lola up. "So tell me, will you go home to Ireland for Christmas?"

"Of course," said Cara. She turned towards him and met his eye, unaware of how physically close they were. "I couldn't dream of Christmas anywhere other than at Graceland with my family."

She moved away and sat down in the armchair next to the fire while Dylan went to make them some drinks and tried to compose herself while in such divine and easy company. When he returned, she took the steaming cup of cocoa from his hands which were cold to touch and she tried to ignore the way their fingers brushed and lingered just for a second.

"My mother would have a fit if I didn't bring Liam home for Christmas, you know. Irish mothers and their love for their sons is legendary."

Dylan sat opposite her and took Lola on his knee.

"Plus, you've all those punters at Graceland to keep happy too," he said with a smile. "It sounds like an intriguing place. I'm not kidding when I say I want to go there some day."

There it was again. That look in his eyes that Natalie had been talking about. Of course, Cara noticed it much more now that her friend had pointed it out, but instead of making her feel uncomfortable like before, she felt at ease now. As if it was okay now that Natalie had noticed it too.

"So, what are your plans for when your dad arrives?" she asked. "Are you going to just hang out here or do you have some day trips planned? You must be so excited?"

Dylan's eyes brightened. "Well, yes, but obviously I want to just chill out for a while, get to know him again and test the water as to how we're going to get on. Mum will be there of course, and Mark is coming for the first night, so he'll probably insist on taking a run out to the football grounds so Dad can see where I spend most of my time, and then a nice meal on the evenings that they're here. Here, at home, preferably with just the five of us, like I say, to get to know each other again. Sophia has never met him."

Cara sensed an opportunity. "Does that make you nervous?"

She sensed that Dylan was unsure. But he answered her genuinely.

"To be honest, yes. I'm not sure that Sophia has a lot of interest in anything – only the here and now and the good times. Oh, I'm not being hard on her by saying that, am I?"

"No," lied Cara. Give it to her, she thought. She's a self-centred cow!

"It's just that, well, we may have to take the rough with Dad before we get to the smooth. She mightn't be able to deal with that."

Oh, I could say so much, thought Cara as she watched Dylan stroke the lovely Lola who Sophia despised so much. But she knew her place.

"Well, hopefully, she'll prove you wrong," she said.

They spent a while chatting at ease about each of their childhoods, swapping stories, both funny and sad of love and loss from grandparents to pet goldfish and they laughed uncontrollably one moment, then sat in mutual silence the next. Before they knew it, it was almost eleven.

"Gosh, look at the time! I guess I'd better go and do some housework," said Cara. "It's the fire, you see. Once I sit down I can't stop talking and reminiscing. I hope I didn't bore you."

"Well," said Dylan, "I didn't like to say but how you could mourn over a guinea pig for longer than a goldfish is beyond me. It just doesn't make sense."

"Huh! And you who didn't shed a tear over that

poor piranha you kept in a tank just so you could terrorise your friends. The cheek! Seriously, I'm sure you didn't intend spending your entire morning off chatting to me."

She stood up and Dylan held her gaze and he looked like he was pondering a smart answer.

"Hey, do you normally only wear one earring, Cara?" he asked and stood up, then reached over and pointed at her earlobe.

"Oh," she said, lifting her hand to her ear and it brushed against his for what seemed like a lifetime. He was so close to her now she could hear him breathing and she took a step back, afraid she might have reached the point of no return. Lola jumped from his arms and joined Buster at the fire, as if she recognised when she'd overstayed her welcome.

"Er, I must have lost it around here somewhere," she said, her eyes skirting around the room. "Not to worry. It will turn up. Look, I really should be going – to check – to check on Sam."

She made for the door.

"Cara," he called and she stopped, then looked behind her to where he stood in front of the fire.

"Yes?"

He smiled at her then pursed his lips like he was holding something back. "Thanks."

Cara had to remind herself to breathe. This was a dream, she said inwardly. This was a dream she had been in before and that dream had turned all too quickly into a nightmare. She couldn't put herself through all of that again.

"For what?"

"For listening," he said and she felt a surge of heat rush through her entire body.

"Thanks for listening to me too," she said as her heart pounded and her speech began to slur and race ahead of her, "Look, as I said I'd better go check in on Sam. He'll be watching the clock for that bowl of stew I promised him. I'll be back soon. Bye."

She could feel his eyes watch her as she left him by the fireside and ran out of the house, down the laneway to Sam's cottage until she was well and truly out of breath.

Sophia was more pleased with herself than she could ever have imagined. This was a genius of an idea she had came up with and it was going to make her popularity soar. She had the perfect plot from start to finish and even those useless overpaid tartlets at Assets PR agreed that it would work a treat if it went to plan. Sophia had no doubt it would go exactly according to plan because this was a project she was going to dedicate the next two weeks of her life to. And she had the perfect front all signed, sealed and delivered. All she needed to do now was to sell the glossy side of her thinking to her unassuming boyfriend.

She arrived home with a full folder of samples she had been given at the printers and whizzed into the kitchen where Dylan was – *ew!* – was he *cooking*?

She noticed Dylan was still wearing that stupid grin on his face.

"What on earth are you up to now?" he asked, spotting the folder.

"You'll see. Oh, don't tell me *she* is still here!"

"Who?" said Dylan.

"That stupid waste of space some people might call a dog. I thought she had conveniently run off. That's it! The pound for her tomorrow. I must tell Cara. And why oh why are you attempting to cook? Isn't that what we pay Cara for?"

Dylan continued to stir the meat and tomato sauce in the saucepan. Cara was teaching him how to make lasagne and he was well pleased with his speedy progress.

"Lola has spent a few days keeping Sam company so yes, she is still here. And, yes, we do pay Cara to cook our evening meal but I thought, since I had a day off, I would at least give her a hand."

"So she is still here too? Good. Where is she?"

Cara emerged from the utility room with a basket of fresh vegetables, looking like the perfect little domestic goddess, all bright-eyed and cheerful when realistically she was doing what Sophia considered one of life's most mundane chores.

"Well, sorry to interrupt this broadcast of *Ready*

Steady Cook," said Sophia, "but I have an announcement to make and it's best if you both hear it as I'm going to need your help to make it a success."

"This sounds exciting," said Cara, leaving the vegetables by the sink.

"Believe me, it is." Sophia stood in the centre of the kitchen, her eyes dancing with excitement. "I am going to throw our very first party. Here, at Summer Manor!"

Dylan and Cara glanced at each other. Sophia was going to actually do something that involved entertaining other people? This was a first. There had to be a catch.

"What type of party? When?" asked Dylan in bewilderment.

"Well, since I have been doing the rounds of some of the best events London has had to offer in some of the most plush, posh and even some pathetic venues and homes, I have learned quite a bit so I've decided that I can do much better myself. I am going to throw a Hallowe'en party. What do you think?"

Dylan thought it had to be a joke at first, and Cara wished she hadn't been included at all in this escapade. Had Sophia totally forgotten about Dylan's family visit over Hallowe'en? How could she be so selfish?

"Sophia, hold on a second. Let's just slow down," said Dylan. "You know that we already have plans for Hallowe'en weekend, so how can you possibly think about arranging a party at the same time? Sometimes you don't listen or even think past your own needs and desires, do you?"

Sophia tapped her foot on the kitchen floor. Cara was staring at her as if she had just committed a mortal sin and Dylan looked like she had just slapped his face. He dropped his spatula into the saucepan and Cara took over, wanting to keep busy. "It's not what you think. I'm not trying to steal your thunder at all, honey," said Sophia. "Quite the opposite, really. I wanted to throw a party for your family, that's all. Maybe invite a few neighbours and friends around. You know, make them feel welcome. Let them see how we live around here. Cara, why are you looking at me like that? Stop it."

Cara couldn't help herself. She had been staring in bewilderment. She had to find an escape route.

"I think I'll just leave you two to it," she said, turning down the heat and removing her apron. "I have things to get from the office upstairs and then I'll be gone. If you need me to do anything for you at your party, just let me know. Hope the lasagne turns out okay."

25

Devil in Disguise

"A party? Sophia, are you totally off your rocker?" Dylan wanted to scream.

"Settle, petal! This isn't going to be any old party," said Sophia. "It will be a welcome to Summer Manor party for your dad and mum and Mark. Imagine how special it will make them feel. I'm going to throw a party in their honour."

Dylan paced the floor until he noticed his cookery lesson had been abandoned and his saucepan was beginning to burn.

"Will you for once get your head out of the clouds, *please*? My father is a fucking alcoholic who has just spent the past few years of his life almost in the gutter! My mother is so traumatised by his behaviour that she doesn't leave the house! Why oh why do you

314

think that when I am on the verge of forgiving him for his wrongdoings and helping him get over this horrible, diminishing disease that I would want to throw him a party? Why?"

Dylan's voice bellowed off the walls and Sophia feared her plans were scuppered before they'd even got past the first hurdle. Dylan never shouted at her. Never. She was being backed into a corner and she had to think quickly. Time for plan B . . .

"I thought it would be something we could do together. You know, you and me. Yes, I might need Cara to do some of the dirty work like the cooking and cleaning in the run-up and a bit of administration, but you and I could draw up a guest list, decide on invitation designs, book in the entertainment. Together. We never do anything together any more."

Should she cry now or wait to see if this was enough to win him over? Sod it, she would cry now. She swallowed hard until her eyes watered, just like she used to when she was a child and her mother didn't give her enough attention. Sure enough, the waterworks came in perfect timing and she added in an odd sniffle or two for good measure.

"You're right, Soph. We don't do anything together any more."

Dylan's voice was softer now as if the tears had done the trick. Sophia almost sighed aloud in relief.

"We don't," she said. "And we really should."

"No," said Dylan. "If the truth be told, maybe I don't feel we should any more."

What? What did he just say? Sophia's emotional act turned into a blind panic as she let his words sink in. This wasn't right. How dare he? Who did he think he was? No! Who would she be without Dylan Summers? That would well and truly be the final blow on her career as "a celebrity". She had to fight hard to make things up to him.

"Baby, don't say silly things like that! You know we are just two very hard-working individuals who perhaps have drifted apart lately, but we can't give up on us just like that."

She had read that once in a magazine – "don't give up on us" – and thought it sounded dramatic and meaningful and was delighted she had remembered to use it right now.

"We want totally different things, Sophia."

"I wouldn't say that!"

"I would!" he said. "You have changed so much lately. The sweet girl I once knew and loved has turned into a fame-hungry monster who I don't know any more. We can't go on like this. It's not working."

Sophia was certain she was on the verge of a panic attack. Could her life possibly get any worse? All of her efforts, all of her hard work of late to make a name for herself in the media-hungry public of Britain was slipping from her fingers faster than Emily Evans' single was hurtling towards the Number One spot! She had to stop Dylan from leaving her in the gutter with the sewer rats of celebrity who had merely sniffed a whiff of fame on some reality telly show only to be back at their day job as quick as the viewers flicked through their channels.

"Dylan, please don't do this to me," she sobbed. "You are everything to me. Summer Manor is everything to me, and Sam and – and Buster and Lola." She knew she would go to hell for bringing the elderly and animals into it, but desperate times and all that.

"Sophia, just give me a break, eh? I can't be bothered with this nonsense any more. I want you to go."

"Go? Oh Dylan, surely you are overreacting!"

"I mean it, I want you to go. We are over."

But Sophia had a huge problem. She couldn't just go. She had nowhere to go. Before she met Dylan she had shared a grotty bedsit with a struggling actor she worked with in a nightclub who had been stalking her since childhood and there was no way she would go back there. Her parents lived in a Council house in Sheffield and that was like Outer Mongolia in comparison to where she had climbed to, plus what would all her snotty cousins and old school mates say as they watched her plummet back to her roots with all the grace of an elephant?

"Dylan, no! Please, just forget I ever mentioned the

stupid party. Forget I said one thing about what we should do when your father arrives. We can do it your way. Anything you say. Please."

She looked at Dylan who for the first time looked stubborn and restless, irritated almost at every word she said. He looked so handsome still, with his strong jaw line and piercing eyes which she had genuinely fallen for when she first saw him. Yet, she had taken him so much for granted lately and had truly thought he was too wrapped up in his football world to even notice.

"It's too late, Sophia. I'm sorry, but you're too late."

Sophia's eyes widened while Dylan avoided her stare.

"But why? Why am I too late? What have I done that is so bad?"

"Bad?" Dylan laughed. "I don't think you're bad at all, Sophia. No, no. I think you're sad, really. You don't care about me. All you want is your face in the paper, to have a purpose in the eyes of the public and you would sell me and everyone you know to get that far. I've been slowly realising it ever since you moved in here. So go and find some other mug to use as your stepping-stone, Sophia, because this rung on your ladder has just snapped!"

Sophia tried to breathe. So he was serious, then. It looked like she had well and truly blown the nearest thing she had to security in her life and she had absolutely no idea where to turn.

But then, just when she thought her life was over, she remembered how she had another fantastic idea in reserve. Another, much more ruthless plan had emerged of late, and it was just about to be promoted into pole position.

Sophia had been saving it for a moment like this, like an ace up her sleeve. Oh no. Sophia Brannigan was far from beaten yet.

Cara reminded herself to move. She had been rooted to the same spot outside the kitchen door for almost five minutes now for fear of interrupting and every time she heard a gap in the conversation between Dylan and Sophia, they would start to shout again and she couldn't just burst in. She even tried fake sneezes and light coughs which had begun to hurt her throat but they were too busy arguing to notice her. All she wanted to do was to say she was going home, but they were in the midst of a "breaking up" argument!

The scene reminded her of when she had broken Sophia's shoe all those months ago. How awkward she felt back then at Summer Manor in comparison to recent months when she had almost made herself at home in her multiple role as writer-cum-housekeeper-cum-dog-minder-cum-nurse-to-Sam and sometimes confidante to Dylan.

She eventually turned on her heel and made her way across the hall, towards the beautiful doorway and out into the early evening drizzle towards her car, not knowing if she had a job to come back to the following morning.

So, Sophia and Dylan were no more. Why oh why did she feel like she was somewhat to blame?

She knew she should go home and leave them to it, but instead of getting into the car, she ran down the lane and banged on the door of Sam's cottage.

"Sam. It's me, Cara. Sam, are you there? Can I come in?"

She heard Sam shuffle towards the door and she barely gave him time to open it wide enough to let her in before she pushed through.

"What on earth do I owe for this visit? Isn't it past your home time?"

"Oh Sam, I think I need to say goodbye to this place once and for all. I seem to have caused so much trouble."

She almost tripped over Lola who lay beside Buster at Sam's front porch and she walked ahead into the kitchen and flicked on the kettle switch. She spied a bottle of Irish whiskey she had bought for him still untouched and was sorely tempted to crack it open to drown her sorrows, but instead she made her way back to where he sat by the fire which crackled and spat in the hearth.

"Are you going to tell me what has got you into this state, hen, or am I going to have to guess?"

Cara sat in the cosy armchair adjacent to Sam and curled her legs underneath her, just as she had sat on so many mornings when Sam was too unwell to do anything for himself and she'd tended to him when Sophia was not around to tell her otherwise.

"Remember I told you once of the man I loved back at home in Ireland?"

"Ah, yes. Michael the Married Man. Is he back in your life?"

"No!"

"I thought you were well shot of him, Cara. Don't go down that messy road again, you hear!"

Cara couldn't help but laugh at how Sam remembered to give Michael the Married Man his full title. He may have suffered a bit of a blow with his old ticker, but Sam's brain was in full, spritely working order.

"He, well, he . . . I knew he was married of course. Right from day one I knew he belonged to someone else. I should have walked away, but instead I walked straight bang into a disaster that I could have avoided if I had followed my head and not my stupid, gullible, vulnerable, naïve heart."

She heard the kettle click and went to make a pot of tea, then changed her mind and made them a hot toddy each. She needed something to settle her nerves.

"Ah, now I like the look of this," said Sam, his eyes

dancing when he saw the steaming, golden liquid in the glass coming his way. "I had hoped we could share that bottle at some stage. It's no fun having a drink alone. Now, go ahead. Get what it is off your mind."

"Well, no matter how many times I told myself I was doing wrong, that I was on a path of hurt and humiliation, I plodded on, telling myself that it was meant to be. That I couldn't help who I fell in love with and that these things happen every day, but when it eventually went public that we were seeing each other, I could never have imagined the trouble that it caused. Devastation doesn't even describe it."

Sam knew only too well of how devastating betrayal in a relationship was, but he couldn't bring himself to add fuel to the guilt of Cara's confession.

"Did it shock you how bad you felt when it was all exposed?" he asked.

"Shock? I was numb to the bones," said Cara. "I couldn't look my parents in the eye. I was a scarlet woman, a home-wrecker, a sneaky young upstart who had nothing else to do only bed-hop with married men who were vulnerable and weak and, oh, don't get me started . . . I had to, well, I had to run away. And look where I ended up. Here!"

Sam knew that eventually Cara would let him know what had brought her outburst of confession on, but it didn't take a rocket scientist to take a guess.

"And you're afraid that history is going to repeat itself all over again if you stay here at Summer Manor?" he said.

Cara took a tissue from up her sleeve and wiped her eyes. "Oh, Sam," she said. "I think it already has."

26

Hellhouse Rock

Sophia sat in her hotel room and wondered how long it would take for her telephone to ring. It was 7 a.m. now. Dylan would be in the shower back at Summer Manor. In approximately thirty-five minutes he would leave for his morning run into Wimbledon Village and would arrive back in time for breakfast with the morning papers. It was funny how much she realised now that he truly was a creature of habit. In her world "routine" translated as "boring", but today it would prove invaluable to her best-laid plans.

Oh, how the tables would turn today, she mused.

Now, what should she have for breakfast? A full English to celebrate her latest conquest of fame? A continental to give a perky start to what promised to be a very busy day ahead? Or perhaps a bit of both to congratulate herself on her big brainwave? Yes, it would have to be both.

With the help of half the contents of the mini-bar, she had slept like a baby the night before in her king-size bed, which she deliberately spread right across to get her full money's worth. Every few moments she would anticipate the headlines and a wry smile would curl over her face.

"Today is the day I conquer the hearts of the great British public and it was a whole lot easier than I thought." This was her morning mantra and theme of the day and she chanted it to her reflection every time she walked past a mirror.

A gentle courtesy knock on her door startled her and she sat upright in the bed, then like an excited child on Christmas Day she scrambled across the floor in realisation that her early morning newspapers had arrived. She opened the door to find a young European lady balancing a hideously large bouquet of flowers in both hands instead of the bundle of tabloids she had requested.

"For me?" said Sophia and then in a dramatic swoop, she burst out crying, much to the girl's dismay.

"Oh, madam! I did not mean to make you cry. Flowers are for happy days. Not sad days. Is this a sad day, madam?"

Sophia needed all the witnesses she could find if she wanted to stretch the mileage out of her story so she decided to divulge a few details.

"Oh, it's my boyfriend. He is a very famous footballer. We broke up and I am very, very sad. Now, perhaps, he is saying sorry with this beautiful bouquet. Thank you so much!"

She noticed the hotel lady gulp in realisation at what she had just witnessed, on recognising Sophia's face. So she had obviously read the morning papers. Sophia closed the door and took the flowers to the window of the room. It was an unexpected gesture, but a great start to her day which she anticipated would be more than hectic after all her hard work with Penny from Assets the night before. The PR firm had even paid for her hotel room for a week, they were so sure of making a mint out of the story.

An envelope was nestled in the softness of the autumn bundle, and Sophia tore it open with more vigour than she thought she could have at this time of the morning. She had butterflies in her tummy and her heart pounded in her chest in a rush of adrenaline and excitement. Who could they be from? Could it be Dylan? Or even better, Jake?

"Call Me xXx," it said and a number was scrawled beneath the distinctive handwriting.

"Crap-dog-shit!" she squealed in disappointment. It wasn't Dylan. It wasn't Jake. It was just Tom. "Shit!"

Cara awoke with an empty feeling inside her stomach and a pounding sound in her head. She tried to touch the roof of her mouth with her tongue but it felt like a razor-blade scraping on a blackboard, so she attempted opening one eye at a time, but it felt even more dry if that was humanly possible. She had been dreaming of a water fountain but in her dream when she went to take a sip of water, Michael the Married Man's deranged wife would snap the cup from her hand and she would look around to the scary, distorted faces of her former work colleagues who laughed and jeered at her pathetic life.

"Oh Lord in heaven please help me," she muttered.

A faint smell of rose spray moistened her brain ever so slightly and when she eventually regained some sight, her hangover was shoved to the back of her mind and a wave of panic set in instead. She patted the sides of the bed to check if she had company and then darted upwards, so hard she thought her head might burst, and when the dizziness subsided she realised where she was.

She was in bed in Sam's cottage. Oh shit. And she'd drunk almost a full bottle of whiskey. Oh shit shit!

It was still quite dark outside so Cara anticipated she hadn't slept in too late but then she remembered that since Sophia was probably gone by now, she really wouldn't have a job at the big house to go to this morning.

Liam was probably an hour or two from wakening back at her apartment and Natalie would no doubt call the police and report her as a missing person if she didn't contact them soon. Her clothes were a wrinkled mess and she got a faint whiff of whiskey when she stood up, giving her a flashback of spilling a glass down her front as she sobbed to Sam about why she always caused trouble because of her Master's degree in Bad Judgement that Natalie reminded her of so often.

"Oh, mercy, mercy me," she mumbled to herself as the memories zapped her brain, one by one. Yes, she had told Sam about how touched she felt when Dylan said he would give Liam a temporary job; yes, she told him of how convinced Natalie was that he looked at her in *that* way; yes, she told him how they had embraced earlier that day when Dylan told her his good news about his family and yes, she had told him of how he had thanked her for listening to him earlier that morning. And yes, oh yes, she had told Sam that she feared she had fallen for a man who once again belonged to another.

And all the while, Sam just nodded, never judging one thing she said, but just listening to her problems and reassuring her that she was a good person beneath all of her tendencies to fall for the wrong men and send all of the Mr Perfects like Tom back to the Mr Perfect factory with their packaging still intact just because he had what was called by that good old modern-day term – baggage.

She wondered how long she could stay locked in this tiny bedroom with its floral curtains and floral walls and floral bedspread. It was so cosy and heart-warming here with Sam that she felt wrapped in a safe cocoon where life was rosy and slow-paced and making the dinner was the highlight of the day.

A distant crunch on the gravel outside awoke her senses and she reached across to the curtains which, when she pulled them back, she realised looked right out onto the main gates of Summer Manor.

She couldn't see anything or anyone at first, but then a silhouette in the dusky light caught her eye and her heart stopped when she saw not one but four men crouched outside the gates.

And Jesus, they were pointing something towards Summer Manor! Guns?

A few high-pitched sounds escaped her mouth before her hand finally reached it to smother any further hyena-like yelps that might alert the gunmen.

She quietly opened the window.

Then one of them spoke and she concentrated to hear over her panting and the sound of her heart racing at a record rate.

"What time did that stupid bimbo say he was due to leave for his early morning run? It's almost seven thirty and I'm starving. Who wants to do a breakfast run?"

"Not me," growled his mate.

Cara wished she had a brown-paper bag to help her breathe. She stretched out one arm, with the other one still clamped across her mouth, and fumbled until she found her mobile phone at the side of the bed. She would call the police and tell them to get around to Summer Manor right now. She lifted the phone and tried to punch in the number but her fingers wouldn't do what they were told and she kept slipping and sliding them all over the buttons. In an extra stroke of bad luck, her mobile phone gave three faint long bleeps and then the light disappeared. Cara's phone was dead. Oh, God, what was she to do now?

"Get your own breakfast," said another gunman. "If you think I got out of bed at this hour to miss this shot that could earn me enough to pay off my mortgage for a month or two, then think again. I am not going to miss out on this for the sake of a soggy sausage bap. You do whatever you want, mate. I've got my priorities right."

It was a hitman. Sophia had ordered a hitman. No, she had ordered two, three, *four* fucking hitmen. Cara glanced up at Summer Manor with the sun rising faintly in the distance behind it and looked around for Sophia's car. It was gone. Definitely gone. For a moment, Cara wished that Sophia and Dylan had kissed and made up and this whole nightmare had never begun. Could Sophia really be so cruel as to hire someone to kill Dylan as he sprinted out of his own home and into Wimbledon Village as he did every morning at the exact same time? He had told Cara how his morning routine had always given him time to think about the day ahead, especially coming up to a big game. It helped him to focus and release some of the pent-up nerves he might be feeling about his performance on the pitch. No, there must be some mistake. Not even Sophia could be so cold-hearted.

But perhaps they had some sort of agreement about the house or his money and, with him bumped off, Sophia would be the grieving girlfriend with no one to know about the row they had the night before. No one but Cara, but then who would believe *her* with her track record back at home?

She had to alert him. She just had to, even if it was all just a big mistake and it was going to be that prankish footballer who played tricks on other unsuspecting Premiership stars and she would look a merry fool in front of a crowd of famous people who had gathered to take the piss out of Dylan. No, that couldn't be it. No matter how crap some of the pranks on that Rio Ferdinand show were, they wouldn't resort to weapons, would they?

It was getting brighter now, and Cara heard a noise coming from the kitchen. It was the radio. Sam was up.

She tiptoed out into the living area and waved her arms so as not to give Sam the shock of his life by creeping up on him. The last thing she needed in this whole scenario was another heart-attack victim to resuscitate when she was on the verge of witnessing a crime of passion!

"Morning, wee hen. How's the wee head?"

"Shh!" whispered Cara. "It's, er, really, really sore. Why don't you go back to bed and I'll fix you some breakfast?"

She almost shoved Sam back into his bedroom. She only had a few more minutes if Dylan's timekeeping was as accurate as he claimed.

"No, no, no," said Sam. "I always rise at this time of the morning. And anyhow, Dylan always pops in with my newspapers on his way back from his run. You could set your watch by him. Mind you, he hasn't even left yet. I'd say he's due to leave the house in, er . . ." Sam squinted at his watch and then glanced up at the giant clock on the wall for reassurance.

"When?" asked Cara in desperation.

"I'd say he's about halfway down the drive now, in fact."

"*No!*"

Cara turned in a flash and raced back to the flowery room where she had slept, not worried about Dylan seeing her with panda eyes and sticky-up bed-head hair, not to mention revolting, whiskey morning breath. This was a life or death situation. She would call to him through the window of the cottage bedroom in a bid to grab his attention so he could run for cover.

Of course they might shoot her to silence her.

In a fight or flight moment of decision-making, Cara knew she had to take a chance. She prised open the old-fashioned window further and screamed at the top of her lungs.

"No, Dylan! No! Don't come down here! They're trying to get you! Turn! Go back!"

But, in the haze of flashes in her direction and then in Dylan's as he stood like a rabbit in headlights in the middle of the driveway, Cara realised that she had made a terrible mistake.

For the gunmen weren't hitmen at all.

They were the paparazzi. And Cara had just made sure that, like Dylan, she had made front-page news.

27

Mean Woman Blues

Sam opened the front door of his cottage and was almost blinded by the early-morning flashes that followed Dylan inside. It reminded him of days gone by when Dylan used to be followed everywhere he went by crawling photographers who couldn't get enough dirt on his upbringing and family history. Dylan had shunned so-called celebrity events and parties since Davina's kiss-and-tell and Sam was under no illusion that this new invasion of privacy was not the young man's own doing. He locked the door firmly behind Dylan.

"Ah, hello, my little Lola! And hello, my big old Buster," said Dylan, kneeling down to greet his canine companions.

"What the hell have you done to cause this, son?" said a perplexed Sam. "We haven't had one photographer at the gates in ages and now they're almost scrambling over them to get a snap at you. Who sent them here? What's going on?"

"I have no idea," said Dylan. "But just give me a second and I'll find out *exactly* what is going on."

He dialled Sophia's number and tried to remain cool and calm as he waited for her to answer his call. She did but only on his third attempt and by this time his temper was well and truly sizzling.

"Hey, good morning, sunshine," she said in a tone that took him completely by surprise. "I take it you got your wake-up call."

"Sophia, perhaps you can tell me exactly what you are playing at?"

"Oh, baby, you know me by now."

"Unfortunately, yes I do! Is your hunger for fame so insistent that you would set me up with a bunch of lepers at my gate first thing in the morning? You don't waste an opportunity, do you?"

He heard a male voice in the background and it made his blood reach boiling point.

"You are absolutely right," said Sophia. "The first rule in courting publicity is never, *ever* to miss an opportunity. I have been waiting for something major to happen that would get me into the spotlight. Columns, perfumes, clothing ranges – hell, I even chased up a television show when all the time my big opportunity was staring me right in the face!"

"You really have set me up here, haven't you? Sophia, how could you be so childish about all of this?"

"Dylan, darling. You mess with me, I'll mess with you. It's as simple as that."

"This is nasty, Sophia. Whatever happened to bowing out with grace?"

Sophia gave a nasty cackle. "Don't tell me you weren't playing about behind my back, Summers. I have known it for such a long time but I was willing to be the typical footballer's girlfriend, happy to sweep your infidelity under the carpet so I could keep my place somewhere down the pecking order of your luxurious lifestyle."

"What? This is ridiculous?"

"Oh, but then you ruined it all by trying to get rid of me, didn't you? Well, it's just as well I was doing my homework as I went along because I know more about our mousey little housekeeper than you do, and now the rest of the country knows just what a sucker you've been, too."

Sophia hung up and left Dylan in limbo.

"What a bitch!"

Sam had joined him by now in the sitting room, his frail hand holding a cup of strong morning coffee which he gave to Dylan and then they both sat down in silence, waiting for one of them to put the pieces of Sophia's latest escapade together.

"Why is Cara here?" asked Dylan, remembering the blurry vision hanging out of the window that had tried to save him from the spider-men on the gate. "I noticed her car was still at the house, and then –"

"Oh. Well," said Sam. "Well, last night she called and we had a few drinks so I put her to – I mean, she couldn't drive obviously so she stayed in the spare room. She's worried about her job here now that you and Sophia are . . . I hope you don't mind but Cara told me what she'd heard last night. Is it true that you and Sophia are over?"

"Oh, we are *over*, loud and clear! You have my word on that. Especially after this little game she's playing, setting the paparazzi on me. I thought my days of being hounded by the press were long gone."

Sam let out a long sigh and rested back on his chair. Dylan didn't deserve all of this again and Sophia knew how much he had suffered before when the press first dug up some of his father's messier moments with booze and women and the odd brush-up with the law, not to mention his previous girlfriend's false allegations. Dylan thought he had left that all behind him when he moved to Fulton and the press eventually moved on to their next sitting duck until now, in a twist of irony when he was about to patch things up with his dad, Sophia had chosen her moment to perfection and landed him right back in the spotlight.

"I knew she was media hungry but this just takes it

to a new level," said Sam. "Do you think the papers have got wind that your father is coming here next week?"

Dylan looked at Sam as the pieces of Sophia's plan slotted together in his head. She couldn't be so malicious, could she?

"That makes sense, you know. Yes, now it all makes sense. She came to me last night with this crazy notion of throwing a huge Hallowe'en party at the house when Dad and Mark come to visit. She wanted to invite her bloody magazine and every low-life celebrity she and her PR firm could get their grubby hands on, but now I realise that she had planned to leak the story of how she had arranged it all in honour of my making up with my dad. What a conniving, self-centred, shallow bitch!"

Sam stood up and walked over to Dylan. "Now, now, we don't know all that, do we? As much as Sophia is down my list of favourite people, I'm not totally convinced she would stoop so low. Until we know more, let's give her the benefit of the doubt and not jump to any conclusions. You're only working yourself up into a state and that won't do you any good."

But Dylan's brain was like a runaway train. He had watched Sophia transform lately from a young girl with ambitions and dreams into a media whore who would go to any lengths to get where she wanted. She was out of order. Bang out of order this time.

"But her plan didn't exactly work, did it, Sam? Her

plan to expose my father's recovery from the depths of despair and blame it all on some twisted journalist from the *Daily Whatever* fell flat on its face when I turned her offer down. Now, she's pulled another little cracker out of her witch's hat. Yes, now she's accusing me of playing away and is staking her claim as the first so-called 'WAG' to refuse to stand by her man. If it didn't stink so much, it would almost be genius!"

Sam didn't like what he was hearing at all. "*You* playing away? Where did she get that from?" he asked. "Where is her proof? And who on earth were you supposedly cheating on her with? It's not as if you are the party type who spends night after night away . . . oh Jesus . . . it's Cara, isn't it? She's pointing the finger at Cara!"

"Yes, Sam. It's Cara. She is accusing me of cheating on her with Cara. And the media will just love it."

They both envisaged the dirty headlines. It had all been done before, but the public couldn't get enough of scandals within the lives of those who aired their dirty linen in public. Nannies, PAs, hairdressers, housekeepers. It had all been done before.

"No. That's just not fair, now," said Sam. "Poor Cara doesn't deserve any of this. She has been nothing but loyal to Sophia. And to you."

After his lengthy conversation with Cara the night before, of her turmoil over how she felt about Dylan and how wrong she knew her feelings were, and now, in return for walking away and following her head for once, it had all blown up in her face. How would the girl cope with being thrown into such a media frenzy over nothing? It could ruin her. It probably would ruin her. She wasn't one of those kiss-and-tell girls who saw a few column inches as a ticket to fame.

"So, do you want to warn her, or will I?" said Dylan, fearing that Cara was as much a victim of this mess as he was.

"I think it might be better coming from you."

"That makes sense, I suppose. I'll have a chat with her and then we'll go up to the house and check the newspapers online to see exactly what damage Sophia has done."

Sam nodded and held his head in his hands. "That sounds like a good idea, son. She's in the spare room."

Cara sped down the country lane from Summer Manor and darted through Wimbledon Village, all the while racking her brain as to how the press had found out about Dylan and Sophia's break-up in such a short space of time. She wished her mobile phone had been charged so she could phone Natalie or Liam to tell them that a) she was still alive and they had could call off their manhunt and massive reward for her safe return, and b) to tell them of the excitement she had witnessed with the paps that morning and of the drama of mistaking them for hitmen or terrorists ... oh, and c) that she might be in the evening paper but thankfully she would be unrecognisable as she was hung-over and disguised by a fizzy mop of hair and morning-after-the-night-before make-up.

She had watched carefully as the paps packed up their gear from the gates of Summer Manor, all smug and satisfied that they had caught poor Dylan unexpectedly that morning – they'd probably been hoping to catch him looking happy while they snapped Sophia looking forlorn and well, dumped.

Of course Cara felt horribly guilty having sneaked out of the cottage before she had spoken to Sam or Dylan and allowed them to thank her for trying to warn Dylan about his awaiting predators.

As much as she would have loved to join Dylan and Sam for a cosy gossip about what a bitchy cow Sophia was, having obviously set him up in such a vindictive manner, there was no way that she would allow him to see her properly in her whiskey-stained clothes and un-straightened hair. As much as Sam worshipped the ground she walked on, Cara knew that she had put the fear of God in him when he witnessed her morning image.

Plus, she was beginning to feel ever so slightly nauseous now that the excitement had died down and to say her face was a nasty shade of grey was an under-statement. How could she let Dylan cry on her shoulder when he had just jumped out of his morning shower and she was so obviously smelly and not her new-found glamorous self?

Natalie of course would be chomping at the bit for all the juicy gossip of the break-up once she got over her anger that Cara had stayed out all night and Liam would be offering his services to listen to Dylan's woes since they were, after all, bezzie buds.

With her head buzzing with all of the morning activity, and spinning on its axis after all of the night-before whiskey consumption, Cara knew that she had to distract her overactive mind or else she would end up in a ditch and Natalie would be setting up a manhunt for real.

She turned on the radio and flicked through the channels, hoping for one of those chirpy breakfast presenters to perk up her weary body in advance of the pumping shower she would have when she got home, followed by a banana and strawberry smoothie to boost her vitamin intake, but her ears pricked when she heard Sophia's name mentioned in conversation on Radio One in what appeared to be a campaign in her honour. *Go Go Sophia!* they were chanting and Cara turned it up.

"I ain't no wimpy WAG," said Sophia in a pre-recorded vox pop. "I ain't the type to forgive and forget just to build a brand or live a certain lifestyle. She can have him if she wants him. After all, they're two of a cheating kind!"

"We'll keep you updated, folks, in this Affair of the Horny Housekeeper!" said the delighted DJ.

The rest of the journey home was a blur as Cara let Sophia's comments sink in. She pinched her left arm with her right hand and then did the same the opposite way round to convince herself that all this was real, that it wasn't a nightmare she had been through once before on a much smaller scale. Only this time, she was innocent. But who would believe her?

Not the crowd of awaiting photographers and journalists who stood by the door of her apartment, that was for sure.

28

Rip it Up

"Leave her alone!" shouted Natalie and she ran to meet Cara on the steps of the apartment block and then hauled her through the gang of leeches who shouted and quizzed her as she made her way through.

"Did you set all of this up?" asked one Lois Lane wannabe and she shoved a dictaphone in Cara's face. "Is it true you came to London in a bid to become a WAG?"

"What? Where did you . . .?" Cara was stunned.

"No comment!" shouted Liam who had appeared at the front door and seemed to be somewhat enjoying all of the fuss. "Just say 'no comment', sis. That's what all the rest of them say."

"How long have you been seeing Dylan Summers, Miss McCarthy?" asked Lois.

"Do you deliberately target men who are attached, or are you really in love with Dylan?" asked a camp-looking Clark Kent sidekick.

"And how do you feel being called a home-wrecker all over again?"

Cara kept her head down and pushed her way in through the front door.

"No fucking comment!" said Liam and he slammed the door shut, and then followed the girls into the sitting room of the apartment.

"Oh my God, can someone please just tell me what the hell is going on?" asked Cara. Her hands were shaking so hard she wasn't sure if it was shock or if it was the dreaded DTs from alcohol abuse, but all the same she welcomed the glass of brandy her brother had shoved into her shaking hand. Whiskey for supper, brandy for breakfast. She reminded herself to apologise to her liver later.

"It's for the shock," said Liam, watching while she sniffed the glass and swirled it around a bit. "At least that's what they take on the telly when someone has an affair and are found out and if it's good enough for *EastEnders*, it's good enough for me."

Natalie sat down beside Cara and put a blanket around her shoulders.

"You should have told me, Cara," she said. "If you had just told me you were sleeping with him I would have seen all of this coming. I mean, I can't say I blame you. He's an absolute stud. Every woman's dream. Not to mention how much you have changed since you met him. I thought about it, from time to time, that it might be true but I should have *known*. The clothes, the new image, the confidence. Now, it all makes sense."

"What makes sense?" asked Cara. "What the hell makes so much sense to you two about my life? I wish it all made sense to me."

She wanted to go back out to the trolls on her doorstep and scream her innocence so loudly that everyone including that know-it-all disc jockey on Radio One would hear her. What had he called her? The Horny Housekeeper? Bastard!

"I have to say, sis, even I was a bit suspicious," said Liam. "But I really didn't think you'd risk going through all this again. Of course, this time around, not only have you shagged a celebrity once more but you have fucked up on a much, much bigger scale. I mean, this is *international* media we are talking about. This is an international celebrity as opposed to that ageing newsreader the last time!"

"Oh, would you just shut it, Liam!" said Natalie, rubbing Cara's back as she spoke. "I am sure you're making your sister feel much better now by reminding her that the whole of the UK is talking about her now as opposed to the whole of Northern Ireland when she almost wrecked Michael Bradley's marriage!"

Cara chose that exact moment to let out a scream that would have wakened the dead. Then she yelled, "Yes, I did almost wreck Golden Balls Michael Bradley's marriage! But this time I did not do anything wrong! I did not do anything with Dylan Summers! And can I just add that it's so nice to know you both have used the time of my absence to put two and two together and come up with a million and one, just because I had an affair with a married man before and it was splashed all over the newspapers for everyone including my very own granny in Kilshannon to read! Do you think I would do it again? *Do* you?"

They both stared at her in great pity.

"You do! Jesus, I don't believe this! I am totally alone amidst all this nonsense."

Natalie and Liam both felt terribly sorry for her. Cara could deny it until she was blue in the face (they both noted she was a sea-green colour already from the drink the night before) but it was already a closed case. She was guilty. Trial: the media. Judge: the public. Victory: Sophia Brannigan.

"So you have decided to believe Sophia, then? I thought there were two sides to every story," squealed Cara and she stood up, peeped out of the curtains and then closed them shut again. "How come you two and half the country are all so buck-sure that I was playing around with Dylan, eh? You have no evidence. There is *no evidence*! Show me the fucking *evidence*!"

Natalie's face didn't change expression. Her head just cocked to the side ever so slightly and she stared at her friend as if she was slightly deranged in her denial of the truth. She looked at Liam and gave him the nod to do as he was asked to do. Show Cara the evidence.

Liam let out a dramatic sigh and, as he forced out his breath for effect, he held out a copy of the *Daily Mirror* and without looking her in the eye handed it to his sister.

"I'm afraid there is evidence, Cara," he said. "Plenty of it. It's all there in black and white. Actually, now that you mention it, it's also in colour on page 3 in the *Sun*. Sorry, sis, but it doesn't make pretty reading at all."

Cara's face changed colour again as she stared at the photo on the right-hand corner of the front page of the *Daily Mirror*. It had been taken from a distance but with the help of a zoom lens the image was crystal clear.

The photo was taken the day before at Summer Manor. It was of her embracing Dylan when he told her the news about his father coming to stay and it was taken from behind at a wonderful angle that made it look as if they were both embroiled in the snog of their lives, rather than the innocent hug that it was to celebrate good news.

There was another, more grainy picture of Dylan

chatting to her outside her apartment on the day he had returned her car.

The photos were manipulated, carefully plotted and perfectly timed, but as bad as they looked, she was confident she could explain herself.

But when Cara read the headlines that framed the photos and scanned through the article that accompanied them, she had to run to the bathroom where she violently vomited up her whiskey and her brand-new brandy.

Sophia's telephone hadn't stopped ringing all morning and she was glad she had her partner in crime manning the hotel landline in her room to answer calls on her behalf should she be on the other line.

She had already been invited to appear on the BBC's number one Friday night chat show to talk about how she dumped her millionaire footballer boyfriend to go homeless rather than put up with his cheating ways like the other WAGs did so they could keep up their luxurious lifestyle.

GMTV were lining up an early-morning interview on how she had found out about his affair with their housekeeper (she was working on the content of this one as she wasn't too sure of this at all) and *Fab!* magazine's biggest rival, *Today*, had offered her a problem-page-style pullout with a full-page photo where she would advise members of the public who had also been humiliated by their spouses and their cheating ways.

In the space of a few hours, she had bounded from zero to hero status and she was lapping every single piece of it up as she watched her life-long ambitions come to fruition at long last. But she couldn't have done it alone. For that she was (as far as Sophia Brannigan could possibly be) grateful to her old room-mate Tom who had been feeding her with information about Cara McCarthy for the past few months, even if he had mucked up his "relationship" with Cara by having pretended to have two young children to make him seem more modern-day. He had been so sure she would like him all the more, but had been badly mistaken – he even told her their names where Tom and Sophia! How bloody thick!

"It's him," said Tom, almost vomiting with excitement. "He's on line two here! What will I say? Quick, what will I say?"

Sophia's heart did a cartwheel. This was her big moment. Just as she had hoped, the mountain had come to Mohammed at last.

"Give it to me, give me!" she said and snapped the phone from Tom's hand. "Actually, no. Let him wait."

Sophia flung the phone back to Tom who was blowing a cut on his hand from where Sophia had slashed him with her acrylic nail.

"You mean you aren't going to talk to him after all?

Sophia, darling, are you having a mental breakdown? This is your time to shine, honey. Take the call."

Tom was astounded. This was Sophia's life-long dream, to have all of this media attention and now the king of them all was gagging to speak to her and she was asking him to wait? He had stalked Cara on Sophia's behalf, pretended he liked football, even pretended he had kids to appeal to her so-called "soft side" – and for what?

"No. I won't take the call. Not for a moment. He has led me on a merry dance for long enough, so let's give him a piece of his own medicine and let him wait. Tell him I'm on the phone to *Today* – no, *This Morning* – no, BBC actually. Tell him BBC are casting for a new celebrity reality show and I'm being headhunted to be the star. I don't want Jake Johnston to think I am all his just yet. He can suffer for a while like I have had to all these years as a struggling artiste waiting for him to show me some attention."

"Okay," said Tom somewhat reluctantly. He put on his most pleasant, polite voice and explained to Jake Johnston that he was in a queue and that Sophia would take his call when she had finished speaking to the imaginary BBC representative but, just as Tom had suspected, Jake hung up and said he would "catch her later".

Sophia's face turned a dull shade of grey.

"You muppet! Why did you exaggerate so much,

Tom? I didn't say to tell him his call was in a queue! What do you think we are running here, a bloody call centre? You were just supposed to make him hold for like thirty more seconds. Thirty seconds on hold to Jake Johnston is like half a day to you or me! Sometimes I wonder why I bother with you at all."

She tossed a hairbrush in his direction and he caught it, then threw her a dagger look. She knew she couldn't boss him around as much as she used to when they were penniless and combined their weekly income from dancing and drama, but she still had a hold over him that she was prepared to use to her maximum value.

To be fair to Tom, Sophia knew he had done quite a good job tracking down Cara in a pub, pretending he was a football fan (as if) and taking her out to the cinema to glean as much as he could on her personal life in case she ever grassed on the fact that she wrote Sophia's column. No one would care about that now, though. The girl's name was mud and Sophia had came up smelling of roses. Good job, Tom.

"Shall I try and get him back on the line, Fifi?"

"No, you shall not and stop calling me Fifi. You know it makes my stomach curdle. We are not fifteen any more, Tom. You need to grow up."

Tom's face crumpled and Sophia felt just a little tinge of guilt. After all, he was her childhood sweetheart who had never really moved on, but what did he really think she was going to do? Trade a life of fortune and fame for the semi-detached lifestyle that she had been reared in back in Liverpool? No way. The dream may not have worked out with Dylan Summers, but Sophia would gladly hold out for another love match that would keep her in the comfort she had become accustomed to. Tom would just have to keep on clinging to her coat-tail and she would use him as she needed to, just like the old days.

"Now, which of these headlines do you like best, Tommy boy? I think the *Sun* has summed it up to perfection. And I have to say, brownie points to you for capturing the photo opportunity. We couldn't have staged that one if we tried. Picture perfect."

Tom's face brightened and he sat down beside Sophia on the bed.

"You know I'd do anything for you, Fifi. I always will, even if you do treat me worse than you treated that little mutt Lola I sourced for you. But I just wish you could show me some feelings back, just now and then, you know?"

"Oh Tom. I do love you, honey, you know I do," said Sophia and she pinched his cheek. "Now, I'll just go and freshen up and then we'll think of a plan for how I'm going to get an audience with Jake Johnston since you mucked it up the last time. Oh, and tidy up this place for goodness sake. A celebrity like me cannot live in such a pigsty."

29

There Goes My Everything

"She's a journalist, Sam. Cara is a fucking journalist! Do I have the word 'gullible' stamped on my forehead? What is it with women that I have such bad judgement? I really thought she was different. I thought she was a friend."

Sam shook his head in disbelief. Dylan had spent the past hour or so sifting online for the combination of stories Sophia had sold to the press but Cara's past was the one that he kept going over and over.

"Oh, you know what the tabloids are like more than anyone, Dylan," said Sam. "Everything is twisted and exaggerated and the only people who are gullible are those who are thick enough to believe them. I'm sure Cara's background is nothing like what they have reported. She's a good girl. You know that. I know that."

"I really did believe she was," said Dylan. "You know, Sophia has really dished the dirt over the past twenty-four hours with her claims that I had been cheating on her with Cara, but I can see right through her little game. She has the media eating out of her hands and she'll be hoping to make a career out of this because, after all, being my girlfriend wasn't really cutting it for her. But Cara! I can't believe she would keep this from me. I thought I knew her really well. It's like she was working here undercover!"

Sam stood up when the phone rang. "Shall I get it?"

"No, it's okay, Sam," said Dylan. "It's probably Mark. Anyone else would have called my mobile. I'd say my mother is having a mini-breakdown over another family scandal all over the press."

Dylan was right and it took him almost twenty minutes to reassure his brother about the facts behind the headlines. He spoke to his mother who was evidently distraught as she despised the attention his career sometimes brought onto her doorstep. He endured her usual lecture to keep his head down and stay on the back pages instead of the front pages of the press after all the hurt it had caused her before when his father's life story was splashed across every gossip page in the country.

"That was rough," said Dylan to Sam who looked like he was about to nod off on the couch in the conservatory after all the morning's trauma. The rain pelted down now onto its glass walls and reflected both of their dark moods with the way the day was panning out.

"I can imagine," said Sam. "It's just a shame we didn't know in advance and we could have warned your poor mother at least."

Dylan pulled a sweater on over his T-shirt and searched around for his trainers. Despite the scandal, he had a training session ahead of him and he wouldn't let some smutty newspaper allegations get in the way of his career.

"They feel better now they've heard the truth," said Dylan. "Of course, Mum gave me the 'Beware of Gold-diggers' sermon again and said I should have learned my lesson with Davina and all of the heartache she caused."

"Davina and Sophia were accidents waiting to happen, if you don't mind me saying so, but Cara is a sweet girl who loved being around here and, might I add, was getting very fond of your company. Don't put her in the same category as those other two socialites who were obviously just using you as a launch pad for their own publicity."

Dylan lifted his kitbag and flung it around his shoulder.

"Sam, Cara lied to us. She lied to me and she lied to you," he said. "It's a bitter pill for me to swallow as much as it is for you, but the bottom line is she was hired here under false pretences and, as much as I thought I knew her, she has let me down by keeping this from me. God knows what the next chapter will be when she decides to put *her* storytelling techniques to the test."

"Is she breathing?" asked Liam and he poked his sister in the ribs with a tennis racquet, then plonked himself down on the bed beside her.

"What do you mean is she breathing?" barked Natalie. "Of course she's breathing. She just isn't talking. Cara, can you hear us? Are you still with us?"

Natalie was getting just a little bit worried about the state her friend was in and was getting a bad case of déjà vu. When the news had broken about Cara's fling with Michael Bradley, Northern Ireland television's news anchor and husband of media darling Maeve who ran her own bridal business, the country had been flabbergasted. Cara was a junior reporter on the news team, a background runner no one really took notice of until she was exposed as Bradley's mousey, plain bit on the side and the media went mad to reveal the less wholesome side of his family-man image and the irony of how he was having an affair with a girl-next-door type and not the stereotypical glamour girl normally exposed in such situations.

"Do you think we should call the doctor?" asked Liam. "Or should we call Mum? What do you think, Natalie?"

Natalie was just about to answer when Cara shot up on the bed.

"Do not, and I mean do *not* phone Mum, Liam. I mean it, do *not* phone her. I mean it —"

"She means it," said Natalie in earnest.

Liam stifled a fit of laughter that he always got when he was nervous. His sister was behaving like a pure space cadet and Natalie was only about two steps behind her, but he was only trying to help.

"Oh holy crap," said Cara and tossed back down onto the bed, not noticing that she had come within inches of taking her ear off by almost clipping the side of the bedside locker.

"Let's try and put all of this into perspective," said Natalie, doing her very best practical, motherly impression. "What is the absolute worst thing about all of this? We have got to put this into perspective."

The three of them sat on top of Cara's chequered duvet cover as their minds ticked hopefully over to realise that the splashes in the tabloids were not the end of the world.

"I'd say losing her job *again*, having a fling with a married man, and being caught *again* and Dylan Summers finding out she was a journalist rather than the domestic goddess he thought she was . . . er, I'd say it's all pretty bad really," said Liam and the girls stared back at him, horrified. "Well, you did ask."

"I was asking Cara," said Natalie, "not you, but

thanks anyhow for really helping the situation with your executive summary on Cara's life as we know it!"

"Don't mention it," said Liam. "It's good to remind ourselves of the current state of play so we can assess the situation."

"Just leave me alone," said Cara, her eyes wild and black with yesterday's mascara and her face a blotchy mess. "I don't need you two tearing pieces out of me when I am well fit to do that myself. Please, just leave me alone for a while so I can get my head around how I'm going to show my face again in public."

Liam shrugged and left the bedroom but Natalie stayed put.

"Cara, this will be old news tomorrow when Amanda Stewart breaks a fingernail or Emily Evans gets another boob job, and you know that more than anyone. How about you lift the phone and speak to Dylan if that would make you feel better?"

"Are you nuts? There is not a remote chance of me doing that! He probably hates my guts!"

"Explain to him that it's not what he thinks! Tell him about our crazy plan to switch off our brains for a year. Tell him the truth. Tell him that you were running away from Bradleygate and you needed anonymity and how you didn't know when you applied for a cleaning job that you'd end up working for someone like Sophia. Tell him the truth!"

Cara met Natalie's eye for the first time since she took to her bed that morning.

"I can't tell the truth, Natalie. I'd be too mortified to go into all that detail with Dylan, but you know what?"

"What?"

"I think I already told Sam the whole truth and nothing but the truth in my drunken stupor last night. I think I've just made a prize dickhead of myself and I'm just trying to deal with that right now. I've been so stupid."

Natalie lay down on the bed beside her friend and threw an arm around her waist.

"Don't be sorry about telling the truth, Cara. It always comes out in the end anyway, and from what I've heard about him, I'm not sure that Sam would be the type to speak out of turn."

Cara let out a sniffle and tried to disguise the fact that she was crying a river of snot and tears all into one.

"He isn't. He is such a great man and now he thinks I'm a liar as well."

"But you just said you told him the truth? You told him you were a journalist, right? Or did you tell him about Michael Bradley? Which truth did you tell him, Cara?"

Cara reached for a tissue from her bedside locker and blew her nose to try and disguise her watery eyes with a fake sneeze.

"I think I told him, no, I know I told him . . . Oh, pants, why does alcohol turn you into an honest person sometimes, Natalie? I mean, why do you say things through drink that you wouldn't normally say even if it was St Peter you were talking to and the Pearly Gates were rammed shut until you confessed everything from copying homework to having an illicit affair with a smarmy newsreader? Why?"

Natalie pulled a strand of Cara's hair back from her face. "I don't know, but it happens to the best of us," she said. "Do you remember the time I got really drunk and told my holier-than-the-Pope stepmother that her son was a fan of coke, and I wasn't talking about the fizzy shit that comes in a bottle and makes you fart?"

Cara began to giggle at the thought of it. Natalie was the very person who could nurse you through the worst hangovers as she always could beat your stories hands down. "Or the time that you told everyone at my twenty-first birthday party that you had an explicit dream about Mrs McKenna who ran the laundrette in Kilshannon? We were all convinced it should have been renamed your 'coming-out' party!"

Natalie lifted a cushion and whacked Cara over the head for bringing that up again. It was an official no-go area, but hell, it was lifting her mood.

"You're a good person, Cara. You would never intentionally hurt anyone and despite what the papers say, or what Sophia Brannigan says, we know you had no intention of being embroiled in her smutty scandal."

"Well, she sure has done some deep digging into my past. I bet she was delighted when she found those few old skeletons of mine lurking around the closet."

"I can imagine!"

"I wonder how long she has known about Michael Bradley? I am so humiliated. I feel like a scarlet woman all over again."

Natalie pulled the curtains and let some afternoon daylight into the bedroom. It was still raining outside and she was due to start at the Juicer in just under an hour, but she couldn't leave Cara in this state.

"You are not and you never were a scarlet woman. As we all now know, Michael Bradley has been having flings behind the lovely Maeve's back for years. You were just naïve to believe in his charm and empty promises. You thought you were in love with the man, for goodness' sake, though I can't for the life of me imagine why."

Cara laughed at the look on Natalie's face. "He isn't that bad looking."

"I didn't say he was ugly, but he could do with shedding a few pounds around the waistline. And those teeth are not his own. *And* don't tell me he doesn't use a sun-bed 'cos he has been well and truly tangoed. And he has spray-on hair."

Cara's tears turned into laughter and before she knew it, she and Natalie were rolling about the bed as they threw insult after insult at Michael Bradley who had no idea how therapeutic his pathetic traits actually had turned out to be.

"I really can pick them, eh?" said Cara when they finally drew breath.

"Oh, don't be so hard on yourself. I would say you've been very selective in your choice of men down the years. I mean, it's not as if you're a slapper who takes every man who comes your way. You've just been selective with the wrong man once – or twice if you count your crush on Dylan."

"I suppose you're right. Do you think I'll always be punished for Bradleygate?"

Natalie chuckled at how Cara now referred to her brief fling as Bradleygate without batting an eye.

"No. Of course you won't. And don't beat yourself up for falling for Dylan. Any woman with a pulse and a heartbeat would have done the same so you can't blame yourself for that, and you still have the lovely Tom to see again if you're interested. He was nice."

"Yes, I really messed him up too. I think I have about ten missed calls from him. Oh, Natalie, you have got to believe me," said Cara. "Nothing happened with Dylan. Nothing."

She looked downwards and fiddled with the edge of her duvet.

"But . . ." said Natalie. "Why do I feel there is a 'but' coming up?"

Cara glanced up and then looked Natalie directly in the eye.

"Oh, Natalie, you have no idea how much I wanted something to happen between us," she said. "You have no idea how much I still do."

30

Moody Blues

Jake Johnston drummed his fingers on his desk. No one kept him waiting more than two minutes. No one. Just because that jumped-up little bimbo Sophia Brannigan had been given a whiff of celebrity she thought she was on track to be the next Emily Evans. Not a chance. As much as Sophia could write a feisty column or two, there was no way she was up there in Emily's stakes. The difference was, Emily had likeability and Sophia, well, Sophia did not. The public could see straight through her efforts as she clawed and clamoured up the ranks only to slide right back down again to where no one remembered who she was.

This was probably her last chance to make a go of a media career and if she didn't show up within the next thirty seconds, Jake would send her packing back to oblivion.

"Jake, Jakie, I am so sorry to have kept you waiting," said Sophia only seconds later, scrambling through the door in skyscraper shoes with a pleasant-looking young man by her side. It hadn't taken her long to replace young Summers, that was for sure.

"I was just about to give up on you, Sophia. I'm a busy man," said Jake and shot her a look that said "and don't you forget it".

"Oh, no, believe me this will be worth your while. I have such big ideas as to how I can really stretch all of this publicity to the limits if you just give me a chance and –"

"Leave the ideas to me, Sophia," said Jake sharply. "I know how this business works. It's fickle and it's cruel. You get one crack of the whip and one crack only and I need you to show me that, if I give you a crack of the whip, you will not let me down. Who's *he*?"

Jake stared at Tom who squirmed in his seat under his powerful glare.

"This is my friend, Tom Sutherland."

"We were flatmates once," said Tom and Sophia dug her stiletto heel into his toe so hard that tears came to his eyes.

"Irrelevant," said Jake and he switched his gaze back to Sophia. "Now, let's get down to business. I have been thinking long and hard about what we discussed some months ago. The *Fab!* TV channel is just weeks away from its first broadcast and we have a fantastic line-up of programmes, but we do have some gaps."

Sophia sat up straight and then pouted to give herself a sultry, attractive image. She thought of this meeting as her final audition and she had to give it her best shot. He had gaps. Gaps were good.

"Sounds exciting," said Sophia and she looked at Tom for reassurance but he was huffing and was truly considering the fact that his toe might be broken.

"I don't like to beat around the bush so I'll cut to the chase. I've scrapped your features show," said Jake, biting the end of a pen, and he heard the inevitable sharp intake of breath from Sophia's direction.

"Oh," she said, disappointment crawling all over her face. "I thought you loved that idea."

"I did. I still do, but the difference is, instead of being called *So Sophia* I've decided that the title will be *Forever Emily*."

Sophia looked as if she had been hit on the head with a hot poker.

"Forever Em . . . So, so what exactly do you have in mind for me, then?" she asked and poised herself for bad news.

"You, my dear, will be Emily's roving reporter. You'll be out on the road, bringing in the stories, feeding them through from pre-recorded broadcasts and generally edging your way in until you prove that the public want to see more of you."

Tom let out a snigger at the sneer on Sophia's face as it sunk in that she would be merely a side-kick to her nemesis rather than lead her own show.

"But, um, I'm not so sure about this at all, Jake."

"Well, as your, er, former flatmate friend here told me earlier on the phone, you seem to have other offers to consider, no?"

Sophia squinted her eyes across at Tom in a look that could crucify.

"I *do* have other offers, but since I have my column and features with *Fab!* I really wanted to stay loyal to the company and –"

"About the column," said Jake and he lifted a sheet of A4 paper from a drawer in his desk. "You haven't submitted your piece for this week, have you?"

"No, but under the circumstances –"

"Under the circumstances just doesn't cut the mustard, Sophia. Absence of my columnists doesn't sell magazines. This is exactly why I don't feel you're ready to front a television show. Toughen up a bit. Get your column written. Prove to me you're worth a gamble and I'll make sure you reap the rewards. I promise."

Sophia's lip curled into a smile as Jake lowered his eyes and stared deeply into hers when he spoke his final words to her. Just what type of rewards did he have in mind for her? Sometimes the intensity of his stares were enough to make her legs crumble beneath her and this was one of these moments.

Tom cleared his throat to remind the two of them that he was still in the room, but he was ignored.

"I will prove it to you, Jake," whispered Sophia in her most well-rehearsed, seductive voice. "I will prove it to you that not only the public but also you will want me so, so badly it will hurt."

How was she going to write the damn column without Cara? She would worry about that minor detail later because her next move was to get those smouldering eyes and powerful gaze into her bedroom and the sooner, the better.

With Natalie at work at the Juicer, and Liam perched in front of his latest television quiz show, Cara spent the evening checking out flight times and prices back to Belfast. There was no way she could stay in London any longer under the circumstances and she longed for the security of Graceland and all its punters who knew her well enough to guess she wasn't what the big city buffs had made her out to be.

Every time she thought of Dylan and all of the precious moments they had shared she felt a lump form in her throat. There had been so many times when she wanted to tell him all about her real life back in Ireland so that he would know her through

369

and through, but her foolish decision to keep it from him would haunt her forever now that she was portrayed as an undercover, money-grabbing home-wrecker who had a history of hooking up with highly successful, high-profile men in steady relationships.

She considered writing to him but feared what the consequences would be should her thoughts and feelings fall into the wrong hands. She lifted the phone every few minutes and her hand shook as she dialled his number, only to hang up before it rang through. She even considered making contact with Sam to beg him to set the record straight and to keep her night of confessions to himself.

With her head in a muddle, she fished her credit card from her purse and out fell a small scrap of paper. When she lifted and examined it, she didn't recognise the writing at first but then it clicked.

It was Amanda Stewart's telephone number.

She quickly typed in her details to secure her flight home to Kilshannon the very next weekend as there was no way she could stay cooped up in the claustrophobia of the apartment for much longer, and before she could think twice about it, she dialled Amanda's number.

"Amanda speaking," said the Super-WAG's sweet voice.

"Amanda. I have some explaining to do to you."

There was a few seconds of silence before Amanda spoke.

"Andrew, honey, keep an eye on the girls while I take this call. It's important."

Cara could hear her shut a door in her Hertfordshire home.

"Sara, or Cara should I say?"

"Amanda, I never meant to lie to you. I was just messed up too much in Sophia's life. I'd like you to hear me out on this."

Cara prayed she could make a convincing plea of innocence to at least one person in Dylan's wider circle.

"Go on."

"If I tell you something that no one else knows, please will you keep it to yourself?"

"Cara, I'm not really sure I want to get involved. What you and Dylan get up to is entirely your own business. Believe me, I have witnessed scandals worse than this since they turned footballer's wives into so-called celebrities."

"This has nothing to do with Dylan. In fact, I had nothing to do with Dylan."

"Okay . . . go on."

"I write, sorry, I wrote Sophia's column. That's why she made me tell those lies. That's why I was at all of those parties. I'm not sure what she will do now, but just watch her piece in *Fab!* and, when you see the difference, you will know I'm telling the truth. I am not the home-wrecker or slapper she says I am. I was her housekeeper and I was her ghost writer. I hope you can believe me. Bye, Amanda."

Cara hung up and printed off her flight details, then sat them carefully on her bedside locker.

"Hey, did I just see what I think I saw?" said Liam over her shoulder.

Cara jumped, then shoved her credit card back into her purse and closed down the airline's website.

"Christ, Liam, what are you, the invisible man? Don't creep up on me like that!"

"Don't tell me you're going to run home?" he said and plonked down onto the bed.

Cara bit her lip and nodded. There was no point denying it to Liam. She wanted to run away from all of this and forget everything she had learned in London.

"I have to, Liam. I think I've caused enough trouble around here. In fact, I seem to cause trouble wherever I go lately, so I'm going home. That's the one place I think I can lead a low-key, unassuming life that I was meant for. A life of fishing boats and Gaelic football and serving up pints at Graceland, just as Natalie and everyone else always predicted was right for me."

Liam sighed. "Balls! You and I both know that you have changed in the past four months. You have seen a different side of life and if you're honest there are parts of it you really like. Don't walk away from it just because someone like Sophia Brannigan is trying to ruin you. You're a bigger and better person than she is."

"Well, I sure am bigger," said Cara. "A celery stick is bigger. A kitchen skewer is bigger."

"Ha ha. You know what I mean," said Liam. "Look at all you have done for me over here. Back home I was on a fast track to becoming a junkie loser with my 'sod it' attitude and my druggie so-called friends. We're both taking a break from a wrong turn in our lives – you with your job in journalism and me with my anti-social networking. You said you'd give it a year and you're going to quit partway through?"

Cara picked up her dressing gown and wrapped herself into its warmth and comfort. She sat down beside her brother and rested her head on his shoulder.

"Well, right now I need a break from *this* break, if you know what I mean. I've booked my flight so I'll go home for a while and see how I feel after Christmas. I'm sure you and Natalie will think of enough reasons to coax me back over here for another while and so I'll be back before you even notice I'm away."

"That sounds fair enough," said Liam. "I suppose we'll all be going home for Christmas anyhow, but I can think of one good reason already why you'll want to come back."

Cara sighed. "So can I. It's just a shame that, as always, the man that I want is totally out of my reach."

"Oh, now I wouldn't say that. Young broadcast journalists from the backwaters of Ireland bag themselves famous Premiership footballers all the time. These things happen."

"Oh shut up," said Cara. "No, I've decided it's about time I got my head out of the clouds and back to reality. Now, I need you to do me a favour."

"What's that?"

"Before I change my mind, I need you to come with me to Summer Manor."

"Are you serious?"

"Totally serious," said Cara and she grabbed her coat from the back of a chair. "Take me to Summer Manor so I can at least try to clear my name."

Dylan had taken the smart-ass comments on the chin at his training session that afternoon and now, as he sipped a cold beer and stared out onto the floodlit grounds of Summer Manor, he vowed that he would never be caught out by a woman ever again. Davina's revelations had almost forced his mother into a nervous breakdown when she read about her husband's dalliances with Dylan's youth-team physio, of his affair and of his other drunken romps with cling-on starlets as Dylan's early career took off.

When Sophia came along, Dylan had vowed to stay out of the limelight and at first he thought she was happy to do so too, but as soon as she filled her dressing room with designer gear at his house, and attended a few weddings and christenings of other footballer's wives, she caught a whiff of the good life and like a drug she couldn't get enough of it.

Paul Henderson had been sympathetic as always that day at training. Even his old mate Andrew Stewart had called him to see how he was and to get the true side of the story and Dylan valued their solid friendships, knowing their concern was genuine.

"Shit," he said, when he saw a car approach the gates of Summer Manor. He couldn't figure out who his early evening visitor could be. Sophia had already made arrangements to clear the house of her "stuff" the following weekend under Sam's supervision and, after speaking to them on the phone, he knew it wasn't any of the lads.

The monitor buzzed in the kitchen and Dylan pressed it, and then muttered a cautious hello.

"No, you speak," said a familiar Irish accent and Dylan listened carefully. Was it Cara?

"Would you hurry up and say something before he thinks we're feckin' stalkers," said a male voice that was unmistakably Liam McCarthy's.

"Cara? Is that you?" said Dylan.

"Yes, it's me. It's me. Look, can I please have a quick word? We need to talk."

Dylan shook his head which was already throbbing sore. He couldn't chance seeing Cara face to face right now. He was afraid he might crumble when he saw her and he couldn't risk it, no matter how hard he yearned to hear her out.

"I don't think so, Cara. I'm really confused right now and I don't think it will do either of us any good to go over everything that has happened now. It's all too soon."

"Please, Dylan. I just want you to know the real story. I never meant to hurt you like this. It's not like what they said in the papers. You know I'm not like that. Please, can I just see you for a few moments? Give me a chance to clear my name."

Dylan punched the wall and gathered his thoughts. Davina's damage and all Sophia's kiss-and-tell allegations had haunted him all day, swimming through his head and he knew that as much as it felt like the right thing to do, he couldn't afford to follow his heart this time.

"Cara, it's been a long day. I have a lot going on at the moment. Please understand. I can't do this. Sorry. Goodbye."

He waited for her reply.

"I just wanted to tell you to follow your heart, Dylan. Don't be afraid to follow your heart. Please don't let all of this put you off finding a good person to spend your life with. I'm so, so sorry for letting you down and I'll really miss you from my life. Goodbye."

Dylan couldn't speak, so he walked to the window and watched Cara McCarthy drive away, out of his life, and already he felt like part of him was missing.

31

Viva Kilshannon

Cara felt a glow as warm as the colours of the last days of October as Graceland came into view. With its stone walls and roadside positioning, it was as far from the home of Elvis as Tennessee itself, but its site on the outskirts of the Donegal fishing port of Kilshannon meant it was a true attraction for passers-by at all times of the year.

"I can't tell you how glad I am to be home," she said, already feeling soothed by her familiar surroundings. The roads were quiet and the trees were bare but she felt welcomed by the familiarity of the slow pace of her own territory.

"You'll have to share a room with our Olivia," said her father as they approached the brow of the hill that Graceland stood on.

He said it as if it was a threat, despite the fact that Olivia and Cara had shared a room since they were children and it didn't bother them in the slightest. What was more worrying was that it was the third time he had said it on the journey from the airport.

"It won't be for long, Dad. I'll be going back to London to finish my year out after Christmas, though what I'm going to do when I go back there, I have no idea."

Gerry McCarthy yanked the handbrake on his modest estate car and grumbled to himself as he let himself out and walked to the boot to fetch his daughter's luggage. Cara followed suit and took one of the bags from her father's hands. If she was big enough to carry them from London, she was big enough to carry them a few feet into the house.

A gust of wind blew her hair back from her face and she closed her eyes against the elements which reminded her of earlier times when she waited for the school bus outside the doors of the bar.

"I've said it to you before and I'll say it again," said Gerry. "All I'm asking is that you keep your private business private as it's much easier dealt with if you get into a spot of bother. I mean, for feck's sake Cara, what is it with men off the telly that you can't resist?"

Cara wrapped her coat around her and shut the boot of the car.

"Would you lay off, Dad? Believe it or not, I didn't come home for another lecture. I've spent the past week and a half waiting for the hyped-up lies about me to die down and now you're throwing it all back at me. Please, please give it a rest."

Gerry McCarthy was definitely not one to give it a rest. No wonder her mother avoided telling him half of what was going on in their family down the years. When he got a bee in his bonnet, the world had to know his opinion.

"All I'm saying is, if that Bradley bastard was a fisherman in Kilshannon you'd never have looked twice at him. But put a microphone in his hand and you go weak at the knees. This time it's a footballer. Who will it be next, Elvis feckin' Presley himself?"

Cara rolled her eyes. "God knows I wish Michael Bradley had been a fisherman from Kilshannon because, if he had, my life would be a whole lot easier now. It looks like I'll be serving my purgatory here on earth for the rest of my days for one moment of weakness with him!" She made for the door of the pub.

"Now, as for your other man, the footballer," said Gerry as he puffed and panted behind his daughter. "I can definitely see what you found attractive in him. He's like one of those Hollywood actors with his Italian looks and he's got buckets of talent and as for his wallet – well, that's another big attraction."

Cara approached the double doors of Graceland.

The pub had a separate doorway that led upstairs to the family home but she walked past it, wanting to say hello to her mother who was no doubt serving up stew or soup to the regular punters like she did at this time every day.

"Enough," said Cara, with her hand on the door of the pub. "That is really enough. Believe it or not, Daddy, I am relying on you to support me through this over the next few days until the neighbours find someone else to talk about. I can just imagine that old razor-tongued witch Mary MacAvoy when she gets a hold of me. Now, come on in till I see my mother and I hope to God she has a stiff drink waiting for the both of us."

There was only a handful of people propping up the bar in Graceland when Gerry and Cara walked in. She scanned the place for her mother and was met with a beaming smile when Margaret spotted her younger daughter coming through the bar. A roaring turf fire blazed in the hearth under the only picture of Elvis that had stood the test of time, and three men on bar stools had their heads buried in the local newspaper.

"Welcome home, love," said Margaret and she hurried across the slate floor with her arms outstretched. Cara noticed how tired her mother looked and she felt a pang of guilt at all the stress she had caused her over the past few days.

The heads at the bar turned on hearing the

commotion and Cara waited for the inevitable reaction.

"Well, if it isn't the wannabe WAG back in town," said one from behind the rustle of a newspaper. "I thought you'd be arriving here by private jet, Cara."

"I did," said Cara with a wry smile. She could take their comments lightly after the wrath of the British tabloids.

As she greeted her mother, she heard the door open behind her and in bounced her older sister, wrapped up like an onion against the late autumn weather. Cara winced at what Olivia's reaction would be. She was usually as subtle as a sledgehammer across the head.

"Cara! It's so good to have you home!" she squealed. "Come, come and tell me all about the delicious Dylan Summers! I cannot believe that you had sexual relations with him. Was he good in the sack? Spill the beans!"

The men in the bar buried their faces in their pints and Cara's face went a deep shade of puce at her sister's frank questioning.

"Olivia, would you give the girl a chance to get her bearings before you ask her personal questions like that? Now, would you like a bowl of stew, Cara?"

"I would love one, Mum, and if you don't mind I'll have a swift gin and tonic and one for my dad too. He looks as if he needs it."

Gerry McCarthy had turned pink at such explicit conversation between the female members of his family.

"So how is that son of mine behaving?" he asked under his breath. "I'm almost afraid to ask."

"He's doing great," said Cara with a proud beam. "Our Liam is doing just fine."

"Has he grown up at all since he went to the bright lights of London or has it sent him over the edge like I thought it would?" asked Olivia, pouring herself a glass of orange juice.

Cara noticed that Olivia had put on a bit of weight since she had last seen her, and her father had lost some in contrast. She pulled up a stool by the fire and nestled her gin and tonic in her hand. Despite the embarrassing welcome, it was good to be home.

"Honestly, you would be so proud of Liam," she said. "He is working with Natalie in a shopping-mall juicer –"

"A what?"

"It's a yuppie drinks counter with smoothies that cost an absolute fortune," said Olivia knowingly. "They have them in Dublin and Galway and all the big towns and cities. Pure rip-off merchants the whole lot of them."

"Right," said Gerry and he rolled his eyes. "Maybe that's what we need to move into then, as this place is so feckin' dead."

"Well, he has really, really settled and I think he might have even *matured* quite a bit since he left here."

"No *way*," said Olivia and she shook her head so her dangly earrings jangled. She was always one for oversized accessories. "Our Liam? Matured? I'll believe it when I see it."

The bell above the door rang out and all heads turned as usual to see who was entering. Mary MacAvoy, the neighbourhood gossip and part-time cleaner of Graceland, came into the bar sideways, lugging a mop and bucket and taking the last drag of a cigarette before she let it leave her bony fingers out onto the street.

"That's littering, Mary," said Gerry and he nudged Cara knowing that in return he would get a lashing from Mary who had the sharpest tongue in Kilshannon. "What sort of cleaner do you call yourself when you throw your filthy fag-ends at the very door?"

Old Mary's face twisted as she thought of a response to the bold Gerry's comments. He always tried his hardest to rile her when she came in every other day to clean around the place but he rarely matched her tongue that would whip the devil. She had been found out with her cigarette butt and feared she might struggle for once to respond, but then her eyes widened in delight when she saw the younger of the McCarthy girls had arrived home after all her shenanigans in London with rich and famous footballers.

"D'ye know?" she said in her thick Donegal accent. "If it had been that Olivia one I would have believed it straight off. She is definitely fond of the men and has a reputation that would put any man to shame, but that other lassie, I always thought butter wouldn't melt in her mouth."

"Now, I was only messing with you Mary about the litter," said Gerry, standing up in defence. "There's no need to be nasty to my girls."

"All I'm saying is that I would have thought Cara, with her tomboy style, would have been more likely to be playing *football* with the boys than *playing* away with the *footballers*, if you know what I mean. It's the quiet ones you need to watch, as my mother used to say."

She gave out a raspy cackle and dragged her mop across the floor, then coughed and barked until she could laugh no more. Gerry McCarthy sat back down on his chair and looked sadly at his daughters.

"She got you there," said Olivia.

"She has a point," said Cara.

"Aye," said Gerry, shrugging his shoulders. "I suppose she does."

Then the three of them clinked their glasses and burst out laughing.

"All we need now is our thug of a brother here and

we'd make a right motley crew!" said Cara and Mary
MacAvoy gave her the filthiest look that she could
find from behind her wrinkly eyes.

"Who invented the text message?" asked Cara as she
lit candles in a row of pumpkins along the window-
sills of Graceland. Since she arrived she had thrown
herself into making the place look a little more lively
and knew that, with it being Hallowe'en weekend, it
was as good a time as any to make use of her somewhat
sterile creative skills.

"Where the heck did that question come from?"
asked Olivia, who was reluctantly serving out bowls of
monkey nuts to old men who would probably choke
at the very sight of them.

"Well, I would just like to un-invent them, that's
all," said Cara. "You see, if there was no such thing as
a text message, or a mobile phone for that matter, I
wouldn't have the urge to do something I would later
regret."

"I'd hardly call you the impulsive type," said Olivia,
delighted at a conversation that might get her out of
working in the pub for five minutes. She had zero
interest in Graceland and all its revellers, preferring
much more to go clubbing in the nearby Donegal
town or to outdoor dance festivals in the summer
time. The very sight of the place made her yawn,
unlike her younger sister who seemed to bring the

place to life with her very presence. "Apart from your taste in men, of course. To whom or why do you want to send a text message that you will regret?"

"Dylan."

Olivia used a stool as a hurdle and almost knocked an old man's false teeth down his throat to get over to the window where Cara was threatening to burn the entire building down with a match in her hand. Cara had point-blank refused to talk about Dylan Summers since she arrived home and now, out of the blue, as she lit up a pumpkin, she was feeling the urge to contact him.

"His family are coming to visit him today for the first time in ages and I'd just like to wish him luck," she said.

Olivia snapped the burning match from her hand just before she created an inferno.

"Well, go on then. Do it. Trust your instincts!" said Olivia, delighted that the first sign of feelings for Mr Wonderful were starting to come through. She had already made a list of the top ten single footballers she would like to be introduced to, should she ever have the opportunity of meeting the sex god himself. All of the young people, male and female, at the youth club where she worked thought Dylan Summers and Co. were gods and she couldn't have agreed more.

"I don't think so," said Cara and she lifted the box of matches again. "He doesn't want anything to do with me since he heard of my journalism background and the affair with big man Bradley. He thinks I'm like every other money and fame-grabbing bimbo he has let into his life."

"Our Liam says he's a cool guy," said Olivia. "And anyone who lets our Liam around his house to help out has my vote. Even Dad wouldn't let him loose around this place for fear of him stealing anything that wasn't nailed down."

Cara sighed and surveyed the glowing pumpkins, then glanced about, admiring the good job she had made on the bar in such a short space of time. It had become somewhat dilapidated since she was last home and she was determined to give it back its old sparkle and attract some new clientele in the run-up to Christmas.

"Well, he *is* a cool guy," she said to Olivia who had parked herself at a table and was helping herself to some monkey nuts. "Come on, sis. You're the one with all the experience with men. Tell me what to do. Should I text him or am I on a fast track to making a fool out of myself?"

Olivia applied a layer of lipstick and looked at Cara. Much as she wanted to encourage Cara to chance her luck with the mighty Dylan, she was her sister and she owed her the truth. "Cara, honey," she said, waving her lipstick in the air as she spoke. "As much as I would jump the bones of some of those hunks in trunks in the world of football, this is where you belong. Here, in Graceland, Kilshannon. Not Graceland, Tennessee, or Wimbledon Village in London for that matter. We all knew you were never cut out for the world of television when you left here for Belfast all those years ago, and you're not exactly typical of one of those glamorous WAGs you read about in the papers."

"But I've changed, Liv. I'm not as naïve as I used to be."

"As much as you say you have changed, I know that in reality shopping to you is for groceries, parties are for birthdays and clothes are for comfort," said Olivia. "If it were me, on the other hand, I'd have had my eyes on the prize from the very moment I entered those doors. You're way too slow, Cara."

Cara sniffled and lifted a dishcloth from the table, then wiped away a spray of nutshells and made her way toward the bar.

"You're probably right, Olivia. Just keep reminding me of that, won't you? I'm way too slow. I didn't have my eye on the prize and if it were you . . . now, Billy," she said to an awaiting customer. "What can I get you? The usual?"

32

All Shook Up

Dylan checked around the sitting room one final time. He couldn't believe how nervous he felt at the thought of his own family coming to visit but it had been so long. He had lit a fire in the hearth and had contemplated lighting a few candles, but decided against it as Mark would probably use it as an excuse to slag him off. He sat down on an armchair and then stood up again, cursing himself for feeling so unsettled. They were due in twenty minutes and he longed for the awkward waiting to pass and for them to arrive and get any formalities out of the way so that they could just get back to being a family once again.

A brandy would settle him down, he decided. Sam had offered to be there to act as an icebreaker but he had declined the offer, knowing he had to do this for himself. Now, as the big moment grew closer, he felt so alone and wondered what it would have been like if things had turned out differently with Sophia. How would she have warmed to his brother who worked in a normal nine-to-five job, to his father with his sordid history and determination to make up for his flaws, and his mother who was so fragile and uncertain of people she didn't know? This was probably the most important moment in his life in the past year, and deep in his heart he knew that Sophia would have wanted absolutely nothing to do with it.

He bent down and opened the drinks cabinet doors and searched for a bottle of brandy and a glass. He would have to conceal any signs of alcohol when his father arrived, but he had just about time for a swift one for himself. He reached for the bottle and a glimmer caught his eye on the second shelf. There, right beside the brandy, was an earring and when he took it in his hand he knew it had to be Cara's.

He grasped the small piece of silver and smiled, as the day she lost it flooded back into his head. How they had laughed that day together about next to nothing, and then he had confessed his fears to her of the day when he would be reunited with his family. Today was that day, and finding this tiny piece of her made him feel more settled than any alcoholic drink ever could. He closed the drinks cabinet and locked its doors, then slipped the earring into his dark shirt pocket and closed his eyes as memories of her soothed his heart.

She had listened to him when no one else would, she had soothed his fears and laughed at his jokes. She had seen past what he was and got to know him for who he was, and then he had let her go without giving her a chance to explain her side of things when she had called one week ago today.

The doorbell stirred him and he realised he was so lost in thought he hadn't even heard the car in the driveway or the monitor from the gate. Sam must have let them in. With his heart pounding in his chest, Dylan walked to the front door of the house and pushed his regrets of how he had let Cara go to the back of his mind. He couldn't deal with that now. He had other mistakes to make up for.

"You could teach your brother a thing or two," said Marian Summers as Dylan served up a platter of coffee and scones in the conservatory. "I don't think he knows how to boil a kettle, do you, Mark?"

Dave Summers gave a nervous laugh and put his hand on his wife's in a sign of appreciation of her efforts to lift the tension in the air between his family. It was more than he deserved.

"Hey, I have been known to rustle up a pizza and salad for the kids when I had to," said Mark in defence, knowing too that his mum was trying her best to lighten the mood.

"You think this is impressive," said Dylan with a faint smile. "Wait till you see what I've prepared for tea. All my own work, too. Move over Jamie Oliver."

"Oh, go on, really stick the knife in me, why don't you?" said Mark.

"I mean it. You will be impressed. I've learned to make a mean lasagne," he said. "And with all the trimmings too."

"I never thought I'd see the day," said Marian. "Who taught you how to cook?"

"Em, an old friend. Anyhow . . ."

"Yes, now, sit down, Dylan, and have your tea and then you'll have to give us a grand tour of the house," said his mother, not wanting any awkward silences. "It has changed so much since we were last here."

"It has, Mum. A lot of things have changed since you were last here," said Dylan. "It's amazing how much has changed, really."

"I hear Paul Henderson is getting married soon," said Mark. "Is it true he sold the rights to a magazine for over two million quid?"

"Oh, we don't talk about that type of thing on the pitch," said Dylan. "But if it is true, it will help him pay the £2000 fine he picked up for taking a call from his future wife during training! I got one too for chatting to Mark."

"No way!" said Marian. "Isn't that too extreme? Two thousand pounds?"

"It's an absolute disgrace," said Dave with a grunt. "There are people in this country who don't make two grand a month and in football terms these figures are bandied about like monopoly money."

"That's hardly Dylan's fault," said Marian, and Dylan and Mark glanced at each other as the components of a row began to brew.

"See," said Mark, "you should have been a mechanic or an electrician after all, little brother. Save all these debates about phones and fines and the like."

"Oh, I didn't say that," said Dave. "Don't be putting words into my mouth, lads. Now, how about we finish up our tea so I can get a look around this place once and for all? The last time I was here, I was a bit worse for wear and my memory of the occasion isn't totally clear."

"All's going well, so far, kid," said Mark later in the evening when his parents had gone to the cottage to bring Sam up for tea. "I think this has been a great success, don't you?"

Dylan reached into the oven and lifted out his masterpiece. The pasta sheets were a bit crispy around the edges of the dish, and the cheese had melted into a colour that was slightly on the wrong side of golden brown but it smelt good and as a first attempt on his own, he was mighty proud of the lasagne.

"I didn't think he would even look me in the eye, Mark, but he has managed to make direct conversation on a few occasions," said Dylan. "He was even referring to his drinking in a roundabout way which I didn't expect."

"Me neither."

"He looks really good, too. He says it's a struggle but I sense a steely determination about him this time."

Mark grabbed some cutlery and napkins and laid them out on the table. As fancy as Summer Manor's facilities were, this was a casual, relaxed family occasion and there was no need for formalities.

"He is so determined to put things right," said Mark. "I swear, he was like an excited child on the drive down here. Nervous as a kitten, mind, but excited too."

"Shit, Mark, if you think Dad was nervous, imagine how I felt. I was just reaching for the brandy bottle when you guys arrived."

"Really? Were you that bad?"

"Worse," said Dylan. "I was so afraid that things would turn angry and Mum would get upset at Dad and me arguing and you would have to intervene as usual but then I found something that made me change my mind."

Mark stopped what he was doing and looked at his brother who was staring into space. "What do you mean you found something?"

"Oh, it sounds stupid, but I took it as a sign, that's

all. It was something belonging to Cara and I had talked to her about this so much that I took it as a sign she was supporting me through this today. I'm turning into a real mush here, aren't I?"

Mark nodded. Dylan had loved and left more women down the years than he could add up, and now after a range of high-maintenance beauties and models that had almost ruined him, he was falling for a girl who was his housekeeper?

"Jeez, mate. You definitely are a changed man."

"Shit, Mark, but how can I ever learn to trust a woman again? I've seen enough of my dirty linen being aired in public with my last two relationships and the pressure it puts on my family at the same time."

"Do you love her?" asked Mark.

Dylan stalled. "Oh, don't beat around the bush, bro'! Just go ahead and ask the million-dollar question, no holds barred."

"Well, do you? If you do, maybe she is worth taking the risk? Who says she is like the others? You can't live the rest of your life in fear of Sophia and Davina clones."

Dylan laid out the lasagne on the table and went back to the fridge to find the pre-prepared bowl of salad. He put it beside the lasagne and then leaned against the table.

"She *has* changed me, you know. She has opened my eyes to how two people should feel when they are together. She has made me realise that I never loved

Sophia, and that Sophia never loved me. We loved the *idea* of each other, that's all. But do I love Cara? Well, I like her a lot. I really like her and I miss her terribly but I know I'm too sore at the moment to know if what I feel for her is real. I'm trying to do things right this time and, to do so, I need to lay the ghost of Sophia and all of her damage to rest first."

"*Cut, cut, cut!* Miss Brannigan, the word is 'phenomenon'. Say it! Phe-nom-e-non."

"Phe-nom-e-non," said Sophia like a child at kindergarten. "I *can* say it, Piers!"

"See! It's easy really when you know how. Now, from the top! Just read what it says on the autocue! Thank the Lord this isn't live television or we wouldn't last a second."

Sophia smacked her lips at the director of *Forever Emily* and practised saying the word "phenomenon" again in a whispered tone. How could she grovel at Emily Evans' success and describe it as a phenomenon when she hated the very sight of the plastic bimbo and hated her whole phenomenon in the first place! But she had to do it. She no longer had her column so she had to make this work.

"I am doing my best here, Piers! It's just not easy with you staring at me and miming each word with me as if I'm totally thick," she grumbled to the wormy man she was made to answer to.

"The thought never entered my head. Now, from the top!" shouted Piers, rubbing his forehead and tapping his toes in irritation at Sophia's prima-donna behaviour.

Sophia was equally irritated. With his squeaky voice and tiny feet, Piers was laying the blame for absolutely everything on her and had told her that, because of her incompetence, *Fab!* TV's launch date was more likely to be dragged into the New Year rather than its November target.

"Emily Evans. Glamour model. Novelist. Style icon. Mother. And now, television host," said Sophia into the camera. *So far, so good.* "Emily's success in the space of two years has been nothing short of a phemonem – fuck!"

"Christ! Where is the scriptwriter?" yelled Piers and he fired his clipboard on the studio floor. "Can someone please get me the scriptwriter? *Now!*"

"I will get it this time, Piers" said Sophia. "Just give me one more chance. It is my first day after all."

"Look, missy," said Piers, pointing a pen in her direction, "I have missed my coffee break twice by giving you chance after chance to pronounce that word and, as well as caffeine withdrawal symptoms, I just buried my cat yesterday so you, Miss Brannigan, are not helping me do my job today at all!"

"But isn't it a bit harsh to call in a scriptwriter? How humiliating!"

"Harsh? You don't know the meaning of the word

'harsh' and you certainly don't know the meaning of the word 'humiliating' but you soon will. We are two hours behind schedule and when Jake Johnston arrives here in approximately seven minutes, whose arse is going to get kicked? Whose? No, not yours! Mine! My arse will be kicked around this floor in the finest of fashion!"

Sophia made a face behind Piers' back as he strutted away from her to find his precious scriptwriter and Tom emerged from the wings and came in Sophia's direction. He was carrying a water bottle with a determined look in his eye and, just as Sophia was about to ask him what he was up to, she was sprayed with a cloud of facial mist.

"Piss off! Piss off! What are you doing to my make-up, you ponce?!"

"It's facial mist, Fifi. I thought you needed freshening up, that's all. Can't have you perspiring on camera, can we, duckie?"

"Tom," said Sophia through gritted teeth, "take your facial mist and your Fifi and get the duckie out of my face! You are suffocating me, Tom. Smothering me and I can't stand it. Now skedaddle! Go!"

Tom walked away with his tail between his legs and Sophia's anger turned into a beaming smile when she spied Jake Johnston arrive on set. He was dressed to kill as always in a dapper white shirt and a pinstripe suit and his snow-coloured teeth almost glowed from afar. Sophia powdered her nose and admired her own perfection in her compact mirror, then sprayed a quick squirt of perfume on her wrists and stood in anticipation of Jake's greeting.

"Sophia, baby. How is your big debut coming along? You look amazing!" he said as he marched over towards her. "No cold feet, I hope?"

"Piers says I'm a natural," she said with a radiant smile. Natural-born bimbo was what Piers had said, but Jake didn't need to know that minor detail. "I'm really loving it, Jake. I think it's my destiny to be on camera."

"Excellent," said Jake with a flash of porcelain. "Look, honey. I know you were disappointed that I gave the show to Emily, but in a few months' time, if you play your cards right and if *Fab!* TV is a success, you and I will have much bigger fish to fry."

Jake led Sophia a few steps into the studio lighting and, putting a finger under her chin, he raised her face up to his.

"I – I'm going to make you really proud of me, Jake," whispered Sophia and she closed her eyes in anticipation of a kiss as his face moved closer to hers.

"Good," he said. "That's just what I like to hear. Now, go and get Make-up to look at your face while we wait for Piers, because if my eyes don't deceive me, you have the makings of a humongous blackhead on your chin."

33

Are You Lonesome Tonight?

November had gone by in a blink and her life in Summer Manor almost seemed like years away as Cara scraped a pile of snow away from the front doors of Graceland with a shovel. She blinked as a cold, wet flake landed on her nose. It was a beautiful crisp evening in Kilshannon and, as she looked down the hill that led to the village, she noticed flickers of light as her neighbours' homes lit up as darkness drew down. She kicked the snow off her boots, then made her way back indoors to the cosy warmth of the bar where a modest crowd had gathered, all determined to get into the Christmas spirit as early as possible and, if the truth be told, to see what all the fuss had been about Graceland being given a well-overdue face-lift.

As soon as Liam had arrived home for the holidays,

she had handed him a paintbrush and between her and Natalie and with a pinch of assistance from Olivia, they had transformed the place into a small haven the King of Rock 'n' Roll would have been proud of.

Each booth was named after an Elvis song, and the bar stools had caused great conversation as they were named after each member of Elvis' extended family. Liam had great *craic* with some of the regulars who almost fought over who would be first to sit on Priscilla! A huge fluffy white Christmas tree dominated the lounge area, with more silver bling than a WAG's wedding, and the new jukebox was proving a real hit with the regulars.

"Hey, Cara! Have you seen the evening paper?" whispered Liam from behind the bar. He looked extremely handsome and grown-up in his black T-shirt and jeans and, without his facial piercings and bleached Mohican, he cut a fine barman. His winter smoothies were going down a treat with the lunchtime traffic.

Cara's heart galloped when she looked at Liam's face. Had more rotten stories reared their heads on the mouth of Christmas when she had finally begun to settle into her life in Kilshannon and lay the ghosts of London to rest?

"It's nothing, really," said Liam and he flicked through the pages. "I just thought you might like to see his picture. I can read it out to you if you want?"

Cara leaned her head in her hands and, though part of her wanted to walk away and let the newspaper go to the recycling bin where she didn't have to look at it, something urged her to just take a quick glance at the man who held her heart so many miles away.

Nothing could have prepared her for how she felt when she raised her head and saw Dylan's photo. He was dressed in a navy suit with a matching shirt underneath it, opened at the collar. His dark hair was cut short but was swept back at the front and he wore a beautiful smile that she traced with her fingers, not realising how sad she looked as she stared at his face. At his side were Andrew and Amanda Stewart and Cara realised that the occasion was the much-hyped wedding of Dylan's team-mate, Paul Henderson.

"Just read some of it to me and I'll tell you when to stop," she said to Liam who was awaiting her response with bated breath. "I don't know why but I feel like a punishment beating, so get it over and done with."

"Okay," said Liam. "Here we go: '*Fulton's finest Dylan Summers mixed with Arsenal's Andy Stewart today at the wedding of team-mate Paul Henderson in a church in Surrey. With photo rights snapped up by* Today *magazine, the* Evening Telegraph *managed to scoop this exclusive pic of the three main guests as they left a nearby pub en route to the celebrations. Summers, who recently split with Fab! TV's Sophia Brannigan was unusually chatty when questioned* about his alleged relationship with Irish broadcaster-turned-housekeeper, Cara McCarthy –"

"Stop!" said Cara. "Enough already. I don't need to hear any more!"

"Oh, but I think you do," said Liam and he continued over his sister's insistence that he shut up.

"*The extremely private winger for Premiership side Fulton said he had 'no regrets' about his relationship with McCarthy, despite Miss Brannigan's allegations of an illicit affair behind her back and the revelation that Miss McCarthy had a similar relationship with Northern Ireland news anchor, Michael Bradley. Summers said he had a "true friendship" with McCarthy and when asked if he would be seeing her again he said he 'sincerely hoped so'.*"

Cara gulped. "Now read the right version, you punk! Don't mess with me like this, Liam."

"Okay, so I made some of that up. But, look at him, Cara. He looks miserable. And he did say most of those things."

"He's smiling like a Cheshire cat, you liar!"

"For the cameras! He's so faking it! Don't you think it would be worth contacting him again? I'm sure he has calmed down by now. Admit it to yourself. You have thrown your whole time here into decorating the bar for Mum and Dad, putting a false face on for customers – and I'm not talking about Hallowe'en – and you've even banned soccer from the telly in the bar so you can avoid seeing him play. You love him,

Cara, and from what I could see when I was clearing up around his house, he has feelings for you too."

Cara closed the paper shut and threw it into the bin. "Well, I have tried to talk to him and he didn't want to listen so just drop it, Liam, won't you? And please don't show me any more pictures of him in the paper. I don't need to be reminded of how fucking gorgeous he really is!"

"Where are you going?" asked Liam as Cara fled through the bar, grabbing her coat on the way.

"To town with Natalie. You can look after this place for a change, Liam. I'm going to get pissed."

Dylan downed his fourth vodka shot at the bar and his head was beginning to spin. He hadn't drunk so much in months but it wasn't every day his best mate got hitched, he reminded himself, and ordered another from the bar.

"Steady on, mate," said Andy Stewart who was pacing himself with a pint of lager. "I don't fancy cleaning up when you puke all that up later on, kid. What's the problem? All this wedding shit getting to you?"

"Ha!" said Dylan. "I'm having a wonderful time, Andy. Me and the bar make a beautiful couple, don't you think? No pressure from my date to dance or to make small talk with the guests or to go home when I don't want to. I highly recommend it."

Andy shrugged and left to join some of the others

on the dance floor and his presence was replaced by his wife Amanda.

"Hey, sunshine! You missing your other half?" she said, playfully linking Dylan's arm. "You're like a lost soul without her, really you are, and no amount of vodka shots will convince me otherwise."

"Amanda, have I told you how stunning you look today?" said Dylan. "Tell me something. How is it that Andy met a genuine sparkler like you and I end up with climbers who just want to use me to get a job on television or a column in a magazine, eh?"

"You didn't answer *my* question," said Amanda, leading Dylan to a nearby table as most of the other guests danced to the live band that had been flown in from America especially for the occasion. "Are you missing her? I can see it in your eyes, despite the attractive shade of bloodshot they are swiftly turning."

"Amanda, I am missing Sophia like a hole in the head, if you know what I mean. I am missing her like I would miss a terminal illness, or a car-crash injury. I think it's fair to say that I am very, very happy to be right here, right now, on my own. With my one or two vodka shots, or three, or four –"

"Or seven," said Amanda, lifting the drink from his hand. "And who said I was talking about Sophia in the first place? She was never cut out to be your other half. You can do much, much better than her, can't you?"

Dylan looked up from the table and blinked a few times slowly. The alcohol was kicking into his system at last.

"This, this is shit," he said to Amanda. "Shit, shit, shit with a capital *shit*."

"It doesn't have to be," she said. "If you really want her, you could still fix things, you know. She isn't what the papers said she was, Dylan. From the first day I met Cara, I knew she was so different to what Sophia was putting her up to be. I got to know her. She's a fantastic person and is so right for you. And she's such a talented girl. I can't believe that she was writing that genius column for Sophia all the time! She must have been well cornered by her to live such a lie. I honestly don't think the poor girl realised the extent the social climber she was working for would go."

"I know, I know," said Dylan in a slight slur. "And you wanna know how I know? 'Cos every time I take a drink here today, I think of her more and more and more. Every time I go into a room in my house I see her. I think of her playing the piano, of her laughter or her voice and shit, Amanda, I've never felt this way before, but I've been sold up so many times and I'm afraid of it happening again."

"You know it won't happen with Cara."

"Of course it wouldn't," he agreed. "That's just my sorry excuse because I've left it too late."

Amanda shook her head. "I can't believe you have

let it go so far if you feel the way you say you do. Didn't she try to explain to you before she went back to Ireland that she wasn't the lying, vindictive home-wrecker Sophia had made her out to be?"

Dylan nodded and reached for his drink. "Oh, she tried all right. But I chased her away. I chased her away in her little green car and she went without saying a word. I, Dylan Summers, am officially a first-prize asshole."

"You can say that again."

"Okay, then I will. I am an asshole. Now, do you want to dance because if I don't do something other than drink myself into oblivion, I fear your good husband might be dealing with a sorry mess of puked-up booze in a just under a few hours' time."

"Call her," said Amanda. "Just look her up and call her."

Dylan nodded for a few seconds in a drunken haze.

"D'you know what, Amanda? I just think I will. Tomorrow I will call her."

But Amanda had a funny feeling that without a little help, Dylan's courage to call Cara tomorrow might never come.

34

It's Now or Never

With everyone at *Fab!* TV in the Christmas spirit, Sophia knew she would have to make an extra effort to grab Jake Johnston's attention at the end-of-year party.

"How do I look?" she asked Tom and she sashayed past him in a festive red halter-neck dress with a plunging neckline and sequinned front. His penthouse apartment was like a shoebox in comparison to the acres of space she'd had at Summer Manor, though to the average Londoner it was vast and luxurious with its views over Canary Wharf. Poor Tom had no idea that he was merely a gap-filler until she moved on to bigger and better things, but she needed him for the near future until her next victim came along.

"You look stunning, as always, Sophia," said Tom.

He stood up and dutifully buttoned her dress up at the parts she couldn't reach as she held up her mass of hair above the nape of her neck. "Now, what should I wear? I have my tux if you think traditional is best, or perhaps I should be suited and booted in a black Galliano with a red tie to match your dress?"

Sophia twisted around like her head was on an axis. "Tom, we are not a couple so stop acting like we are."

"I never said –"

"Like I have told you before, get your head out of the clouds and stop fantasising. It's a millionaire I am after, not a crummy theatre actor who can't keep me in the lifestyle I have grown accustomed to. Now, get back into the real world and order us a cab, then get dressed in whatever you find first."

The Christmas party was a who's who of work-starved reality-television stars, PR gurus hungry for their next client and models and dancers ravenous for a rich man. Sophia's eyes were agog and Tom almost choked on an anchovy when he saw Emily Evans in the flesh. She was blonde, curvy and hot to trot and she knew it. He was terrified of Sophia seeing him stare at her monstrous cleavage so he forced himself to look away.

"Can you see him anywhere?" Sophia hissed under her breath.

"Who?"

"Who do you think? Robbie Williams? *Jake,* of

course! And for goodness' sake will you stop stuffing your face like you've never been fed. It's highly embarrassing."

"I am bloody starving," said Tom. "I told you we should have stopped for a burger on the way here if you were going to be so precious over a few prawns."

"Oh, shit, there he is. Right, disappear, Dumbo!"

Tom popped another prawn into his mouth in protest as Sophia left him standing on his own amid a sea of familiar faces with no names and he felt his temper boil over.

He glanced around him, then lifted a napkin and filled it with as many hors d'oeuvres as he could squash into it and pushed past the posing wannabes out into the frosty evening where he hailed a cab and settled into its warmth. As the car pulled off, Tom smiled to himself when he realised that Sophia didn't have a key to his apartment. He had just done exactly what she had told him. She could find some other mug to suck blood out of, because where Sophia Brannigan was concerned, Tom had just disappeared.

Jake Johnston was surrounded as always by a bevy of scantily clad admirers and Sophia could feel herself begin to perspire. She hovered around the table next to him, pretending she hadn't noticed his powerful presence which radiated wealth, arrogance and charm and prayed that her make-up was still intact.

Those silly little bimbos reminded her of her life

pre-Dylan Summers and she shuddered at their naïvety. She sneered at one of them deliberately when she caught her eye while pretending to be scanning the place for a friend.

Ten minutes passed and Jake still hadn't taken any interest in her and by now she could feel a panic attack come on. She would allow him another few seconds and then she would take a breather and find Tom to hide behind for a while. At least he was good for something, the little clag.

"Excuse me, are you Sophia Brannigan?"

Sophia swung around meet a googly-eyed, Bambi-like creature who fiddled with her golden curls as she spoke and Sophia's breast heaved with pride as she greeted her first fan. She was recognised, at last! Was it as a columnist? WAGs were *so* last season.

"I certainly am. Would you like an autograph?"

The girl raised an eyebrow then laughed so hard she showered Sophia with her champagne.

"Autograph?" she spat. "Hell *no*. I don't want your autograph! I was just going to say how ridiculous you must feel having let your stunning boyfriend slip through your fingers, and all for a blink and you'll miss it flash on *Fab!* TV. All of my set are laughing our legs off at you every evening on the telly!"

"Excuse me, but who are you to be insulting my career? What exactly do you do for a living? Starve yourself?"

"For a while, yes. But, I'm a WAG, like you once were. I'm on my second Vauxhall Conference player but I'm moving my way up to the Premiership."

The juvenile delinquent went off, swinging her bony hips to the beat of the hip-hop music that filled the air and for a split second Sophia wondered if she was ever as pathetic as the vile creature she had just encountered.

"Well, if it isn't my little lady in red?" said Jake Johnston and he pretended to look behind Sophia as if something was missing.

"What is it, Jake? You don't like my dress?" she asked, her hand clamped on her chest in distress.

"I love your dress, babe. I was looking for what's-his-name, your 'former flatmate'? You two are like Ant and Dec lately."

Sophia gave out a girly giggle and rested her hand on Jake's arm with her mouth almost gaping at the sight of his huge Rolex that weighed more than a small car.

"Jake, can I remind you that I am a single, carefree, career woman and I am loving it? Though, there *is* one man for me and one man only, and tonight I plan to get exactly what I want, because that is the type of girl I am."

Jake put his arm round her delicate shoulder and she shivered under his touch. The man had more pull than a magnetic force and she was well and truly under his spell.

"And who, might I ask, is the lucky man?" he asked with a light smirk. "Anyone I know? Perhaps I could put in a word for you."

This was exactly what Sophia had hoped he would say. Her moment had arrived and he had replied just as if it had been written in a script for him. Who needed dumb footballers when there were media moguls like Jake Johnston to lure into her web?

She reached into her tiny purse and in record time she produced a compact mirror and held it up to Jake's face, then awaited his response with a smile.

Jake jerked ever so slightly. "Why are you holding a mirror up to my face, Sophia? I do know what I look like."

Sophia clamped the mirror shut, then stuffed it back in her handbag, feeling her heart race faster if it was humanly possible. As well as she had practised this moment in her head, she had not rehearsed the part where he failed to catch on to what she was telling him.

She composed herself again and then whispered into his ear, rubbing her lips against the softness of his lobe as she spoke.

"Jake. Don't make me state the obvious. It's *you*."

Again, he pulled away. "I know it's me," he laughed. "I admire myself in the mirror every other minute of the day. What exactly are you saying, Sophia?"

He was teasing her. Two could play that game, she thought, so she turned to face him directly so that their bodies pressed together in the dimly lit surroundings.

"The man – the one man that I want, more than anyone else – is *you*," she said, looking directly into his hazel eyes which she believed had undressed her on so many occasions over the past few months. "It's you."

Was it her imagination or was he sniggering?

"Ah, Sophia, no. No! Poor, poor Sophia," said Jake, holding her arms in his hands and gently pushing her away from him. "I didn't know you felt like this, but I'm glad you've been so honest . . ."

"You are? That's great. I'm glad you're glad," she said, grasping at straws as she felt her plan deflate around her. She took a quick look around for Tom but he was nowhere to be seen. This was not working out at all! She was horrified.

"No, no. It's not great at all," said Jake. "In fact I'm highly embarrassed. Sorry, but I just don't think of you that way. I never have."

Sophia wondered if she had ever felt so darn right stupid in all her life. He looked *angry*.

"But I thought . . ."

"Whatever you thought was wrong. You're an employee here at *Fab!* and I had high hopes for you, but knowing you have a schoolgirl crush on me is a bit, well – let's just put it down to a cringe-worthy office-party moment. It's all we can do."

Sophia felt hot tears sting her eyes and applauded

herself for buying very expensive waterproof mascara when she last had use of Dylan's credit card.

"Now, run along and enjoy the party," said Jake with a patronising smile. "I'll see you on Monday at 8 a.m. sharp and we'll forget this ever happened."

"Okay," said Sophia like an obedient child. "Monday at 8 a.m. Sharp."

"It's a date. Oh, and bring Wellington boots," he said, loud enough for the benefit of the nearby coven of bimbos to hear. "You're reporting from a local turkey farm."

When Jake was well out of her sight, Sophia stomped her foot so hard in bad temper that the heel of her shoe snapped off and she slumped down onto the nearby dance-floor on her petite derriere, feeling a humiliating sense of déjà vu.

Dylan was stretched out on the sofa and casually flicking through TV channels when the doorbell rang. He wasn't expecting visitors but he had noticed a higher volume of people coming to see him now that Sophia was gone. Either they feared he was lonely or they couldn't stand Sophia more than they cared to admit to.

"Who could that be, Buster?" he asked the dog who was in his primary care in Sam's absence on his Christmas visit up north, as was Lola who lay in front of the blazing fire, looking peaceful and content now that the lady of the manor had gone.

415

It was almost six thirty and Dylan had a flight to catch to Spain that evening but it was too early to be his cab or the dog-sitter he had arranged to stay while he was away.

He sauntered out to the front door and did a double take when he saw Andy and Amanda Stewart on his doorstep, laden with a Christmas hamper, and a child at each side of them.

"Sorry to call unannounced, Dylan but we were doing the rounds and thought we'd pop in to see how you've been since the wedding," said Amanda as Dylan stood aside to let them into his home.

"I'm great," said Dylan and Amanda looked at him in disbelief. "Honestly, I'm very content. Buster, Lola and I are sharing some bonding time before I go to Spain and get pissed. Oops, sorry, the kids!"

"Don't worry, they've heard worse," laughed Andy as he took a seat and his wife followed suit. "If a word sounds naughty at all, my daughters love to say it on repeat. And always when there is a judgemental adult within earshot."

"You didn't call her," said Amanda. She knew it was almost bedtime for her children and wanted to concentrate on the job in hand.

"I, er, I didn't call her," said Dylan. "Look, I don't know, I think I'm afraid she'll tell me where to go. You shouldn't listen to me when I'm drunk."

"Just call her and find out," said Andy. "At least if

she does tell you to piss off, then you know where you stand."

"Piss off!" said Abigail from a corner where she had found Buster skulking away from his uninvited guests. Lola was curled under his belly.

"Shit, do you see what I mean?"

"Shit!" said Meg with a devilish giggle.

"Andy's right," Amanda continued. "Just call her and I can guarantee to you that she will not turn you down. She feels the same for you, believe me, and is kicking herself for everything that has happened."

"How on earth can you be so sure?" asked Dylan. Amanda was like a dog with a bone, but he wanted to hear more.

"Because I spoke to her. Today," said Amanda. "I gave her my number ages ago and she called me when Sophia's story was splashed all over the press. Sophia had her well and truly hammered, but that's not the full story. Cara is as miserable as you are and as stubborn as you are too. She has been covering Sophia's ass for months with that column and God knows what else and I just know she is a genuine, loving girl who didn't know who or what she was dealing with. Just lift the phone and give her a call. You'll regret it if you don't."

Dylan saw his guests out into the frosty night and wondered if he could do what he most wanted to do.

Cara was back with her family in the famous Graceland and he tried to imagine what she was doing now. Amanda was adamant that he had nothing to lose and everything to gain and he knew what he wanted more than anything now was to see her again. It was two days to Christmas. He had a flight booked to join his family in Spain for the holidays but the very thought of stepping on the plane was pulling his heart in the wrong direction.

He opened the fridge and cracked open a beer, then decided to open one of his Christmas presents to lighten his sullen mood. Sam's humble gift sat amongst his usual gifts from friends who had made him promise not to open them until Christmas, but Sam had given him strict instructions to open his sometime before then.

He lifted the box, a small unassuming bundle amongst the array of presents his parents had left for him to make up for the lost time of the past few months. Ripping the paper open, he recalled how excited Sam had been before he left for Scotland where he would spend the festive season with his own daughters.

"I want you to accept this gift from me and when I come home I want a lot of changes in you, young man," he had said in his soft border accent.

Inside the box was a CD and Dylan wondered what all the fuss could be about. When he looked at the cover he smiled. It was an Elvis collection of greatest hits and Dylan wondered why opening it before Christmas Eve could make any difference, but when he flipped open the cover, a sheet of paper fell out.

Reading Sam's careful instructions, Dylan's heart stopped at his old friend's kind words and thoughtful efforts.

He decided not to call Cara after all. Sam had just made sure he didn't have to.

"I'm sure your girlfriends would rather spend the evening here at my Karaoke King night than swan off to some glamorous nightclub in town," said Liam from behind the bar to his sister who was rearranging tables for the big night ahead. He really was beginning to fancy himself as a *Cocktail*-style Tom Cruise figure and between his infectious cheerful manner and Cara's rock 'n' roll décor, they had managed to attract quite a different clientele into Graceland.

Tonight Liam had planned an evening of karaoke featuring the best of Elvis Presley's hits and the whole of Kilshannon had pledged their support – all except his sister, that is.

"Gosh, Liam, you know I'd love to but it's not my call. Natalie and some of the girls from school have arranged this night out ages ago as a sort of Christmas reunion and I can't dictate where we should go. I do wish I could stay here, believe me. A busy evening behind the bar would help take my mind off other things."

Liam leaned his strong arms on the bar and shook his head. "I meant you could come here for your night out, not that you should stay here to work, you clown. You need to let your hair down, sis. In fact, you'd also need to get your hair done! It looks like you're slipping back into your old tomboy ways, Cara McCarthy."

Cara threw a dishcloth at him and it hit him full whack on the cheek. She looked into the huge Guinness-branded mirror to her right and saw that what he said was true. Her hair was lank and faded, she wore her old glasses and her pale face made her look just as she felt.

"I just don't feel like glamming up any more. What's the point?"

"Do it for you. That's the point. Do it to make *you* feel better, not because Sophia Brannigan says so, or so that Dylan Summers might look your way. Look, sis, I hate to sound like a wet rag here, but I've been thinking that maybe it's time you moved on. It's been a while since you left London and unfortunately it looks like Dylan Summers has forgotten all about you, doesn't it?"

"I know, I know. I'm trying to but it's so hard. But what about my phone call from Amanda yesterday? She said Dylan was utterly miserable at Paul Henderson's wedding, despite all the glowing photographs and she said he's drinking a lot. I'd just love to talk to him, you know. Make sure he's okay."

"Listen to yourself. He's a big boy. You did try to explain yourself to him before you left London and he wouldn't hear you out. Go out tonight and paint the town red and find yourself a real-life man, not some fantasy figure whose life is worlds away from life as you know it."

Cara looked at her handsome younger brother and knew he was right. There was no point in wasting her time fantasising over a man who would never be hers. After all, she had been there, done that with Michael Bradley.

"You're right. I'll give Nat a ring and see if she can call around and weave some of her magic again before we go out. You never know, it might perk me up a bit."

"That's the spirit. Just don't turn into our Olivia. There is a happy medium to hair and make-up," laughed Liam.

"Don't worry, that will never happen. So are you all set for tonight?"

"I'm all set. Menus printed, tunes aplenty, promotions done. Now all I need is the crowd to show up."

"They will. And the whole place looks fantastic, Liam," she said, admiring the pub's new funky style with its Elvis-themed drinks menu and brand-new framed pictures on the wall. A small stage area was located to the far side where Liam had set up the new karaoke machine he had convinced his parents to invest in as an attraction over Christmas. Outside, they had tidied up the signage with some fresh paint and already the compliments were flying as to how the new-look Graceland was just what the village needed in the run-up to the holidays. Cara and Liam had injected new life into the place and their parents were delighted.

"It does look great and it feels great too," said Liam.

"It does. Okay, then. I'll be off then to try and transform back into a human again. New attitudes and new beginnings all around," she said and made for the door.

"Cara!" called Liam as his sister walked away. She stopped in her tracks and turned to hear him out. "You know I would never have got to where I am today if it wasn't for you."

Cara gulped. This was quite unexpected. "What?"

"You've been a real star to me, sis. If it wasn't for you I'd still be a drug-taking, anti-social delinquent whose only future was in some grotty prison cell. I'll never forget you for this. You deserve the best and if Dylan Summers doesn't see you for what you are, that's his problem."

Cara was moved by his honesty. The old Liam would have shown his affection or appreciation with a playful thump on the arm that might have left you in the A and E department.

"Look at you going all mushy," said Cara, wiping a stray tear from the side of her cheek. "Now you've got me started."

"I'm serious," said Liam. "For God's sake don't put me off my track of being nice now that I've only realised how to. I really was in the gutter when I went running to you in London and I know it put strain on you and Natalie having me around at the start. But it worked, you know. I'm a different person now and it's thanks to you for giving me a chance when no one else would. Thanks, sis. You're the best."

Cara walked back towards the bar and grasped her brother's hand.

"You're not a different person at all, Liam," said Cara. "I think it's called growing up. You've grown up, that's all, and I'm really proud of you, you know that."

"I know you are. Now go and get all spiced up for your big night out and I don't want to hear Dylan Summers' name mentioned around here again unless he walks through that door and sweeps you off your feet, do you hear?"

"Okay, it's a deal," she said with a smile and then her eyes lit up. "You are so right. In fact, I'm just going to knock them dead in Donegal tonight. Men everywhere beware! Cara McCarthy is back in town!"

The group of girls tooted the horn for Cara and Natalie at eight o'clock on the button.

"I'm frightened to think of what shape that lot will come home in," said Gerry McCarthy as his two daughters, together with Natalie and at least four others began to pile into a tiny grey Renault van, all heels and hair and make-up.

"I'm frightened to know how they're all going to fit into that wee van," said Margaret, her arms folded in disbelief, but wishing behind it all she could be part of the *craic*. They were laughing hysterically already as they hauled each girl into the back of the tiny vehicle, one by one. Kelly, the designated driver, obviously had the patience of a saint.

"You look beautiful," said Gerry to Cara and she almost tripped in her stilettos at her father's compliment. "I never thought I'd see the day when you'd get out of your jeans."

"People change," she said and winked at her brother who joined them in the doorway. "I never thought getting dressed up would make me feel so good."

"Good luck with the karaoke, Liam," shouted Natalie with a bottle of alcopop swinging dangerously in her hand. "We'll be back in time to do a duet, me and Cara."

"Oh yeah? And what will that be? 'Heartbreak Hotel'?" shouted Liam and Cara gave him a "ha ha" grin.

"I was thinking more of 'Hard Headed Woman'," she laughed and she piled into the van which was gone in a flash, with only a flurry of grey and a beat of dance music fading into the distance.

"Now, son," said Gerry McCarthy, "let's go and get ready for our big karaoke night. I've been practising all day for my party piece and, if what I'm hearing is true, even old vinegar-tits MacAvoy is getting into the spirit and is pulling out a pair of flares for the occasion. We may even have to put out extra seats."

Liam beamed with pride at his father's approval of his first event, not to mention his new-found trust in his only son.

"It's a long time since we had to put out extra seats, Gerry," said Margaret and her heart glowed as she watched the two men in her life walk arm and arm into Graceland.

The grey van scuttled along the windy roads that led out of Kilshannon village towards Donegal town. Cara forced herself to join in on the festive spirit, but her heart wasn't in it.

"Why the long face, Cara?" asked Katrina who was just back from the States and had developed a trans-Atlantic accent. "You look amazing but you don't seem to be your normal bubbly self. What's up?"

"She's fine," said Natalie from the front seat. "Just some man trouble but we are on a mission tonight to find her a new man and we won't settle till we do. I'm on a man hunt myself. *Whoop whoop!*"

"Turn the van, Kelly," said Cara and the girls stared back at her in shock. "Really, I'm so sorry, Kell. Just turn the van. I don't want to ruin your night by being a party-pooper so I'd rather just go back and let you all get on with it."

"Cara! Don't be silly," said Natalie. "You're always the life and soul of our Christmas party. Please don't go home!"

"I have to. Please, Kelly. Please just take me home. There's something I've been meaning to do and I want to do it now before I ruin everything by doing it when I'm drunk and emotional when we come home at silly o'clock in the morning."

Kelly pulled the van into a halt and turned around in her seat to where Cara was squashed into the back surrounded by legs and handbags galore.

"If you're sure it's what you want, babe?" she said.

"I'm sure," said Cara, and Kelly locked the car into reverse and headed back to Graceland.

35

Burning Love

Dylan Summers pressed his face against the windscreen of the car in an attempt to see beyond the flurry of snow. Was it left then right or right then left? He couldn't remember.

He blindly searched for the CD cover that Sam had presented him which lay on the passenger seat, all the time keeping his eye on the winding roads that were coated with a fine shimmer of ice. With a flick of his wrist he prised the cover open and shook it so that the sheet of paper fell out onto the floor.

"Shit," he said, and then leaned downwards to grab the sheet from the floor, wishing he had managed to hire a car with Sat Nav.

Sam's directions had so far been easy to follow but

in this worsening weather he was beginning to struggle and, as fate stacked against him, he wondered if this random arrangement by Sam was going to work out after all.

Earlier that day, he had almost turned for home when he learned that the plane to Belfast was delayed due to severe weather warnings and then when he got to his destination two hours later than intended, the car he had pre-booked wasn't available so instead he was stuck with a modest people-carrier that made him feel like he was driving a mini-bus.

A few minutes and one or two hairpin bends later he came to a junction and sighed with relief, but closer inspection showed the signs to be covered in snow. For the past twenty miles or so, he had barely met a car let alone a human to ask for directions and he began to fear he was well and truly lost.

He turned the radio on for company and said a quick prayer that he had made the right decision, then in a hasty move he indicated left and was relieved to see a gathering of people with car trouble on the side of the road. Directions at last.

"Excuse me!" he shouted from the car window as a gust of wind blew into the cosy interior, but none of the four girls gathered around their flat tyre could hear him. "Do you need any help?"

A tall girl with dripping-wet curly red hair waved him on and another who was dressed totally inappropriately for the month of December yelled back at him from inside the van.

"Girl power! We can change our own tyres, mister."

"Speak for yourself, Katrina," said a blonde girl who seemed to be doing most of the work. She ran towards him and leaned her head in through his window.

"Don't listen to my friend," she said. "It's a kind offer, but right now all I really want to do is just leave the van here till morning and find a nice warm pub. Any chance of giving us a lift instead?"

Dylan looked behind him into the six empty seats and shrugged.

"Sounds like a good option to me," he said. "Jump in. Oh, and maybe you could help me out along the way? I'm looking for a pub called Graceland. Do you know where that is?"

"Of course, the karaoke night!" shouted the girl against the elements and she waved to her friends who grabbed handbags and bottles from the back of their little grey van and sprinted towards his car.

"What karaoke night?" asked Dylan.

"The Elvis karaoke night in Graceland. The whole village is going to be there. Come on girls, get a move on!"

Dylan felt the car rock as the gang piled in and then realised he was playing the Elvis CD Sam had bought him. The girls probably thought he was some weird fanatic who travelled to Elvis tributes in the blinding snow! He had texted his brother to say he would be joining his family in Spain later than expected, but his journey west instead of south had nothing to do with karaoke!

"Thank fuck for that," said one of the girls as she scrambled into the back seat with a shiver. "Whoever you are, you're a life saver. Girl power my ass! I couldn't change a tyre in the blazing sun, never mind in the middle of bloody December."

Dylan laughed at the girl's honesty and he knew right then he had made the right decision. The girls' accents were identical to Cara's and now more than ever he couldn't wait to see her.

"Ooh, heat at last," said another. "My bloody hair is a total fuzz-ball. Seventy euro this hairdo stung me and I'm not going clubbing like this."

Dylan turned up the heating full blast and waited for Kelly, the driver of the van, to lock up and join them in his monstrous vehicle.

"Right," she said to Dylan, jumping inside then closing the door with a bang. "So you want to go to Graceland?"

"That I do. Am I at least going in the right direction?"

Kelly laughed and shook her head so that Dylan was sprayed with flakes of melting snow.

"I'm afraid not. It's about two miles back. But don't worry, we'll get you there. Hey, you look really familiar. Should I know you?"

"Don't think so," said Dylan, realising that this was not the time to be recognised.

"Mmm. Okay, ladies!" shouted Kelly to her frozen companions in the back. If this babe was going to Graceland, then they were too. Sod the night clubs. "Who fancies a bit of Elvis karaoke?"

"I do, you hunk of burning love," said a voice from the back and Kelly cranked up the Elvis CD as Dylan turned the car back towards the village of Kilshannon.

Cara had traded her heels for flat shoes and was beginning to relax into the music as the crowds of revellers packed inside the walls of the pub. It was all hands on deck as she served pints of beer and hot whiskies by the dozen and Liam's famous alcoholic smoothies were flying off the shelves. His new Elvis-themed drinks menu had everyone intrigued as they tried "Suspicious Limes" and "Kiss Me Quick Strawberry Pop" amongst others.

The local drama group ensured the karaoke got off to a fine start and Liam was dividing his time between sorting out songs for them and carrying trays full of drinks down to tables.

"Check out Dad," said Cara to Liam when he finally got a quick breather. "He thinks he's flippin' Peter Stringfellow."

"So he does," said Liam. "He'll be looking for a franchise on this place after this."

The look on their father's face was priceless as he

carried out stacks of chairs to accommodate the growing crowds, while their mother kept disappearing into the throng on the excuse that someone had to welcome some of the new faces to ensure their return during the long, hungry month of January.

"So, did you do what you came back to do?" asked Liam, pouring a triple "All Shook Up" for old Mary MacAvoy who was pissed as a fart already.

"No, not yet," said Cara.

Liam rolled his eyes. "You should have had your night out with the girls as planned. I could murder you for arriving back here like that and I feel horribly guilty."

"Don't be. I knew you'd need the help," said Cara and the door opened again to let another group of people in. She was just about to do the rounds for empty glasses when Mary MacAvoy took the mike to sing "Always On My Mind".

Suddenly the very song that reminded her of Dylan had more association with a crucifixion as old Mary croaked out an ear-bleeding version and Cara took it as a sign to bite the bullet and make the phone call she had been longing to for weeks.

"Hold the fort, Liam," she said. "I'll be back very soon. It's now or never!"

"Are you sure that's a good idea?" called Liam but Cara had disappeared through the door that led to the storeroom of the bar.

She nestled the phone in her hand and scrolled

down to find his name on her contacts list. With her heart about to jump out and join her on the floor of the dusty storeroom floor, she pressed the button on her mobile and closed her eyes tight. Please pick up, she thought. Actually, no, don't, I don't know what to say. Yes, do. No, don't.

She was on the verge of hanging up when she heard his voice and it automatically brought a smile to her face.

"Cara?"

"Dylan. Yes, it's me. Hi. I just wanted to –"

"Cara, where are you?"

Dylan sounded like he was in a bar. Maybe this was a bad time. Shit, what if he was on a date!

"I'm in Graceland. Look, is this a bad time?"

"Good," he said. "Boy, am I glad to hear that you're in Graceland! I thought you said people could sing around here?"

Cara paused and listened in wonder. From Dylan's end of the line she could hear a poisonous version of their song, and then she held the phone away from her ear and realised that it was Mary's excruciating rendition from the other side of the storeroom door.

"Dylan, where are you?"

"I'm in some Elvis tribute bar in Donegal," he said. "Took me ages to find it. It's a nice place but the service is crap and I'm just dying to try an 'Always On My Mind' Super Juicer."

433

With the phone still pressed against her ear, Cara stood up and slowly opened the door of the storeroom. He was right in front of her, sitting on Priscilla Presley but she could tell him that later!

She stepped out of the storeroom.

"Coming right up, sir," she said across the bar to where Dylan was now flanked at either side by Natalie and the group of girls from the van.

Her hands shook as she poured the concoction of alcohol and fruit juice into a tall glass, then topped it with ice and set it in front of the man of her dreams.

"I told you I'd come here some day, didn't I? So, how have you been?" he asked, his hand finding hers and their eyes locking and the noise from the stage and the bar fading away into the background.

"Miserable."

"Me too," he said. "And now?"

He lifted her hand and held it to his face. His face was cold.

"Better," she whispered. "I just can't believe you're here. How on earth did you find the place?"

"It wasn't easy, but your good friends helped me out."

Cara looked at Natalie who seemed as shocked as Cara was that the man who had given them a lift was Dylan Summers. At first she had been too busy giving out as usual to notice if it was Jack the Ripper's car that had rescued them. The other girls just stared in awe and one or two made rude gestures behind Dylan's back, illustrating in a very crude fashion in no uncertain terms just what they would like to do if they were in Cara's shoes.

"You see, some time ago a very good friend of mine told me to follow my heart," said Dylan. "But I was too afraid to take her advice. Then, with a little help from Sam and his carefully timed Christmas present, I did it today. I followed my heart and it led me to you, Cara McCarthy. It led me right here to you."

"I'm really glad it did," whispered Cara into her sleeves. Her eyes filled up and she smiled at him from behind the bar, biting her lip to stop her tears in case she ended up looking like a panda bear. Her father looked across at her from the side of the stage and gave her the thumbs-up, while Liam looked as if he had got the shock of his life as he stared from behind Mary MacAvoy who was now wrecking "Can't Help Falling In Love With You". Her mother was too star-struck to notice and Olivia was downing her fourth cocktail now that her parents were preoccupied.

"I'm glad too," said Dylan and he walked behind the bar and lifted Cara into his arms, then kissed her so hard she forgot her entire family was watching and savoured every single moment of his warmth. When he finally let her go, Cara realised the entire bar-room was staring and cheering and had their new Christmas cameras at the ready. But she didn't care, and neither did he.

"You hungry?" she asked, longing for an excuse to take him away from prying eyes and flashing lenses. She had had quite enough of that in London. "I can make you some lasagne?"

"No way," said Dylan with a glint in his eye. "I've been living on that for weeks now."

Cara felt sorry for him but was delighted her cookery lesson had been put to use.

"Really," she laughed. "So what else do you fancy? Irish Stew?"

He opened her hand and placed her earring into it, noticing that she still wore its match after all this time.

"You know, I never did get to sample any of that. It was always saved for Sam."

Cara put the earring into her ear and then led him through the cheering crowd and out through the doors of Graceland into her family home.

"It's on tap here, especially at this time of year."

"Excellent," he said. "Oh and by the way, is there a piano in Graceland? I want to hear you play again when we go back into the bar. I did say I'd get you to play that for me again."

Cara shook her head. "Oh no. Not a chance of that happening. Like you said, my piano-playing is our little secret. Like your fascination with Elvis."

"Well, can I tell you another one?" asked Dylan and he held her in his arms. Cara felt so safe, so sexy and, like Natalie had predicted, it was all so comfortable.

"Of course you can. Go for it. I'm all ears."

Dylan lifted her chin and closed his eyes, then kissed her firmly in a slow passionate way. His fingers traced her spine and she shivered in delight.

"The secret is," he whispered, gently lifting her hair off her face, "that I have been longing to do that for months now."

"Me too," said Cara, secretly pinching herself. "Me too."

Cara snuggled in to Dylan and walked into the living area of her family home, stopping only when they heard the sound of Mary MacAvoy screeching "Always On My Mind" for the second time round in the background.

"That's our song," said Cara, "and she's absolutely crucifying it."

"Do you know what?"

"What?"

"I love it anyway."

He put his arms around her and they danced in front of the Sacred Heart picture, a McCarthy family photo that was at least ten years old and an ancient photo of Cara with her bruised knees on her Communion day, which she discreetly turned on its face as they shimmied past.

She pinched her own arm behind Dylan's back. Yes, it was true. Cara "Plain Jane" McCarthy, the local tomboy who was destined to settle down and marry a fisherman in Kilshannon had found fashion, make-up and the love of a good man. And she was genuinely as surprised as the hundreds of revellers who gathered in Graceland, one or two of whom were phoning the Big Newspapers in Belfast at that very moment with the biggest scoop Kilshannon had witnessed since the robbery of the post office.

Well, it wasn't every day a celebrity came to town, you know.

THE END

Also published by Poolbeg.com

Beyond Sin

Emma Louise Jordan

(A.K.A Emma Heatherington)

Your Daughter is Missing. Your Son is
a Suspect. Your Husband Blames You.

The picture-perfect O'Neill family is both admired
and envied, near and far. But in the week leading up
to Andrea O'Neill's high-profile society wedding,
life-changing trouble is suddenly brewing and sinister
cracks begin to show in the previously solid
foundations of the O'Neill household.

When the bride's angelic sister Jessie disappears
from the wedding reception and is still not found days
later, the finger of blame switches from person
to person as the hours before her vanishing are
scrambled together in a jigsaw full of missing pieces.

Could Jessie have been living a double life, unknown
to those who love her? And could anyone hate her so
much that they would make her suffer the ultimate
punishment for her dreadful secret sin?

978-1-84223-399-3